Oh, Charity." Flanna clutched the newspaper and its dread news to her chest. "What are we going to do? This is terrible news, just terrible."

"We could go home." Charity lifted one brow in mute supplication. "We don't belong up here, Miss Flanna."

Flanna lowered the paper to her lap, her mind spinning with bewilderment. Her father hadn't had time to write of this incredible news, but he would, she was certain. Would he demand that she come home immediately? *Should* she go home? She was so close to finishing her degree, but what would her father's friends think of a man who allowed his daughter to live among and consort with Yankees? A cold knot formed in her stomach as she realized that she was now in a foreign country, a place no longer affiliated with home.

We are one country, Flanna, one sacred Union.

Not anymore.

Flanna pressed her fingers to her temple as another thought hit her. *Roger!* If Papa were caught up in this wave of secession hysteria, he'd no sooner correspond with a Yankee Republican than he would with Abe Lincoln himself. He would never approve of Flanna's engagement. Indeed, he might even reply to Roger's initial letter with a surly response, destroying any chance of what might have been a suitable match.

And finishing her degree elsewhere was not an option. There was only one medical school for women in the South—Graefenberg Medical Institute in Dadeville, Alabama—but her father had not been impressed with that school's facility. In Boston Flanna had enjoyed access to a vast array of resources: a real skeleton, lab equipment, and an entire room of normal and pathological specimens in glass beakers. Graefenberg did not even have a decent medical library.

Dear God, what should I do?

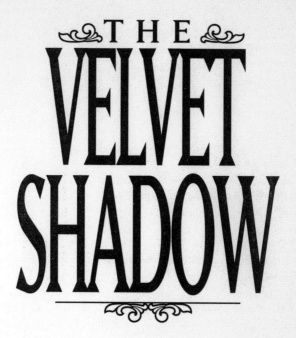

THE
VELVET
SHADOW

ANGELA ELWELL HUNT

WATERBROOK
PRESS

THE VELVET SHADOW
PUBLISHED BY WATERBROOK PRESS
5446 North Academy Boulevard, Suite 200
Colorado Springs, Colorado 80918
A division of Random House, Inc.

Scripture quotations, unless otherwise noted, are from the *King James Version* of the Bible.

Some of the characters and events in this book are fictional, some historical. For further information on the historical basis of the book, see pages 405-6.

ISBN 1-57856-131-0

Rosetta Wakeman's letter on page viii was taken from Lauren Cook Burgess's *An Uncommon Soldier* (New York: Oxford University Press, 1994).

Printed in the United States of America
1999—First Edition

10 9 8 7 6 5 4 3 2 1

*With thanks to Gaynel and Sharon Wilt
(who gave me "flippin' her eyelids at him"),
and Rick and Frani Rivers,
who volunteered their time to make sure I got it right.*

The Heirs of Cahira O'Connor

Book I: The Silver Sword

Book II: The Golden Cross

Book III: The Velvet Shadow

Book IV: The Emerald Isle
(Available Fall 1999)

Contents

I have just thought of something new to Write to you. It is as following.

Over to Carroll Prison they have got three women that is Confined in their Rooms. One of them was a Major in the union army and she went into battle with her men. When the Rebels bullets was acoming like a hail storm she rode her horse and gave orders to the men. Now she is in Prison for not doing accordingly to the regulation of war.

The other two is rebel Spies and they have Catch them and Put them in Prison. They are Smart looking women and [have] good education.

I Can't think of any more to Write at this time. Write soon as you get this letter.

Rosetta Wakeman,
Alias Pvt. Lyons Wakeman,
153rd Regiment,
New York State Volunteers

The
Heirs of Cahira O'Connor

Book 3

Prologue

Three months passed before I saw Taylor Morgan again. What had seemed at the outset to be a promising relationship faded like the colors of autumn when the fall semester began. As the oak leaves in Central Park toasted golden brown, Taylor's schedule picked up its pace, and I, too, stayed busy with schoolwork and my part-time job at the bookstore.

I've never been one to mourn the passing of what could have been a promising relationship. When Jeff Knave broke my heart in the ninth grade, I decided then and there that if a guy couldn't see that I was something special, I'd say good-bye with no regrets. Not that I think I'm more special than anyone else, mind you. But if a thing is not meant to be, I figure it's just not part of God's infinite plan.

So I moved on, and I buried my fascination with Cahira O'Connor and her descendants with as much determination as I put away my interest in Taylor Morgan. When I had researched Anika of Prague I'd been giddy with enthusiasm, and I had been thoroughly infatuated with Taylor while I investigated the story of Aidan O'Connor. But since Taylor had drifted away, so had my eagerness for the work of reading, researching, and writing. I hadn't even thought about Cahira O'Connor in several weeks because thinking about her reminded me of *him*...

I was surprised, then, to find Taylor sitting on the steps of my apartment building one afternoon just before Christmas break. He wore a heavy overcoat with the collar turned up against the wind, and for a split second my adrenaline surged at the sight of a stranger at the door of my apartment. But then those blue eyes flashed in my direction, and my knees turned to water.

"Hello," Taylor said, his voice faintly muffled by the collar and the scarf at his throat. "It's good to see you, Kathleen."

I pressed my lips together and hoped he wouldn't notice that my cheeks were burning. "Taylor? What on earth brings you here?"

He flashed me a brief smile and clapped his gloved hands together. "I just happened to be in the neighborhood."

That was a lie, and we both knew it. Taylor divided his time between his apartment and the college, and both were located on the Upper West Side. Taylor wouldn't come to the Village unless he really wanted to see me.

I shifted my grocery bag from one hand to the other, not exactly sure what I should say next. After a brief season of dating last summer, we'd gone our separate ways. So, did friendship require that I invite him in for a cup of coffee, or should I be truthful and tell him that my Chaucer class met in half an hour?

I looked away from those compelling blue eyes and remembered my resolution to forget him. "Taylor, it's good to see you, but—"

He cut me off with an uplifted hand. "Kathleen, I didn't come here to intrude." His voice deepened in apology. "But I thought you should know about the professor."

"Professor Howard?" I smiled, remembering the soft little man who had first introduced me to the legend of Cahira O'Connor. He'd set me on one of the great quests of my life. "What's the professor up to these days? Did he earn another doctorate?" I pasted on a look of exaggerated astonishment. "No—don't tell me, they've just awarded him the Nobel Prize!"

My voice dripped with sarcasm, and inwardly I cringed. I was behaving like a jilted lover, but Taylor Morgan had never made any promises, never said anything to imply that we were more than just friends. So why was my heart pounding like a kettledrum?

Taylor stood and jammed his hands into his coat pockets, then lowered his gaze to the sidewalk. "Professor Howard is dead, Kathleen."

A curious, tingling shock numbed my brain. The professor couldn't be dead. I'd had lunch with him just six months ago, and he'd looked fine. And he wasn't old, certainly not more than fifty-five or so. "Dead?" I forced the word through my tight throat.

"He'd been having heart problems." Taylor's square jaw tensed. "I found him in his office this morning. He was sitting there with his head on his desk, and his hand was resting on this."

Taylor pulled a manila envelope from the pocket of his overcoat and handed it to me.

I frowned at the sight of my name printed in the professor's neat handwriting. In the center of the envelope, beneath my name, was another: Flanna O'Connor. Cahira's last heir. The one I'd relegated to a mental back burner and hoped to forget.

Caught up in a vague sense of unreality, I looked up at Taylor. "What does this mean?"

"I'd like to come in and tell you about it." Taylor glanced down at his shoes again. "It was important to the professor, so I thought you ought to know. If you have a few minutes to spare."

My heart twisted in compassion as I studied his face. Taylor Morgan usually looked like a confident, dashing young intellectual, but the sorrow in his countenance today revealed how much he'd thought of his teacher. And no matter how disappointed I was that Taylor and I had never developed a romantic relationship, he was still a friend.

I decided to borrow notes from the girl who sat next to me in the Chaucer class. Being here with Taylor was far more important than studying *The Canterbury Tales.*

"Come on in." I tucked the envelope beneath my arm and climbed the steps. After unlocking the door, I led the way inside and pointed toward the sofa in the living room. "I'll be with you in just a minute," I called, carrying my groceries to the kitchen. "Let me get us something warm to drink, and then you can tell me all about it."

Taylor moved silently past me toward the sofa. And as he passed, I thought I saw a shimmer of wetness on his cheek.

Ten minutes later, I had two steaming cups of tea on the coffee table and the professor's envelope in my hands. Barkly, my guardian mastiff, had given the package a perfunctory sniff and then stretched out beside the window, content to watch our guest from a cautious distance.

Taylor sat on the sofa and picked up his mug. He held it with both hands, all signs of false cheer gone from his eyes. He looked like a man who'd just lost his best friend, and I realized I had underestimated the bond between the older man and his protégé.

"I'm very sorry about the professor," I said, sinking into the wing chair facing him. I wanted to reach out and pat his arm, but felt too awkward to attempt it. "I know he meant a lot to you."

"He was like a father." Taylor's gaze moved from me to the carpet. "Forgive me if I seem addled. I suppose I'm still in shock. This day has been a nightmare, with the questions and all the arrangements." A muscle clenched along his jaw. "I have to handle everything. Professor Howard had no family. He never married, and his parents are deceased."

"How awful. How did you know what to do?"

"I found an envelope at the front of his filing cabinet, and in it were all his last requests. His library is to be donated to the college, his personal effects are going to Goodwill, and he wanted his body cremated. He wanted no memorial service, no fuss."

I couldn't help frowning. "Sounds awfully Spartan."

"That's what he wanted." Taylor's gaze shifted to the envelope on my lap, and his icy blue eyes seemed to thaw slightly. "Since that package was on his desk, I thought he might want you to have it as soon as possible. It looked to me like he was clutching it when he died."

A tumble of confused thoughts and feelings assailed me as I looked at the wrinkled package. Though the envelope looked new, it had picked up the smell of musty paper and old attics. It bulged at the sides, straining to fit around whatever the professor had slipped inside.

"What do you suppose it is?" I asked, almost afraid to open it. "He wasn't still checking up on Cahira O'Connor for me, was he?"

"He may have been." Taylor stretched one arm along the back of the sofa as he shifted to watch me. "I know he was disappointed when I told him you hadn't mentioned anything about plans to work on Flanna O'Connor's story. I know he was most curious to learn as much as he could…as quickly as he could."

My blood ran thick with guilt. I had not even begun to work on Flanna O'Connor, reasoning that two novel-sized manuscripts on the O'Connor heirs was more than enough research for one lifetime. After all, I had a job, college classes, and a *life,* for heaven's sake. And though the professor had been fascinated by the story of Cahira's deathbed prayer, I didn't really want to believe I was one of her long-lost relatives. The first time I met him, the professor had been quick to point out that all Cahira's noteworthy heirs had red hair with a piebald white streak, just like mine. But surely that was coincidence, the whim of chance, or a one-in-every-two-hundred-years caprice of nature.

"Aren't you going to open it?" Taylor's voice, though quiet, had an ominous quality that lifted the hair on my arms.

"I know what this is about," I said, flipping the envelope. "Professor Howard thought that I was—that I *am*—one of Cahira's descendants. Just because I have red hair with a white streak, he is—he *was* convinced that I'm going to do something of earth-shattering importance with my life. Well, I'm not. I'll be lucky if I get a job at a newspaper. I'm no hero, I'm just me. I told him several times that I was only the writer, the one who could chronicle the stories of Anika and Aidan and—"

"But you stopped before the job was done." His tone rang with a strong suggestion of reproach.

I opened my mouth to give him a sharp answer, then thought better of it. No sense explaining that I was tired of reading and writing and research. People like Professor Howard and Taylor Morgan never wearied of such things. Taylor would rather spend the evening in a library than at a movie; maybe *that* explained why we never progressed past friendship.

"I'm sorry." I offered the words as a heartfelt and belated apology to Professor Howard. "If I had known he wanted to know—that he only had a few more months…"

"Open it," Taylor urged, his voice flat.

My fingers trembled as I undid the clasp and slid the envelope's contents into my lap. The envelope contained a book, its leather cover brittle and clouded with age, and a single sheet of letterhead stationery from New York University. I recognized Professor Howard's tidy penmanship immediately.

> *My very dear Miss O'Connor,*
>
> *You may never know how gratified I was to learn of your work on the biographies of Anika of Prague and Aidan O'Connor! Taylor read your first manuscript and sat through what I understand was an invigorating depiction of your second, and he is most complimentary of you and your efforts. Kudos to you, my dear. You have done excellent work.*
>
> *I also understand that you have taken a sabbatical from your work on the O'Connor descendants. While I can understand your need for a change of pace, I begin to fear for you, Kathleen. With every sunset, we are brought closer to the new millennium, and you must face the dawning of the next century as an heir of Cahira O'Connor. I cannot begin to imagine what wonders and terrors the next century will hold, but I know you will not meet the challenge unprepared. Through your work, I trust you have acquired Anika of Prague's spiritual strength and Aidan O'Connor's creative joy. I pray you will exhibit both these qualities as you face your future.*
>
> *There remains only Flanna O'Connor of the nineteenth century. I confess I was afraid you might begin your study of*

*this young woman on a day when I would be unable to aid
you, so I have done a bit of research to help you make a good
beginning. We are fortunate, you see, for journal keeping was
a favorite pastime of women in the Victorian era, and our
Flanna was no exception. God has smiled upon us. Enclosed
is Flanna's journal, which I discovered in a Boston museum
and purchased for your use.*

*I would not send you into the future unprepared, Miss
O'Connor. You are but two-thirds equipped for the task that
lies ahead of you. Take then Flanna's journal and glean from
it the lessons you can. And know that I bear every good wish
for your happiness and success in your endeavors.*

*With great affection and every prayer
for God's blessing,
Henry Howard*

"He bought this…for me?" I dropped the letter on the coffee table
and ran my hand over the rough journal, inhaling the scents of age
and dust. If the book had come from a museum, the professor must
have paid a high price. Astounding, the thought that he'd do something like that for me.

"I believe," Taylor's mouth tipped in a faint smile, "that the professor had begun to think of you as a daughter. He often spoke of
you, and he cherished the few notes you sent him about your
research."

The few notes. I cringed, wishing I'd made more of an effort to
stay close to the professor. Months ago, when we first met, I had
thought him an eccentric old man with a naughty penchant for red-
heads. Later I'd discovered he was a brilliant history professor with
more compassion than the rest of my teachers put together.

Once he learned that the heirs of the Irish princess Cahira
O'Connor were linked by a common thread, the professor grew terribly concerned for me. On her deathbed, Cahira begged heaven to
allow her descendants to fight for right in the world, and thus far each

woman who inherited her red hair and white streak had also been bequeathed an unusual destiny. Anika of Prague, who lived in the fifteenth century, became a knight and fought against spiritual corruption in the Bohemian Hussite wars. Aidan O'Connor disguised herself as a common sailor to flee the corruption of Dutch Batavia's wharf and later became a world-famous artist and philanthropist. And Flanna O'Connor...

My mind darted back to the single bit of information I'd gleaned from the World Wide Web: *Flanna O'Connor, a nineteenth-century Charleston woman who disguised herself as a soldier and fought in the Civil War at her brother's side. Commonly known as the Velvet Shadow, she was as well known for her ability to rescue wounded comrades from behind enemy lines as for the singular pale streak which ran through her red hair.*

Now I held the Velvet Shadow's diary. I shivered at the thought, then turned the book and riffled through the pages. Line after line of a flowery script filled the yellowed leaves, the ink faded but still legible.

"I don't know how complete the journal is." Taylor tapped his fingers on his knee in a meditative rhythm. "But surely there's enough material to get you started. And I must say that I agree with Professor Howard that you've no time to waste. It's nearly Christmas, with the new year not far behind." He leaned toward me, his eyes soft with compassion and kindness. "What will you do, Kathleen, if you're confronted with some great calamity in the near future?"

"Do you really believe I might be?" I gave him an uncertain smile. My heart warmed to think that Taylor Morgan cared, but I couldn't help feeling a little disconcerted by the knowledge that he feared for my future.

"I don't know what tomorrow holds," Taylor said, rubbing a hand over his face, "and neither did the professor. But he had a great instinct for knowing how people would react in a time of trial, and you must admit that Cahira's heirs rose triumphantly to face their unique challenges." A faint line deepened between his brows as he sorted through his thoughts. "The professor would never claim to be a fortuneteller, but he often said that each age holds its own trials—each decade, for that matter, suffers from its own troubles. The Vietnam War dominated thinking in the seventies; terrorism influenced the eighties; natural disasters made news in the nineties. The coming decade will hold its own tragedies, and how do we know that you will not find yourself involved in something of vital importance? Professor Howard wanted to be sure you'd be prepared for whatever might come your way as an heir of Cahira O'Connor."

I lowered my gaze, then tucked my legs under me, making myself comfortable in the wing chair. While Taylor sipped his tea, I opened the journal's cover and turned a few pages.

The first entry was dated December 24, 1860. A slanting feminine hand had written,

> *This book is such a lovely gift! Roger Haynes never ceases to surprise me! Tonight I dined with Mr. Haynes and his mother at their fine house in Beacon Hill, and my homesick heart was greatly cheered by their merrymaking and many kindnesses to me. I could almost stop missing Papa, Wesley, and Charleston, but every time the wind blows I find myself listening for the pounding of waves on the bulkheads, the chattering of palmetto leaves, and Wesley's boisterous laughter. How strange it is to celebrate Christmas so far from home!*

Engrossed in spite of myself, I read on.

Boston

They talk about a woman's sphere,
As though it had a limit.
There's not a place in earth or heaven,
There's not a task to mankind given...
Without a woman in it.

KATE FIELD, 1838–1896, AMERICAN WRITER

One

We're so glad you could take time out from your studies to be with us, Miss O'Connor."

Flanna shifted her eyes from the sparkling crystal and gleaming silver in order to meet her hostess's gaze. "I am deeply honored by your invitation," she answered, inclining her head toward the venerable older woman who stood at the head of the table. "Indeed, I was afraid I would spend Christmas alone in the boardinghouse with my maid."

"Your maid." The thin line of Mrs. Haynes's mouth clamped tight for a moment, then her stringy throat bobbed as she swallowed. "You're referring to the colored girl who accompanied you this evening?"

"Relax, Mama. Charity is a free Negro," Roger answered smoothly, pulling Flanna's chair out from beneath the mahogany table. "Flanna does not own slaves." With a flourish, he extended his arm. "My lady, your chair awaits."

Flanna managed a tight smile and maneuvered her voluminous skirts into the narrow space between the chair and the table, then sat down. The butler seated Mrs. Haynes, and the older woman's blue eyes narrowed slightly as she watched Roger take the empty seat between her and Flanna.

"I assumed," Mrs. Haynes said, her hand idly playing with the spangled jewels at her neck, "that everyone in South Carolina held slaves. After all, the gentlemen from South Carolina in Congress are most vociferous in their support of slavery."

"Mother, I assure you there is no reason for this concern." Roger frowned. "Flanna is from Charleston, and her father is a physician. Charleston is a metropolitan port; there is no room for plantations like those populated by your Uncle Tom and Eliza."

The woman's thin mouth softened slightly. "I suppose one should not prejudge another on account of where one was born. Miss O'Connor, I'm very glad to know your people aren't slavers. I believe in speaking up for the downtrodden, whether they be women or people of color."

"That's very gracious of you, ma'am." Flanna smiled and folded her hands in her lap. Roger had warned her that his mother had become an ardent abolitionist ever since reading *Uncle Tom's Cabin*.

"Do you read much?" The lady lifted an elegant brow.

"Quite a bit, actually," Flanna answered. "Mostly medical texts. I'm in my last term at the medical college."

"You ought to read *The Equality of the Sexes and the Condition of Women*, by Sarah Grimké." Mrs. Haynes unfolded her napkin with an emphatic snap. "I suppose you've heard of Sarah's sister, Angelina? She was born in Charleston, too, but is *persona non grata* there now, from all reports. Of course, I'm not surprised she would no longer be received in the South. Her book urged Southern women to speak out against slavery. A remarkably brave lady, Angelina Grimké."

Flanna drew in a deep breath and released it slowly. Of course she'd heard of the Grimké sisters—all of Charleston thought them remarkably boorish women. They had moved to the North and begun to publish literature that bemoaned the state of women in general and slaves in particular. Gentlefolk in Charleston ignored them, but many Northern women had elevated the sisters to an almost saintly status.

After nearly two years in Boston, she'd grown tired of caustic remarks about slavery. Common sense and good manners dictated that she let the subject pass, but she couldn't resist explaining the true situation to this sheltered Boston lady. After all, Roger *had* assured her that his mother was quite broad-minded.

"The truth, Mrs. Haynes," Flanna said with a tolerant smile, "is that less than one-quarter of Southern people hold any slaves at all.

My father is a physician and has no need of field hands. Charity is my maid, of course, and Papa has a valet, but we hired them from among Charleston's free brown population."

"You see?" Roger crossed his arms and beamed at his mother. "Your sensibilities are safe. Now call Howard to bring in the soup. I'm famished."

"One moment, please, Roger." Flanna put out her hand so that it barely brushed the sleeve of his coat, the only touch she might risk toward a man who had not yet crossed the line from suitor to betrothed. "Your mother is an intelligent lady; I am certain she would appreciate hearing the complete and honest truth."

Roger shot her a warning glance, but Flanna decided to ignore it. "My older brother," she said, again smiling at her hostess, "is a rice planter just outside Charleston. I believe Wesley owns over a hundred slaves, and the last time I visited him I found them quite happy under his protection. Regardless of what you may have heard about life on a plantation, I can assure you that my brother does not beat his slaves, nor does he allow those who are married to be separated."

Mrs. Haynes's face twisted into a horrified expression of disapproval. "So your people *do* own slaves!"

"Mama, remember your delicate constitution," Roger cautioned. "Are your smelling salts at hand?"

"Yes. My brother owns slaves, as do most gentlemen in the country," Flanna went on, lightly tapping her fingertips together. "In my brother's view, slavery is wholly without justification or defense. He will admit that it is theoretically and morally wrong. But my brother and my statesmen did not *choose* slavery. It was consigned to their supervision by a premeditated policy drafted by our forefathers."

A door swung open. Flanna looked up, hungry and ready for dinner, but Howard, the Irish butler, took one look at his mistress's face and froze with a steaming tureen in his hands.

Mrs. Haynes seemed not to notice that the first course had arrived. "Your brother," she leaned forward and paused for emphasis, "has surely *bought* slaves on occasion."

"Why, yes, he has."

"Then how can you say he does not support slavery?"

Flanna lifted her chin until the full weight of her netted hair rested upon the back of her neck. Regarding her hostess with a level gaze, she said, "If Wesley had not bought them, what would have become of them? You cannot believe they would be better off with a slave trader in a less civilized area! We are not ignorant of the brutal barbarians who abuse colored people, but on the other hand, neither am I ignorant of certain people who brutally abuse their children. Should we forbid families to rear children because some of them will be whipped or unloved? How can you then forbid slavery on the grounds that a few masters are cruel?"

"Because slavery itself is cruel! Because the black man wants to be free!"

Flanna's eyes caught and held Mrs. Haynes's gaze. "With all due respect, ma'am, I don't believe you can know what colored people want. You cannot understand that race until you have lived with them."

Mrs. Haynes's silver brows knitted in a frown as her bosom rose in indignation. "I understand them very well! I read Mrs. Stowe's book, and I regularly correspond with some Quaker folk who risk their lives and fortunes sending innocent runaways over the border into freedom."

Flanna shook her head slightly, then smiled at her empty soup bowl. Something in her wanted to rise up and shout out against the unassailable prejudices of these Northerners, but she was a lady and a guest in this house. Years of training in the graceful arts of gentility could not be discarded in one evening. Let the Yankee abolitionists and suffragists dispel their boredom by raging against things they did not understand. Flanna would hold her tongue, for she'd be leaving this Yankee city soon enough.

But something in her couldn't resist raising one final point.

"Mrs. Haynes." She paused to temper her voice and her rising exasperation. "Have you ever reflected upon the consequences of committing two or three million people, born and bred in the dependent state of slavery, to all the responsibilities, cares, and labors of freedom? My brother's slaves cannot read or write; they are accustomed to having all their needs met. Many, I fear, would find a life of freedom far more terrifying and taxing than the life they enjoy on his plantation."

"A pampered valet is no less enslaved than a brutalized field hand." A faint glint of humor sparkled in the lady's eyes. "Would *you* prefer a life of pampered slavery to the life you now lead, Miss O'Connor?"

Flanna felt the corner of her mouth twist in a half-smile. On several occasions growing up she *had* felt a bit like a pampered captive. Aunt Marsali, who had helped supervise Flanna's transformation from a spindly tomboy into a young woman, had continually chided her with admonitions about what proper young ladies simply could not do.

She tilted her head in acknowledgment of a point well made. "I believe it was Thomas Jefferson who wrote that slavery was like a wolf we held by the ears." She smiled and folded her hands in a tranquil pose. "We can neither hold him, nor safely let him go."

"Well, let us hope the wolf will not huff and puff and blow our house down."

Roger took the brief lull in conversation as an opportunity to wave the butler into the room. "Look, ladies, the soup is ready! Come, Howard, before it grows cold. Serve Mother first. She likes her chowder hot."

Flanna caught the chiding look Mrs. Haynes shot her son, and repressed a smile as she studied the elegant dining table. Wealthy, civic-minded Mrs. Haynes was probably wondering what sort of Southern infidel her son had brought home, and for a moment Flanna wished she were out in the kitchen with Charity and the other servants. The opening salvos of a battle had been fired, however gently, and only the Lord knew how far Mrs. Haynes might carry the conversation.

Flanna removed her napkin from the table and spread it in her lap, dreading the advent of what might become a heated discussion.

She had enjoyed many rousing debates with her father and brother, often taking positions she did not personally support just to see how well she could argue against their masculine mind-sets. But family arguments were one thing; dinner conversation with a matriarch of Boston society was altogether different. She would *not* allow herself to be drawn into an argument about slavery. She had no personal involvement and little interest in the subject, but everyone from her landlady to her classmates felt it necessary to chastise Flanna for the perceived faults and injustices of the entire South.

"Mother, Flanna is at the top of her class, did I mention that?" Roger leaned across the table to squeeze his mother's hand, nearly upsetting the butler's ladle as he attempted to fill Roger's bowl. "She is a very bright young woman."

"An outspoken young woman, at any rate." Mrs. Haynes pressed her lips together as the butler served Flanna. "Apparently you hold unconventional views in several areas. I applaud you for attempting the study of medicine."

Flanna smiled to cover her annoyance at the woman's use of the word *attempting*. "Yes ma'am. I've always wanted to follow in my father's footsteps, and months ago I realized that a female partner could be of great use to him. Many ladies are too modest to call for a male doctor when they are ill, and a midwife cannot handle every medical difficulty."

Mrs. Haynes's mercurial dark eyes sharpened. "I must say, I've always thought the idea of women doctors to be a most appropriate notion. I shudder every time I have to visit a male physician, and my husband, the General—God rest his soul—was most adamant upon being present whenever a physician had to attend me. A male doctor's attention detracts from female delicacy." She smiled at Flanna with a faint light of approval in her eyes. "I congratulate you, my dear, for choosing a worthy profession. And I hope you find a really good doctor to oversee your efforts in case you encounter some serious situation."

Beneath the table, Flanna flexed her fingers until the urge to throttle the older woman had passed. "I thank you for your approval," she said, noting Roger's chagrined expression from the corner of her eye, "but even though I will assist my father, I do not think I will require his help should a serious case arise. My education at the medical college has been quite complete. When I graduate, I expect that I would be able to attend you without resorting to any other professional. Technically, I should even be able to treat"—her eyes lifted and caught the butler's startled gaze—"Howard."

"My goodness!" The dowager's hand flew to her jeweled neck, and after an instant she let out a throaty laugh. "As if I would allow a slaveholder near one of my sturdy Irish servants!"

"Madam, I do not believe my presence is required here," the butler stammered, a dark flush mantling his cheeks.

"She was only making a point, Howard," Roger said, waving the butler away. He placed one elbow on the table and gave his mother a conspiratorial smile. "Now, Mother, Flanna has already told you that she owns no slaves and that she finds the practice abhorrent. And you must admit that she is determined enough to join your corps of suffragists."

Mrs. Haynes's penetrating eyes swung back to Flanna. "How do you feel, my dear, about women and the right to vote?"

Flanna hesitated, wavering between honesty and discretion. She would love to tell this woman exactly what she thought, but she had already said too much. "I believe," she said, keenly aware of the older woman's scrutiny, "that women know much more about politics than men give them credit for knowing."

She smiled, congratulating herself on her tact, but Mrs. Haynes pressed on. "But what do you think about women and the vote? We are citizens of this country, so shouldn't we be able to cast our vote as freely as American men?"

Flanna glanced at Roger, hoping for his assistance, but his eyes were fastened to the tablecloth, his cheeks flushed. The coward.

"Mrs. Haynes." Flanna forced a demure smile to her lips. "Most women I know are happy to be under the authority of their husbands and fathers. They do influence the vote, they do play a role in politics, but they influence matters through the hearts of their men."

Mrs. Haynes sank back in her chair, her face frozen in an expression of incredulity.

"Ladies." A grin overtook Roger's handsome features as he straightened and looked at Flanna. "My two favorite women in all the world, you are both strong in mind and opinion. But in the spirit of Christmastide, can't we put aside our differences and lift our thoughts to peace on earth?"

Mrs. Haynes reached for the crystal goblet at her plate. "We already have, son. Only the spirit of the season could enable me to sit at a table with one whose family owns slaves."

"Blessings on you, Mother, for your generosity," Roger answered in a wry voice. He gave Flanna a warm smile, then extended his hands, one to her, one to his mother. "Give me your hands, ladies, and let me ask God to bless this meal. And I will pray that our conversation may be more amiable for the rest of the evening."

❧

"I'm afraid you may have cast a sour spell on your mother's holiday, Roger," Flanna said, slowly making her way over the snow-dusted walkway outside the Haynes house. "Your mother heartily dislikes me."

"No, she doesn't!" Roger protested, laughing. The sound of his laughter echoed over the quiet street as he extended his hand and helped Flanna to the carriage block. Behind him, the four-story brick house loomed like an ancient and forbidding presence, the lamp-lit windows shining like Mrs. Haynes's disapproving eyes. "She thinks you are quite…original."

Flanna paused for a moment to make certain Charity had been safely seated on the dickey at the rear of the carriage, then squeezed Roger's hand as she stepped from the block into the creaking phaeton. The four-wheeled conveyance, with its folding top extended to shelter them from the winter wind, reminded her of her father's buggy, and for an instant homesickness smote her with the force of a physical blow. She steeled her heart and reminded herself that she'd surely spend *next* Christmas at home, then slid to the end of the upholstered bench as Roger climbed in beside her.

"Excuse me, my dear."

Flanna lifted her arms, allowing Roger to arrange a carriage blanket over her skirts, then sighed in simple relief when he lifted the reins and clucked softly to the horse. She was so thankful that this night was just about over.

"Sorry to have spoiled your Christmas, Roger." She rubbed the tip of her nose, certain that it had gone red with the cold. "I shouldn't have spoken so freely. Your mother probably thinks I am the worst sort of influence on you."

"My mother abhors the idea of slavery, but she adores you." Roger guided the horse onto the narrow street that separated the row of stately houses from Louisburg Square. "She admires strong-minded women. You should hear her carry on about equal pay for women who do men's work."

"I wouldn't know much about that," Flanna admitted, her eyes following the bare tree limbs that stretched overhead like a black and skeletal canopy. "I don't care how much I'm paid; my father takes care of all my needs. I only care that women receive the medical help they need."

Roger looked down at her, his dark eyebrows arching mischievously. "Mother probably wouldn't admit it to you, but she is actually quite an admirer of Dr. Elizabeth Blackwell. She has followed that lady's career for several years and was quite pleased when Dr. Blackwell established her women's clinic in New York."

"Dr. Blackwell was from Charleston too." Flanna's thoughts turned wistfully toward home. "I wonder if she missed it as much as I do."

"Flanna, darling, don't fret so." Roger transferred the reins into his right hand, then slipped his left arm around her shoulders. "You have only to give me some sign, and I would agree to take care of you forever. You could have a wonderful life here in Boston. I would be able to recommend you to the finest ladies in the city, and you could cure feminine diseases to your heart's content. And when you have grown tired of medicine, you and I would have children, as many as you want."

With a skill derived from years of divining men's intentions, Flanna gently steered the subject away from matrimony. "Are you so certain of your influence, Mr. Haynes?" She injected a smile into her voice. "I'm not certain your mother would seek me out as her physician."

"Give me time, darling." His arm fell from her shoulders as he shifted the reins to negotiate a difficult turn. "My influence can only grow once I enter politics. Mother says Judge Whittier is ready to place my name upon the next ballot, and it's reasonably certain I shall be successful in this district. Why, the folks from Beacon Hill alone could carry the day, and no one has greater influence than those people."

"Perhaps, then, you should reconsider our friendship in the light of your political aspirations." Flanna's eyes drifted out to the rows of dignified stone houses that lined the street. They were passing Pemberton Square, Beacon Hill's eastern mate to Louisburg Square. Golden light from the gas street lamps pooled on the snowy sidewalks, injecting occasional notes of warmth into what would otherwise be a cold and alien landscape. Charleston rarely saw snow, but twice in the last month alone Flanna had wondered if Boston would be buried in it.

"Flanna, why should I reconsider you?" Roger turned to give her a look of pure disbelief. "How could I, when we are the perfect pair? You represent the modern woman, one as useful as she is beautiful, and I am the forerunner of a new political movement that will mend the fractures in our grand and glorious Union." He snapped the reins. "No, my dear, together we are an unbeatable team. You are a lady of the South, I am a man of the North. You undoubtedly feel strong loyalties to Charleston and South Carolina, while I desire to give my life in service to the people of Boston and Massachusetts. Others will see us as friends and partners and realize that it is possible for two people to put sectional and philosophical differences aside in order to work together."

"Philosophical differences?" Flanna tilted her head to look up at him. "What philosophical differences? In all the time I've known you, Roger, you've never contradicted me. I thought you shared my views."

His broad mouth quirked with humor. "No couple shares every view, my sweet. But just as you and Mother were able to eat a peaceful meal without resorting to unpleasantness, so you and I shall sometimes disagree and yet present a peaceable appearance. In truth, you shall have your work, and I shall have mine. I doubt our differences of opinion will ever amount to much."

Flanna didn't answer, but looked out at the street, uncomfortable with Roger's implication that they had come to some sort of understanding. She was returning to Charleston after graduation from medical school; she had told him so time and time again. And though she considered him a fine friend and a man of admirable qualities, she had no desire to rush with him to the altar. She wanted to be a doctor, but Roger seemed to think her ambition was nothing but a schoolgirl's foolish daydream.

"Mother wants you to come tomorrow, of course," Roger was saying, his eyes intent on the road. "We'll have our big Christmas dinner at one o'clock." He gave her a quick smile. "We have a surprise for you—my brother is coming from West Point." He pulled back on the reins, halting the horse, and gave her an oddly keen, swift look. "What do you say, Flanna? Will I be able to tell my brother that he is meeting the future Mrs. Roger Haynes?"

Flanna squinted in embarrassment and looked away, certain that he had momentarily lost his good sense. But though this unexpected proposal had caught her off guard, she did not want to react hastily and offend him.

"Thank you, Roger," she said, smoothing the irritation and shock from her voice. She looked up and met his bright gaze. "I am not unaware of the honor you are bestowing upon me, but I have told you that I am not presently interested in marriage. I have to finish my education, I have to pass my medical examinations, and I have promised my father that I would return to Charleston and assist him in his practice. And since you feel strongly that you must remain in Massachusetts—"

"We are one country, Flanna, one sacred Union." He dropped the reins and reached across the lap blanket to enfold her gloved hands. "And you and I should be one flesh. I understand your commitment to your father, and I admire you tremendously for the strength of heart and will that motivated you to make it. All right, finish school. Return to Charleston, and give your father one year of your time. But consider that I am willing to wait for you. As you work, I will build a constituency that will propel me to a position in the governor's office before you can return from Carolina! We can be wed in the governor's mansion, or anywhere you like, but say you'll be my wife, Flanna O'Connor!"

His steady gaze bore into her in silent expectation, and the intensity of his look made her pulse pound. This was not her first marriage proposal, but Roger was by far her most persistent suitor. For two years he had escorted her to events around Boston, providing an introduction into fine homes and social events she would never have graced without his influence. Flanna had to admit she enjoyed walking into a luxurious drawing room on the handsome lawyer's arm.

But to live in Boston? The people here seemed alien, cold, and stuffy compared to the warm and gentle folks of Charleston. As much as she enjoyed Roger's company, she did not think his conversation and ready wit could compensate for the loneliness she would feel without contact with her brother, her father, her Aunt Marsali, and her seven strapping cousins. Why, she could not have endured the lonely college terms if not for Charity's company and the knowledge that she could go home during the summer months.

"These things," she began, speaking slowly as she searched for words which would protect their friendship and yet cool Roger's ardor, "are not announced casually over family dinners. And you have forgotten one very important step—you must write my father and ask his permission and blessing before I can give my consent. I am a dutiful daughter, and if I were to assent to your plan without consulting my father, my actions would break his heart."

"Don't you like me, Flanna?" Roger looked down, the fringe of his lashes casting moonlit shadows on his cheeks. "Would marriage to a lawyer be so terrible that you cannot contemplate it? Or is it me you find objectionable?"

"You are being foolish." She softened her voice, trying to verbalize feelings he would not understand. "I'm very fond of you. It's just—Roger, may I be honest?"

"I would accept nothing less than honesty from you."

"Good." She paused, her gaze flicking toward a passing buggy. "Should we be sitting out in public like this?"

"We're chaperoned." Without taking his gaze from her face, he called out, "Charity?"

"Yes, Mr. Haynes?" The girl's voice echoed over the street.

"There." Roger tightened his grip on Flanna's hands. "Your maid is here, and we are safely under observation. So tell me what is in your heart."

Flanna shifted in the buggy. "I am terribly fond of you." That much was true. After several miserable weeks in Boston, Flanna had met Roger at a social sponsored by several college supporters. He had at once become her escort and her friend, and she had reserved every spare moment for him without wanting to think of the consequences. Now she was about to disappoint him, perhaps for the last time. But she had never intended to give him her heart, only her friendship.

She looked directly into his dark eyes. "Roger, I must go home to Charleston. I promised my father that I would assist him once I became a doctor. And I miss Charleston. My family is there."

"I will be your family if we are wed." Roger spoke in an odd, yet gentle tone. "And Flanna, think of it—I may one day be president of the United States! What greater destiny could a woman wish than to marry a man who has devoted his life to public service?"

"She might wish to devote *her* life to those less fortunate." She squeezed his hand, hoping he would understand. "Roger, I never told you this—I suppose I was a bit embarrassed—but my grandfather owned over a hundred slaves. One of them was my Mammy, and I have never met a more modest woman, black or white. My mother died when I was a baby, so Mammy was everything to me, the only mother I ever knew."

"I don't care that your grandfather owned slaves."

"That's not the point, Roger." Flanna looked down at his hands, so tightly entwined with hers. "Mammy became ill, you see, but she was so demure, so shy, that she would not allow a male doctor to examine her."

She breathed deep and felt a sharp stab of memory, a painful remnant from the past. "She died one night as I held her in her bed. When I lifted the blanket I discovered that she'd hemorrhaged from her female organs. A doctor could have stopped the bleeding and saved her life, but she would not let a strange man come near."

Roger made a small, comforting sound. "Why didn't your father tend her?"

Flanna shook her head. "She would have died from embarrassment before she'd let him examine her. Despite her unrefined language and her status, she was by nature a lady, far more genteel than I could ever hope to be." Her mouth twisted in a wry smile. "She was always fussing at me for roughhousing with my brother and my cousins. She thought I'd grow up to be a tomboy."

"Darling," he said, his voice silky, "there is absolutely nothing of the tomboy about you now."

"That's because of Mammy. When I was fifteen, she and Aunt Marsali brought me in, pulled my hair up, and let my dresses down. They taught me to be a lady, and by that time I was ready to learn." Flanna paused, then continued in sinking tones. "And on the night Mammy died, I vowed that I would become a doctor so no woman, black or white, would have to suffer because she would not visit a male physician. I can't break that vow."

"Women die in Boston too, Flanna," Roger said, with a significant lifting of his brows. "You could fulfill that vow here, in Washington, anywhere."

"But my father is in Charleston. And when I left for medical school, I promised to come back and work with him."

Roger sighed heavily and released her hands. "I understand, dear Flanna. So be it. I will say nothing to my brother."

"Thank you."

"But"—he held up a warning finger—"at the earliest opportunity I will write your father and ask for his blessing upon our future marriage. You promised you would work with him. You did not promise him a lifetime."

Flanna sat in silence, considering his words. Perhaps she would be unwise to completely reject his proposal. She had given little thought to her life beyond her future as a doctor, and handsome bachelors like Roger did not come along every day. He was a catch; all the girls at the boardinghouse said so. Her vision was still colored with the memory of Mammy, and she could just see the woman rising up, her face as stern as granite, rebuking Flanna for being penny wise and pound foolish. *"You's always disregardin' tomorrow for the promise of today."*

"If you write my father, perhaps you should introduce yourself first," she suggested. "I shouldn't think he would respond favorably if you ask for my hand outright. I've mentioned you in my letters, of course, but he will want to know you on a personal level."

"Doubtless he'll want me to visit Charleston," Roger said, taking up the reins, "which I will gladly do, but only because you are the only woman in the world for me. And while I am winning your father's good faith and his blessing, you shall take your final examinations and pass them. Are we agreed?"

Flanna stared at him, her thoughts scampering frantically. Why not agree? Roger was as persistent as a mosquito; he would give her no peace until she assented to *something* in his favor. And though her father undoubtedly would approve of Roger Haynes, he had little time for correspondence, so it might be months before he answered Roger's letter and granted permission for an engagement. By then Flanna would be back home in Charleston, fulfilling her promise. Roger might lose interest; he might even forget her altogether. Certainly his mother would do *her* part to make sure Flanna was forgotten. But if Roger persisted, if his feelings for her endured through time and separation and distance, then perhaps he really *did* love her as a husband ought to love a wife.

Flanna sighed and closed her eyes. She would pray for God's will, but in the meantime there was little she could do to resist Roger's relentless energy.

"Are we agreed then?" Roger sat still, the reins suspended in midair, awaiting her response.

"I believe we are—but I must pray about it."

Roger caught up her hand and pressed it to his lips in a fit of rapture, and Flanna smiled at his impertinence. Roger was all flash and flair, the most charming companion she had ever met, and one of the most considerate escorts. If by some miracle he did forget her once she returned to Charleston, she would certainly never forget him.

Flicking the reins, he urged the horse forward. Flanna pressed her hands together as the carriage moved slowly down the street. Who could tell? Perhaps Roger's plan actually made sense. She could work with her father for a year, and if Roger was still determined to marry her, perhaps he'd even consider a move to Charleston. They were one Union, he'd said. One country. He could fill a political seat in Charleston as well as in Boston; charming, gregarious men like Roger developed a following wherever they went.

"Whoa, Gertie."

Roger pulled back on the reins as the carriage drew up outside the tall wooden building that housed sixteen of the forty students at the New England Female Medical College. Flanna noticed a light burning in the parlor window. The housemother, Mrs. Davis, probably rocked there by the fireplace, mentally checking off each girl who returned. In another hour she would bar the door. Any young lady not satisfactorily accounted for would be expelled from the boardinghouse and the college on the grounds of moral turpitude.

Flanna shifted to face Roger. "You may call for me tomorrow but not a word about your future plans. Remember, before we can plan to marry, you must not only win my father, but your mother must approve of me." That roadblock would probably grant Flanna another year's grace, for Mrs. Haynes obviously believed that all Southern women were slaveholding monsters.

"Don't mind Mother." Roger lowered his head until his forehead brushed the brim of Flanna's bonnet. "She spends too much time reading the newspapers. She's upset by all this talk of secession. But I will not allow the word *slavery* to be uttered tomorrow. One should not talk of politics on Christmas Day."

"Agreed. I will not speak of slavery, or secession, or women in medicine. I will do nothing but sit by your side and try to charm your mother." She gave him a heartfelt smile. "I may even tell her I'm willing to stand with those noisy suffragists, if that will charm her."

"Don't forget my brother—he'll need charming too. He wrote that he couldn't believe I could lose my heart to a girl from South Carolina." His breath gently warmed her face as he tilted his head. "May I be so bold as to ask for a kiss before I walk you to the house?"

"Miss Flanna?" Right on cue, Charity's voice rang out from the back of the carriage. "Are we goin' in now?"

Flanna pulled away from Roger as she turned to answer. "Yes, Charity. Hop on down, and Mr. Haynes will walk us in."

"You can't blame a man for trying." An easy smile played at the corners of Roger's mouth. "After the official engagement then." He stepped out onto the carriage block, then extended a hand to help Flanna alight.

"After the wedding, you mean," Flanna answered, taking his hand and descending as gracefully as she could. "A lady does not kiss a man until the wedding band is on her finger."

"Is that so?" One of his dark brows arched devilishly. "Then three-quarters of the young women in Boston aren't ladies."

"That may be, sir," Flanna answered, falling into step beside Charity as the maid moved toward the house. She turned and flashed a bright smile over her shoulder. "But you may rest assured that I am."

⊷◦⊶

Flanna pressed her hands to her cold cheeks as she stamped her feet on the entry rug to dislodge any lingering clumps of snow. The rhythmic creak of the housemother's rocker halted for a moment, and Flanna called out, "It's only me, Mrs. Davis. Charity and I are safely returned from the Haynes house."

Charity helped Flanna slip out of her pelisse, then gathered it in her arms as Flanna smoothed the wrinkles out of her skirt. Mrs. Davis liked her girls to look modest and tidy at all times, for the widow had a sterling reputation to maintain. Though she had probably found it difficult to swallow the idea of a female medical college, for the past twelve years her girls had lived and studied under intense scrutiny without a single moral failure. Practically every time Flanna went out the door, Mrs. Davis's farewell included a cheery reminder that the college's fate and reputation rested upon her students' shoulders.

Flanna lifted her chin and walked through the parlor, pausing politely before Mrs. Davis's rocker.

"A nice evening, my dear?"

"Very nice, Mrs. Davis, thank you for asking. Mrs. Haynes is a gracious hostess."

The widow nodded, her white cap framing her pinched face. "You've been seeing quite a lot of her son. How long have you two been keeping company?"

"Oh, about a year and a half, I suppose." Flanna gave the landlady a careful smile. "Long enough for me to know he is quite a gentleman. You need not fear when I am out with him, ma'am."

"A woman can never let her guard completely down." The old woman's voice rattled like the wind against the windowpanes. "Shouldn't he be writing a letter to your father soon?"

Good grief, had the woman been listening at the window? Eager to retreat from the prying questions, Flanna shifted her weight toward

30

the staircase. Her bell-shaped hoop skirt swung forward, betraying her eagerness. "I expect Roger will do whatever a gentleman should do. But he understands I intend to finish school and return to Charleston."

The old woman closed her eyes and shook her head slightly. "I suppose it's his mother that's preventing him from proposing. She cannot approve the match."

Flanna had taken a forward step, but at Mrs. Davis's last comment she halted, shocked by the woman's bluntness. "Why would she not approve the match?" Though she knew from firsthand experience that Mrs. Haynes did not approve of slavery, she *did* approve of Flanna's plans for a career in medicine. And despite Flanna's conviction that tonight's dinner had not gone entirely well, she had not yet met a person she could not charm—if given enough time.

Mrs. Davis let out a three-noted cackle. "A proud son of Massachusetts marrying a Charleston girl? It could never happen. Not anymore. Why, at this very moment the name of South Carolina is as reviled as the devil's." The smile she wore was no smile at all, just a wrinkle with yellow teeth in the midst of it. "In a month you'll be fortunate if you're received in a single parlor in Boston."

Flanna stared at her landlady in total incredulity. "Why ever not?"

"Have you not heard?" Mrs. Davis's skinny frame fairly vibrated with eagerness. "No, I suppose you haven't. South Carolina seceded from the Union four days ago! It was in the evening paper. Did no one tell you?"

Shock tore through Flanna, numbing her toes and tingling her fingers. Unable to respond, she looked back at Charity, then shook her head as confused thoughts whirled in her brain. It couldn't be true! Oh, Wesley had written about a group of politicians who had threatened to secede if Lincoln won the presidential election, but she had never dreamed they'd actually proceed with their plan.

Aghast, Flanna glanced about the room until her eyes fell on a folded newspaper. "May I?"

"Of course, you certainly should take it." Mrs. Davis's age-spotted hand quivered as she lifted it in permission. "Read what your countrymen have done. And know that if trouble arises between you and Roger Haynes, the fault can be assigned to those hotheaded slaveholders in South Carolina!"

With the older woman's tirade ringing in her ears, Flanna scooped up the newspaper and tucked it under her arm as she fled for the safety of the stairs.

❧

Flanna thought her heart must have stopped when Mrs. Davis told her that South Carolina had seceded, for it now began pounding much faster than usual, as though to make up for a few lost beats. By the time she and Charity reached her room it was knocking in her chest like a swampland woodpecker.

Her dark eyes wide with alarm, Charity laid the mantle on her bed and searched Flanna's face. "Miss Flanna, what's wrong with South Carolina?"

"I'm not sure," Flanna whispered, half-stumbling to her own bed. She fell on the creaking mattress, mindless of her dress and the medical books strewn there. With trembling fingers, she shook open the newspaper and read the screaming headline: "South Carolina Secedes!"

"It can't be."

"What can't be?" Charity had a round, cheerful face whose natural expression was a smile, but that face was blank now, all traces of humor wiped away.

"South Carolina," Flanna murmured, thinking of her father, her brother, her aunt, and her cousins. "My state—*our* state—has seceded from the Union."

"Seceded?" Charity knelt at Flanna's feet to unlace her walking boots, but she paused and looked up. "Miss Flanna, I don't understand."

"Pulled away, withdrawn," Flanna whispered, reading the article. "South Carolina and Charleston are no longer a part of the United States."

Charity responded with a strange gasping sound, but Flanna scarcely heard her, so intent was she upon her reading. According to the newspaper article, calls for secession had been circulating ever since the news of Lincoln's election reached Charleston on November seventh. The foreman of the grand jury in the federal court, Robert Gourdin, refused to conduct any further business "as the North, through the ballot box has swept away the last hope for the permanence of the Federal government of these sovereign States." Within days other officials resigned, including Judge Andrew G. Magrath, the United States District Attorney, and the collector of the port.

"Great heavens," Flanna whispered, only half-feeling Charity's tug on her boots, "they are quite serious! I never believed it would come to this!"

Secessionist leaders, she read, were comparing themselves to the early American revolutionaries. Palmetto and Lone Star flags, the beloved emblems of South Carolina, were sprouting like wildflowers throughout the state. Many gentlemen of Charleston had decorated their lapels with cockades—gold badges with the palmetto tree, a lone star, and a coiled rattlesnake superimposed on a blue silk ribbon.

"What are they going to do?" Charity's brown eyes were wide and slightly wet when Flanna looked down at her. "Does the paper say?"

"I'm afraid I don't know," Flanna answered, a wave of apprehension sweeping through her. South Carolina *couldn't* be an independent country. On a surge of memory, Roger's words came back to her: *"We are one country, Flanna, one sacred Union."*

What were these secessionists thinking? And why had they done this crazy thing right *now,* right before Christmas, right before her exams? What if the examining board looked at her file and saw that she was from South Carolina? What if Mrs. Davis warmed to the idea of tossing the secessionist student out of the boardinghouse? Flanna's dreams would vanish like a pebble in a dark pond, dropping out of sight forever.

"Does the paper tell you anything about the home folks?" Charity's fingers struggled clumsily with the bootlaces, and Flanna suddenly realized the girl was worried about her parents. They were among the three thousand free Negroes in Charleston, many of whom held slaves themselves. Ever since Flanna could remember, an uneasy peace had existed between Charleston's white elite, the free browns (so-named because many of them were mulatto), and the city's white working class. If the city was in turmoil over slavery and secession, this might be a dangerous time to be black in the South—slave or free.

"Leave my shoes. Let me read." Flanna scanned the page again. "This article says that the city of Charleston was united in its calls for secession…and that on December seventeenth more than 160 delegates from South Carolina met in Columbia to decide whether or not the state would secede. Charleston sent 23 representatives, but an outbreak of smallpox sent the convention back to Charleston. There, in St. Andrew's Hall, the delegates unanimously adopted the Ordinance of Secession from the Union. That night they signed it at Institute Hall."

"The colored folks…did they sign it too?"

"I don't know, Charity." Flanna read on. "Well—here's something. Eighty-two brown aristocrats sent a message to the mayor of Charleston that read, 'We are by birth citizens of South Carolina; in our veins is the blood of the white race, in some half, in others much more; our attachments are with you.'"

Charity's dark eyes filled with disbelief. She sank back, resting her weight on her heels, and Flanna hoped the information would satisfy her curiosity for a while.

She read further, of church bells ringing as the news spread through the city, of Union flags thrown to the breeze, of artillery salutes thundering in the night. The reporter also mentioned that Charleston officials, fearful of a slave uprising, sent nightly patrols through the city to quell any sign of black unrest.

"Oh, Charity." Flanna clutched the newspaper and its dread news to her chest. "What are we going to do? This is terrible news, just terrible."

"We could go home." Charity lifted one brow in mute supplication. "We don't belong up here, Miss Flanna."

Flanna lowered the paper to her lap, her mind spinning with bewilderment. Her father hadn't had time to write of this incredible news, but he would, she was certain. Would he demand that she come home immediately? *Should* she go home? She was so close to finishing her degree, but what would her father's friends think of a man who allowed his daughter to live among and consort with Yankees? A cold knot formed in her stomach as she realized that she was now in a foreign country, a place no longer affiliated with home.

We are one country, Flanna, one sacred Union.

Not anymore.

Flanna pressed her fingers to her temple as another thought hit her. *Roger!* If Papa were caught up in this wave of secession hysteria, he'd no sooner correspond with a Yankee Republican than he would with Abe Lincoln himself. He would never approve of Flanna's engagement. Indeed, he might even reply to Roger's initial letter with a surly response, destroying any chance of what might have been a suitable match.

And finishing her degree elsewhere was not an option. There was only one medical school for women in the South—Graefenberg Medical Institute in Dadeville, Alabama—but her father had not been impressed with that school's facility. In Boston Flanna had enjoyed access to a vast array of resources: a real skeleton, lab equipment, and an entire room of normal and pathological specimens in glass beakers. Graefenberg did not even have a decent medical library.

Dear God, what should I do?

Flanna's gaze fell on her anatomy textbook. She had nearly memorized the entire text, and in just four weeks she'd be tested on the material. That anatomy examination was the last hurdle, all that stood between her and a bona fide medical degree. If they went home now, all her hard work would count for nothing. Surely God would not want her to toss away two years of an expensive and hard-won education.

"We can stay a few more weeks," she whispered, running her hand over a map of the human body's arterial system. "Let's wait until all this excitement dies down. Besides, Papa wouldn't want us traveling while things are so…undecided." She drew in a deep breath and released it slowly. "Surely this will pass, Charity. It has to."

The maid's face fell in disappointment, but the touch of the textbook calmed Flanna's pounding pulse. Apparently South Carolina had worked itself into a dither while she lost herself in her studies. If she immersed herself in her studies again, perhaps God would lead South Carolina to straighten itself out. What good would worry do? Her father had sent her to Boston to earn a medical degree, and she could not let him down. He needed her at home, but he needed her as a doctor.

With that decision made, Flanna's mind shifted to practical matters. Until this secession business had been settled, her father must not know about Roger Haynes and his intentions. News of that development could wait. If it took the better part of a year for the dust to settle, so much the better. She would have earned her degree and begun to fulfill her promise to her father. Roger seemed to have enough ambitions to keep him busy, and if in the interim he found some nice Massachusetts girl who'd make him a better wife, that would be fine. She'd miss his wit and his charm, but if God closed one door, he was certain to open another.

"Charity, bring me pen and paper, please." Flanna tossed the newspaper to the floor and resolutely pushed South Carolina from her mind. She had to write her father and assure him she was well, and tomorrow she'd have to tell Roger to postpone his letter indefinitely.

Until South Carolina came to its senses, matrimony would just have to wait.

Two
⁓⁓

Meagan, the Hayneses' Irish maid, sat at the shiny new piano and began to play "I Dream of Jeanie with the Light Brown Hair" for the third time. Sipping her tea, Flanna caught Roger's eye over the rim of her cup. He was seated on the sofa by his mother, his head propped on his hand, his eyes dull with displeasure.

He hadn't handled the news well. When Flanna told him that an engagement could not possibly be arranged until after the storm of secession had ceased, he'd been clearheaded enough to see the wisdom in her words, and politician enough to protest. His howls had filled the carriage as they rolled through the Beacon Hill district, and Flanna rolled her eyes, knowing that Charity, safely seated on the dickey, had to be giggling at his ridiculous display of disappointment.

Now Roger's gaze roved over the flickering fire while his foot absently kept time to the tinkling piano. Flanna knew he was weighing the advantages of not having a Southern fiancée against the disadvantages of campaigning without a fiancée at all. A genteel woman would give him added polish and respectability when he ran for office. His mother was a virtual queen among the Boston elite, but to fulfill his aspirations Roger's appeal would need to extend far beyond Beacon Hill.

"People expect a politician to have a family," he had told Flanna one afternoon as they walked around Louisburg Square, the garden cul-de-sac across from his mother's house. "How am I to identify with a working man and his family unless I have a family of my own?"

"And how can you relate to women, unless you are on friendly terms with one other than your mother?" Flanna answered, half-teasing.

Roger nodded, apparently missing the joke. "Indeed! I'm so glad you understand! You see, Flanna, what a benefit you are to me! You are bright, beautiful, and kind. I could not ask for a more gracious hostess or a more beautiful confidante."

She had understood his intentions almost from the beginning, and if he was using her as a beautiful charmer, she had continued to see him for reasons equally as selfish. Roger Haynes was respected, his mother a doyenne of impeccable breeding. The stately brick house symbolized all that was proper and acceptable and good in Boston society. As a newcomer in the city, Flanna had been so desperate to belong, to be among people like those she had known at home, that she had gladly accepted Roger's invitations.

The final strains of "I Dream of Jeanie" drifted away from the parlor, then Meagan stood and curtseyed in front of her mistress. "Shall you be wanting to hear it again, ma'am?"

"No, I believe we've heard enough," Roger said, straightening on the sofa. While one hand fell to his mother's shoulder, he pulled out his pocket watch with the other. "It's half past one already, Mother. Obviously something has delayed Alden. Shall we go in to dinner without him?"

"No." Mrs. Haynes pulled her lips into a straight, disapproving line. "You are always in a hurry, Roger. You know how undependable the train is."

"But we've waited half an hour."

His mother's eyes narrowed. "A polite person would wait all day. Now be patient and be quiet. I find I must address an issue that concerns your dinner guest."

Stiffening in her chair, Flanna felt a rush of warmth flood her cheeks.

"I trust, Miss O'Connor," Mrs. Haynes said, folding her hands at her waist, "that you have heard the news? Have you seen a newspaper?"

Flanna forced her lips to part in a curved, still smile. "Yes ma'am, I have. I read one yesterday."

Mrs. Haynes gave her a bright-eyed glance, full of shrewdness. "What say you to your countrymen's rash decision? Those rebellious traitors have spat upon the blood of our forefathers and disavowed themselves of our glorious Union. Are your people in league with these renegades?"

Feeling tired, hungry, and irritable, Flanna ran her hand over the rich upholstery of her chair and tried to think of a diplomatic response. She had lain awake most of the night, staring into the darkness and forming answers to the remarks she knew she'd encounter in the days ahead. How unfortunate that the comments had begun in this house on Christmas Day.

"I couldn't say for certain," Flanna drawled, a light note of mockery in her voice, "but since my father and brother live in South Carolina, I imagine they will support South Carolina's actions. And those forefathers of whom you spoke, ma'am, are the ones responsible for a great deal of this trouble. It began years ago and has finally bubbled to the surface. Perhaps the time has come to deal with it."

"Our forefathers?" Shock flickered over the woman's face like summer lightning. "How can you say such a thing?"

"Does not the Constitution itself allow slavery?" Flanna persisted, a reckless feeling rising in her soul. "Does the Constitution not state that a slave who escapes must be returned to his owner?"

"The men who wrote the Constitution wanted to eliminate a necessary evil." Mrs. Haynes showed her teeth in an expression that was not a smile. "They included a provision to end the importation of slaves in 1808, did they not?"

"Mama knows her history." Roger gave Flanna a rueful smile. "I think she was there when the forefathers wrote the Constitution."

"Then perhaps she can recall what happened in Washington only three years ago." Flanna shifted her gaze from Roger back to his mother.

"Do you remember the momentous Supreme Court decision *Dred Scott v. Sandford?* President Buchanan claimed that the court would settle the issue of slavery once and for all, and the court ruled that no black man, free or slave, is a U.S. citizen and therefore has no rights under the law."

Flanna inclined her head in an exaggerated gesture of respect. "When it comes down to facts, Mrs. Haynes, slavery is a choice the law allows us to make. Is that not one of our precious American liberties, the freedom of choice? Any man may choose whether or not he wants to own slaves. And this same freedom of choice has allowed my countrymen, as you call them, to withdraw from a union that no longer represents their interests. In 1776 thirteen states came together to protect each other; now South Carolina wishes to withdraw and protect itself. Would you forbid my family and statesmen the liberty to choose for themselves?"

"My very dear Miss O'Connor." Roger's hoarse voice held a note halfway between disbelief and pleading. "Will you join me for a walk in the garden? I daresay this waiting has grown tedious for you, and Mother's garden is the toast of Boston."

Flanna hesitated, then caught the gleam of desperation in Roger's eye. Belatedly remembering her manners, she lowered her head in assent, then gathered her skirts and allowed him to help her to her feet.

As soon as they passed the parlor doorway, he bent to whisper in Flanna's ear. "I don't blame you for feeling edgy after hearing that confounded song three times in a row, but raising an argument at Christmas is a bit much, don't you think? I thought we agreed we would not discuss politics today."

Flanna pasted on a polite smile as a servant stepped out of a hallway, then held her tongue until they had stepped out into the garden. The winter wind nipped at her cheeks, but she scarcely noticed it, so fierce was her rising indignation.

"Roger!" She whirled on him in an Old Testament mood, unwilling to turn the other cheek just yet. "I will not allow your mother to deposit this entire issue at my feet. I don't know what she thinks *my people* are, but we are not barbarians! If the truth be told, the politicians in Washington have done more to stir up this present unpleasantness than any slaveholder I know!"

"But must you sharpen your tongue on my mother's ears?"

He reached out, and she shivered as his hands fell upon her arms. He'd been in such a hurry to escort her from the parlor that he'd neglected to bring her mantle. His eyes softened when he saw her tremble.

"How thoughtless of me," he said, releasing her. He began to slip out of his own coat. "You must be freezing."

"Roger, don't be foolish, you can't let the servants see you half-dressed. Don't give them something else to gossip about." Rubbing her hands over her thin sleeves, she nodded toward the door. "I'll be all right. Just go inside and fetch my mantle. This brisk wind is probably just the thing to cool my temper."

His tight expression relaxed into a smile. "Right you are. I'll be back in a moment."

He stepped away, his long stride carrying him back into the house in three steps. Flanna rubbed her hands over her arms again, then moved into a patch of sunlight that stretched between the house and the garden wall. Roger's suggestion of the garden was an obvious excuse to get her away from his mother, for the spindly rose canes and banked flower beds alongside the house were pitiful and bare. A weathered wooden bench sat in an alcove beneath the parlor window, but Flanna had no desire to sit in the chilly shade. Instead she walked briskly in the sunlight, hugging her arms as she attempted to balance the chilly temperature of her skin with the fiery resentment raging in her heart.

At the north end of the garden a wrought-iron gate opened to the sidewalk at the front of the house. The clopping sounds of passing carriages enticed Flanna, and she moved toward the gate, wishing she could hail a hansom cab and retreat to the boardinghouse. But a lady did not run away from difficulties, and Flanna would not give any Yankee woman an excuse to criticize her manners.

Shivering, she rubbed her hands together, then froze as the muffled sound of voices broke the garden's winter stillness. Even through the closed glass and heavy parlor draperies she could hear Mrs. Haynes's strident tones.

"You have no right, Roger, to bring a secessionist woman into this house! Your father would turn in his grave if he knew a Rebel, one who would happily spit upon the Union flag, will sit at his Christmas dinner table!"

"She is not a Rebel, Mother, and Flanna doesn't spit. Now calm down; let's discuss this. Where are your smelling salts?"

"She is a slaver, if not in practice, then at heart. You heard her defend the practice! How do you know her people don't beat their slaves? You will stand before God Almighty and be judged for this, son, but the Lord will know that I sought to turn you from this path."

"She is not a slaver, Mother; she is my guest. Would you like me to have Meagan play again? Does she know any other tunes?"

Mrs. Haynes spoke again, but the words were too low for Flanna to hear. She shuddered, filled with humiliation at the thought that she had brought discord to this house on Christmas. Guilt flooded over her, and she turned toward the gate, ready to forfeit her reputation and walk home, but the sight of a uniformed officer on the sidewalk stopped her in midstep.

He stood just beyond the gate, his blond hair gleaming in the winter sun, his gloved hand resting formally on the hilt of his sword. He wore a blue uniform of fine wool, with knee-high boots and a matching leather belt at his waist. Bright gold braids adorned his shoulders and complemented the braiding on his collar. A police officer?

Flanna took it all in: the confident set of his shoulders, his firm features, the neatly clipped moustache, and his compelling blue eyes. She was surprised to see him smile at her. "Is there some trouble in the house?" he asked.

Her mind whirled at the odd question. "I beg your pardon, sir?"

His eyes raked over her, and Flanna pulled her thin, decorative shawl tightly about her in response to his gaze. "I am not accustomed to seeing elegantly attired young women loitering outside the house unless there is some trouble within—a fire, perhaps, or a raving lunatic."

He lifted a brow at this last comment, and Flanna realized he was teasing. She gave him a relieved smile. "Mrs. Haynes may be raving at the moment, but I wouldn't call her a lunatic. She does seem opposed to my presence at Christmas dinner, however, so her son felt it advisable for me to step outside."

This answer seemed to amuse the handsome officer, for he thrust his hands behind his back and smiled. "I know Mrs. Haynes. And you are quite right, the lady is most opinionated, especially when it comes to the young ladies her son brings home. But I've never met a more righteously sane woman in my life."

"Oh?" Despite the sunlight's warmth, Flanna shivered as a gust of wind blew upon her bare neck and shoulders. "Have you encountered her as you patrolled this neighborhood?"

"Not exactly." His blue eyes sparkled as they met hers. "Mrs. Haynes is my mother."

Flanna felt her cheeks blaze as though they'd been seared by a roaring fire, then the door behind her opened. "Flanna! My goodness, you must be freezing!"

Too mortified to answer, she cringed in embarrassment as Roger approached and saw the man standing by the gate. "Alden!" Infectious joy rippled in his voice. "Brother, it is good to see you! Have you met Flanna?"

Flanna nodded in mute greeting as Roger draped her mantle around her shoulders, then she stepped back as he opened the gate.

"Flanna, I'd like you to meet my older brother, Major Alden Haynes, an instructor at West Point." The grooves beside Roger's mouth deepened into a full smile. "Alden, allow me to introduce Miss Flanna O'Connor of Charleston."

"We've met, though not formally," Alden answered. He grinned at Flanna again, his eyes gleaming wickedly. "And since you have the liberty to use her first name, I assume this is the young woman you mentioned in your letters."

"The very same."

"Then, brother, you ought to return to school." The bold look in Alden's eye made her pulse skitter alarmingly. "Your words did not begin to describe this lady's loveliness."

He bowed and lifted Flanna's frozen hand to his lips, making the back of her neck tingle as his warm mouth brushed her skin. She knew she ought to say something witty and charming, but her addled brain could think of nothing more clever than, "I am very pleased to meet you, Major Haynes."

With a possessive smile, Roger took her hand from Alden, then linked it through his arm. "Come, Alden, and let Mother embrace you. She's been frantic with worry that you'd be detained in New York."

"Then let me put her at ease," Alden answered, politely standing aside as Roger and Flanna led the way. "I came as quickly as I could, leaving my trunk at the station. I'll send a servant for it later, but first let me assure Mother that I am alive and well."

As they moved toward the house, Flanna kept her gaze lowered, acutely aware of Alden's crunching footsteps on the frozen ground behind her. She did not dare look back at him. Simple humiliation and embarrassment undoubtedly accounted for her fluttering heart and damp palms. Once she had an opportunity to properly apologize, she *might* be able to look him in the eye again.

Three
≈≈≈≈≈

December 26, 1860
Dear Papa,

How dreary this Christmas seemed without you!
Mrs. Haynes and her son Roger invited me to dine
with them, but the experience was not quite the
Christmas I would have kept with you and Wesley.
Boston folks seem intent upon making the day a
perfunctory celebration, not at all like the merrymaking we know from home. Boston public schools
held classes yesterday, and for a few hours the
Haynes family feared the oldest son, Alden, would
not arrive from West Point in time to join the family
at dinner. He finally appeared, though, and
brought much rejoicing to his mother's heart.

He is a singular fellow, though not much like
Roger. In many ways the brothers are opposites.
While Roger is witty and talkative, Alden tends to
be quiet. He scarcely uttered more than a hundred
words at dinner, but when he speaks, even the
butler stops to listen. Alden seems to think that
South Carolina's secession will lead to fighting, but
deferred to my feelings and declined to discuss the
subject when his mother pressed him.

Flanna paused and tapped her pen against her chin, recalling the scene at the dinner table. Alden Haynes had been seated across from her but next to his mother, and when Mrs. Haynes asked when the army would move south to teach the Rebels a lesson, his eyes momentarily caught Flanna's. A spark of some indefinable emotion—was it compassion?—filled his gaze, then he smiled and remarked that while there was certain to be a skirmish or two, he hoped matters could be settled without bloodshed. Roger had been quick to add that issues involving government should be settled in the halls of Congress, not on the battlefield. He had been about to launch into his favorite speech on the duty of a politician (a discourse Flanna had heard a dozen times before), but Alden lifted his hand and cut his younger brother off with a single determined gesture.

"I joined the army in order to defend our country against her enemies." Alden had spoken with quiet emphasis. "But I find it hard to think of men from South Carolina as my foes." He gave Flanna a wavering smile. "I do hope you won't fear my sword or my calling, Miss O'Connor. I would not harm you or your statesmen. My soul is wrapped up in my country, and I will do my duty just as my father did his in the Mexican War. But I have no wish to fight my brethren in South Carolina or any of the slaveholding states."

Mrs. Haynes's face turned as red as a robin's breast, and Flanna lowered her gaze to her plate, knowing a stream of accusations and challenges lay dammed behind the lady's pinched lips. But Alden's presence seemed to be a restraining influence, and for the first time Flanna had begun to relax within the Haynes house. Mrs. Haynes might wish to curse the secessionists and deport them all to Hades, but she'd hold her tongue as long as her beloved Alden remained in the room.

But Alden Haynes was a soldier, stationed in a distant city. He would not be around to protect Flanna forever.

Flanna sighed and dipped her pen in the inkwell.

I fear, Papa, that I have come to a crossroads in my life. I have prayed for the Lord's guidance and would beg for yours as well, though I know you will tell me that God gave me a brain for a purpose other than holding up my hat. But this is a puzzle I cannot reason out.

I am fond of Roger, and—I must be honest— he has recently spoken to me of a future we might share. His mother cares nothing for me at this time, but I truly believe her dislike springs more from hatred for South Carolina than from any personal antipathy toward me. Indeed, Roger assures me that she supports female doctors and women's rights, and she is listed as a patron of the New England Female Medical College.

Secession alone, then, has caused Mrs. Haynes to look upon me as a pariah. And while the people here are whispering of war (I know they are, though the girls at the boardinghouse are not so bold as to speak of it in my presence), I implore you and Wesley to do what you can to maintain peace in Charleston. I know the situation will never come to war, and in time all things shall pass. Soon slavery shall vanish from the earth, like all evils, and one day women and slaves shall have the same opportunities as free men.

Did you know, Papa, that several Boston women have been discovered masquerading as men while working in the factories? Boston is a manufacturing city, and the newspapers frequently delight in exposing damsels who dress as men in order to earn men's pay. It is beyond my comprehension to understand how a company can pay a man a dollar a day for operating a press whilst paying a woman only thirty-five cents for the same duty. They say, of course, that men are responsible for the feeding and care of a family, while women are not. I suppose they speak truly, but what wages would they pay a widow who is the sole support of five children? One such woman, dressed as a man, was recently exposed and dismissed from employment.

On the other hand, it is also beyond my comprehension to understand how a woman could willingly lay aside the particular graces of her sex, her gowns and hairnets and all the particular feminine distinctives to which we are accustomed. Such an act must be born of a desperation I have never known. God has been good to me, Papa.

I suppose that when I am a doctor, I shall have to accustom myself to the notion of receiving half wages. I shall therefore have to find an able-bodied husband to support the absent half of my livelihood! I wonder if my patients would think it fair if I treated them only half as well, or completed only half a surgery...

I am rambling too much, Papa. How I miss the discussions we used to have about these things! Give my love to Wesley, and remember to wrap a strip of flannel around your throat if you develop a cough. Write when you have the time, and know that I am studying most devotedly. Charity is fine, and reads my textbooks nearly as well as I do. Pray for me during my exams, during which I shall endeavor to do you honor.

I am, most ardently, your loving daughter.

Flanna

Flanna folded the letter, slid it into an envelope, and sealed it. She searched among her papers for a sheaf of stamps, then wondered if the letter would even reach her father. Now that South Carolina had declared itself independent from the United States, would the postal service deliver mail to Charleston?

"I pray you will find your way home," she whispered, pressing her lips to the heavy vellum. Then, turning around, she called Charity from her mending and asked her to post the envelope.

⚬≈⚬

Three days later, Flanna stood with Alden, Roger, and Mrs. Haynes outside the majestic brick house. Alden's four-day pass was about to expire, and Roger had invited Flanna to his brother's farewell luncheon. Flanna enjoyed the meal very much, for Mrs. Haynes's attention was focused almost entirely upon her soldier son. She had little time or energy, it seemed, to fret about Flanna.

Now Flanna shivered inside her elegant blue velvet mantle and leaned closer to the curving brick wall at the front of the house. She tapped her toes beneath the hem of her gown, hoping this public good-bye would not take long.

Roger stood next to his mother on the front steps, his arm supporting her while she wept into a lace-trimmed handkerchief. Standing stiffly and rather awkwardly in front of the house, Alden Haynes nodded one final time at his brother.

"Take care of her, Roger." He turned the catch in his voice into a cough, then lifted his hand. "I may be back soon. Until then, farewell."

Mrs. Haynes burst into fresh weeping and burrowed her head into Roger's chest. Patting her shoulder, Roger glanced helplessly at Alden, then mouthed a silent apology to Flanna.

"Miss O'Connor." Alden turned to her with a snap of his heels. "My brother has asked me to see you home. Since the train station is near your residence…"

"Thank you very much," Flanna answered, understanding Roger's reasoning. He was doubtless eager to have Flanna away from his distraught mother, who might say anything once Alden had departed.

Flanna stepped forward and corked her hands firmly into her muff, more than ready to leave the sorrowful scene. Alden saluted

49

his brother, then picked up his bag, a gesture that evoked even louder weeping from Mrs. Haynes.

"Shall we go?" Alden led Flanna away at a brisk pace, not slowing until they had left Louisburg Square. "I'm sorry you had to witness that," he said, pausing at a street corner. He waited until a passing carriage had moved through the intersection, then looked down at Flanna. "Mother is not usually this emotional. But with all this talk of war—"

"Major Haynes," Flanna interrupted, giving him an understanding smile, "you do not need to explain. If our situations were reversed and my brother were going off to a military post, I think it highly unlikely that my father would be able to restrain his feelings." She softened her tone. "He would not cry, I don't think...but his heart would break, just the same."

"Indeed." Alden's expressive face became almost somber. "I wish I knew how my father would feel about these present difficulties," he said, walking again, "but I am certain he would do anything to preserve the unity of these United States."

"He was a patriot?"

"He was a general in the army." His voice brimmed with pride. "A fine soldier, and a brilliant strategist. He gave his life in the Mexican War. I was fifteen at the time."

"I'm very sorry." They walked in silence for a moment, then Flanna turned her head and looked up at him. "Is that why you chose a military career? Are you following in his footsteps?"

His eyes warmed slightly, and the hint of a smile acknowledged the accuracy of her intuition. "I suppose you're right, though I have never considered my motivations. When he died, I knew I had to act as the head of the household. And being a soldier—being like him—was all that ever occurred to me."

He studied her face for a moment, then offered her his arm. "I hope I am not being too forward to proffer you this assistance. In private, Roger told me that you two have come to an understanding. And if you'll forgive my boldness, Miss O'Connor, I'd like to say that I am touched by your commitment to your father. You are, I believe, a rare woman."

"That sort of boldness is easily forgiven." Flanna laughed softly. Hesitantly, she pulled her hand from her muff and placed it in the crook of his arm, then allowed him to lead her across the street.

"I must say," he went on, his eyes scanning the cobbled sidewalk as they walked, "that you are not at all what I expected to find when Roger told me he'd been courting a Southern belle. I'd always heard that Southern women were rather vain and insipid creatures. Spoiled, in fact."

"No doubt some of them are," Flanna said as she looked up at him, "but the South has no monopoly on vain women or gallant men."

He smiled, and she thought she detected rising color in his cheeks. "Roger warned me that you were charming." He looked away toward the street. "I suppose I had better watch my heart lest I lose it to my own brother's sweetheart."

"I'm acting under direct orders," she replied lightly, breathing more quickly to keep up with his brisk pace. "Roger told me to charm you."

He stopped so abruptly that she feared she had offended him. She searched his face, hoping for some clue regarding his thoughts, but could find nothing but cool detachment behind those ice blue eyes.

"Have I, then?" Her heart fluttered wildly beneath her corset. "Have I fulfilled my orders?"

"Completely." His expression was serious, but one corner of his mouth curled up in a dry, one-sided smile. "I have the feeling that you, Miss O'Connor, are much like whiskey—pleasing to the eye, warming to the heart, and the source of the world's worst headaches."

Flanna blinked. "Whatever do you mean?"

"I salute you, miss." He released her arm as he backed away. "And I bid you farewell."

Flanna looked to her right and saw that she stood before her own boardinghouse. She'd been so intent upon their conversation that she hadn't even realized that he'd walked her home.

"You cannot leave me like this, sir!" she called, her voice suddenly hoarse with frustration. What had he meant by his last-minute insult? Was this his way of teasing her?

Alden Haynes only laughed softly and turned toward an intersecting street, then broke into a slow jog as he hurried to catch his train. He obviously had no intention of coming back to explain himself or beg her forgiveness.

Feeling restless and irritable, Flanna stamped her foot. At least Mrs. Haynes was honest enough to insult her openly. What had Alden Haynes intended, behaving like a sweet gentleman until the last moment, then likening her to a headache and hurrying away?

Flanna shook her head and turned to climb the boardinghouse steps. "Until my dying day, I shall *never* understand Yankees."

Alden proceeded into the train car and took a seat by the window, eager to be alone with his thoughts. A train butcher paused in the aisle and offered to sell Alden a newspaper or dime novel to pass the time, but he waved the boy ahead, preferring to close his eyes to the sights and sounds of his fellow passengers. The porter had shoved a log into the wood stove at the far end of the car, and the air was thick with the scent of smoking hickory—a log far too green, Alden suspected, to burn without smoke.

"Do you take tobacco?" a man asked.

Alden opened one eye. A man wearing a dark suit and bowler stood at his elbow, a thin stream of dark juice running down his bearded chin.

"Never developed the habit," Alden answered, frowning.

"Then you won't mind if I take the window?"

"Not at all." Alden stood so the whiskered man could take the window seat. Better to have the man spitting out the window than over his lap for the space of the journey.

Once the man had settled himself, Alden took the aisle seat, stretched out his legs as far as the cramped arrangement would allow, and folded his hands over the buckle of his uniform. Whispers of boulevard traffic drifted in through the open windows, and a trio of children ran down the aisle, leaving a trail of laughter in the smoky car. Passengers were still moving about, and as he looked across the aisle he caught sight of a pretty little girl no more than five years old. Her red hair, a mass of copper-gold curls tied with bright ribbons, reminded him of Flanna O'Connor's. But Flanna's hair had that beguiling white streak near her temple, a flash of brightness not unlike her spirit.

The little girl offered Alden a shy smile, then dove for the security of her mother's lap. Alden looked away as a feeling of homesickness tore at his heart. A military career was not a difficult life in peacetime, and he truly desired to serve his country. But the dark clouds on the horizon were more threatening than his family realized, and his stomach twisted in misery at the thought of Roger's Charleston sweetheart. Why couldn't Roger have set his cap for a nice Boston girl?

Strange, how God had placed the two brothers on two separate paths. Alden followed in his father's footsteps on the path of duty and honor, while Roger followed his mother's course of public service. And while Alden enjoyed his disciplined way of life and his work, sometimes he envied Roger's freewheeling social life. Spiritually, as well, the brothers differed. Roger saw God as a benevolent king, lovingly protecting his subjects. In the army, Alden had seen more of God's justice than his mercy, more wrath than love.

Alden parked his chin in his palm and smiled as his thoughts drifted toward Flanna O'Connor. She had been insulted when he likened her to a whiskey-fed headache. He'd meant no real slight, for he'd found her charming, bright, and cultured—everything a politician's wife should be. She was probably resilient too. Butter wouldn't melt in her mouth, nor would criticism hurt her, for women that polished usually held a high opinion of themselves. The concerns of others rolled off them like dirt off a shovel. He had always been amazed at the cool composure with which his mother and her friends distributed food baskets for the poor during Christmas week and turned a blind eye to the needy during the rest of the year. That same quality, no doubt, enabled them to rail against the enslavement of Negroes while they treated their Irish servants with less respect than their horses.

But Flanna O'Connor seemed quite unlike the other young women who moved in Roger's circle. Her voice was not the girlish, empty-headed whisper that so many other young ladies cultivated these days. She spoke in low and dusky tones that would send shivers of awareness down any man's spine. And she was Southern. But while Roger undoubtedly considered her geographical heritage an advantage in his long-range ambition to rise to the presidency, geography could not completely account for her uniqueness.

When she had spoken of her father, Alden had seen a glimpse of real compassion in her eyes. What other quality would lead a gentlewoman into the demanding and indelicate study of medicine? She seemed too refined and feminine to suffer from a masculine desire to prove herself, and at lunch she had visibly recoiled when his mother boldly stated that women ought to doff their skirts and crinolines in favor of bloomers. Alden had seen a woman dressed in that silly costume once—the lady walked on the street in baggy trousers and a shortened, full-cut overdress that fell just past her hips. The overall effect only served to make the woman appear blowsy and plump. After that, Alden decided he could do without seeing another bloomer costume...unless Flanna O'Connor could be persuaded to promenade in one. For a glimpse of that lady's ankle, he'd—

No. Exhaling deeply, he put a halt to his imaginings. In them, he realized, lay the real reason for his cutting comment as they parted. If Roger's Southern sweetheart thought Alden rude and ill-mannered, perhaps she'd keep her distance from him...and he'd be better able to preserve his honor and maintain his brother's trust.

Alden closed his eyes against the nauseating sight of his seatmate's chewing and spitting and turned toward the aisle, hoping to sleep.

Four

Sunday, December 30

In Mrs. Davis's dining room tonight, one of my fellow students, Mary D., began a violent attack upon "this mischief-making South Carolina." I said not a word in defense of my native land. Another girl, Jane, came in while Mary was pouring her beliefs upon me. Jane asked if she did not know I was a Carolinian. Mary flushed very prettily and reversed her tack, praising the beauty of Charleston, etc., but I knew the true bent of her opinions.

I cannot wait to be home and away from all this. I dare not speak the things that are on my mind. Heavenly Father, make the days pass quickly!

Roger Haynes celebrated the new year in a flurry of politics and merrymaking. He proudly escorted Flanna to three different holiday balls, and at each he danced far less than he debated. Like a brilliant cardinal among a flock of gray doves, Flanna sat sedately with the other women and gracefully tolerated Roger's impassioned speeches in favor of national unity. Each time he saw her lovely face he congratulated himself again upon his fine taste in women. When they were married, they would influence the country like no other couple in history.

The new year was scarcely nine days old when Mississippi became the second state to secede from the Union. Florida followed within hours, then Alabama. By the close of January, Georgia and Louisiana had joined the secessionists. People in Boston were so busy counting the Rebel states that they scarcely noticed when Kansas joined the Union as a free state on January 29.

Roger knew Flanna had been too engrossed in her studies to notice much of anything. After the last ball on New Year's Eve, she settled into her textbooks and said she could see him only on Friday evenings— and then only for one or two hours at most. She was determined not only to pass her examinations, but to graduate first in her class. "I will not have people thinking I received my degree on the strength of my father's reputation," she told him, her chin lifting in determination. "They must know that I am a physician in fact, not in name alone."

Though Roger admired her determination, he knew she could not entirely cut herself off from the world. And so with a heavy heart he climbed the steps to the boardinghouse on Wednesday afternoon, February 6, hoping she would not be so surprised by his unannounced visit that she would refuse to see him. He had an urgent message, one that might bring her pain.

Pausing on the wide front porch, he tucked the morning newspaper beneath his arm. With one hand he yanked on the bell pull, then he stepped back and waited for the door to open.

The white-haired landlady opened the door a moment later, her eyes squinting over the rims of her spectacles. "Yes?"

"Good afternoon, madam." He doffed his top hat. "I am Roger Haynes, and I'd like permission to speak with Miss Flanna O'Connor."

The old woman peered at him as if he were some obnoxious species of insect. "Miss O'Connor is in her room. She has asked not to be disturbed."

"But it is important." The corner of Roger's mouth twisted with exasperation as he pulled a calling card from his pocket. "Please give her this and tell her I must speak with her. I would not have come unless the situation were urgent."

The door opened a bit wider, then a birdlike hand snatched the card from his fingertips. "Wait there," she called, before closing the door again.

Roger moved to the edge of the porch, then thrust his hands behind his back and rocked slowly on his heels. Surely she would see him. Their time together last Friday night had been pleasant. She had listened with a distant look in her eye as he spoke of all the causes he would adopt once he was in office. Her faraway look intensified as he continued, leading him to suspect that she was mentally rehearsing her lessons instead of listening. But when he mentioned that Alden had written and inquired after her health, she brightened to a most becoming shade of pink. Roger congratulated himself; she had heard every word.

The heavy door screeched in protest, and the landlady appeared again, staring at Roger with eyes too hard for beauty. "Miss O'Connor will see you in the parlor," the woman announced, frowning at Roger as she stepped back. "You will sit in the wing chair, she on the sofa."

"Certainly," Roger answered, following the lady into the small foyer. A single bench and a table with an oil lamp stood at his right hand; an assortment of beribboned bonnets and cloaks hung from pegs on the wall at his left.

Still frowning, the landlady moved to stand before him. "Follow me," she said in a voice of steel. Like an army private behind his commander, Roger followed her into a small parlor, where a faded rose-colored couch faced the fireplace and a series of mismatched chairs stood sentinel around the room.

"My wing chair?" Roger asked, waiting for permission.

The woman pointed a bony finger toward a brocade chair near the sofa, then lowered herself into a rocker by the fire. Humming gently, she took up a ball of wool and her knitting needles, resuming her work on what appeared to be a stocking.

Roger perched on the edge of the wing chair and placed his top hat on his thigh, a little chagrined to discover that his hostess apparently planned to remain for the duration of his visit. The boardinghouse parlor was not the place he would have chosen to have this talk, but perhaps the stilted atmosphere would work to his advantage. Flanna would undoubtedly keep a tight rein on her emotions with this frowning gargoyle in the room.

A moment later he heard the soft rustling of skirts, then Flanna herself appeared in the doorway, her hair long and flowing over her shoulders, restrained only by a thin ribbon tied at the crown of her head. Her eyes were wide, and her lips parted at the sight of him. "Roger! What brings you out today? Is there some terrible news?"

Keenly aware of the housemother's steady gaze, Roger rose, took Flanna's hand, and bowed formally. "Miss O'Connor, it is good to see you. No, the news is not terrible, but it is serious. I simply had to come."

Her lovely face clouded with concern. "Is it your mother? Your brother? Is someone ill?"

"No." Touched by her compassion for his family, he smiled and gestured toward the sofa. "Be seated, won't you, while I compose my thoughts?"

After casting a troubled glance in the landlady's direction, Flanna sat on the sofa while Roger paced before the fire. Glancing up, he saw that the housemother's needles had fallen silent. Her hard little eyes had fastened to his face with the intensity of a searchlight.

"Flanna." He turned to his sweetheart. "Have you been studying very hard? I imagine that you have not had time to read a newspaper."

She shook her head. "Of course I haven't, Roger. I've been studying anatomy."

"Then let me be the first to tell you." He took a deep breath, shivering with the dark thrill of being the first to deliver the news. "I know you believe that South Carolina and the other Rebel states will agree to a compromise of some sort, but two days ago—"

He paused, trying to frame the news in delicate words, but could find none.

"What happened two days ago?" Flanna asked, her voice flat. "Tell me, Roger! Surely they have not gone to fighting!"

"No, my dear." He gave her a fleeting smile. "Two days ago representatives from the seceded states met in Montgomery, Alabama. They formed a new union, calling themselves the Confederate States of America. It is rumored that Jefferson Davis of Mississippi will be elected president. It is nearly certain, for no one has come forward to run against him."

For a long moment Flanna's expression did not change, then his words fell into place and the color left her cheeks. "The Confederate States of America," she whispered slowly, as if trying to translate the words. "The Confederate States—the C.S.A." She looked up at him, her eyes alive with calculation. "I am now a citizen of the C.S.A.? What does that mean?"

"You have nothing in common with those Rebels," he said, moving to her side. He dropped his hat to the floor, about to sit next to her, but a loud snorting sound from near the fireplace reminded him of Mrs. Davis's rules. Rolling his eyes, he moved toward his assigned wing chair and sat on the edge, then leaned forward, his elbows on his knees, his hands outstretched to Flanna. "Don't fret, my dear, I believe this is for the best. Don't you see? Now that South Carolina and the others have officially banded together, you are free from your promise to your father. Your father is now a traitor. Love him if you must, but do not think of serving him! Disavow your heritage as a child of South Carolina and vow your loyalty to the Union. Everyone will know that you do not agree with those fools in the Confederacy. What I'm trying to say..." He hesitated, clearing his throat and casting a pointed glance in the old woman's direction. Mrs. Davis saw it, understood, and merely lifted a brow in reply.

"Flanna, dearest," Roger continued, turning back to the only woman who mattered, "why should we wait to be married? The Confederate States have committed this rebellious action without your participation or your knowledge. You have spent most of the last two years in Boston. Surely you belong to Massachusetts as much as to South Carolina."

She looked up at him, her eyes large and liquid and as distant as the stars.

"Marry me, Flanna." He reached out to take her hand. Mrs. Davis cackled and coughed, but Roger ignored her, pressing forward with his suit. "Forget the past and become my wife as soon as you graduate. No one will think ill of you, but they will say I am the luckiest, most fortunate man in all creation."

"Roger, I can't marry you!" Her words flew from her like breathless birds released from a cage, and her expression darkened with unreadable emotions. "I won't be married in Massachusetts! I'll only be married at home, in Charleston, with my brother nearby and Father standing at my side. Forget the past, my family? How could I? They're my home, my heritage, and I have promised to make them part of my future!"

"Flanna." Roger squeezed her hand, his determination like a rock inside him. "Charleston, U.S.A., is gone forever. The city you knew is no more. That place is now a foreign country, populated by Rebels with whom you have nothing in common. They have chosen to leave us, they have stolen American properties and lands, they have scoffed at our liberties and forfeited their claims upon our hearts! I hear the Rebels are even planning to adopt our American constitution, excepting any clauses banning slavery!"

She jerked her hand from his and swallowed hard as tears began to slip down her cheeks. "Roger, don't talk like that about my family! My father, my brother, and my cousins are not traitors. They have stolen nothing—they are only struggling to keep the things they've worked for!"

"Flanna, I—" Roger stopped, swallowing the harsh words that sprang to his tongue. He had to remember that Flanna was living under intense pressure. His news had surprised her. She needed time to think, to reorient herself to a world that had drastically changed over the past month.

"My dear girl," he said, standing. "I am terribly sorry for any pain my news has brought. I know it was a shock, and I have probably been unwise to spring this news on you without warning. Promise me that we shall meet this Friday night, as always. We will talk again then."

She had lowered her head to hide her tears, but he saw her nod.

"Till Friday then." He walked toward her, stooping to pick up his hat, then resisted the urge to run his hand over her silky hair. He nodded briefly at the old woman near the fire.

"Ladies, I wish you a good day," he said, then left the room.

Roger let himself out, then paused at the steps of the boarding-house and glanced back toward the lace curtains, half-hoping to see Flanna's face at the window. He should have predicted her response; he should have known her better. He had suspected she would be upset about the fledgling Confederate States of America, but he had not expected her dismay to spill out on his marriage proposal.

He had been too hasty, but the sands of time would cover his blunder. And as he waited for time to do its assuaging work, he would encourage Flanna to keep up her studies and earn that blasted medical degree, since it seemed important to her. And after she had accepted that diploma of medicine, he'd propose marriage again. She would be caught up in the rapture of the moment, and she'd agree to marry him. Perhaps they could have a summer wedding, as early as June.

As he sauntered down the street, he reminded himself to write Alden and suggest that he plan ahead and request a weekend pass for the month of June.

Roger wanted his brother home for the wedding.

Five

April 12, 1861

    Friday night, and I did not allow Roger to visit. My thoughts are far from him, far from Charity, far from everything but my studies and the exam that looms like a steep mountain before me tomorrow. I have never felt lonelier, yet this is a self-imposed loneliness, a situation I must endure until my examinations are done.

    Will I remember all that I know is true? And will the things I have learned from my father conflict with the things I have been taught here?

    My father's favorite verses come to mind: "Trust in the Lord with all thine heart; and lean not unto thine own understanding. In all thy ways acknowledge him, and he shall direct thy paths." I know what Papa would say were he here now—"Flanna, me girl, just because you're not to lean on your understanding doesn't mean you're not to use your God-given brain. Use it, darlin', and work hard. Work like everything depends on you, then pray like everything depends on God."

    I can only pray that God will bless his truth and my efforts. I have worked so hard to please him.

The Boston winter melted into spring, and the day of Flanna's final examination arrived. On Saturday morning, April 13, she stepped outside the boardinghouse and stared wordlessly at the changed aspect of the street. Trees that had been bare and leafless when she last noticed them had begun to frill themselves like glorious gold-green parasols. The air carried hints of warmer days to come, and brilliant sunlight washed the sidewalk under a clean blue sky.

Flanna glanced at Charity, then laughed softly. "I knew we were working hard," she said, lifting her skirts as she descended the stairs, "but I had no idea how hard."

"It will all be over soon," Charity promised, following with Flanna's notebooks and medical bag. "Just a few more hours, Miss Flanna, and we'll be making ready to go home."

"Right you are," Flanna answered, moving briskly toward the street. In honor of this auspicious occasion, Roger had arranged for his mother's closed carriage to drive Flanna and Charity to the college. The driver waited on the street, his eyes lighting in a look of admiration as Flanna approached.

She allowed him to help her into the carriage, then slid to the end of the bench and waited for Charity. She took a deep breath and counted to five, her father's old trick to calm an unsettled stomach. She would soon stand before a committee of five doctors, all men, and all determined to expose her every weakness.

Charity climbed in, and the door closed. "You ready, Miss Flanna?"

"Yes."

"You want me to pray for you?"

Flanna reached out and squeezed her maid's hand. "Please."

Charity closed her eyes and moved her lips in a soundless prayer. One of the horses whickered as the carriage lurched forward, and the jangling sounds of horse and harness rattled Flanna's nerves.

She looked down and stared at her hands. For two years she had given her attention to the study of medicine. For the past four months she had invested nearly every waking moment in preparation for this examination council. While the world outside her window raged with news of secession and strife, she had concentrated on anatomy, chemistry, toxicology, physiology, obstetrics, gynecology, and surgery. While the other girls had spent their leisure hours gossiping about "that Carolina girl," Flanna had given particular attention to the study of hygiene—a discipline not endorsed by current medical experts, but one her father supported and Dr. Elizabeth Blackwell routinely practiced. Clean patients, Flanna believed, were healthier patients.

At last the carriage pulled up outside the college. After asking Charity to wait in the vestibule, Flanna walked immediately to the large lecture hall. The five doctors were already present, and they peered at her curiously as she opened the door and thrust her head into the room.

Dr. John Gulick, chairman of her examination committee, looked up with an unwelcoming, cold, and piercing eye. "Come in, Miss O'Connor, we are nearly ready. It is good of you to appear promptly."

Flanna took a deep, unsteady breath, then moved toward the empty table in the center of the room. She waited beside it, her hands clasped, as the doctors shuffled papers and skimmed various documents, ignoring her.

She eyed the empty table at her right hand. One solitary chair sat behind it, and once she had assumed that examination seat she would not rise until she had either proved herself capable or failed completely.

The thought of failure was anathema. How could she go home if she failed her exams? She knew her father regularly boasted of her progress to his patients, and all of Charleston expected her to follow in Elizabeth Blackwell's hallowed footsteps. That bright daughter of the South had established herself in no less intimidating a place than New York City. The folks at home expected something equally spectacular from Flanna O'Connor.

She shifted from foot to foot, then looked down at the floor and forced her mind to run in mundane, less worrisome channels. Despite the political unrest, mail was flowing between the two nations. Since the news of Texas's secession and Jefferson Davis's election as president of the Confederate States of America, Flanna had received one letter from her father. In it, he encouraged her to concentrate on her studies and keep her mind fixed to her task, but he also bragged that South Carolina had seized the former Federal properties of Fort Moultrie, Castle Pickney, and the arsenal at Charleston. "Our eyes turn now to Fort Sumter," he had written, "which sits off our shore like a beacon in the night. Federal soldiers still guard the garrison, but it will soon be ours. Why should we tolerate the presence of foreign soldiers on South Carolina's shores?"

"We are ready, Miss O'Connor." Flanna flinched at the sound of Dr. Gulick's raspy voice. "Please relax and be seated. You may take your time as you answer these questions."

Flanna smiled to cover her embarrassment and moved to the chair. Gracefully maneuvering her expansive skirts around the legs of the table, she took her seat, then folded her hands atop the table.

A balding man she did not recognize lifted a bushy brow. "I hope you did not misunderstand, Miss O'Connor. You are allowed to use notes. Have you forgotten to bring them?"

"No sir." Her voice, like her nerves, was in tatters, and she took a deep breath to strengthen it. "No sir, I did not forget. But I believe I can best prove my abilities and readiness without notes. After all, not every doctor has access to his notes and journals when he or she encounters an emergency situation."

Dr. Gulick's full mouth dipped into a deeper frown. "Perhaps you are unaware that the purpose of this college is to *encourage* women. It is our belief that no woman can pass this examination without notes." He leaned back in his chair and folded his hands across the paunch at his belly. "We would be pleased to recess for the space of a few moments if you wish to fetch yours."

For a moment Flanna was tempted to ask Charity to bring her notebook, but the look of malign satisfaction on Dr. John Gulick's face quelled that urge. She had never liked him as a teacher, for when he wasn't half-drunk he patronized his students, talking to them as if they were children. Her father had treated her with more dignity when she was ten years old.

She would not reinforce Dr. Gulick's prejudices.

"With all due respect, gentlemen," she said, keeping all expression from her voice, "I am ready to proceed without notes. I would not want to waste your time fetching props I do not need."

A thunderous scowl darkened Dr. Gulick's brow; another doctor laughed. "All right then." Gulick spat out the words as he lifted a sheet of questions. "Shall we begin?" He hesitated, seeming to measure her for a moment. "Tell me, Miss O'Connor, in full detail, what implements you will carry in your medical bag if this committee is inclined to award you a degree."

Flanna mentally listed the items in her father's medical bag, then took a deep breath and began to recite them: "Castor oil, calomel, jalap, Peruvian bark or cinchona, nux vomica, splints, forceps, and my stethoscope. I, sir, would also carry a scalpel, with an adult dose of either chloroform or ether, in case I had to perform a surgical procedure."

"On what occasions would you use jalap as treatment?" the bald doctor asked.

"Whenever a powerful cathartic is needed." She returned his gaze. "What else may I answer for you, gentlemen?"

"I have read your paper on aseptic techniques." Dr. Gulick's eyes darkened and shone with an unpleasant light. "Why would you waste time with such foolishness? Why would you splash your patients with cold water and insist that physicians wash their hands before surgery?" He held up his burly hand, displaying veins that squirmed across the skin like fat blue worms. "Is there something on my hand that will harm a patient? Do you believe in hexes and superstitions, Miss O'Connor? If not, why would you resort to all this foolish hocus-pocus?"

Flanna's pulse began to beat erratically at the threatening tone in his deep voice, but she inhaled deeply and counted to five. She had been expecting this attack. Her views on cleanliness were unconventional, but her father had practiced hygiene for years with great success. One of his medical professors had been a devout Jew, and that doctor insisted that his students follow the ritual cleansing practices outlined in the Old Testament.

"Oy, if God himself tells us to wash our hands, shall we not trust him?" Flanna murmured, mimicking her father's oft-repeated motto.

"What's that?" Dr. Gulick asked. "Speak up, I can't hear you."

As casually as she could manage, Flanna began to frame her answer. "Sirs, I base my opinion about hygiene on two things: God's Holy Word, which you would not want to refute, and my father's record of success. He has been using water to clean wounds and instruments for years."

"I'll not accept the record of any Confederate doctor," Gulick snapped, his voice sharp with fury.

Flanna turned her gaze toward another examiner, the pleasant fellow who had laughed earlier. "Consider, then, the record of Dr. Elizabeth Blackwell of New York. She follows the techniques of cleanliness advocated by Trotula and Hildegard, who outlined such practices in ancient times. The rate of puerperal fever among Dr. Blackwell's patients is far lower than the rate of a similarly located New York hospital where doctors do not wash their hands between patients. Dr. Marie Zakrzewska has established similar good results with hygienic methods."

"A confounded waste of time and effort," Gulick countered, his mouth twisting unpleasantly. He opened his mouth to say something else, but the examiner Flanna had addressed cut the professor off.

"Dr. Gulick, when are you going to give the rest of us an opportunity to learn from this remarkable young lady?" he asked. When Gulick remained silent, the pleasant doctor gave Flanna a look of faint amusement. "Thank you, my dear, for explaining why you believe cleanliness is important. If you want to bathe your patients, I've no doubt that it will do many of them good. Now"—he paused and looked down at his notes—"can you please explain for me the function of the human circulatory system? Take your time, my dear. Even the most advanced healers do not fully understand it."

Flanna took a deep breath, then began. "The circulation of blood, Doctors, originates with the human heart..."

❦

Two hours later, Flanna thanked the committee and moved toward the doorway. Once she reached the hallway, she closed the door and leaned against it, her heart beating in a staccato rhythm. She had passed! Try though they might—and they had tried, most sincerely, to trip her up—they could find no fault in her preparation. Even dour Dr. Gulick had awarded her a passing score. Soon she would receive a diploma with her name etched in broad, black strokes— Dr. Flanna O'Connor!

She looked around, anxious to share her news. Charity was waiting downstairs in the vestibule, no doubt, and Roger might have arrived by now. Flanna hurried down the stairs with a quick step and a light heart, feeling as though her feet might begin to dance at any moment. She had succeeded!

Charity lay curled on a sofa in the entry, her knees drawn up on the cushions, her head pillowed on her hand. Flanna stooped and woke the girl with a fierce hug.

"Gracious, Miss Flanna, what's come over you?"

"We did it, Charity." Flanna felt a blush of pleasure rise to her cheeks. "I passed my exams. You are looking at the youngest doctor in the family."

"Sakes alive, you really did it?" Charity's arms slipped around Flanna's neck, and they shared a tight embrace, one triumphant heart beating against another. "Oh, Miss Flanna, your papa will be so proud!"

"I can't wait to write him." Flanna pulled out of Charity's embrace and wiped a tear of joy from her cheek. "Or should I wire him? We could stop by the telegraph office on the way home." She looked around the small vestibule. "Have you seen Roger? He said he would be here when my exams were done."

"I haven't seen hide nor hair of Mister Roger." Charity shook her head for emphasis. "Not a glimpse, and I've been sitting on that sofa nearly all day."

"Well then." Flanna tried to smile, then closed her eyes as a flash of loneliness stabbed at her heart. A woman ought to have friends around when she had good news to share, but the people who mattered most to her were far away. Papa and Wesley would hear her announcement through an impersonal telegram, then they'd run across the street to share the news with Marsali and her boys. While Roger, who ought to be here, had undoubtedly been detained by some fascinating political gossip spilling in a tavern somewhere.

Flanna opened her eyes and gripped Charity's arm. Her maid, at least, was near, and if Charity's was the only friendly face in town, so be it. "Let's go to the telegraph office immediately." Flanna pushed her dark thoughts aside. "And tonight we'll ask Mrs. Davis for some of that delicious ham she keeps squirreled away in the larder. We'll have a feast."

"Miss Flanna?"

About to stand, Flanna stopped short, caught off guard by the expectant expression on her maid's face. "Yes, Charity?"

"Does this mean we can go home now? I'm awful tired of living here with these Yankees. I want to go home and see my folks."

Flanna paused and looked out the window. Boston and all its glory lay outside, cobbled streets crowded with fancy buggies, busy people, and prosperous traders. Roger had nearly convinced her that this city might hold the promise of her future, but in the last few weeks she had felt the sting of its scorn. Her fellow students, her landlady, and the members of society who had once enthused over her dresses, her slender waist, and her wit—none of them had spoken to or inquired about her in past weeks.

She had hidden herself away, to be sure, but she had kept her weekends free, and not a single invitation had been delivered. She suspected her lack of social acceptance had more to do with her origins than her study habits. And if Boston society thrust her out, Roger would soon desert her too. In the heart of Massachusetts, how popular could a Rebel-loving politician be?

It was time to go home. Now that she'd accomplished her goals, she could be the doctor she had always wanted to be. She had made her father a promise, and she fully intended to keep it.

Turning from the window, she stood and gave her maid a broad smile. "Yes, Charity. We'll go home just as soon as we settle things in Boston."

"Flanna!" Roger burst through the doorway, his eyes blazing and his body as tense as a bowstring. Flanna lifted her chin, ready to brace herself against his list of excuses and rationalizations.

"Flanna, dearest!" His eyes brimmed with emotion as he came forward and grasped her elbows. "I came as soon as I heard. I knew you'd want me to be with you."

"How could you hear so soon?" Flanna asked. "I've only just learned the news myself."

A tremor passed over Roger's face. "You've heard already?"

"Of course I've heard. I was there." She repressed the urge to stamp her foot in exasperation. "You weren't. You promised you'd be here when I came out of the examination room, but—"

"Your exams!" A sudden spasm of grief knit his brows. "I'm sorry, dearest, but this is far more important than your test!" His grip on her arms tightened. "Darling, the Confederates have fired on Fort Sumter! At four-thirty in the morning yesterday the Rebels opened fire, and the garrison surrendered! The Union flag was lowered in defeat, dishonored!"

Flanna hesitated, blinking with bafflement. "So this means—?"

"War, darling." Roger relaxed his hold on her arms and brought his hands to her cheeks. "It's unavoidable. So kiss me now, before I go see Mother. She's certain to be in a dither at this news, and she can never find her smelling salts when she needs them."

Before Flanna could protest or answer, his mouth covered hers hungrily, taking the kiss he had sought for months. When he pulled away, he patted her cheek. "I'll make arrangements for you, Flanna, before I go. You can stay with Mother while we put an end to the trouble, then we'll be married in the wedding you've always dreamed of."

"Roger—" She tried to speak, but words would not come. Her anger had evaporated, leaving only confusion, and Roger was moving away, toward the door and the bustling street.

"I'll come to you tonight," he promised, walking out the door. "Wait for me."

While she watched through the window, Roger climbed into the waiting carriage and ordered the driver to go.

Mixed feelings surged through Flanna as she and Charity walked back to the boardinghouse. The major event of the morning—her examination—seemed a lifetime removed, like an event from a distant past. The breaking news about Fort Sumter traveled through Boston like a wind-whipped grassfire; drivers called out to one another, and women gasped in delighted horror as they greeted each other with the news. In a sudden epidemic of patriotic fervor, merchants rifled their storage rooms for bolts of red, white, and blue bunting. The storefronts along Washington Street seemed to have bloomed in a patriotic frenzy since breakfast.

"Miss Flanna," Charity whispered, edging closer to her mistress's side, "I'm scared. If those Yankee girls at the boardinghouse were mean to us before this, how mean are they gonna be now?"

"I don't know, Charity." Flanna lowered her head as they quickened their steps. "But I don't want to tarry and find out."

Outside of T. R. Burnham's, Flanna caught sight of Mrs. Gower, a close friend of Mrs. Haynes's. Since Flanna had welcomed the new year at Mrs. Gower's holiday ball, she smiled and attempted to greet the lady, but Mrs. Gower stared right through her. Flanna felt the pressure of the woman's hard gaze as she and Charity passed.

"Law sakes, did you see the look that woman gave you?" Charity's voice rose to a screeching pitch as they hurried down Washington Street. "If she'd had an egg in that shopping basket, she'd a thrown it at you, Miss Flanna. We've got to go home, as quick as we can."

"I know." The serpent of anxiety curled around Flanna's heart slithered lower, to twist around her stomach. *Could* they go home? Now that fighting had broken out, could they travel safely?

She breathed a huge sigh of relief when they finally reached the boardinghouse. Mrs. Davis opened the door without comment, but the two girls they passed in the hall stared at Flanna as if she had suddenly sprouted horns.

Flanna and Charity raced up the stairs, ducked into their room, and slammed the door. Flanna tensed at the sight of a letter on her bed, then nearly wept with joy. Though the ink was smudged, she recognized her father's handwriting.

Falling on her bed, she ripped open the seal and began to read:

> April 1, 1861
> Dearest Daughter,
>
> My prayers are with you as you prepare for your examinations. Rest assured that Wesley and I have every confidence in you. You are a remarkable young woman and a most talented physician, and we are certain we will be rejoicing with you when your day of testing is done.
>
> I don't know what sort of news reaches you in Boston, but these are trying times in our beloved South Carolina. Spirits are high, and our young boys are certainly rarin' for a fight. Those who are most eager to bear arms against their brothers in the North have composed an entire list of grievances. Among their many complaints is the fact that the Yankees refuse to honor the Federal law requiring the return of runaway slaves. Northern politicians consistently close their eyes to the beneficent aspects of slavery, choosing to believe fairy tales rather than investigate the truth for themselves. They are quick to make heroes and idols of foolish caricatures like Mrs. Stowe's Uncle Tom, and they choose to look upon Christian, law-abiding slaveholders as Simon Legrees. Even more unforgivable,

Yankees had contributed money and support to the murderer John Brown, whose proven purpose was the murder of innocent Southern women and children. Most heinous, and I myself cannot understand Yankee thinking on this point, when John Brown was legally executed for his crimes, our Northern foes crowned his vile head with martyrdom.

If you hear of trouble—and unless I am sadly mistaken, you soon will—know that the rascal Lincoln has engineered the situation. Fort Sumter, which sits like a beautiful diamond off the shores of our own city, is the foremost object of contention. Our men have demanded that the Federal commander surrender this South Carolina fort to South Carolina men, but thus far the officer, a Major Anderson, has refused. (Let it be noted, daughter, that Major Anderson is from Kentucky and has owned slaves himself. He is surely sympathetic to our cause, but is bound to the Union as long as he wears a uniform.) We suspect that Lincoln will reward this stubborn soldier and send Federal troops to reinforce him, thereby forcing our hand. We cannot allow the soldiers of a foreign country to keep us from property that belongs by right and by nature to South Carolina.

It will be a fight, dearest daughter, so if you hear news of trouble, you are not to come home. The rails may not be safe, and the water routes are likely to be even more dangerous. But we are confident that our boys can meet this challenge and settle it within a few weeks. So wait where you are until you hear from me again.

It appears that a battle looms on the horizon, and I shall be needed. Though the forces and fury of war may separate us for a few days, know that I love you...and that I pray God will keep you safe in the palm of his hand.

If it comes to a fight, may God help the right.

Your loving father,

Donnan O'Connor, M.D.

Six

Sunday, April 14

Yesterday I became a doctor, a full and confident woman, and last night I woke in the dark weeping like a child in the throes of a nightmare. I feel so alone! Charity is with me, of course (I would be lost without her), but what if something happens to her? I am living in a crowded house in a crowded city, and yet I am as lonely as the moon. I miss Wesley and the cousins. I miss Papa and Aunt Marsali.

I have never missed home more than now, when I cannot return to it.

Boston rocked with the news of Fort Sumter. On Sunday, April 14, the city's pulpits thundered as preachers of every denomination denounced the rebellion. Reserved congregations who would have thought it irreverent to cough during a sermon stood and applauded the calls for war. Flanna sat with Mrs. Haynes in the family pew and shrank in her seat as the Presbyterian minister roared that the coming contest would be waged over one issue alone: slavery.

On Monday morning the city's smoldering sense of patriotism burst into bright flame when Lincoln called for seventy-five thousand volunteers to serve for three months. Flanna knew her people would interpret Lincoln's call as a declaration of war; the North received it as an affirmation that war had already begun. Every soul in Boston knew that Southern Rebels had affronted the glorious flag. Valiant soldiers of the U.S. Army had been forced, under hostile fire, to surrender a Federal fort and march out in shameful defeat. Under the sting of humiliation, the North rose like a screaming eagle, eager to avenge her lost glory.

By Tuesday morning the sounds of drum and fife filled every street corner. Recruiting offices opened in each city district, and volunteer militiamen began to pour into Boston, escorted by cheering crowds. Merchants and clerks rushed from their shops and stood bareheaded in the drizzling rain to salute passing wagonloads of eager recruits. Women leaned out their windows to wave handkerchiefs damp with tears. Horsecars, carriages, and omnibuses halted for the passing of these would-be soldiers, and the air rang with acclamation.

Drawn by curiosity and dread, Flanna and Charity donned their bonnets and mingled with the crowd, following a parade of volunteers to Faneuil Hall. As a parade of men—young and old—filed into the building, the supportive crowd roiled in fervent excitement.

One man standing near Flanna suddenly pulled his bowler from his head and placed it above his heart. "God bless it," he cried, his eyes lifting upward. Flanna followed his gaze and saw the American flag rising to the top of the staff.

The crowd responded with a tumultuous roar. Old men and tearful women lifted their gaze as well, reverently saluting the sacred emblem, while the young men cheered and waved their hats in a loud hurrah. Flanna felt a stirring in her heart, but her mind reeled with confusion. She loved her country, but she loved Charleston too. Was it wrong to love both?

A uniformed officer stepped outside Faneuil Hall and lifted his hands for silence. The crowd gave him their attention, and in a loud, confident voice he announced that complete preparations were under way. Army rifles had been ordered from the Springfield Armory. The Boston banks had offered to loan the state three million, six hundred thousand dollars without security, and a host of military and professional men were donating their services to the Massachusetts regiments. "By six o'clock this evening," the officer told the crowd, "three regiments will be ready to start for Washington, and new companies are being raised throughout the state."

The applause lifted in great waves, and Flanna wept silently as she clung to Charity's arm and wished she were home.

❦

In mid-April Virginia followed the other slave states into secession, and within days of that action Lincoln ordered a blockade of Confederate ports. That news sent a shiver through Flanna, for much of Charleston's livelihood depended on the exportation of sugar, rice, and cotton.

With her education complete, Flanna no longer had the luxury of work to occupy her time. Each morning she and Charity stayed in their room until the other students had departed the boarding-house; only then did they dare creep down to the dining room. While Charity scraped breakfast together from leftover scraps in the kitchen, Flanna scanned the newspaper for any sign that they might be able to return home.

The news was anything but hopeful. The newspaper reported that from every corner of the Union, men were rushing to arms with camp-meeting fervor. Recruiters held mass enlistment rallies in churches and auditoriums, where leading citizens regaled audiences with speeches rich with allusions to country and flag and fatherhood. Breathing defiance at slaveholders and traitors to the glorious Union, these orators ultimately ended with the challenge, "Who will come up and sign the roll?" Scores of young men, fathers, and teenagers rushed forward to heed their country's call.

The appeal went out to Northern women too. Fiery abolitionists reminded wives, sweethearts, and mothers that their duty lay in urging their men to defend the country. Patriotic women challenged their sisters to work for the cause. Emboldened by the thought of their brave young men marching off to face bloodthirsty traitors, Boston women, including Mrs. Davis, rose to participate in the fray.

Flanna watched her landlady's efforts with quiet amusement, but she dared not protest lest she be evicted for insubordination. Having heard much about the tropical, steamy climate of the South, Mrs. Davis succumbed to the common view that the only practical headgear for a southbound soldier was a cap named for General Henry Havelock, whose soldiers in India adopted a cap featuring a flap at the neck to protect the skin from sunburn. Mrs. Davis and her boarders set to work with a vengeance, sewing havelocks at all hours of the day and night. Charity often remarked that since the firing on Fort Sumter, the house felt far more like a factory than a home. Flanna said nothing, but spent her mornings sewing the silly-looking hats.

Schools and universities suspended classes in order that young men might enlist and young ladies might work for the cause. At social gatherings, including several that took place in Mrs. Davis's parlor, young women gathered around the piano, pressed their hands to their bosoms, and stared at young men who had not yet enlisted while soulfully singing "I Am Bound to Be a Soldier's Wife or Die an Old Maid." Uniformed veterans of the Mexican War offered benedictions in Boston's leading churches, while women's sewing groups adopted military companies and worked until their fingers bled to provide uniforms, nightcaps, and socks. Each morning private homes, churches, and public rooms buzzed with the sounds of sewing machines and determined women who spent the entire day producing hats and uniforms.

Flanna was horrified to read that anything that smacked of Dixie was trampled in the rush to Northern arms. In Bangor, Maine, a group of schoolgirls pounded a Southern boy who came among them wearing a palmetto flag. At Pembroke, a lawyer of alleged Southern sympathies was threatened with a dunking in the river, and in Dexter, a group of volunteers rode Mr. Augustus Brown out on a rail for saying he hoped every one of them would be shot. In other cities, suspected Southern sympathizers were pelted with rotten eggs.

Such stories haunted Flanna's nights. She feared to venture out of the boardinghouse after dark, even in Charity's company. Roger, once her faithful escort, had made himself scarce. She had not seen him since their meeting at the college the day of her examination. That evening, instead of meeting her as he had planned, he had sent a note apologizing for his absence. The militia needed him, he had said, and the opportunity to lead men was too valuable to ignore. "Trust me, dearest, this unpleasantness will be upon us and forgotten before we know it," Roger had written, "and a stint of military service is the most wonderful opportunity that could present itself to a future states-man. Let me go and do my part to whip the Rebels. I will return to your side in three months, ready to continue with our plans."

Not at all surprised by Roger's defection, Flanna had tossed his letter on the heap of textbooks beside her bed. With every passing day the future he had planned looked less bright and more unlikely. As she pondered the events that had trapped her in Boston, she peered into the likely future and saw life with Roger as a series of missed appointments and hurried mealtimes. While she understood his devo-tion to patriotic duty, she was bothered by the fact that he did not consider her feelings as he prepared to "whip the Rebels." Those *Rebels* were her family and fellow Southerners, and Roger seemed intent upon forgetting her heritage. He seemed to think that by the sheer force of his will she could become a Bostonian.

She would never understand these people. Her graduation cere-mony, which had nearly been canceled in the frenzy of war prepara-tion, had consisted of an invitation to enter the college president's office. There she lifted her right hand, took the Hippocratic oath, and received a simple rolled diploma. That diploma now lay atop a pile of newspapers in the corner of her wardrobe, and Flanna could not even summon the enthusiasm to untie the ribbon and look at it.

Across the room, Charity lay asleep on her cot, a clump of dark hair covering her face. The lamp glowed softly, gilding the bureau and desk in a golden light. Outside the noise of revelers was broken by the occasional sharp pop of firecrackers. Boston was preparing for war with the fervor of a young girl planning her coming-out party.

Grief welled in Flanna, black and cold. Sitting on the floor beside her bed, she pressed her hands to her eyes and wept silently, not wanting to wake Charity. Why had she worked so hard? She had prayed for that medical diploma. She had studied throughout sleepless nights. She had sifted through countless theories and risked the censure of her professors by adhering to eternal truth instead of pretending allegiance to commonly accepted medical wisdom.

How had God rewarded her efforts? With war. Division. Strife. And the death of her dreams.

She dropped the reins on her mind and let it wander back to a time when Mammy lived and Wesley was a mischievous older brother who liked to pull Flanna's braids. Each morning Mammy came in and tamed Flanna's hair, working the bronze hanks into manageable plaits, then tying the ends with silk ribbon. When she had finished, Flanna always hopped up on the bed behind Mammy and tossed her arms around the woman's neck as Mammy plaited her own daughter's hair. One morning, as Mammy twisted and tied little Lulu's spongy curls into more than two dozen stalk-straight pigtails, Flanna had run her hand over Mammy's close-cropped hair and asked, "Why does Lulu get so many ribbons, Mammy, when you don't wear any?"

Mammy's broad black face widened in a smile. "Miss Flanna, don't you know nothing? Little girls wear their dreams in their hair ribbons. Old women like me—well, we've given up on such foolishness."

Flanna picked up her own braids, eyed the floppy wide ribbons dangling from the ends, then frowned. "So why does Lulu get lots of dreams, and I only get two?"

"'Cause, honey"—Mammy had swatted Lulu on the behind and sent the child scurrying out the door—"your dreams are a lot bigger than hers."

Mammy's words echoed in the black stillness of Flanna's mind as a damp breeze blew in through the cracked window. Were her dreams too big? Flanna had no idea what sort of things Lulu had dreamed of, but she'd earned her freedom and married a nice man in Charleston.

"All I ever really wanted," Flanna whispered, the words scraping her throat, "was to become a doctor and help my father. There are women, Lord, who need me. I am ready to serve, and yet you have closed the door. You have brought this terrible conflict upon us—why?"

She listened for an answer, but heard nothing but a few smothered laughs from the street outside. God was going to be silent, then, as his children both in the North and South begged him for victory. Perhaps a wise parent did not take sides when his children squabbled, and if God was anything, he was wise.

She hugged her knees to her and rested her head upon them, letting her tears fall upon her pantalets. What was she supposed to do? On the day of the examination Roger had suggested that she live with his mother for the duration of the trouble, but Flanna knew Mrs. Haynes would not be happy with that suggestion. And it was not entirely proper, for she and Roger were not engaged. But where else was she to go? Her father wanted her to remain in Boston, but Mrs. Davis would not want a Rebel in her boardinghouse any more than Mrs. Haynes would want one in her guest room. At least Flanna's room had been rented through August, for her father had thought she might like to work a short term in the Boston Hospital for Women before coming home. Fortunately for Flanna, Mrs. Davis's pragmatism outweighed her patriotism—she would not evict the devil himself if it meant losing money.

Flanna smiled in appreciation of her father's foresight. He'd probably paid the extra rent to give her a little time to sort through her feelings about coming home. Several of his letters had hinted that she shouldn't feel obligated to return to his work. If she found a promising position in Boston or New York, he wanted her to consider it.

But Flanna couldn't imagine living away from her family for long. She and Wesley had always been close, and Aunt Marsali had stepped in as a second mother after Mammy died. And then there were the seven cousins, Marsali's rambunctious brood, named in alphabetical order: Arthur, Brennan, Carroll, the twins Dillon and Erin, Flynn, and Gannon. All were strong young men, and all old enough to fight for the Confederacy…

Flanna's gaze drifted to the desk and the last letter from her father. How had that letter found its way to her? He had mailed it before that disastrous shelling of Fort Sumter, obviously, but—

She lifted her head, instantly alert as something clicked in her brain. If a letter could cross the boundary, surely she could too. Her father had told her to remain in Boston, but he had no idea how difficult and lonely life in a Yankee town could be.

She folded her hands under her chin, thinking. Roger wouldn't care if she left the city—he might not even miss her for several days. And Mrs. Davis would still have her precious rent money. Flanna had no reason to remain in Boston—absolutely nothing held her here.

In the morning she would tell Charity to pack a bag with only the bare necessities for travel. She would go home to Charleston, in a baggage car and standing up if necessary, but she would go home.

On the last Saturday in April, Flanna and Charity rose before the other girls and slipped quietly from the boardinghouse. The damp and chilly air held the promise of a spring shower, so Flanna thrust her hands deep into her muff and quickened her pace as Charity scrambled to keep up. The maid had packed only two bags. Flanna hated to leave her ball gowns and medical books behind, but if they were to slip away quickly and quietly, they had to travel without heavy bags. The presence of Flanna's belongings in the room would prevent Mrs. Davis from launching a search until nightfall, and, once they had safely reached Charleston, perhaps the widow could be persuaded to ship the things Flanna had left behind.

"Despite the scandal, she will be glad to be rid of us," Flanna muttered as they walked, "since her house is the only one tainted by a Rebel boarder."

She was nearly breathless by the time they reached the railway depot at Park Square. Flanna stopped to catch her breath and stared at the immense brick building. Yards of red, white, and blue bunting fluttered over the arched windows and entryways. Her stomach twisted at the ardent display of patriotism. What was this, if not a display of determination to crush *her* people?

She couldn't wait to leave.

Gesturing to Charity, Flanna moved through the huge entryway and into the lobby. She paused at the window where a clerk sat on a stool and absently chewed his thumbnail. "Good morning," she said, careful to smooth the Southern accent from her voice. After two years in Boston, she had nearly mastered the trick. "Two tickets, please."

"Is that for you and the Negro wench?" The clerk peered over Flanna's shoulder. "Your maid will have to ride in the colored car."

Flanna gritted her teeth. "Whatever for? She rode with me when we came to Boston."

The man frowned. "Is she a slave then? Slaves ride with their masters, but free Negroes have to ride in the colored car. That's the rule, miss."

Flanna bit down hard on her lower lip, then turned to Charity. "I don't want you to be separated from me," she whispered. "What if there's trouble on the way? You should ride with me, so I may have to say—"

"I understand, Miss Flanna." Charity lowered her eyes. "Tell the man I ain't goin' unless I ride with you."

Flanna turned back to the window and opened her purse. "She will ride with me. Two tickets, please, on the next train going south."

"She's a slave then?"

"She's riding with me." Flanna spoke with quiet, desperate firmness. "Now, may I have those tickets?"

"Final destination?"

"Charleston."

The man stamped some documents, then ticked off two tickets, and shoved the papers through the window. "Two tickets to Charles Town in western Virginia."

"Not west! I want to go south!" Flanna's nerves tensed. "I said *Charleston*. South Carolina."

The clerk gaped at her. "Ma'am, that isn't even funny. I can't get you to Charleston, not for all the gold in California. There's a war on, haven't you heard?"

"It's not a war, and I've heard more than enough." Flanna flushed as her temper began to rise. "Now please give me the proper tickets."

"I can't. Our trains aren't going there. The line is closed south of Washington, and I wouldn't feel right selling you a ticket and knowing you'd be put off somewhere without an escort. A lady shouldn't be traveling alone anyhow."

"I'll take my chances." Flanna's lower lip trembled as she returned his glare. "Please, just give me a ticket for anyplace south."

"I won't." The clerk folded his arms across his chest. "I can't sell you tickets to Charleston, or any place in South Carolina. I wouldn't even sell you a ticket to Maryland. Haven't you heard what's happening down there?"

Flanna shook her head.

"Last week, men of the Sixth Massachusetts Regiment were en route to Washington through Maryland," the clerk explained, his eyes flickering over Flanna's face. "A crowd of Southern sympathizers pelted our boys with stones when they were changing railroad lines. Four men died. Now that part of the country's in a revengeful mood, and here you are, with a black slave, wanting to travel south—" He spread his hands and leaned forward on his desk. "You'd be lucky to make it to Connecticut without trouble. I shouldn't even have offered to send you to western Virginia. Go back to where you've been living, ma'am, and count your blessings that you're safely away from South Carolina."

Flanna rubbed her hands over her arms, thinking. What could she do? She had to get home, but this railway clerk wouldn't lie about the risks involved. She didn't doubt his report—she'd stood in the Boston crowds and heard angry jibes about the Confederacy mingled with jeering laughter and promises of vengeance for Fort Sumter. This clerk was right, she would be lucky to reach Washington.

"Thank you for your time," she told the clerk. Turning, she made her way to a bench, only half-aware that Charity followed like a shadow.

"Miss Flanna, ain't we goin' home? I don't think I can stand it here another day. When you're readin' or studyin', the young ladies at the boardinghouse are always asking how often you beat me. They want to know how many times my master comes to my room in the night. I tried to tell them I am free, but they don't listen. They only hear what they want to hear, and I'm right sick of it. I want to go home. I want to see my ma and pa—"

"Charity, hush!" Flanna sank to the bench, resisting the urge to clap her hands over her ears. It was frustrating to hear her own desires voiced aloud and know that she couldn't do anything to set things right.

She stared at the brick floor as a flash of wild grief ripped through her. How had she, Flanna O'Connor, the bright and capable doctor's daughter, arrived at this situation? In Charleston she had but to ring a bell and Papa's valet arranged for a carriage to take her anywhere she wanted to go. Even in Boston, doors opened easily for a lady. The only real difficulty she had faced was her examination board. She had met that challenge with energy to spare, but now she couldn't even buy a simple train ticket home! When had the rules changed?

A train whistle blew, scattering her thoughts, and Flanna looked up to see a locomotive steaming into the depot, belching smoke and dust. She watched the train with rising dismay, realizing that it might be many months before she saw her family again. If the trains were not even moving south, the crisis was far more serious than she had realized.

The mood in the depot certainly seemed different. Last summer when she had returned from Charleston after a visit with her family, the atmosphere in this place had been as gay as the bright, clear colors of cotton dresses. Soft laughter filled the air as women embraced their loved ones returning from holiday, and a band on the piazza supported those happy sounds with the sentimental songs of Stephen Foster.

Now there was no band, for the musicians had enlisted to serve in the army. Bright, bold patriotic bunting fluttered from every post and pillar, and the few women who waited for their loved ones seemed abstracted and distant, as if they were bracing themselves for sorrows yet to come.

Roger, of course, had insisted that the strife would end in a few weeks, but he didn't know Southern gentlemen. Flanna did. They were not errant children who would fall into line after a severe scolding. They were gentlemen of honor, and they would not be easily vanquished. They had tasted victory at Fort Sumter. Moreover, they were fighting for their homes, their loved ones, and the right to remain independent.

Her face burned as she recalled John Brown's last statement, published in an antislavery paper called *The Liberator.* Mrs. Haynes subscribed to that rabble-rousing rag, and the last time Flanna visited the Haynes house, Roger's mother had made a point of reading the quote aloud. "I, John Brown," the murderer of five slaveholders had written on the day of his execution, "am now quite certain that the crimes of this guilty land will never be purged away but with Blood."

A suffocating sensation tightened Flanna's throat. Oh, let the guilty be punished, but God was righteous, so surely he would spare the innocent! Her family—Papa, Wesley, and all seven of her cousins—were innocent!

A swarm of disembarking travelers spilled from the train cars and moved past her. Flanna swiped at the tears wetting her lashes, not willing that a single Yankee should see her cry.

"Miss O'Connor? Can it be you?"

Flanna blinked and lifted her head. Alden Haynes stood before her, his uniform brushed and gleaming, a pistol at his right side and a sword at his left. He hesitated a moment, then bowed deeply, doffing his black hat in the first sign of respect offered her in many days.

"Major Haynes, how nice to see you." Flanna spoke calmly, but with the sense of detachment that comes from an awareness of impending disaster. Alden would tell Roger he had seen her at the station, and Roger would be horrified to learn she'd attempted to travel home. And if Mrs. Haynes learned that Flanna wanted to return to South Carolina, she'd spread the news that Flanna O'Connor was a Southern sympathizer.

Already Flanna had heard faint rumblings of danger. A few paranoid Boston officials had written newspaper editorials calling for the arrest and confinement of all "secesh" in Boston. A terrifying realization washed over her—the next moments were crucial. Her life and liberty might depend upon the story she now told Alden Haynes.

"Are you taking a trip?" His gaze roved over the carpetbags at Charity's feet, then returned to meet Flanna's eyes.

"No." She managed a small smile. "Just delivering some donations to the Boston Female Anti-Slavery Society. They are looking for supplies to outfit the soldiers."

"I know the group; Mother is a member." A flicker of a smile rose at the edges of his mouth, then died out. "The society's office is blocks from here, isn't it? So what brings you to the depot?"

Flanna's eyes widened in pretended surprise. "Why you, of course! Didn't Roger write you? When I heard that you were coming home—"

"No one knew I was coming." He gave her a warning look that put an immediate damper on her spirits. "I intended this visit to be a surprise."

"Well." Flanna lifted her hands in frustration. "*I* wanted to surprise *you*, and now you've ruined everything! Of course I knew you'd be coming home! Uncle Sam is not so heartless that he'd send his boys away without so much as a farewell to their families. Roger assumed you'd be coming sometime soon. I thought I'd stop by the depot this morning on my way to the society office, just to see if you'd be on this train."

"You came to meet me?" Disbelief and hope warred in his eyes, and for an instant Flanna floundered beneath a wave of guilt. This elaborate lie would certainly trap her later, and probably not one in a hundred men would believe such a haphazard tale. Alden himself probably didn't believe her, but as long as he thought her harmless…

"Well, this is quite an honor." He turned and formally offered his arm. "Shall we go then? I'll walk you home by way of the society office, and you can leave your donations there."

"But, Miss Flanna—" Charity protested.

"How very thoughtful of you," Flanna interrupted, rising. Taking Alden's arm, she gave her maid a warning look. "Isn't it nice, Charity, to have an escort through town?" She gave Alden the warmest smile she could manage. "How long will you be in Boston, Major?"

"Two months, perhaps longer. I've been ordered to help organize a regiment and lead them south to Washington."

"How thrilling!" Flanna patted his arm again, then lowered her eyes while he picked up his bag and led her through the milling crowd. They didn't speak, but one phrase kept replaying itself in Flanna's mind: "*Lead them south.*"

The train could not take her south to Charleston, but the army might.

⚜

Throughout the night, the idea burned like a fever in Flanna's brain. Why not join the army as a doctor? Pleas for able-bodied army physicians filled the newspapers, so why couldn't she offer her services? Though she had never expected to treat male patients, she could diagnose diarrhea and dispense doses of castor oil as well as any man.

Why not enlist? She tossed on her bed, thumping her pillow as the question hammered at her. She could join a regiment, travel south with them, and offer comfort as needed. And when they were close enough to South Carolina that she felt confident of finding her way home, she and Charity could petition for a pass to cross into Confederate territory. If that seemed impossible, they could slip away in the night. They'd endure some discomfort, to be sure, but if they fled in the temperate weather of summer they could sleep under the stars and travel during the daylight hours. No one would dare molest a gentlewoman traveling with her maid.

Sighing, Flanna turned and flattened herself upon her mattress. She stared at the ceiling, imprinting the swirled plaster with images of her loved ones. If this plan worked, she might soon see them again! She had come north to become a doctor, and somehow it seemed reasonable that being a doctor should provide her a way home.

Her heart swelled with hope, and finally she was able to sleep.

Rising early the next morning, Flanna penned a letter, addressing it to the War Department in Washington. In it she truthfully explained that although she was a South Carolinian by birth, she felt indebted to Massachusetts for providing her medical education. "If I may repay this debt by being of service to sons of this fair state as they venture south," she wrote, "I would be honored to do so. I ask only that my maid be able to attend me and that I be allowed to depart the regiment once we near South Carolina."

After double-checking her message, Flanna slid the letter into an envelope and sealed it, trusting that her intentions would be appreciated and well received.

If the Union was as desperate for qualified doctors as the newspaper ads seemed to suggest, she and Charity might be attached to a unit and moving south within a matter of weeks.

Seven

Two days after his return home, Alden Haynes turned before the mirror in his mother's upstairs hallway and soberly studied his reflection. After thirteen years at West Point Academy, four as a student and nine as an instructor, his stiff military bearing had become second nature. Did women like Flanna O'Connor find it attractive—or stuffy?

He glanced behind him to make sure none of the servants stood in the hall, then leaned toward the mirror and coaxed a smile to his lips. The result, he decided, abandoning the effort, was decidedly artificial and hardly worth the trouble. Let Roger charm and sweet-talk the ladies. Alden's manner was probably too severe to appeal to a bright, charming woman like Flanna O'Connor.

Alden turned away from the mirror, resigning himself to the enjoyment of Flanna's company from a distance. He'd taken altogether too much pleasure in the fact that she had been waiting at the train depot when he arrived. Though her flustered explanation was not entirely convincing, he wanted desperately to believe that she had sought him out. Roger, of course, had professed complete surprise at Alden's appearance. Which might mean that Flanna had considered the situation and wanted to meet Alden without Roger's knowledge…or that she was waiting for some other fellow.

Roger dismissed his traitorous thoughts. Her reasons for appearing did not matter. She had been waiting and he had enjoyed her company, but she was still Roger's sweetheart.

Now she was coming to dinner. Alden straightened his uniform dress coat, glanced in the mirror one final time, then moved to the window where she would soon appear. Though Roger had taken the buggy to fetch Flanna and would pretend that the evening was his idea, Alden had been the one to suggest that the Hayneses ought to invite Flanna to dinner to celebrate her graduation from medical school.

When he mentioned the idea at yesterday's lunch, his mother had nearly required her smelling salts. "Merciful heavens," she had whispered, a melancholy frown flitting across her features, "I couldn't have that girl in the house, not now! What would the neighbors think? You cannot know, Alden, how the town seethes with suspicion. If anyone thought I entertained one of the enemy—"

"Flanna O'Connor is not the enemy. She has been a resident of Boston for nearly two years," Alden had interrupted. He had turned to Roger. "And since she is *your* sweetheart, don't you think you should extend the invitation?"

For once Roger was speechless. "Why should we celebrate that useless degree?" he had asked, lifting a brow. "When we're married, I expect her to put all such foolishness out of her mind."

"I thought medicine was important to her."

"She feels an obligation to a dead slave and her doddering old father." Roger had leaned back in his chair as the beginning of a smile tipped the corners of his mouth. "Trust me, Alden, after even a short stint of hospital work, Flanna will be happy to assume her role as my wife. I'd rather not encourage her medical interests."

Indignation flared through Alden's soul. "Private Roger Haynes of the Twenty-fifth Massachusetts Regiment, I am your superior officer and acting head of this household. I hereby order you to do what is right, and may God forgive you your hesitations!"

Outwitted and outranked, Roger had written the invitation and sent a servant to deliver it.

Now the clip-clop of horses' hooves broke the silence of the evening. Alden dropped the lace curtain and stepped back, hiding himself in the shadows. Flanna's husky voice rose from the street, warming the chilly night, and as she alighted from the carriage on Roger's arm, Alden thought her the fairest vision he had ever seen. She wore a green gown that unmistakably matched her startling eyes. Her throat looked slender and graceful above a square-cut neckline, and the elegant spread of her flowing skirt reduced her waist to wasplike thinness.

"If it is treason to love an enemy or your brother's girl," he murmured, noticing how the gaslight sparked the coppery glints of her netted hair, "then I am a fool, and guilty on both counts."

Roger's head inclined toward that burnished crown as he whispered a comment, and a secretive smile softened her lips in return. Alden turned toward the door as bitter jealousy stirred inside his gut. Tonight he would not only have to tolerate his brother's patronizing attitude and his mother's cool indifference, he would also have to fight his own battle of personal restraint. But the effort was a small price to pay for the joy of spending another hour in Flanna's company.

❧

"The table is lovely, Mrs. Haynes," Flanna remarked for the fifth time. Alden rested his chin on his hand and smiled, wondering what she would say if she knew he had ordered that the finest linens, china, and silver be used for this special occasion.

His mother sat at the head of the table, her hands stiffly folded in her lap, her mouth set in a grim line. She had not wanted to do anything for Flanna, but Alden knew how to manipulate the intricacies of her reason. "Set a fine table," he had suggested, "and welcome her with open arms. She will doubtless remain in Boston during this time of conflict, and you know Roger will want to marry her as soon as he returns. So let it be said that you believed in her loyalty to the Union from the beginning. Let your recommendation prove her faithfulness, and you will not only gain a beautiful daughter-in-law, but a female doctor in the family! Susan B. Anthony and Elizabeth Cady Stanton will be so proud of you, they may want to visit and pay their respects."

Roger, of course, was delighted to entertain his sweetheart. Flush with excitement from his day of recruiting men to serve in his company, he was eager to talk about the coming struggle and its political ramifications. Leaning back in his chair, Alden watched Flanna as Roger talked. Her green eyes glittered as he related dull stories of complete insignificance, and for a moment Alden wondered how it would feel to have those emerald eyes light up when *he* spoke.

"Perhaps Miss O'Connor would like to tell us about her final examinations." Alden lifted his glass. "After all, that is the occasion we are celebrating tonight."

A deep flush rose from her square neckline, brightening her complexion to a becoming rosy hue. "It was difficult, but I rather enjoyed the experience." She twisted her hands as she sought Alden's eyes. "I found the examination...most challenging."

"Not quite as challenging as a full day of drill, aye, Alden?" Roger winked broadly across the table. "Those raw recruits are determined to deplete my store of patience! I've been trying to teach a handful of farmers how a gentleman wears a uniform, but they would rather use their dress coats for sunshades than wear them properly!"

Flanna lowered her head, her flush deepening to crimson as Roger continued. Alden ignored his brother, concentrating instead on the forgotten lady who sat across the table. Roger seemed to care only for her beauty, her deportment, and her charm, but Alden suspected that inside that faultless package resided far more woman than his brother could handle.

Roger's silver tongue slowed as Howard came in to clear the table. Alden pushed his chair back, ready to escort his mother to the parlor, but Roger caught his eye and grinned. "I'm so glad we're together tonight," he said, a glow rising in his face. "I have something important to discuss, and cannot think of a better time to broach the subject."

Like a wisp of smoke, a sense of unease crept into Alden's mood. "What could be so important?" He tried to sound casual. "We are here to celebrate. Serious matters can certainly wait until later."

"Not this." Roger pushed back his chair and stood, then dropped to one knee beside Flanna. She looked up, alarmed, and caught Alden's eye for a moment before Roger took her hand and reclaimed her attention.

"My dear Miss O'Connor," he began, one hand coming to rest over his heart.

"Heaven help us," Alden heard his mother murmur. "My smelling salts. Where could they be?" She rose and left the room in a flurry of silk.

Oblivious to his mother's exit, Roger continued. "Surely you know that I have great feelings of regard for you, Flanna." Eagerness and hope mingled upon his face as he gazed up at her. "When this difficulty is over, I want to come back and make you my wife. This is an official proposal, formally offered." Roger cut a quick glance to Alden. "With my brother as a witness, I now present my life and all that I possess to you. Will you have me?"

"Roger, don't." Flanna pulled ineffectively at his hand.

"Don't be embarrassed, my sweet, Alden is family. Speak now, tell me that you agree, and we shall covenant together."

He looked at her with something pleased, proud, and faintly possessive in his expression, and Flanna averted her eyes from his intense gaze. Alden's heart thumped against his rib cage when he heard her reply: "Roger, I'm sorry."

Roger's smile mutated into an expression of shock. "What?"

A look of discomfort crossed her delicate features. "We have spoken of this before. You honor me by this proposal, but I cannot marry you."

Roger sank back to his heels, his face going slack in surprise. "But we talked about it. We agreed."

"We agreed to wait. And that was before Fort Sumter." She tried to smile at him, but the corners of her mouth only wobbled precariously. "I can't marry you, Roger, because I have to go home. I can make no commitments until I know my father and brother are safe. I must go home, I must do what I can for my family. Later, perhaps, when all this is over…"

Her voice faded, and in the silence Alden felt a strange stirring of mingled hope and disappointment. He had wanted to hear that she could not marry Roger because she loved *him,* but that was a fanciful notion, completely insane. Apparently she cared more for her family than for either of them.

"Flanna, you can't go home," Roger was saying now. "It's too dangerous for a woman to travel unescorted."

"I have Charity."

"Your maid is no protection at all. The railroad lines aren't safe."

"I'm not going by rail." A faint smile ruffled her mouth. "I'm going with the army. When you go south"—Alden's heart skipped a beat when she shifted her gaze to him—"I'm going too. Massachusetts gave me my medical degree, and I will repay the state by serving as a physician for as long as I can. When we are close enough to South Carolina, I'm leaving to find my family."

"That's insane!" In his excitement, Roger stood and knocked over his empty glass. Alden merely stared at her, too startled to speak.

"Why is it insane?" Flanna's sweet demeanor vanished, replaced by a glorious indignation. "I told you I had to return to Charleston. Didn't you believe me?"

"You can't—it has never—" Roger's nostrils flared as he sputtered helplessly, then he pointed at Alden. "Tell her, brother!"

Surprised to find himself in the middle of their argument, Alden could not think straight. A thousand random thoughts ricocheted through his mind, and when he heard his own voice again, it seemed to come from someplace outside his body. "You can't go with the army, Miss O'Connor. Even if you were commissioned as a physician, the army takes a dim view of deserters." Pleased that he had managed a coherent sentence, he placed his hands on the table and forced himself to meet her gaze. "The United States has never— and probably *will* never—commission a female surgeon. You may be sure of it."

Flanna's chin dipped in a tense nod of agreement. "That may be. But I'm not asking for a commission. I just want to travel with the army until I am close enough to go home. I don't want to *join* the army; I want to *serve* it for a time."

Alden tapped the table and smiled without humor. "You don't understand the army, Miss O'Connor. Women aren't allowed to travel with a regiment—well, some camp followers are unavoidable, but you wouldn't want—" He cleared his throat and backed away from a most immodest subject. "Let me rephrase my argument. No *respectable* women travel with the army. A few officers' wives may visit briefly, but most gentlemen are wise enough to keep their women at home. An army camp is no place for a well-bred lady, Miss Flanna. You would hear things unfit for a woman's ears, and you would certainly see sights no lady ought to see."

Roger waved his hand. "There are no women in the army for you to treat, so how is it that you wish to serve?"

"I am a physician, Roger." She swallowed hard, lifted her chin, and boldly met his gaze. "I don't expect to operate upon men, but I can administer medicines for routine maladies and digestive upsets. Surely you believe me capable of dispensing castor oil."

Alden stared, amazed by the power in her words and the strength of her defiance. No, she most certainly did not fit his image of a simpering Southern belle.

"Doctor O'Connor." Alden deepened his voice as he stood. "If you are wise you will accept my brother's proposal, remain in Boston until this matter of secession is settled, and live your life as a happily married woman. I should think that is the best course for a woman in your situation, and I would advise you to take it."

"Would you now?" He heard defiance as well as a subtle challenge in her tone.

"Indeed," he answered, bowing slightly, "but something tells me you will not listen."

He left the room before she could inflame his senses again.

⌘

Flanna's hope faded with spring's blossoms. As she waited to hear from the War Department, Alden's words echoed in her memory: *"The United*

States has never commissioned a female surgeon." Apparently he was right, for each day Flanna asked Mrs. Davis for her mail, and each day the widow gave her a wintry smile and replied that nothing had come.

Occasionally on quiet Saturday mornings, Flanna and Charity walked the streets around Boston Common and watched the fledgling Massachusetts regiments drill. Since Roger had taken the initiative of forming his own company, he ensured himself a captaincy. Within three weeks of his enlistment, he had procured the names of one hundred men from Beacon Hill and the outlying districts, more than enough for a company. He and his men were officially designated Company K, part of the Twenty-fifth Massachusetts Regiment. According to a newspaper article Flanna read, Mrs. Ernestina Haynes had personally agreed to financially support Company K, supplying uniforms, guns, and supplies for Roger's one hundred men. A note near the end of the article added that Major Alden Haynes, Mrs. Haynes's eldest son, had been appointed to oversee Company K and nine others in the still-forming regiment.

Flanna felt a lurch of excitement within her as she ran her finger over Alden's name. She certainly had no business feeling this strange attraction to him—he was Roger's brother, an officer in the enemy army, and thoroughly beyond her power to charm. He tended to turn his head when she looked his way, and only heaven knew what he really thought of her. And yet there was something about him she found irresistible and intriguing. "In another time and place perhaps," she murmured, folding the newspaper so that his name lay safely out of sight. "But not now. And not here."

Roger steadfastly maintained his belief in their forthcoming marriage. He wrote her nearly every day, accepting her reluctance to become publicly engaged during wartime and understanding her concerns for her loved ones at home. "When this war is over," he wrote again and again, "then we shall be wed, and then everything will be wonderful. You will see, Flanna. Wait and see."

No matter how hard she tried to concentrate on finding a way home, Flanna often thought of the brothers as she walked past the military training grounds on her way to the hospital. With no word from her father and no other means of financial support, she had accepted a part-time position at the Boston Women's Hospital. Each morning, after a perfunctory hour spent with Mrs. Davis's havelock seamstresses, she and Charity went to the hospital where Flanna assisted with childbirth cases, changed bandages, and listened to a litany of female complaints. Any competent nurse could have performed her duties, and Flanna knew the administrator's reluctance to trust her had less to do with her youth or gender than with her Southern heritage.

She walked a thin line, and she knew it. If by word or deed she did anything to insinuate that she favored the Confederate cause, she risked being cast out of the boardinghouse, her workplace, and Boston society. Though she didn't particularly care about society, out of respect for the Haynes family she spent an hour after her hospital shift volunteering for the Sanitary Commission. The hours she spent rolling bandages went far to dispel the suspicion that Ernestina Haynes had harbored a Rebel in the bosom of her family. Though Flanna was thoroughly exhausted at the end of every day, she hurried back to the boardinghouse and forced her heavy eyelids to stay open while she searched the papers for news of home.

In May, Arkansas became the ninth state to secede, followed by North Carolina. Within days, representatives of the Confederate States of America named Richmond as their capital. June brought another secession as Tennessee became the eleventh state to join the Confederacy.

After eight weeks and four follow-up letters to the U.S. War Department, Flanna became convinced that Alden Haynes was right—the United States Army would not only reject her offer of assistance, they would not even dignify her letters with a reply. She cast about for another opportunity to serve the army, and in June learned that a female powerhouse, Dorothea Dix, had been appointed Superintendent of Women Nurses and authorized to hire women to nurse wounded soldiers. Flanna immediately sent another letter to Washington, this one addressed to Miss Dix. The answer arrived in mid-July: "Nursing is a serious profession," wrote Miss Dix. "Only serious young women over the age of thirty and plain in appearance need apply."

Unjust! At twenty-four, Flanna knew more about medicine than Miss Dix ever would, but she would not even be allowed to serve as a nurse!

As Flanna struggled to overcome the gloom that pressed upon her, an equally gray cloud settled over Boston as the two armies met for the first time at Bull Run, near Manassas, Virginia. Within days reports of heavy Union losses filled the city, and the gay wartime gatherings turned grim. By late July belligerent Boston had been thoroughly sobered by the realization that the Union forces under General Irvin McDowell had been soundly defeated by the ragtag Rebel troops.

Flanna waited until Mrs. Davis and her seamstresses had dimmed the lamps and gone to bed, then she sneaked downstairs for a newspaper and took it up to her room. By the dim glow of that single flame, she anxiously skimmed the newspaper accounts of the battle.

"They came at us, yelling like furies," one soldier told the reporter. "There is no sound like that Rebel yell this side of the infernal region. The peculiar corkscrew sensation that it sends down your backbone under these circumstances cannot be described. You have to feel it, and if you say you did not feel it, and heard the yell, you have never been there."

"That day, July 21, will forever be known as Black Sunday," wrote the reporter. "We are utterly and disgracefully routed, beaten, whipped by secessionists." Horace Greeley, the Republican editor of the *New York Tribune*, urged Lincoln to make peace with the Confederacy and give up the struggle for unity. "On every brow sits sullen, scorching, black despair," he was quoted as saying. "If it is best for the country and for mankind that we make peace with the Rebels, and on their own terms, do not shrink even from that."

Flanna scanned each page, reading every item, until she finally found the information she sought—a listing of brigades and regiments engaged in the battle. The list of Confederate regiments actively engaged at Bull Run included the Second South Carolina under Colonel

Kershaw, the Third South Carolina under Colonel Williams, the Seventh South Carolina under Colonel Thomas Bacon, and the Eighth South Carolina under Colonel E.B.C. Cash, all part of the First Brigade. Reports indicated that ten men from those units had been killed.

Flanna smoothed the newspaper on her desk and clenched her eyes shut. Had Wesley enlisted in one of those regiments? She had heard nothing from her father since mid-April. Wesley was as enthusiastic as any of the Boston blue bloods; he had probably signed up long before the warning shots fired on Fort Sumter. He could easily be serving in the First or Second Brigade. Oh, if only she knew the name of his commanding officer!

An image of Wesley's broad freckled face dropped like a rock into the pool of her heart, sending ripples of fear in all directions. He'd been her playmate and best friend for as long as she could remember, and she couldn't bear the thought of losing him. Panic like she'd never known welled in her throat, but she fought it down, knowing she could not release it.

She had a part to play, and so did Charity. No matter how badly they wanted to return home or how desperately they feared for their loved ones, they could not let one unguarded word or emotion slip the bonds of their hearts. They were prisoners in enemy territory, and, like a wounded bear, the foe was smarting from the unaccustomed sting of defeat and apt to turn vicious.

Both Flanna and Charity noticed that their reception at Mrs. Davis's havelock sewing circle grew decidedly more chilly after the Battle of Bull Run. For a moment Flanna was tempted to stop her volunteer work, then she realized that any weakening of her resolve would only be interpreted as proof of her Southern sympathies. So she persisted in aiding the people who had become her adversaries, wrapping bandages and sewing havelocks until her fingers were chafed and sore.

And each day she read the newspaper, searching its pages by candlelight to see if she could discover any opening through which she and Charity could find their way home.

Eight

Thursday, July 25

 I dreamed tonight that Aunt Marsali came into my room and kissed my cheek. When I opened my eyes, she took my hand. "A great battle has been fought," she said. Though she smiled, a tear slipped down her cheek. "Jeff Davis led the center, Joe Johnston the right wing, Beauregard the left wing of the army. Your brother is all right. Arthur is wounded, Brennan is safe, Carroll is missing, Dillon and Erin are safe, Flynn is wounded, shot in the leg." Another tear fell, and I felt its wetness upon my hand. "Gannon is dead, Flanna. I have lost my youngest and most precious son."

 I said nothing, knowing that it had to be a dream, and after a moment Aunt Marsali continued. "President Davis says it is a great victory. But there are dead and dying all over the field. The Lynchburg regiment was cut to pieces, and three hundred of the legion are wounded."

 I strained to hear her; her voice was lighter than air. "Be certain of what you pray for, Flanna. The army is no place for a woman."

 She vanished then, like a puff of steam, but I

knew it was the way of dreams. I turned in my bed,
forcing myself to wake, and when I sat up, in truth
my hand was wet with tears...but they were my own.

"Get her away from me!" The pale, sweating woman lifted her head and peered out over the rounded bulge of her belly. "I'll not have any Southern trash touching me! Get her out of here, now!"

"Mrs. Scott." Dr. Bartlett stepped forward and gave her a bleak, tight-lipped smile. "I assure you that Dr. O'Connor—"

"I heard about that one! Irish trash from Charleston, that bed of vipers! If you let her touch me, I'll have my husband call you out! You'll think differently about sending some traitor in to tend me when you're staring down the barrel of his pistol."

Flanna looked up, expecting Dr. Bartlett to take a firmer approach with his patient, but the bleary-eyed physician gestured for her to leave the ward. For a moment Flanna hesitated, torn by conflicting emotions. She was far more capable of delivering the baby than this spineless doctor, but the older man was in no mood to argue the point. "Miss O'Connor," he murmured, eyeing her with an aloof expression, "fetch one of the midwives. Let her deliver the brat."

Flanna snapped her mouth shut and stepped out of the ward, her lips puckering with annoyance. Why had she bothered to go to medical school if no one would let her work? She was more than qualified to tend that woman, but men like Dr. Bartlett would rather work drunk and rely on midwives than admit that women made perfectly capable physicians.

Shrugging in mock resignation, Flanna crossed her arms and leaned against the plastered wall. This was only the latest of her indignities. The word had filtered out, and no Boston woman—even the poor ones who came to this hospital—wanted to be attended by a Southerner. No one cared that Flanna had graduated first in her class; it mattered far more that she had been born in Charleston and employed a black maid rather than a sturdy Irish girl.

Swallowing the lump that had risen in her throat, Flanna pulled herself off the wall and moved down the hallway, thinking that she would be more likely to find gold under her pillow than to work in this city.

"Miss Flanna!" Alarmed at the urgency in Charity's voice, Flanna spun on her heel and faced the wide double doors at the end of the hallway. Charity was running down the hall, her skirts stirring up dust as she approached. Flanna's mouth went dry when she saw Alden Haynes trailing in Charity's wake.

Flanna's heart skipped a beat. She had not seen Roger or Alden since that horrible night when Roger proposed. He continued to write her newsy little notes, boldly assuming they would resume their courtship as soon as this "difficulty" had passed, but Flanna knew things would never be the same between them. In the space of a single moment that night—when Alden had tried to congratulate her and Roger had brushed her accomplishment aside—she had seen both brothers for what they were. And in that moment woven of eternity, she had realized with heart-stopping clarity that she had bestowed her affections on the wrong man.

Turning away, she wiped a bead of perspiration from her brow and smoothed her apron.

"Miss Flanna," Charity called again. "The major needs you. He's got a sick soldier, and the man wants you to come."

"Me?" Flanna's voice rose in surprise as she looked at Alden. "Is this some sort of joke, Major? Why would one of your recruits want a doctor from the women's hospital?"

"Good day to you, too, Dr. O'Connor." Belatedly reminding her of her manners, Alden bowed slightly. "I hope you are well."

"As well as can be expected." Irritated by his mocking tone, Flanna wiped her hands on her apron again and struggled to smooth the annoyance from her face. "Now, sir, perhaps you can tell me what sort of joke this is. A Massachusetts man would never call for a female doctor."

"He says he's from Carolina—that's why he wants you." Alden's appreciative eye traveled from her hair net to the toe of her scuffed slippers. "And though he's enlisted to fight for the Twenty-fifth, he'll not let our surgeon touch him." His eyes were alight with mischief and inspiration when his gaze caught hers. "Truthfully, Doctor, I can't say I blame him. Our regimental surgeon has been in his cups ever since signing on. I'd let Roger cut on me before I'd let John Gulick into my tent."

The shock of discovery hit her full force. "Dr. John Gulick is your surgeon?"

"You know him? Apparently he signed on because his wife badgered him to enlist, but we haven't had a sober hour's work out of him since he arrived in camp."

Flanna's mouth twisted in a wry smile. "So, your man in camp would rather have a woman attend him than a drunk?" It was a compliment, but not much of one. "Major Haynes," she managed a small, tentative smile, "thank you for coming. I appreciate your man's confidence in me, but I am a female doctor."

A smile tugged at his lips. "I noticed."

"No, I—" She paused as the blood began to pound in her temples. "I mean, I tend female patients. I trained to work with women." Her fingers fluttered to her neck. "I wouldn't feel comfortable working with a man—especially since you have pointed out that the army is no place for a lady. I could dose him, but if he needs a full examination—"

Alden tipped his head back and looked down at her. "Are you saying that you can't doctor a man?"

"No." Flanna lifted her chin and boldly met his eyes. "I could, of course I could. But I'm a lady, and I wouldn't—"

"Feel comfortable." Alden finished her thought, his voice soft with disbelief. He pinned her with a long, silent scrutiny, then his eyes narrowed. "Well then, excuse me, Dr. O'Connor." The grim line of his mouth relaxed as he thrust his hands behind his back. "I was under the impression that you were a woman who valued compassion above comfort, who cared more for humanity than the silly and false ideals of our self-anointed nobility. More than that, I thought you could handle any emergency. But I see now that I was wrong."

With a brief nod to Charity, he turned to leave.

His words had cut Flanna, spreading an infection of guilt. "Wait," she called.

Why should she care if her reputation were further damaged? Let Boston society rot. This stranger from Carolina, God bless him, was the first patient who had sought her out. He deserved the best she could offer.

"Charity, fetch my bag—you'll find it in the office. Then follow as quickly as you can." She took a step toward the admitting desk, about to tell the nurse she'd been called away, then realized it didn't matter. The only people in this hospital who could abide her touch were unconscious or too sick to care. None of them needed her now.

"Major Haynes," she said, noting Alden's look of amusement as she turned to face him, "lead me to your patient."

A heat wave lay over the city like a heavy shroud. As Alden escorted her up Tremont Street, Flanna wondered how men could abide living outdoors in such humidity and heat. The high ceilings and shuttered windows of most Boston buildings cooled their interiors somewhat, but these men had been living outside ever since Massachusetts began to form her regiments.

Alden apologized that he had brought no carriage, but at present he had no horse. "I would have waited until a horse was available," he added, "but Private Fraser's condition seemed rather urgent."

A tremor of mingled fear and anticipation shot through Flanna. This did not sound like a case of diarrhea or fever. It might be serious, even a surgical situation, and she had never intended to place herself in a position where she might have to operate on a man.

"If it was urgent," Flanna asked, the hair at the back of her neck rising with premonition, "why did you not take him to the hospital? Surely one of the other surgeons could put him at ease."

"He wouldn't go," Alden answered, his voice flat. "I told you, he's from Carolina. He was afraid his accent would reveal his roots."

Flanna listened, then nodded in sympathy. She couldn't blame the man. If she were sick, she wouldn't want to depend upon the mercy of a Boston doctor either. Especially not so soon after Bull Run.

"So he sent for me? Why?"

"Oh, the men hear all sorts of things in camp." Alden's mouth curled in a one-sided smile. "Roger talks about you often enough. There's one group of soldiers that loves you for being bright and beautiful, and another that hates you for being Southern and female. So I'm guessing that between Roger and the gossips, Private Fraser decided you wouldn't do him harm. Better to have a Carolina lady doctor than a hateful Yankee drunk."

Flanna stopped short, alarmed that an entire regiment might know her name—and that half of them might hate her. "When you speak of 'the men,'" she said, her nerves at a full stretch, "how many men do you mean? Ten? Twenty? A hundred?" She took a deep breath and reached for his arm. "Major Haynes, if it's not safe for me to go into this camp, perhaps you should give Private Fraser my regrets."

"I assure you, you will be safe." He took her elbow and gently guided her along the sidewalk. "Are you familiar with military organization?"

Flanna shook her head.

"Ah, well, that'll take some explaining." He smiled, and Flanna noticed that he seemed relieved to have found a topic of conversation that would not upset her. "A volunteer infantry regiment like the Twenty-fifth Massachusetts is comprised of nearly a thousand men—our unit has enlisted 786 at present, with 39 officers. These soldiers are divided into ten companies, and from there, the men tend to divide themselves into smaller groups called 'messes.'"

Flanna frowned. "Because they are untidy?"

Alden's smile deepened into laughter. "No, because they eat together. But I've seen some of the meals they concoct from their rations, and perhaps your interpretation of the word is appropriate. They usually gather around a common fire as friends and family do, and in time most men become quite attached to their messmates. I didn't know about Private Fraser, your patient, until one of his messmates reported that he was ill. Fraser is in Company B."

"Roger has a company, right? He said he had recruited nearly a hundred men."

"Yes." A suggestion of annoyance hovered in Alden's eyes as he dropped her elbow and thrust his hands behind his back. "Things were a bit confused when Lincoln called for troops, so the army is allowing nonmilitary men to lead the companies they recruit. So Roger is captain of Company K."

She saw the snap of his eyes. "You don't think he should be."

"No." His brow wrinkled. "He has no experience, no training, no knowledge of military affairs. Roger's greatest gift is his golden tongue, and while that may be invaluable in persuading men to enlist and even to fight, it may do him more harm than good on the battlefield. I just…I don't know how he will handle the pressure of a real fight."

Flanna silently digested this news as they walked. Until this moment she had not imagined that a spirit of competition could exist between the two brothers. Opposite in temperament, they had always seemed to accept their differences. Would Alden's apparent disapproval of Roger affect them in camp?

"Which company do you lead?" She raised her eyes to find him watching her.

"I'm not tied to a company; I serve the entire regiment." He inclined his blond head toward an older gentleman on the sidewalk, who bowed respectfully at Alden's approach. "I assist the lieutenant colonel and the colonel who commands the regiment. Our regiment is one of four that make up the Second Brigade. Three or four brigades make a division, two or more divisions make a corps, one or more corps make up an army."

"That's quite enough, thank you." Flanna held up her hand in protest. "Surely you don't expect me to remember all that?"

"Roger said you were bright." Alden's mouth curved into an unconscious smile. "You cannot tell him I said so, but he thinks you are more intelligent than he."

"Really?" In spite of her nervousness, Flanna laughed. Roger would never admit such a thing to her, but it was nice to know he appreciated her gifts…especially since no one else in Boston seemed to.

"We're almost there." Alden paused on the sidewalk across the street from Boston Common, then turned to her with a decidedly serious expression on his face. "I would not bring you here if I were not extremely worried about Private Fraser. In a few moments you are likely to see men gambling and hear language unfit for a lady's ears."

"Major," Flanna gave him a wavering smile, "I assure you, vile language is the least of my worries. Please, transfer your concern from my ears to our patient." She looked behind her and smiled when she saw Charity scurrying toward them with her medical bag. "Now that my equipment has arrived, I suggest we tend to your sick soldier."

Alden pressed his lips together, then extended his arm toward the edge of the camp. "After you then, Dr. O'Connor."

Flanna lifted her skirts as she stepped from the sidewalk to the street, then crinkled her nose as the first scents of the camp reached her nostrils. The smells of roasting meat mingled with the ammoniac odor of horses and the stench of human sewage.

"They should do something about the pits," she said. "Don't they read Deuteronomy?"

"I beg your pardon?" Alden asked, walking by her side.

"The sewage pits." Flanna absently waved her hand toward the outskirts of the camp. "They should be moved farther out. Each man should carry a shovel and immediately dig a hole and cover it. There should be no standing sewage. It's all explained in Deuteronomy, chapter twenty-three."

Alden didn't answer, but his flush receded in a most dramatic fashion, leaving two red spots lingering on his pale cheeks.

"Major Haynes," she continued, ignoring the guards' wide eyes as she entered the camp, "if you are to assist me, I must ask that you leave all false modesty behind. I am a woman, but I am a doctor, and there are few—if any—bodily functions with which I am not well acquainted."

If she had shocked him, he recovered well. "Agreed, madam." He arched one golden brow. "If you will come with me, I will lead you to Private Fraser."

Following Alden, Flanna and Charity wended their way through a maze of canvas tents and campfires. Though Flanna had walked past the camp nearly every day, she had never really been close enough to observe the details of military life. She saw groups of men brushing their uniforms and blackening their leather outside their tents. Others huddled around fires, stirring pots of some food that did little to whet her appetite in terms of aroma or appearance. Through the spaces between tents she saw the parade field, where some fifty or so men marched in a line with rifles on their shoulders. A band consisting of a half-dozen trumpets, a quartet of drums, three violins, and a pair of fifers stood at the edge of the field playing "Yankee Doodle" in a sprightly rhythm.

"Drill." Alden answered her unspoken question. "They must know how to march before we can move southward. The music helps them stay together."

"I understand."

Finally the major paused outside a tent barely big enough for two people. "We put Fraser in here, not wanting the others to disturb a sick man," Alden explained, squatting down by the low entrance. "I can have him carried into one of the bigger tents if you'd like."

"That won't be necessary." Flanna took a deep breath to quell the leaping pulse beneath her ribs. She had managed to stanch her nervousness on the long walk to the camp, but in the last five minutes the very *maleness* of this place had awakened every apprehension. If she had to examine a man, let it be in a small space, with no curious eyes to note her discomfort. "I'd like to talk to the private alone."

She squatted as low as her voluminous crinoline would allow, then smiled as a ridiculous, irrational thought struck her. Mrs. Haynes and those silly suffragists certainly had the right idea when it came to dress reform. Whoever decreed that women should wear four-foot hoops around their legs certainly must have intended that they be confined.

"Charity, help me, will you?" She stood and looked around for a private place to discard the unwieldy foundation garment. But when she glanced behind her, she saw that the dozen or so soldiers around the nearest fire had frozen in a tableau of curiosity, pausing from their work to take an unseemly interest in hers.

"What am I to do, Miss Flanna?" Charity asked, wringing her hands.

"Let me think."

Flanna squatted again, her skirt mounding around her as she peered inside the small tent. A center pole blocked her path; she couldn't even waddle in. She couldn't crawl forward, for the hoop skirt would tilt upward and expose her pantalets to an entire company of curious Yankees.

"Dog take it all!" The crude expression was one of Wesley's favorites, and she felt better after saying it. In a flash of decision, she stood and pulled her apron off, then tossed it to Charity. As the maid watched in stupefaction, Flanna smoothed the fabric of her dress until she had exposed the seam that joined her bodice and skirt. "Scalpel, Charity," she said, extending her hand.

"Miss Flanna?"

"My scalpel, if you please. Now."

Charity draped Flanna's apron over her shoulder and dropped the medical bag to the ground. After fumbling among its contents, she pulled out the gray felt sleeve containing Flanna's surgical instruments, then slid out the sharpened scalpel and gingerly placed it into Flanna's palm.

The touch of the cool metal seemed to steady Flanna's nerves. Without hesitation, she tugged on her skirt with her left hand and sliced the threads with her right, effectively opening the seam three inches. She heard the murmur of voices behind her, and the exclamation, "The fool woman's gone and cut herself! Major, where'd you find this lunatic?"

"Charity," Flanna handed the scalpel back to her maid, "will you please work your fingers into the hole and untie the string that holds my hoop skirt? I'll never be able to maneuver in this."

Nodding, Charity came forward and did as she was told. When Charity had untied the string, the cage-like contraption fell from Flanna's skirt, billowing the fabric of her plain plaid housedress. The soldiers behind her cheered in newfound appreciation for her ingenuity.

"Now, to tend my patient." Flanna stepped over the collapsed steel hoops and knelt to crawl into the tent. Before she could move, however, another spasm of doubt twisted her stomach, and she shuddered.

"You can do this." Alden's hand fell upon her shoulder and gave a gentle squeeze. "And I will do anything I can to help."

"Just stand aside so Charity can hold the tent flap shut, will you? I'll be working on my hands and knees, and I'll not provide any further entertainment for your men."

Alden lifted his hands and stepped back. "A fair request, Doctor."

"I'll hold the door shut, Miss Flanna," Charity said, coming to stand by Flanna's side.

"My medical bag?" Flanna put out her hand, and Charity slid the heavy bag so that the handle rested beneath Flanna's palm.

She took a deep breath. Time to begin.

Her eyes searched inside the tent, and the tenseness in her back eased somewhat when she saw the small figure huddled upon a pallet. Just one sick boy from Carolina.

"Keep the flap closed, Charity." Flanna grasped her bag and crawled into the tent.

⊱⊰

Private Henry Fraser was a small soldier, barely five feet tall, and very young, for no whiskers had yet sprouted upon that pointed chin. He lay curled on his side, his hands clasped between his legs, his head close to his knees. His shaggy golden hair was damp with sweat, and his complexion had gone sallow beneath a dusting of freckles.

"Private Fraser?" Flanna knelt beside him, her medical bag opened beside her.

The boy's eyes fluttered open, then sought hers. "You—you came? You're the lady doctor?"

"Yes, I'm Dr. O'Connor." Flanna lightly rested the back of her hand on the boy's forehead. His skin was damp and warm; his face flushed with a low fever. The sour scent of vomit emanated from his clothing, and as Flanna reached out to mark the pulse in his wrist she felt a rapid, staccato beat.

"Do you have pain?" She lowered her head to look in the boy's eyes.

He tilted his head toward her and nodded slightly. "Yes'm. Right here." Gingerly he reached down and touched his trousers, a few inches to the right of center.

Despite her medical training, Flanna drew back at the strangely intimate gesture. If this was some sort of vulgar joke…Alden *had* said half the men hated her for being Southern and female.

"Why didn't you send for the regimental surgeon?" she asked, her voice colder than she intended. "Most men would rather suffer than have a woman examine their private parts."

"Please, ma'am." The private peered at her through tear-clogged lashes. "I couldn't tell anyone else. They'd send me home, and I need the money. But it hurts, and I'm afraid I'm gonna die."

"Tell anyone else what?" Flanna examined her weeping patient more closely. Was the boy underage? Quite possibly. Lincoln and his generals were happy to enlist anyone they could.

"My name's not really Henry."

Flanna pursed her lips as the light of understanding began to dawn. "You enlisted under a false name? Whose name was it, your elder brother's? Son, if you're too young, you should tell Major Haynes. He might let you sign up with the musicians. I understand there's a brigade with a twelve-year-old drummer boy—"

"My real name," the boy interrupted, shivering under the effects of fever, "is Henrietta. Henrietta Fraser."

Flanna sat back, frozen in a paralysis of astonishment. Private Fraser was a *girl?* Why on earth would a girl want to join this regiment? She drew a deep breath, feeling a dozen different emotions collide. Motivations didn't matter, but one thing was certain—Henrietta Fraser did not belong in the army.

"You're not really from Carolina, are you?"

"No ma'am. But I'm from the country, and don't speak like the folks 'round here. I thought—I hoped—the major wouldn't know the difference."

"All right." Flanna rose to her knees again. "I'm going to examine you, Henrietta, and then I'm going to tell the major what you've told me. No matter what you've heard, war is not a carefree adventure. This excitement and silliness will fade away, and you'll wish you were home soon enough. So let me see the spot that's giving you pain—"

"You can't tell them!" Henrietta tensed, her hand protectively covering her abdomen. "You can't! They'll want the money back, and I've already sent it home. My folks know what I've done, and they placed me in God's hands. And if they have given me leave to stay and fight, who are you to say I can't?"

Flanna shook her head. "What money? A soldier's wages aren't enough for this sort of sacrifice."

"The bounty." The girl hissed in pain between her clenched teeth. "They were givin' a hundred dollars to any soldier who'd promise to serve at least two years. That's more money than my pa makes in a year. So you've got to help me—*ohhh!*"

The girl gagged and vomited. With clinical detachment Flanna noticed that her patient was now spewing forth the thin liquids of an empty, agonized stomach. The symptoms of appendicitis—fever, nausea, vomiting, and pain on the lower right side of the abdomen—were all present. Whether in a hospital or in this tent, Henrietta Fraser would certainly die from peritonitis unless something was done. But what?

Flanna sat back and pressed her hand to her mouth. One segment of her studies had included the medical records of Claudius

Aymand, an English surgeon who had surgically removed a swollen appendix in 1736. As far as Flanna knew, no American physician had yet attempted such an operation. But this girl would die unless someone did.

Leaning forward, Flanna pushed her patient's wavy hair from her damp forehead. "Henrietta—let me ask you again. Will you let me take you to a hospital?"

"No." Clenching her teeth, the girl curled tighter around her abdomen. "My ma and pa would die of shame if anyone found out. I'd die before I'd let you tell on me."

Biting her lip, Flanna looked away. "I have to be honest. You might die. There is an operation—but I've never performed it. I can't promise that you'll survive, but I can promise that I'll do my best for you."

Henrietta Fraser stopped moaning for a moment. A faint flicker of unease stirred in the girl's soft brown eyes, then a tear slipped down her pale cheek. "You do whatever you have to," she whispered, her voice fainter than air, "just don't tell anyone my real name. If I die, you bury me under the name Henry Fraser and write a letter to my folks. They'll understand."

Sobered instantly by the frightening possibility that she might have to write that letter, Flanna reached for the tent flap and hoarsely called for Charity.

⚬⚬⚬

Alden Haynes stood back, feeling oddly helpless as the maid stepped out of the tent and repeated Flanna's requests. "She wants a pitcher of clean water, a high table, a big tent with a bright light, and a cask of the strongest alcohol you've got." Charity's head bobbed in earnestness. "This soldier needs an operation, and he wants Miss Flanna to do it. And she'll do it, she says, but I'm the only one allowed to help her. Everyone else has to stay clean away from the tent."

"Surely Private Fraser would rather go to the hospital for surgery." Alden thrust his hand into his belt and turned away. "I'll arrange for a wagon—"

"No, he don't want to go," Charity insisted, grabbing his sleeve. "I heard him say that he'd die before he'd let any Yankee surgeon take a knife to him." The maid arched her brows into triangles and tilted her head knowingly. "You gots to understand, Major, this is a Carolina boy. He don't trust none of those Yankee doctors."

Alden blew out his breath. Each day brought its own trying situation, but at least Flanna's requests weren't unreasonable. Most of the new recruits were drilling out in the field, so privacy wouldn't be a problem.

He stroked his moustache, thinking. If the man died, no one in Boston would trust Dr. Flanna O'Connor, and he hadn't brought her to camp to further damage her reputation. He had hoped the Fraser boy was only slightly sick, but despite his good intentions, he seemed to have placed Flanna O'Connor in the midst of trouble.

He straightened and clasped his hands behind his back. Sickness was always a problem in the crowded camps. If the boy died, he'd do his best to make certain Flanna's name was left out of the reports. The surgeons had already been bedeviled by a host of diseases; no one would think it strange that another boy had died.

"I'll get the things she needs," Alden said, turning away. "I'll call when we're ready."

"Miss Flanna says you'd better hurry if you want to save this boy's life," Charity called after him. "He's knocking on heaven's door now and will have one foot through the pearly gates before too long."

Spurred by the warning, Alden quickened his pace.

༺ঞৎঞৎ༻

Flanna moistened the strip of cotton with chloroform, then looked into Private Fraser's eyes one last time. "You're sure about this?" she whispered, trying to steady her own voice.

The frightened girl nodded.

"Then you just breathe normally through this cloth, and you'll go to sleep," Flanna promised. "When you wake up, it will be all over."

Henrietta didn't answer, but closed her eyes. Flanna pressed the chloroform-soaked cloth over the girl's mouth and nose, holding it until Henrietta's breathing slowed and steadied.

Flanna handed the bottle of chloroform to her maid. "Charity, if she moves or speaks, you press that cloth over her nose again until she settles down. Understand?"

"Yes ma'am." Charity balanced the cloth on her palm, ready for anything.

Flanna moved to a basin and washed her hands. *Go ahead, Dr. Gulick, scoff.* She scrubbed between her knuckles until her skin glowed pink. *But if God commanded cleanliness, it must be important.*

With clean hands, she moved to her patient and gingerly lifted the sheet she had placed over Private Fraser's lower anatomy. Out of deference to Henrietta's secret, Flanna had allowed the girl to wear her shirt into surgery and had promised to return her trousers as soon as the operation was completed. She had also revealed the truth to Charity, knowing the girl would keep Henrietta's secret forever if need be.

Lifting the pitcher, Flanna poured running water over the girl's abdomen, then held the blade of her scalpel in the lamp flame, reasoning that a heated blade cut more easily. When the blade glowed with heat, she held it over the faintly pink skin and closed her eyes, momentarily imprinting the girl's flesh with diagrams from her medical school texts. *The appendix is a small appendage hanging from the beginning of the large intestine. A tube with no known function in human beings, it is known to burst if swollen or enlarged. Theoretically the appendix could be removed in order to save the patient's life. Much caution must be observed, however. For the intestine is filled with filth, and any seepage can endanger the patient...*

She would have to enter the peritoneum, the clear membrane that lined the walls of the abdominal cavity, so she would have to make at least four incisions—one through the flesh and fat, one through the wall of muscle that enclosed the gut, one through the peritoneum, and a final cut to sever the appendix itself. Dr. Aymand had used silk sutures to close the cuts, and Charity stood ready with the finest needles and silk threads Flanna had been able to procure for her medical bag.

"Father God, bless my hands," Flanna murmured. Then she lowered the scalpel and used the tip to trace a thin line over the spot where Henrietta Fraser's appendix should lie.

*

Watching through a narrow crack in the tent flap, Alden marveled at Flanna's composure. Though he'd been sincere in his belief that she could dose a sick man, some part of him had been quite unwilling to believe her capable of cutting on a Union soldier. But now she moved gracefully, in complete and quiet control of the situation.

Any other female of his acquaintance would have fainted at the sight of the blade, but Flanna seemed to wield it with as much confidence inside Private Fraser as when she ripped the seam in her gown. From his vantage point, Alden could see that she had two fingers inside the soldier's gut and was now lifting a flaming bit of flesh with a huge pair of elongated tweezers—

Alden looked away as his stomach roiled. He couldn't vomit in front of his men, no matter how unsettling the sight he'd just witnessed. And yet Flanna O'Connor, a polite and proper Southern belle, had not only borne the bloody sight without so much as a grimace, but she'd actually initiated the surgery!

Alden sat on a stump and pulled out his handkerchief, blotting the sweat from his forehead. Years before, at West Point, Alden had known another soldier who took to his bed with a gut-ache similar to Private Fraser's. For three days the military doctor bled him and dosed him with everything from laudanum to alcohol, but no one dared suggest surgery. That young cadet had died in unspeakable agony.

Alden leaned back on a crate of hardtack. Roger probably had no idea what he had in Flanna O'Connor, and he would never fully appreciate her. If Roger were not now out on the parade grounds with Company K, he never would have allowed Flanna inside Private Fraser's tent. He would feel that such things wouldn't be proper for a politician's wife, and proper ladies certainly should never look upon another man's body.

No, Roger would not appreciate Flanna's lifesaving skill, but one day Private Fraser might be very grateful that Roger dearly loved drill practice.

Calmer now that his gorge had stopped heaving, Alden stood and peered inside the tent again. Flanna stood at the side of the table, her right hand rising and falling in a regular, graceful pattern, like the women he'd seen at country quilting bees. She was sewing, he realized, holding a needle in another pair of surgical tweezers, moving over the patient's gut in a regular and even rhythm.

He held his breath as Flanna gave another order to her maid. The girl came forward, held a pitcher of water over the patient, and doused Private Fraser's gut with a blasting stream of water. Once that was done, Flanna pulled a sheet up to the private's chin, then stepped back and gave Charity a wavering smile.

"All right, open the tent and we'll let the fresh air revive him," she said, her voice carrying outside to Alden. He stepped forward, lifting the tent flap as he came.

"Major?" Flanna's brow arched in surprise as she moved toward another basin to wash the blood from her hands. "Did you feel it necessary to spy on me?"

"Not at all." He took a step forward, then halted at the odors in the tent—the pungent scent of chloroform, the stale scent of sweat, the tang of blood. "I was merely…curious." He glanced at the covered body on the table, then thrust his arms behind his back and returned his gaze to Flanna. "Did the operation go well?"

"I believe it did," she said, her eyes flitting toward the unconscious soldier, "but time will tell. There is always the chance of infection, though I did everything I could to keep the area clean."

"Is cleanliness so important?"

A thoughtful smile curved her mouth. "Cleanliness is next to godliness, isn't it? I believe it also aids in the practice of medicine."

"Well then." Alden paused, casting about for something to say.

For some unknown reason he suddenly felt as tongue-tied as a boy alone with a girl for the first time. "I was very impressed, Dr. O'Connor. You seemed most capable."

Flanna looked up, her fascinating smile crinkling the corners of her eyes. "We were both fortunate this time, Major. Your soldier— well, he put me at ease." She lifted a towel from a table and began to dry her hands. "I wouldn't want to do this type of surgery every day. But perhaps you should reconsider my offer to accompany your regiment."

"Now, Flanna—" Alden lifted his hand, amazed at her persistence.

"Think about it, Major." Humor struggled with annoyance on her fine-boned face as she looked up at him. "I've heard about Dr. Gulick's so-called work for your regiment. And while I may not share his gender, I can guarantee that I do not share his fondness for taverns and gambling." A tremor touched her smooth, rose-colored lips as she dropped the towel and took a step toward him. "Let me go south with you. You don't have to pay me. I'll go and I'll help your men...because I must go home."

Alden shook his head, unwilling to voice the feelings that had risen in his throat. Again she had asked the impossible, but his reasons for refusing this time were far different than the last time she'd asked. Before he had cited rules, regulations, and the practical impossibility of allowing a woman from South Carolina to act as a Union physician. But now he would not take her for the simple reason that men did not carry beloved valuables to war.

For some reason, she seemed to find his refusal amusing. "Still not willing to consider the idea?" She took a deep breath and adjusted her smile. "Apparently I shall have to wait out this war in Boston. But there may come a time, Major Haynes, when you will wish you had another pair of experienced medical hands—even if they are a woman's."

"Dr. O'Connor," he said, a wry smile curling his own lips, "I fear you may be completely correct."

Nine

Tuesday, July 30

Yesterday I operated on a patient—Pvt. Henry Fraser, of the 25th Massachusetts. The patient seems to be making a good recovery, though I am certain my prayers have more to do with this soldier's health than my pitiful work. But God was good. He steadied my hand and helped me remember all that I needed to know.

I was so eager to share the news with someone—but can't be entirely honest here, of course, for there is no lock on my door! I wrote a long letter home to Papa and Wesley, giving them every detail, and was bold enough to actually mail it. Mrs. Davis drizzled gray disapproval upon the letter and handled it by one corner, as if it would somehow poison her.

Mrs. Davis's niece, a rather prissy-looking girl called Nell Scott, has come into the city from Roxbury. I don't know what she intends to do here besides entrap a husband, for her attentions are almost entirely centered upon the soldiers—and the more braids upon the man's shoulder, the better. She sings "Weeping Sad and Lonely" with an overtly sentimental gleam in her eye that I find extremely *annoying—particularly when she casts goose-eyes at Alden Haynes from across the church social hall. She cannot be the type of woman he likes, though he is far too polite to say anything to offend her feelings.*

Oh, why do I even care about Nell Scott? Father God, please show me the way out of Boston!

As July passed into August, Flanna continued to divide her time between work for the Sanitary Commission and the Boston Women's Hospital, but she also visited the regimental camp every day to check on Henrietta Fraser. That courageous young woman had made a remarkable recovery from surgery and was scheduled to return to light duty at the end of August. A postoperative fever had been halted with generous doses of water and the regular application of clean bandages, and Flanna was confident that no doctor in Boston could have done better. Best of all, no one in the Twenty-fifth Massachusetts suspected that Private Fraser was anything other than the farm boy she claimed to be.

"How do you escape their notice?" Flanna asked one sweltering Saturday afternoon as she visited the recovering soldier in camp.

Fully dressed in a regulation blue uniform, Henrietta was sitting by the fire eating a mash of potatoes and stewed vegetables. The private hesitated until her last messmate finished and left the campfire, then she gave Flanna a shy smile. "Think about it, Doctor." She wiped her mouth on the back of her hand, a decidedly unfeminine gesture she may have picked up either at home or in camp. "All the women 'round here are shaped like thimbles and decorated in bonnets and ribbons. These men ain't never seen a woman in trousers, and most of 'em can't believe that a woman would ever want to stick her limbs in a pair of pants." She looked down, long lashes hiding her eyes. "I reckon another woman would see me for what I am far quicker than most of the men."

Flanna smiled, silently agreeing. Now that she knew Henrietta's secret, it was difficult to see anything *but* a young woman with large eyes and a delicate frame.

"But don't they—" Flanna hesitated, unsure how to ask about private matters. For all her coarseness, Henrietta Fraser was still a modest young woman. "How do you handle the times…when a woman needs to be alone?"

The tip of Henrietta's nose went pink, and she smiled, looking somewhat abashed. "Oh, that." She shrugged. "They just think I'm shy. There's a couple of other shy boys who don't like bathing in the open or relieving themselves in the company sinks."

"But surely Dr. Gulick noticed something when he administered your physical. He can't have been *that* drunk!"

Henrietta's grin shone through her freckles. "Dr. O'Connor, don't you know nothing? Those army doctors got orders not to be too picky. When I steps to the head of the line for my physical, the doctor asks me to hold up my arm, says my trigger finger looks like it works fine, then shakes my hand and tells me, congratulations, I'll make a fine soldier no matter how skinny I am!"

Flanna frowned and laced her fingers together. "I have no trouble believing that few men think a woman capable of fighting a war. But you would think at least one or two of the brighter fellows here would open their eyes to the truth staring them in the face."

Henrietta stood and raised her arms, looking for all the world like a scarecrow in a too-big jacket. "I don't look like much, but I look like a soldier," she said, her blue eyes dark and serious, "and I must thank you again, Dr. O'Connor. You not only saved my life, but you saved my family too. We needed that bounty money to make it through the winter 'cause my pa can't farm much since he broke his leg last summer."

Heat began to steal into Flanna's face. "Never mind that. How's your incision?"

"That scar's just a little red and puffy now, nothing like it was. I promise to keep it clean, just like you said."

"You're doing very well." Flanna gathered her skirts. "I'll be back to check on you in two weeks."

"No ma'am, you won't find me in a couple weeks. The regiment is moving out. We'll be on our way to Washington by next Saturday.

Major Haynes says we've got 930 men now, and as soon as the new ones have a bit of drill training, we'll be heading south."

Speechless with surprise, Flanna stared at the girl. Neither Roger nor Alden had said anything to her about leaving soon.

Next Saturday! The thought of the Haynes brothers' departure made the skin on her arms prickle into gooseflesh. Soon her best friends would be gone, and she would be alone in a city of hostile foreigners. Though no one would be so crass as to openly say so, Flanna knew that only her friendship with the Haynes family had held the secessionist critics at bay. But when Roger and Alden were gone, Mrs. Haynes's polite invitations to church and Sunday dinner would evaporate, and so would the restrained silence that greeted Flanna and Charity wherever they went. The hate and spite that filled the editorial pages would spill out on her, the secesh doctor from South Carolina, birthplace of traitors.

Flanna bade a thoughtful farewell to Private Fraser, then pulled Charity from a group of servants and began the long walk back to the boardinghouse. Apparently sensing her mistress's mood, Charity walked beside Flanna with her head down and her dark eyes fixed on the stone walkway.

Thoughts Flanna had not dared formulate came welling up as they walked, an ugly swarm of doubts, suspicions, and fears. The newspapers overflowed with tales of Southern sympathizers arrested as suspected Confederate spies. Boston readers had been particularly enraged by the story of Mrs. Rose Greenhow, a forty-four-year-old Washington widow who had apparently sent information across the Virginia border and enabled the Confederates to smash the Union at Bull Run. In retaliation, Federal officials were holding Mrs. Greenhow under guard in her home. Forbidden to read newspapers or receive uncensored mail, the dignified widow could only visit with "approved" relatives. According to newspaper reports, Union officials forced Mrs. Greenhow to live in "the full sight" of Union soldiers, "with her rooms open as sleepless sentinels watched and looked at her by way of amusement, all the mysteries of her toilette laid bare to the public eye."

Though Boston had not yet discovered a spy among its own ranks, Flanna feared that once the brothers Haynes left the city, she might be the first target of speculation. Why, she may have already committed worse sins than Mrs. Greenhow without knowing it! In the vain hope that a letter might reach her home, she had written her father about Private Fraser, innocently describing the condition and strength of the army regiment. What if that letter ended up in the wrong hands?

Even if she was not openly accused of a crime, the polite disdain she had thus far experienced would certainly turn to open distrust and suspicion once Alden and Roger moved south. It could take days or weeks, but Flanna knew she would eventually be discharged from her employment. What hospital would allow a potential spy to care for its patients?

And at the end of this month, her father's prepayment of her room at the boardinghouse would run out. With no income, Flanna would have no means to pay her rent. Mrs. Davis would certainly evict her.

Those dire thoughts brought an indisputable realization in their wake, and a chill that struck Flanna deep in the pit of her stomach. She had no place in Boston, she would have to leave.

Before Boston cast her out.

Ball's Bluff

There are bonds of all sorts in this world of ours,
Fetters of friendship and ties of flowers,
And true lover's knots, I ween,
The girl and the boy are bound by a kiss.
But there's never a bond, old friend, like this—
We have drunk from the same canteen.

FROM A CIVIL WAR POEM, AUTHOR UNKNOWN

Ten

Sunday, August 25th

I went to church this morning with Mrs. Haynes. Roger and Alden received liberty to come, too, and I could scarcely look them in the eye, knowing that it would be the last day they worship with us. Mrs. Haynes knows they are leaving; she wept into her handkerchief during the entire service. I could not weep; my thoughts were too heavy for tears. I sat between Roger and Alden and wondered how I managed to give my affection to one and my utmost admiration to the other.

This afternoon, when Charity and I retired upstairs for our afternoon nap, I pretended to sleep while Charity practiced her reading out of the Bible. She read the Scripture we had heard in church that morning: "The Lord is my light and my salvation; whom shall I fear? the Lord is the strength of my life; of whom shall I be afraid? Though an host should encamp against me, my heart shall not fear; though war should rise against me, in this will I be confident. Deliver me not over unto the will of mine enemies: for false witnesses are risen up against me, and such as breathe

> *out cruelty. Wait on the Lord: be of good courage,*
> *and he shall strengthen thine heart: wait, I say, on*
> *the Lord."*
>
> *I know now what I must do. And though my*
> *spirit quails at the thought of it, at least I know*
> *that the Lord will walk with me. I shall not be*
> *alone.*

"Miss Flanna?" Charity's voice floated through the darkness like the whimper of a disembodied spirit. "Miss Flanna, what are you doing there?"

Flanna sat in the rectangle of moonlight that poured from the tall window in her room. The sultry nighttime breeze blew in across her face, lifting the lace curtains and ruffling her hair—what remained of it.

"Miss Flanna, you'd better answer me!"

"We're leaving, Charity." With mathematical precision, Flanna ran her fingernail over her scalp, sectioning off another hank of hair. The scissors bit through the locks with a clean snip, and Flanna let the hair fall to the floor.

"Leaving?" The bedclothes rustled as Charity's voice drew nearer. "What do you mean, we're leaving? The train won't take us home, and the army said they didn't want any lady doctors."

"I've got it all planned." Flanna snipped another lock. "And I'll need your help, so now that you're awake, you might as well come here. I'm having a little trouble with the back of my head. Could you cut it for me in a straight line?"

"You're cutting all your hair off?" Charity stumbled into the moonlight and gazed at Flanna with wide, luminous eyes. "Miss Flanna, are you feeling all right? If you're sick, I could go downstairs and fetch you some tea."

"Charity." Flanna lowered the scissors to the floor and looked up at her maid. "We have to leave Boston, and we'll have to slip away so no one knows where we're going."

"Ain't we going home?"

"Yes. We're going home the hard way, but it's the only way I know. Remember Private Fraser? We're going to do what Henrietta did. We're going to get ourselves some trousers and shirts and pretend to be soldiers." She took a deep breath and smiled up at Charity. "The Twenty-fifth Massachusetts is moving out next week, and when they go south, you and I will be among them."

Charity sank to the floor with a loud thump, crossed her legs, and wordlessly stared at Flanna.

"Mrs. Davis will think we've gone to New York," Flanna went on. "You'll pack our trunks, and I'll leave a letter indicating that they're to be sent to Dr. Elizabeth Blackwell. Mrs. Davis and Mrs. Haynes and anyone else who cares will think we've taken a position in Dr. Blackwell's clinic."

"You think Mr. Roger will believe that?"

"Mr. Roger will be thrilled." Flanna shrugged. "He'll figure I'm expanding his future constituency."

Charity pressed her hands to her cheeks. "Oh, Miss Flanna. What about the folks at the hospital?"

"I'll send a letter of resignation."

"But shouldn't you go and talk to them? My ma says it's rude for a lady to—"

"There's no time, Charity. And where I'm going, I can't act like a lady."

The two women stared at each other across a sudden ringing silence, then Flanna leaned forward and took Charity's hands in her own. "I know it's scary—I'm nearly frightened out of my wits. But I can't think of any other way."

"We could try the trains again. Maybe we could get through."

Flanna shook her head. "No. Last week I read about two women who were hauled off the train in Washington. The soldiers there ripped off their dresses, looking for guns under their hoop skirts." She lifted a brow. "You don't want that to happen to us, do you? The paper didn't say, but I can't imagine that the women's ill treatment stopped there."

"But how can we fool anybody?"

"The Federals are desperate for men; they won't be choosy." Flanna picked up the scissors and offered them to Charity. "Trust me. If Henrietta Fraser can pull it off, we can…as long as you really want to go home." She gave Charity a small, shy smile. "Or you can stay here. You've been a faithful servant and a good friend. I know I'm asking a hard thing. You don't have to go with me…though I don't know what I'd do without you."

Charity hesitated a moment, then set her jaw and took the scissors from Flanna's hand. "Land sakes, Miss Flanna, you wouldn't last a day without me," she answered, rising to her knees as she came around to finish Flanna's haircut. "And if making us look like boys is the way to get us out of this Yankee town, then I'm going to make us look like the best boys in that whole Yankee army."

Flanna exhaled in relief. "That's the spirit," she whispered, resting her arms on her crossed knees as Charity finger-combed her hair.

The first hint of sunrise was touching the eastern sky as Flanna swept up the tangled strands of her coppery hair. She hesitated by the fireplace with the dustpan, tempted to burn the evidence of her trickery, then decided that the stench of burning hair would bring Mrs. Davis out of her bed in terror. Better to wrap the hair in paper and stow it in one of her trunks.

Charity was already dressed, her purse bulging with Flanna's hospital wages, earmarked now for buying men's clothing at the mercantile. The girl paused as the room brightened and made a face as she studied Flanna's new hairstyle. "I couldn't do nothing about that white streak in your hair, Miss Flanna." She crinkled her nose. "I'm afraid anybody who sees it will know it's you they're looking at."

"That's why we're going to always wear a cap, you and I." Flanna raked a hank of the newly shorn hair from her forehead. "Don't forget—buy cheap goods; we'll only need them for a day or two. The army will give us hats and uniforms."

"Yes ma'am." Charity paused by one of the open trunks and ran her hand over the rich sheen of a satin ball gown. "What are you gonna tell Mister Roger? He's going to think it strange if you just take off without a word of good-bye."

"I'm going to write him a letter," Flanna said, searching through the depths of the wardrobe for a bonnet. She finally found a tattered green one and tied it securely under her chin, grateful that the ruffle at the back hid the fact that most of her hair had vanished. "I'll write Roger after I go down and tell Mrs. Davis that we're moving to New York." She waved Charity toward the door. "It will be all right, just get along. And remember—two shirts, two sets of shoes, two pairs of trousers, two hats."

When Charity didn't move, Flanna lifted a brow. "What's wrong now?"

The corners of Charity's mouth tightened with distress, and she looked at Flanna with shiny eyes. "Miss Flanna, don't gentlemen wear something under all that?"

Flanna brought her fingers to her lips, then laughed. She hadn't thought of it, but she couldn't very well wear a corset and pantalets under an army uniform. "Yes, of course," she answered, trying to remember what Wesley had been wearing the time Papa caught him sleepwalking downstairs. "Um, undershirts. And drawers. But it's so hot, Charity. Try to find cotton instead of wool." She frowned. "I wonder if the army will give us socks."

"They'd better." Charity turned toward the door. "That's all the young ladies have been making since the captain told Mrs. Davis he didn't need no more havelocks."

"Better get each of us a pair, just in case. And make sure the shoes are sturdy, in case we have to keep them. I can't imagine walking to the train station in anything less than sturdy shoes."

Charity nodded, then slipped out of the room. The click of the closing door rang like a gunshot in Flanna's ears. She had set her feet upon a path from which there could be no turning back.

She drew a deep breath and forbade herself to tremble. The widow Davis was probably just waking up, and Flanna might as well give her the news while she was still in her nightcap and gown. Mrs. Davis would undoubtedly relish the drama of Flanna's sudden departure, and in weeks to come the story would serve as yet another proof of Flanna's inherently coarse Rebel manners.

She resolutely tightened the ribbon that held her bonnet, then moved out of the room toward the widow's chamber.

⁓

Three hours later, Flanna heard a sharp rap on the door, then Charity entered, her arms loaded with wrapped packages. "I had to go to stores where they don't know us," she whispered, dumping her bundles on Flanna's bed, "but I think I got everything. I sure hope so!"

Flanna dropped her last textbook into a trunk, then dropped the lid. "Let's see." With a rush of rising excitement she hurried to the bed and pulled the twine off one bundle. Inside the wrapping paper were two pairs of butternut trousers and two gray plaid shirts. "Good grief, Charity." She gave the identical shirts a dubious look. "Did you have to buy the *same* shirts? We'll look like twins!"

Charity's eyes widened, then her mouth spread in a slow grin. "What's wrong, Miss Flanna? I always kind of thought we looked sorta like twins, being the same age and all."

"Oh, indubitably." Flanna rolled her eyes. She opened the other packages, then sighed in satisfaction. Charity had remembered everything. There remained only the final packing, the change of clothing, and the exit. Their great escape would have to occur at dinnertime, when all the young ladies would be sequestered in the dining room. She and Charity could slip down the backstairs in their men's attire, and no one would be the wiser.

Charity put her hands on her hips and swayed slightly. "What do we do now, Miss Flanna?"

"We change," Flanna said, running her hand through her hair. She couldn't seem to stop fingering it. The short strands barely reached the tips of her ears and felt strangely light on her head, adding to her feeling of recklessness.

She picked up the canvas cap on the bed and pulled it over her head, adjusting it so the brim rested on her forehead. "Private Franklin

O'Connor, reporting for duty, sir!" She snapped a salute toward the mirror.

"Oh, Miss Flanna," Charity moaned. "I hope you can do better than that! Your voice is too prissy, and your hands—remind me to cut your nails before we go."

Flanna turned her hand and critically regarded her nails. "You're right, Charity. Together we just might pull this off."

By midday, each dress, petticoat, hoop skirt, stocking, and slipper had been packed away in Flanna's trunks. Flanna and Charity sat silently on their beds, each shifting uncomfortably in the too-large men's clothing. The seams of the cotton undershirt chafed Flanna's skin, and the fabric of the shirt seemed suffocatingly heavy.

Flanna had buttoned her journal into the front of her shirt for two reasons. First, the big, flat book did a fair job of disguising her womanly curves. Second, she was unwilling to travel without it. If something terrible happened on the journey, she wanted her father to understand her reasons for acting as she did. She had wanted to take her medical bag, too, but thought she'd be asking for trouble if someone discovered it. Lowly army privates did not carry scalpels and sutures, nor did they know how to use such things. And so her beloved medical bag had gone into one of the trunks, destined now for New York. Inside each trunk she included a note explaining that she'd be calling for her belongings when the strife was ended.

She heard the front door open and shut, then voices rose from the downstairs hallway. In a moment Mrs. Davis would ring the dinner bell, a quaint little ritual the widow thought charming. Anyone not seated when the meal began would miss dinner altogether, for frugal Mrs. Davis would not pursue any tenant thoughtless enough to skip a meal.

"You packed your books?" Charity whispered, her eyes bulging.

"Of course," Flanna replied, her mind a hundred miles away. "And the trunks are addressed and ready to go. I told Mrs. Davis she should send them to the depot at her earliest convenience."

"And Mister Roger?"

"The letter is ready to be posted." Flanna inclined her head toward the desk where Roger's letter lay on the blotter. Mrs. Davis could not fail to see it.

The dinner bell echoed from downstairs, and Flanna tensed at the sound. She stood, surveying the room one last time. Two busy years had passed like a dream, and now it was time to go home.

The muffled sounds from downstairs abruptly ceased, and Flanna knew the diners had paused to pray. She looked at Charity. "Ready?"

"Yes ma'am." Charity stood, but kept one hand on the bed, as if she couldn't balance in her clumsy men's shoes.

Flanna moved toward the door and waited until the murmur of voices began again. Finally the tinkling sounds of silver and china reached her ears, and she opened the door. "Let's go."

As they passed through the hallway, Flanna pressed her lips together, half-afraid she would burst out in laughter. Wesley, no doubt, would find this terribly funny. His sister, the belle of Charleston, dressed in trousers and man-sized shoes, clumping through her own boarding-house like a common sneak.

Flanna hurried toward the back stairway, knowing it would lead her directly to the kitchen and the back door. No one but Mrs. Davis and the cook used this staircase, and the cook ought to be in the dining room, serving the meal. If all went well…

She turned the corner, then froze. Prissy Hillary Owen stood on the second step in the narrow stairwell, her rosy lips pressed to those of some brave boy in blue. Miss Owen's fair eyes were closed, and the soldier was past caring who might be approaching from above. Flanna frantically gestured to Charity, hoping the maid would retreat to the safety of their room.

But Charity must have been watching her feet instead of her mistress. Before Flanna could step back from the threshold, Charity bumped into her, upsetting Flanna from her perch at the top of the stairs. She reached for the banister and caught it, but not before her slick shoes slipped down the polished wooden steps, dragging her body downward amid a tremendous knocking racket. A brilliant pain flashed through her shinbone, and Flanna yelled in dazzled agony.

Miss Owen screamed and stepped back, and the soldier cursed. Obeying an instinctive reaction honed through years of playing rough-and-tumble games with Wesley and her cousins, Flanna righted herself and lowered her head, barreling on down the staircase as she prayed Charity would have the good sense to follow.

"Stop! A burglar!" Miss Owen screamed. "Oh, my heavens, shoot them!"

Flanna hit the back door and yanked it open, then froze as she heard the ominous click of a pistol.

"Stop right there, both of you!" The soldier's voice quavered.

Right behind her, as close as the shirt on her back, Flanna could hear Charity's frantic breathing. This was all Flanna's fault, and Charity should not suffer for it. Flanna lifted her hands and slowly turned her head, looking past Charity's shoulder to see the soldier. The arm holding the pistol quivered in a wide arc, and his breath came hard though his nose with a faint whistling sound. He was just as scared as she was, but he had a lot less at stake.

She opened her mouth, ripping out a yell designed to shatter the eardrums of a pesky older brother, then dove through the open doorway. She hit the ground hard, rolled over the soft earth where the cook had given up trying to grow vegetables, then scrambled to her feet as a gunshot shattered the stillness and a slice of dirt flew up barely three feet to the right of her feet.

The fool had actually fired that gun!

She looked up to see Charity running toward her like a hen dodging the axe. With a burst of hysterical laughter, Flanna joined Charity, and they sprinted together through the back alley.

This was one dinner Mrs. Davis's boarders would never forget.

Eleven

~~~~~

After congratulating themselves on a most spectacular escape, Flanna and Charity walked to the recruiter's office at Faneuil Hall. A police officer patrolled the steps there, and they took pains to avoid his notice, even though it seemed unlikely that word of Mrs. Davis's intrusive vagabonds had reached this part of town.

"You sure Mrs. Davis won't know it was us?" Charity asked for the tenth time, keeping a wary eye on the policeman.

"Hillary Owen was so flustered she won't know what she saw," Flanna answered, squatting on the steps. How comfortable it was to sit like a man! She spread her knees apart and rested her arms atop them, just for the sheer pleasure of doing so. "You can bet that Mrs. Davis is still in a faint. By the time she's roused enough to hear what Hillary has to say, the other girls will be mighty curious about where that soldier came from." Flanna grinned. "By tonight, no one will even be thinking about us. I imagine Hillary's father will get a wire informing him that his daughter ought to be married before the regiment ships out to Washington."

"You don't think that soldier will remember us?"

"Naw." Flanna dragged out the word and grinned. How wonderful it was to *talk* like a man! "Do you remember what he looked like?"

Charity hesitated, then shook her head.

"See? It all happened too quick." Flanna stood up and wiped the last traces of dirt from her trousers. "Now we need to enlist. Let's get it over with."

They walked inside the building and paused before an officer at the desk. "Ah, sure, and I'll be hating to disturb you, sir," Flanna aped her father's broad Irish brogue, reasoning it was the best disguise for her voice, "but the lad and I would like to enlist in this fine army."

The man scarcely glanced up. "Name?"

"O'Connor. Franklin O'Connor."

"Age?"

"Twenty-four, sir."

"State of residence?"

Flanna gave Charity a confident smile. "Well, naturally, 'tis Massachusetts."

The man scribbled her answers on a pad, then ripped off the top sheet. Looking up, he handed it to her, then frowned. "That colored boy can't enlist."

"Why not?"

The man tented his fingers. "Coloreds can't fight. He can go with you as a servant; I hear some of the Maryland men have even taken their slaves to war. But coloreds can't serve in a Massachusetts regiment."

Flanna lifted her chin, not daring to look at Charity. She would never understand Yankees. Why did they want to free the Negroes if they wouldn't allow them to do anything?

"Charles is my servant; he'll remain with me." Flanna gave the officer a polite smile. "He goes wherever I go."

"Right." The man jerked his head toward a door behind her. "See the doctor, and get your physical. You'll be serving in Company M."

Flanna took the slip of paper and moved toward the doorway the man had indicated. "Just stay quiet and stay with me," she warned Charity in a low voice.

"Good thing I bought nice clothes," Charity grumbled, shuffling behind Flanna in her too-large shoes. "Looks like I'm going to be in 'em awhile."

Flanna paused outside the examination room and pointed to a bench where Charity could wait. "Pray that this part goes well," she whispered, placing her hand on the cold brass doorknob. "If we're going to be discovered, this might be the place."

Charity sat down and crossed her arms, and Flanna hesitated as fear blew down the back of her neck. A memory ruffled through her mind, a history lesson in which she had learned that Columbus's men had been terrified to the point of mutiny when they reached the point of no return in the midst of the unknown ocean. As they faced the dark knowledge that they no longer had enough food and water to turn back, surely they must have experienced this same feeling of dismay.

This doorway was her point of no return. She could not go back. They'd think she was a spy for certain if she was discovered with her hair bobbed off and an enlistment slip in her pocket. Exposure now would mean certain arrest and prison, shame, and infamy.

She could only go forward.

Heavenly Father, help me now.

Gathering her courage, Flanna walked into the room. A tall man in a white coat stood with his back to her, and she thrust her recruitment form toward his stout figure. "Franklin O'Connor, reporting for me physical, sir."

She thought she would faint when the doctor turned around. Dr. John Gulick stood before her, his eyes alert and bright. Apparently he hadn't visited the taverns yet today.

He took the paper, glancing at her for only a moment. "Franklin O'Connor," he said, peering at the page through his spectacles. He squinted back at her. "Irish?"

"Well, naturally." Flanna tried to smile. "'Tis a great thing to be Irish."

"So half this city thinks," Gulick muttered. He pulled out a tablet. "Do you suffer from piles or fits, O'Connor?"

"No sir."

"Are you healthy?"

"Yes sir."

"Lift your arms out to your sides."

A cold sweat prickled under Flanna's arms, and she felt her heart begin to pound like a triphammer.

"Don't be scared, boy." Gulick's broad hands moved toward her. "Just stand up straight."

Flanna swallowed hard and obeyed. Gulick pressed his fingertips to her collarbones and shoulders, then told her to turn around. As she waited, paralyzed with fear, he thumped her once on the back.

"You look like a right healthy one," he said, scratching something on his tablet. He marked her recruitment slip and returned it to her. "Congratulations, son. You'll make a fine soldier."

Flanna stepped out into the hall, dazed and a little shaken that she'd actually pulled it off.

<hr/>

The long shadows of late afternoon had begun to stretch across the ground as Flanna and Charity walked into the camp at Boston Common. Little had changed since Flanna had last visited Private Fraser, but she saw the place with new eyes, watching every man who approached, wondering how she would fit into this community of men.

From the color line at the front of the camp a dozen or so standards fluttered in the breeze, along with the regimental colors and Old Glory. The various companies were housed on straight streets branching off the color line. The quarters of noncommissioned officers, company officers, and the regimental commander and his staff stood at the rear of the camp, on three separate streets running parallel to the color line. The baggage trains, partially loaded with supplies, lay behind the commander's quarters.

Forlorn paperboard signs pointed the way to the various companies' quarters, and Flanna finally spied a bedraggled sign that pointed north to a line of tents.

"Company M," she read, following the arrow.

Beside her, Charity shook her head. "I don't know about this, Miss Flanna."

"Franklin. You can't forget. I'm Franklin, and you're Charles."

"Charles! My ma would have a fit if she heard you calling me that!"

"Your ma doesn't have to know."

"What if none of the others has servants? What are they gonna think about you?"

"They'll think I'm a pampered rich boy, I suppose." Flanna gave Charity a lopsided smile. "It's only for a little while. As soon as we get south, we're going home. Just remember that."

Charity nodded without speaking, then Flanna turned onto the street marked for Company M. She peered into the first tent, a bell-shaped structure supported by a center pole. She felt a stirring of confidence, for this was not entirely unfamiliar territory. She had visited Private Fraser in a tent like this one many times.

One young man, a dark-haired youth who appeared to be yet in his teens, crouched inside. He looked up from his haversack and caught Flanna's eye.

"You a new recruit?"

Flanna nodded, not trusting herself to speak.

The boy jerked his thumb toward the street. "You'll need to find the sergeant before you can get your gear. He's a tall, thin fellow, name of Enoch Marvin. Just ask for him anywhere on this road, and you can't miss him."

"Thanks," Flanna answered, muffling her voice as much as she could. She straightened and squinted in the bright sunlight. A tall man with thinning brown hair and a drooping moustache was walking her way, his hands tucked into his belt, his eyes fixed upon the ground.

"Sergeant Marvin?"

The man's eyes lifted to meet Flanna's, then narrowed speculatively. "You new?" he asked, a piece of straw dangling from his lips.

"Ah, sure, naturally." Flanna's voice faded away. The Irish bluster didn't seem to register with this fellow.

"Come on," he said, lazily waving her forward. Flanna fell into step behind him, and when Charity followed, Sergeant Marvin halted.

"You brought a colored boy with you?"

"Yes." She spoke in a firm voice. "He's my body servant…and my friend."

A wry but indulgent glint appeared in the sergeant's eye. "You'll be sorry. You ought to send him home."

Flanna squared her shoulders. "I won't. Others have servants, and I'll not leave mine behind. He's—he's quite useful to me."

Marvin's jaw moved, lazily pushing the straw from one corner of his mouth to the other. "You'll have to share your rations with him 'cause we don't feed servants. And we don't provide goods either. He'll have no blanket, no uniform, no gun." The dark eyes snapped as his gaze shifted to Charity. "Definitely no gun."

Lifting her chin, Flanna met the sergeant's dark gaze head on. "I'll be responsible for him. Just let him stay with me, and you'll have no trouble from either of us."

Sergeant Marvin grinned, then turned away. "It wasn't you two I was worried about," he called, his voice trailing behind him as he walked on.

Flanna and Charity hurried to keep up.

Sergeant Marvin stopped outside one tent where Charity waited outside while another officer handed Flanna a knapsack so heavy she nearly let it slip from her arms. "Hold it tight, boy," the officer in charge called, grinning at her. "That bag's gonna be dearer than your mama and papa real soon."

"What's in it?" Flanna wondered aloud.

"Your haversack, your cartridge box, your bayonet and scabbard." Flanna froze at the sound of the familiar voice. Alden! She could fool anyone in this camp, but not him.

"Your cap box, a rubber-backed woolen blanket, mess equipment, mending kit, and canteen," he continued. "Now get along to the quartermaster, and there you'll receive your rifle and uniform. Hustle, Private, time is short."

"Thank you, sir," Bringing her hand over her face, she coughed the answer and turned her head so that the brim of her cap blocked him from view. Without waiting for directions to the quartermaster's tent, she took off as quickly as she could under the weight of a forty-pound bag.

⚬⚬⚬

Not until sunset had stretched glowing fingers across the sky did Flanna step out of the quartermaster's tent. Charity, who was sitting on the ground outside, looked up slowly, her eyes widening in slow recognition.

"Blazes, Miss—"

"Hush, boy." Flanna shifted her shoulders in her new garb and gave Charity a withering look.

Behind a sheltering screen in the quartermaster's tent she had donned the uniform of a Union soldier: cotton flannel drawers, socks, a shirt, light-blue trousers, and a dark-blue jacket called a blouse. A blue cap with a black visor covered her hair, and two different coats hung over her arm: a long single-breasted dress coat of dark blue with a stand-up collar, and a long blue overcoat with a cape at the shoulder. The quartermaster had offered her a black felt hat for dress parade, but Flanna had refused it, not understanding how she was supposed to carry a knapsack, haversack, and rifle, let alone a useless frippery like a befeathered dress hat.

Now she tossed the overcoat to Charity. "This is for you, Charles," she said, taking pains to make her voice gruff. "Since we have no blanket for you, you can sleep on this and wear it in the rain."

Charity accepted the overcoat with a bewildered look, then shrugged her way into it. Flanna exhaled in relief as her maid settled into the overcoat. The coat completely covered Charity's gray shirt and ought to prevent any zealous sharpshooters from mistaking her for a Rebel in the woods.

"Franklin O'Connor!" Flanna whirled in surprise, then saw the quartermaster gesturing to her. "Forget something, lad? You can't expect to whip the Rebels without a rifle."

The last item of issue was a shiny new .58 caliber Springfield rifled musket. The quartermaster handed it to Flanna with a great deal of pride, remarking that he and some other fellows had recently tested the new shipment. "We put 360 balls into a mark the size of old Jeff Davis from a distance of 600 yards. You'll do right by this gun, lad."

The gun felt cold in Flanna's hand, dark and alien. She did not want to touch or carry it, but every man around her carried a rifle on his shoulder or hanging from his knapsack. From the looks of things, this rifle would soon be her new best friend, no matter how much it repulsed her.

Night had spread sable wings over the camp by the time Flanna and Charity returned to the tents of Company M. A small campfire glowed in front of each shelter, and men huddled around the flames, their faces subdued and shadowed in the fire-tinted darkness.

Avoiding the curious glances that lifted in her direction, Flanna walked steadily forward until she found Sergeant Marvin.

"Private Franklin O'Connor," she said, so nervous she could manage no more than a rough whisper. "Reporting for duty, sir."

One corner of the sergeant's droopy moustache lifted in a half-smile. "Aye." He jerked his thumb toward a tent behind him. "You sleep in there, Private. You and your boy."

Flanna nodded, then she and Charity dragged her equipment into the tent and looked around. Several knapsacks were stowed along the outer rim of the circular tent, so Flanna motioned to Charity and dropped her knapsack in an empty space. After an awkward moment of silence, they sat in the dirt.

"What do we do now?" Charity asked, drawing her knees to her chest.

"We do whatever the others do," Flanna whispered. "But not tonight. I'm not going out there to the campfire."

"Okay." Charity smiled in relief.

"You hungry? We could see what's in that haversack."

"No, I ain't hungry. I can keep till morning."

"Good."

They sat in companionable silence for a long time, listening to the sounds of camp. Flanna heard hundreds of voices—the soft tones of men sharing stories around the campfire, the angry chiding of a captain rebuking a recruit on the next street, a wave of laughter from behind the tent. From somewhere in the distance a violin sang, an astonishingly sweet sound that tugged at Flanna's heart and evoked memories of loving faces at home. The air was so warm that if she closed her eyes and blocked out the voices around her she could almost believe she was already back in Charleston.

"Why'd you join this army, boy?"

Flanna opened her eyes, her heart thumping madly. A tall, thin man stood above her, his hand tucked into his blouse, his sad, droopy eyes fixed upon her face. "What's the matter?" he asked in a low, resentful tone. "Did your father make you sign the roll?"

"No." Flanna inhaled sharply. "I joined because I want to whip the Rebels."

The man looked at her for a long moment, his features hardening in a stare of disapproval. "You look too young to whip anything bigger than a tomcat."

"I'm old enough." Flanna threw back her head and crossed her arms. "Old enough to do what I want, mind you."

He didn't seem angered by her retort. He merely gazed out at the campfire, where a group of men played cards and a handful of others scraped their mess kits clean. "We're all going to die someday," he said, his narrow face firmly set in deep thought. "And to some of us, it'll come sooner than later."

"Och, Valentine, haven't we told you not to pester the new boys?" Another man, a red-haired, freckled youth not much older than Flanna, stooped to enter the tent. A loose thatch of silky hair fell across his forehead, and he swiped it away before extending his hand and giving Flanna a wide smile. "Paddy O'Neil's the name, and 'tis a pleasure to meet you."

"You're Irish." Flanna gratefully shook his hand. "Me too. My grandfather was William O'Connor of Dublin."

"Ah!" Paddy's white teeth shone in the golden light of the single lantern. "Glad to know you, I am. You'll get used to the other fellows in time. Most of them have been here a week, at most. The sergeant says we're to ship out soon, so you're lucky—you won't be drilling as long as the others have been."

"Have you—" Flanna cleared her throat, still a little nervous about speaking. Her voice was naturally low, though not exactly boyish, but so far no one had remarked upon it. "Have you been here long, Mr. O'Neil?"

The man bit his lip, then wagged a finger at her, schoolteacher style. "Never call another enlisted man *mister*." He dropped down to sit beside her. "There's none of that kind of manners in this army, and only military manners matter now. You'll have the others calling you a pantywaist or some such thing if you insist upon respecting your equals, mark my words."

Flanna nodded without speaking. So much to learn! She had so many secrets, so many weaknesses. This disguise might be harder to maintain than she'd thought.

"So who's this with you?" O'Neil gestured toward Charity.

"My body servant, Charles. He's not a slave; he's a free man."

"I expected as much." Flanna blinked in surprise when O'Neil thrust out a hand to Charity. "Good to meet you, Charles. Welcome to our little war."

"Little war?" Flanna turned wide eyes upon the friendly lad.

O'Neil laughed. "Of course. We're going to whip the secesh before Christmas, now that Lincoln's put McClellan in charge. Little Mac will show the Rebs that Bull Run was just a fluke."

"Are you spouting nonsense again, O'Neil?" This came from another soldier who entered the tent with his blanket wrapped around his shoulders. The young man had dark eyes, a riot of curly black hair, and wide, expressive features. His hands, Flanna noticed, were beautiful, long-fingered, and strong. A surgeon's hands, or perhaps a musician's. "War is not about whipping and such," the soldier said. "It's about might and right. It's about truth."

"Well, we're right, isn't that the truth?" O'Neil answered, shaking his fist.

"Time will tell," the newcomer answered, moving to the other side of the tent.

O'Neil jerked his thumb toward the retreating soldier. "That's Andrew Green, our resident poet. The man's been here only two days, and he's written half a dozen poems already, most of them about his ladylove at home."

Flanna smiled as she watched Andrew Green spread his blanket on the ground. She didn't think she would mind having a poet as a comrade.

"You've already met Albert Valentine," O'Neil said, pointing toward the thin, mournful man who'd asked Flanna why she joined the army. "Valentine's a real cheery one."

"So I noticed."

The other men began to enter the tent, and O'Neil made quiet comments as each man settled down for the night. "That man over there, the thin one with the guitar? That's Philip Hart. He's a bummer."

"A bummer?" Flanna lifted a brow.

"A forager, a beggar, whatever you want to call it. He couldn't make a living on his own, so he joined up to rob the army blind." O'Neil chuckled and rested his arms on his bent knees. "Can't say that he isn't useful though. He found that guitar in a pile of trash. Maybe by the time the war's over he'll actually learn to play it."

"That's not likely." Another man, this one with a narrow face, dirty blond hair, and torn trousers, came into the tent and grinned at O'Neil. His hair grew upward and outward in great masses of disobedient curls, and his body seemed as powerless and limp as a filleted fish. He hadn't taken two steps before he bumped into the center pole, causing the suspended lantern to swing in a threatening arc. A riot of oaths erupted, and every eye followed the lantern, waiting to see if it would fall and burn. Gradually the lantern slowed and stilled.

"Sorry," the man murmured, taking the space next to Philip Hart.

"That's Jonah Baker." O'Neil's mouth curled as if on the edge of laughter. "A country boy who's spent his life in a plowed field. You should see him in the drill—he marches like he's still stepping over furrows."

"Can we shut out the light?" Albert Valentine lifted his head from his bedroll. "I'd like to get some sleep before reveille."

"Please, leave the light on, I beg you," another man called. Flanna glanced at him and knew in an instant that he was what Wesley would call a dandy. He wore a uniform of much finer cut and quality than the factory-made garments she'd been given. A paper collar lined the jacket at his neck, and instead of common brogans he wore knee-high enameled boots that gleamed like polished ebony in the lantern light.

"Freddie Smith," O'Neil said, following her gaze. "Don't get dust on his things, whatever you do."

"The light, man, turn out the light!" Valentine roared again.

"Aw, quit your bellyachin'," called a new voice as the quartet of card players came in from the fire.

The biggest of them, a blond, blue-eyed fellow with arms like tree trunks, came and stood before Flanna, his hands on his hips. A black beard bristled on his face like a porcupine's quills, and beneath it he wore an expression of remarkable malignity. "Who's this?" he asked O'Neil, his eyes not leaving Flanna's face.

"A new man," O'Neil answered. Flanna saw O'Neil's body tense, but the lad kept gallantly smiling.

"Why does he need a darkie?" The brute drawled the question. "None of the rest of us have a colored boy to tote our loads."

O'Neil had no answer for this, and from the corner of her eye Flanna saw him turn to her.

She answered over her choking, beating heart. "Charles is a friend of the family. I'm Franklin O'Connor, and pleased to meet you. May I have your name, sir?"

Scowling, the giant looked back at the others. "Lookee here, boys, a real gentleman. He wants to know my name."

The other card players laughed, and Flanna's heart began to thump almost painfully in her chest. She had already messed up, she couldn't even pass one night without being discovered—

The giant put out his meaty hand and grabbed her by the collar. With scarcely any effort at all, he lifted Flanna to her feet. She had the feeling that he could have held her above his head, so great was his strength and determination, but he seemed content to lift her just five inches off the ground until he stared her in the eye.

"My name is Herbert Diltz." He ground the words out between his teeth as his sour breath smote her face. "And I don't like your looks, boy. You look too soft to belong in this company. I've a good mind to pound you into the ground before the Rebs have a chance."

As panic rioted within her, Flanna lifted her hand. "Mr.—um, Diltz, I beg your pardon for anything I may have done—"

"Put the lad down, Diltz." The voice rang with command from outside the tent, and a different kind of fear shot through Flanna as she recognized it.

Diltz hesitated, his small, bright eyes training in on Flanna like gun barrels. He seemed to be weighing whatever punishment an officer might dish out against the pleasure he'd derive from hurling Flanna through the canvas roof.

"Diltz." The voice came closer, and Flanna caught a glimpse of Alden Haynes's familiar form. He now stood in the opening of the tent, his arms crossed, his eyes intent on Diltz. Even in this rough crowd, he exuded an air of command.

"I'm puttin' him down, Major." Diltz's voice was soft, but the venom in it was clear. He set Flanna on the ground, and she turned her head away from the lantern light, turning to her knapsack as if she'd suddenly remembered something important stowed there.

"Take your anger out on the Rebs," Alden told the offender, a silken thread of warning in his voice. "If I hear one report that this company's been fighting amongst itself, I'll have Sergeant Marvin make the lot of you pull double guard duty." He paused, moving into the circle of men. As his shadow fell across Flanna's knapsack, she recoiled as though it were a living thing. "Do I make myself clear?"

"Aye, sir." The reply came from a dozen lips, and Flanna closed her eyes, praying he would soon leave. She heard the soft sounds of footsteps and muffled laughter from somewhere outside the tent; then, without warning, his voice floated down to her from above.

"Are you all right, son?" Alden Haynes stood at her side, speaking to her.

Flanna looked up and caught Charity's eye. Like Flanna, the girl was hiding her face beneath the brim of her cap, afraid to look up at the only friend they had in this camp.

"Fine, sir." Forced through a tight throat, her voice came out hoarse.

"Very good. Get some rest—you'll have a long day tomorrow."

Major Haynes turned and walked away as a bugle began to play in the night. Someone rose and blew out the lantern, and the tent quieted as if by magic. Flanna sat very still, waiting for her eyes to adjust to the lingering light from the campfire.

She brought her thumb to her mouth and absently chewed on her thumbnail—a childhood habit she had broken years before, but it felt strangely comforting now. If she had known this morning that she'd be exchanging more than a dozen snobby boardinghouse roommates for more than a dozen terrifying men, she would never have found the courage to leave her room. The beloved men in her life— her father, Wesley, even Roger—had vanished, and a bizarre assortment had risen to fill the empty spaces.

Under this canvas roof, the strangers stretched out, arranged like the spokes of a wheel, with feet in the center and heads to the outside. The men had rolled up the sides of the tent in order to take advantage of the cool evening breeze, and Flanna felt a moment of gratitude for good weather. If the tent flaps were lowered, the resulting odors from twelve men in various states of cleanliness would be anything but pleasant.

The warm sound of the lonely bugle had no sooner faded than someone began to snore. Flanna unfroze long enough to remove the blanket from her knapsack and unfurl it. She gave Charity her dress coat to use for a pillow, then she lay down, pillowing her head upon her haversack.

As tense as a cat, she lay still for a long time, listening to the muffled sounds of snoring and breathing from the men who were now her comrades. Outside the tent, the waning fire popped and crackled, and occasionally she heard the soft sound of footsteps and muffled voices. Somewhere in the bushes, crickets filled the air with a continuous churring.

Flanna closed her eyes. Alden Haynes had saved her tonight—not only from Diltz, but from the humiliation and exposure she would have suffered if she had lost control and burst into tears. Yet though he had never been as close to her as he would be tonight, he had never seemed so far away.

Thank you, God, she prayed, folding her hands across her chest as her eyes searched the canvas above. *Thank you for bringing us this far, and thank you for sending Alden. Protect him and Roger, please…and see Charity and me through this.*

In her mind's eye she saw God looking down upon two slender forms, two additional cogs in the war machinery. Flanna didn't care whether God supported the North or the South as long as he helped her and Charity make a life in this army for as long as it took to get home.

Twelve

Wednesday, August 28, 1861
Dear Papa and darling Wesley—

I am writing you here, within the leaves of my journal, for reasons you will understand later. Though I am free to write letters—and many of my messmates write two and three a day to loved ones at home—I could not very well post letters to you without arousing suspicion. My heart, therefore, consoles itself with the thought that I am sending myself to you and that my day of arrival comes closer with each rising sun.

I am opening my heart freely within these pages, and will trust the good Lord that my journal shall remain undiscovered as long as I am in disguise. If I am killed, well, there is nothing to be done about it. And if someone reads this journal and exposes me, well—I must trust in the Lord's leading. For he has safeguarded me thus far, and he will continue to direct my paths.

Today I fired my infantry rifle musket for the first time. We did nothing but drill Tuesday; by the end of the day I had grown so accustomed to having the rifle on my shoulder that I scarcely considered the fact that I might eventually have to shoot it. The quartermaster gave me a box containing forty cartridges—my messmates call it a box of "forty dead men." My fingers fairly trembled as I drew a cartridge out—I could not allow myself to believe that I might have to shoot someone. The bullet lies at one end of the cartridge and powder at the other, and a soldier must actually bite off the twisted paper end of the cartridge before loading the gun. As the sergeant demonstrated this for me and a few other recruits, black powder spilled out onto his face, forming a dark circle around his mouth. His appearance grew most fiendish, which, I suppose, was appropriate for the occasion.

It took me ten minutes to prepare my first shot, and Sergeant Marvin said I'd be a dead man ten times over if I didn't improve. A good man, he says, can load and fire two shots in sixty seconds. (I'm afraid I shall never be a good man.)

And the shot! My ears rang for fifteen minutes afterward. The sergeant gave me no time for wonderment, though, for he demanded that I load and fire the rifle again and again. Charity tried to help me, but as the army will not give her a gun, she can do little more than recite the proper order for this killing ritual. So my shoulder is doubtless black and blue from the rifle's harsh retort, my jaws are sore from ripping the cartridges between my teeth, and my face is as grimed as the most seasoned soldier. My messmates laughed at me when I returned, for most of them have grown up with guns and don't need to practice. I explained my ignorance by telling the truth—I grew up with books, not guns.

I saw Roger Haynes today at dress parade. He and his company marched by with great style and flair, and I thought his face looked a good deal browner and sterner than the last time I saw him. But his tongue, apparently, is just as quick—his tales are legendary. Even a few of my messmates have remarked that Captain Haynes of Company K is a "rollicking storyteller."

They do not flatter Alden Haynes as easily, but they respect him far more. I see Alden nearly every day, and though my heart yearns to speak to him, I know I cannot. Yet I wonder—has he sent any farewell messages to Mrs. Davis's house in the hope that I might still be there? Doubtless Roger believes me in New York, and Alden probably does too.

You may think me foolish, Papa. If you knew the things in my heart...but you cannot. So my heart will remain veiled until I can open it to you. Then you will take my sorrows, my longings, and my regrets, and you will make me well. And if your medicine is not equal to the task, God himself will heal me.

Sometimes I think I ought to be miserable in this place and this condition, for I am quite out of my element. But though I miss you desperately, I am content. For I am on my way home.

May God, in his mercy, whisper in your ear the suggestion to pray for me. I need you now.

> *Pvt. Franklin O'Connor,*
> *Company M, 25th Massachusetts*

Flanna's week of training passed in a blur of activity. Each night she fell asleep feeling empty and drained, and each morning the bugle woke her before sunrise, mocking her with its bright reveille.

No matter how early the hour, Paddy O'Neil was always ready to go, laughing at his sleepy comrades as he slipped on his blouse and shoes. On Flanna's fourth morning in camp, when she awoke with her nerves still throbbing in exhaustion, he leaned near her ear and sang with the bugler: "I can't wake 'em up, I can't wake 'em up, I can't wake 'em up in the morning."

"Shut up, O'Neil," she slurred, sitting upright. She blinked, realizing that it hadn't taken her long to shed her ladylike manners. Mammy would be aghast at Flanna's rudeness, but Wesley would be right proud of her.

Charity was awake, too, scowling at O'Neil as she slipped on her shoes. Both girls slept in their trousers and shirts, as did a few of the men. Though the weather was warm, a general modesty pervaded the camp, particularly among the rural recruits. Flanna's worries about privacy had vanished.

"Rise and shine, men, and polish those uniforms!" Sergeant Marvin's head appeared in the tent. "Inspection and awarding of the colors today! Look sharp!"

The men around her groaned, but Flanna said nothing as she studied her hands. Black grime had etched little half-moons under each fingernail, though last night she had tried to scrub her hands in a water bucket. The other men didn't seem to mind a little dirt. But though Flanna could tell O'Neil to shut up and address the others by their surnames with impunity, she didn't think she'd ever be able to get used to feeling dirty.

"Hurry up, we'll be late for roll call." O'Neil tugged on Flanna's sleeve. "Roll out, shake a leg!"

"Coming!" Flanna gave Charity a little smile, then pushed herself up and took off after the lumbering O'Neil. Tardiness to roll call usually meant extra work or a stint in the guardhouse, but because the Twenty-fifth Massachusetts was in an all-fired hurry to get to Washington, tardiness now meant only one thing: extra drill.

Flanna couldn't see the purpose of drill, which consisted mainly of exercises in the handling of arms, various shooting positions, and marching maneuvers. While a sergeant yelled, "Stand erect! Salute! March forward! To the rear!" Flanna shifted her gun from shoulder to shoulder, sweated under her heavy uniform, and wondered if she'd be certifiably insane by the time she reached South Carolina.

But it was too late for second thoughts. She was in the army and could only survive by doing what she was called to do without drawing undue attention to herself. So she worked hard, learning to fire in standing, kneeling, and prone positions, practicing parrying and thrusting with the bayonet (a nasty implement she hoped she *never* had to use), and firing her rifle "in nine times," "in four times," and "at will." After drilling for four days, Flanna wondered if her feet kept tramping in her sleep.

The camp routine itself was simple: roll call, breakfast, and fatigue duty, which meant that she walked around with a gunny sack and picked up trash. After fatigue duty, the musicians sounded the call for guard mounting, where the first sergeant of each company turned out his guard detail for the next twenty-four hours' duty, inspected them, and marched them out to the parade ground. Flanna felt lucky that she was never called for guard duty. In the stillness of the dark night or the heat of the afternoon, she was quite likely to fall asleep, a serious infraction of military law.

The bugle next called her company for drill, which lasted until the midday meal. After a short spell of free time (during which Flanna was obliged to learn about her gun and how to fire it), the bugle sounded again, and Company M fell in for more drilling. Finally, after another roll call and inspection, came a dress parade, a ritual Flanna found especially silly—at first.

Only occasional glimpses of Alden Haynes kept her attention from wandering dangerously during dress parade. Each afternoon, hot, sweaty, and exhausted, the entire regiment drew up in a straight line when the order "Parade rest!" rang out. The drummers beat a regular rhythm, marching slowly in front of the regiment. The officers stepped four paces in front, Major Haynes and the lieutenant colonel in advance of the rest. After listening to the commander's remarks and orders, the officers returned to their posts. As the drummers beat a quickstep march, the regiment broke up into companies, each company tramping back to its quarters. No matter how tired Flanna had been going into the dress parade, the sight of Alden's resolute face always refreshed her spirit.

Supper call came shortly afterward, followed not long after dark by tattoo, a ritual which brought another roll call and an ordering of the men to their quarters. The final bugle call of the day was taps, at which all lanterns were extinguished and all noises ceased.

And each night, as the mournful bugle lifted its silvery notes to the silent sky, Flanna closed her eyes and held tightly to the haversack under her cheek. Each day was one fewer she would have to live away from her loved ones. *Please, God, let it be over soon.*

On Saturday morning, August 31, Flanna and her comrades rose with the bugle and polished their uniforms. Last night she and the others had carefully packed their knapsacks with whatever goods they would need for the long journey ahead.

The Twenty-fifth Massachusetts was moving south.

But first they had to endure the army's love of ritual, and Flanna shivered through fleeting nausea as she checked and rechecked her uniform. She had borne a multitude of inconveniences and trials for this day, but tonight she would lay her head someplace outside Boston. She had begun the long trek home.

"Company M, fall in!" Sergeant Marvin called. Charity helped Flanna adjust the ponderous weight riding her shoulders. Her woolen blanket was draped across her right shoulder, with its ends tied at hip level on the opposite side. Her journal was wrapped inside the blanket, an extra weight, but a necessary one. Her rifle rode her right shoulder, and from her belt dangled her bayonet, cartridge box, cap box, tin plate, cup, and haversack.

Charity stepped back to eye Flanna's efforts, then shook her head. "Land's sakes, Mr. Franklin," she said, a smile in her eyes as she lifted her gaze to meet Flanna's. "You has gone and made a soldier!"

Flanna rolled her eyes, then stepped toward the tent doorway, clanking like a peddler as she walked. "Remember, this is only temporary," she called over her shoulder, "and you're here to help me! So stay close, and don't be left behind!"

Charity could not march in the dress parade, so she hung back with the other camp followers—a few officers' wives, a corps of brazen prostitutes, and the regimental surgeon and his assistant. Flanna followed her messmates, taking her place in a long line that made up the hundred-man Company M, part of the proud Twenty-fifth Massachusetts.

As the band played a spirited song, they marched to an open field on the Common. Flanna recalled that last summer this field had been bright with grass, but the daily drilling of nearly one thousand men had worn it to nothing but dust and dirt. A special platform rose from the worn center of the field, and an imposing array of colorful ladies and stern men sat atop it, their eyes trained on the troops beyond.

The sun glared hot overhead, and Flanna felt a trickle of perspiration run from her underarm down to her rib. The uniform she wore had obviously been designed for winter wear; the dark blue dress coat was as hot as blazes. She envied Charity, who was lounging in the shade with the other servants. She also envied the young women on the platform, who wore lovely dresses of summer cotton, their arms and necks exposed to the light breeze that cooled the hot, dusty field.

Flanna narrowed her gaze. Why, one of those young women was Nell Scott, Mrs. Davis's niece from Roxbury! Nell wore a stunning blue silk dress, cut off the shoulder and most daring for daytime. A white silk ribbon stretched from Nell's dainty waist to her right shoulder, a gorgeous sash to honor the brave men setting off to war. She looked as bright and beautiful as a butterfly, while Flanna felt heavy, dirty, and sweaty. And though she and her fellows had brushed and polished their uniforms and rifles for inspection, there had been no opportunity to bathe. Flanna suspected that sweet Nell would find the lot of them repulsively odorous.

Nell shifted her parasol to shade her fair skin from the sun, and Flanna trembled with a thrill of recognition when she saw the lady standing behind it. Mrs. Haynes stood there in a full-skirted gray silk, a color only two shades away from mourning black. The woman appeared pleasant and content, but the marks of grief were clear, etched in the lines beside her mouth and eyes, thrown into shadow by the slanting sun.

What was she feeling at this moment? She had always been an ardent abolitionist, but did she support the cause as ardently since it had demanded the service of her sons?

The last company filed into place in the hollow square around the platform. The band stopped playing, and the air seemed to vibrate in the stillness as a clergyman stepped forward and lifted his hands for prayer.

After a lengthy benediction, the mayor of Boston rose to address the troops. While he droned on with compliments for the officers and pleas for God's blessing upon this endeavor, Flanna found herself watching the women on the platform. Nell occasionally brought a lovely lace-trimmed handkerchief to the corner of her eye—but just one eye, Flanna noticed, and only when the speaker paused and some disciplined soldier might be tempted to look over the rest of the platform. Mrs. Haynes sat motionless, her hands in her lap, her eyes trained upon the wooden platform. And yet, Flanna knew, both Roger and Alden were somewhere in this crowd. Had either of them managed to embrace their mother in a quick farewell?

After the mayor's speech, Mrs. Haynes stepped forward, followed by Nell Scott and two young ladies Flanna did not recognize. As the three young women unfurled a resplendent silk flag in blue and white, Mrs. Haynes pressed her hands to her breast and addressed the men of the regiment.

"When you follow this standard in your line of march or on the field of battle," she said, her narrow face twisting in a fragile smile, "and you see it waving in lines of beauty and gleams of brightness, remember the trust we have placed in your hands. We will follow you in our hearts with our hopes and our prayers. You are to go forth to the conflict to strike for our noble Constitution, for freedom of speech, for freedom of thought, for God and the right. From her mountain nest, the eagle of American liberty has at intervals given us faint warnings of danger. Now she swoops down on spreading pinions with unmistakable notes of alarm; her cries have reached the ears of freemen, and brave men rush to arms. She has perched on this banner which we now give to your keeping. Let your trust be in the God of battles to defend it."

The men remained at attention, but a handful of observers applauded from the bleachers. Mrs. Haynes wiped her eyes, then clasped her hands again, her eyes settling on one specific form in the line of men. Without looking, Flanna knew that the lady had found one of her sons.

Stepping forward, Colonel Farnham bowed to Mrs. Haynes, then assured her that the trust reposed in him and his men would never be abused. "This flag," he said, his voice stentorian and booming, "will never be given up to traitors, but will be defended by myself and my associates with our lives. Its luster will only be increased by deeds of valor, and our watchword shall be 'The Union, now and forever, one and inseparable.'"

The men around Flanna erupted in cheering. Swept along on a tide of emotion she could scarcely understand, she caught her breath. She was an American, yes, and part of her would always stir at the sight of the red, white, and blue flag, but she was also a Carolinian!

The drum corps began its steady beat. The sergeant called a command, and the band began to play a bright march. Flanna shifted automatically, turning right, and lengthened her step to match that of the man in front of her. A thrill shivered through her senses as she realized that these steps would lead to the depot, where a train waited to carry the Twenty-fifth Massachusetts to Washington. The war might be only a few nights away, but beyond that lay her home.

She forced her mind to focus on these thoughts as she marched, her legs moving stiffly to the steady beat as the men ahead of her began to sing, "John Brown's body lies a-moldering in the grave…"

As he shifted in the saddle and rode alongside the columns of marching men, Alden Haynes's mind kept turning to the image of his mother on the platform. Colonel Farnham had given the Haynes brothers a four-hour pass last night, so he and Roger had gone home to bid her farewell.

His mother had attempted to pretend the occasion was just another family dinner, but though the food was a sight better than army rations, Alden had no appetite. When Howard noticed Alden's mostly untouched plate and asked if everything was all right, Mother burst into tears and fled the dining room.

Alden sighed and watched her go. Obviously, Flanna O'Connor had made the right decision when she decided to leave before the regiment pulled out. She had completely avoided the pain of parting, the floods of bitter and worried tears.

Despite his best intentions to forget his brother's girl, Alden found himself missing her. She had certainly made their family dinners…interesting. It was far better to have Mother fuming about Roger's unsuitable Southern sweetheart than weeping uncontrollably.

He turned to Roger, who sat still and silent in his usual chair. "Did Miss O'Connor weep when she said farewell?"

A deep, painful red washed up from Roger's throat and into his face, as sudden as a brush fire. "She disappeared rather abruptly, I'm afraid." He swirled his half-empty glass and stared at his untouched plate. "I had hoped she'd come see us off, but apparently the strain of my imminent departure was too much for her. She left a forwarding address in New York, in care of Dr. Elizabeth Blackwell."

"You're going to write her?"

"Of course." Roger managed a quick half-smile. "I have been writing her every day. Her example keeps me motivated."

Alden's heart sank. "She writes you every day?"

"Well—no. Actually, I haven't heard from her since she left. But she hasn't had time to write, with the trip to New York and her need to settle in. And there's the matter of the mail taking time to catch up to us." He shrugged. "I meant that she keeps me motivated by the example of her hard work. She labored in medical school to establish herself, and I will labor in this war. When it is over, I shall have the reputation I need for a career in politics." A secretive smile softened his lips. "War veterans are extremely electable, Alden. Surely you knew that."

"No." Feeling restless and contentious, Alden leaned back in his chair. "I never gave it much thought."

Roger glanced over his shoulder, making certain his mother had left the room, then pulled a cigar from his pocket and lit it. "Actually, I think Flanna's move to New York is a good idea. There she'll have an opportunity to get this infatuation with medicine out of her system. She'll be more than ready to marry me when I'm home again."

"I thought she wanted to work with her father."

Roger snorted softly and puffed on his cigar. "Who will want to live in the South once we have chastised it?" he asked, smoke trailing from his mouth. "No, brother. Flanna was smart enough to come north for medical school and go to New York to work with Dr. Blackwell. That same good sense will lead her to stay here."

"Major Haynes!" Jarred from his memory, Alden glanced out at the crowds lining the sidewalk. Miss Nell Scott had pushed forward and stepped into the road. Instinctively, Alden pulled back on the reins and steadied the nervous gelding under him.

"Major Haynes?" The young lady came boldly forward, her hand brushing the hem of his trousers.

Unnerved by the approaching mountain of blue silk, the gelding tossed his head and bounced in agitation. "Easy, boy." Alden settled the horse, then removed his hat out of respect for the lady. "Can I help you, Miss Scott?"

"Yes, Major." Her curved mouth smiled up at him. "May I, Major Haynes—oh, I shouldn't ask, this is so terribly forward of me!"

He forced a smile. "Please speak, Miss Scott. I haven't much time."

"You're so right!" Her hand was now tenaciously fastened to his ankle. "Major Haynes, it would do my heart good to know that you would approve…"

Her eyes fell as her voice drifted away. Alden heard the steady tramping of the men passing beside him, and duty tugged at his heart. He heard a note of impatience in his response. "Miss Scott, please speak freely."

"Major Haynes," her arched eyebrows lifted, "may I pray for you while you are away? On my knees I will pray most devotedly, every night and every morning, for an hour each time!"

Her grip was like iron, and Alden resisted the urge to kick himself free. "Miss Scott, I would be most grateful if you would pray." He smiled down at her in bewildered amusement. "Not only for me, but for all my men. Some of these fellows are yet raw and inexperienced. They will most decidedly need your prayers."

"Thank you, Major." Smiling as if he had handed her the world, Miss Scott released him and stepped back.

Alden replaced his hat and slapped the reins, gently nudging his horse forward. They would need prayers, probably more than these excited patriots realized. This unseasoned army would face the enemy with an abundance of pride and an appreciable lack of experience. Alden himself prayed every night that the Union might be brought together as painlessly as possible, and that he would be able to do his duty without failing in the face of battle.

A snippet of Scripture, a favorite of the West Point chaplain's, filled his thoughts: *"If thou faint in the day of adversity, thy strength is small."*

"Oh, God," he murmured, his eyes roving over the surging crowd by the road, "give me the strength I will need."

The crowds thickened as they neared the railway depot, crowding the sidewalks and tearing the air with cheers. Red, white, and blue bunting fluttered from lampposts and storefronts. A pair of enterprising young lads worked the crowd, yelling "Hot popcorn! Fresh from the oil!" while in the distance a politician stood on a podium outside the depot and thundered at the men as they filed by. Above the noise of the crowd, the regimental band played "The Star-Spangled Banner," inspiring marchers and observers alike.

Alden dismounted when he reached the depot and tossed the reins to a waiting soldier. The disciplined marching formation broke here, each man making his way through the mob as best he could. Young women waved handkerchiefs and embraced every man who passed, while the more cheeky soldiers took advantage and stole kisses whenever possible.

Alden frowned as he watched the mindless merrymaking. Did any of these fresh-faced young men have any concept of war's horror? Probably not, since most of them had not lost a father to war. Or perhaps they did know and had determined to throw restraint to the wind in exchange for allowing Uncle Sam to use their bodies as targets for Rebel sharpshooters.

What would you do, asked a little voice inside his head, if Flanna O'Connor stood here and offered you a farewell kiss? As an officer and a gentleman, he should refuse it, of course, but as one who stood to become her brother-in-law, he could probably accept it in all propriety.

But it was not a chaste, affectionate kiss he yearned to give her.

Abruptly slamming the door on his thoughts, Alden spun on his heel and went in search of Colonel Farnham.

Thirteen

Saturday, August 31
The train to Washington

I can scarce believe it, but Charity and I are on our way home! The glamour and excitement of our glorious send-off has faded to good-natured grumbling and discontent amongst my comrades, but I care not. Let them grumble; I am overjoyed!

These accommodations are a far cry from the luxurious train car in which Charity and I rode to Boston. Gone are the wide seats and soft-spoken stewards—this car was designed for moving cattle, I daresay, not human beings. The car lacks proper ventilation, water, and sanitary facilities. I am sitting on the floor near Charity, while my messmates stretch out around me. If this entry is illegible, 'tis the jostling and constant rumble of the car that makes my handwriting tremble so.

A railroad attendant tried to close the door as the train jerked forward, but Sergeant Marvin thrust the butt of his rifle into the opening, glaring down at the wide-eyed porter. "Leave it open," the sergeant yelled, "unless you want these Union men to suffocate before we reach the war!"

I hope we never reach the war, and Charity agrees with me. She watched our "parade" from the sidewalk, keeping pace with me as we moved through the city. She did make one curious remark, which I shall record here in case something should come of it. My skin crawls to think that Alden Haynes might be attracted to a vain creature like Miss Nell Scott, but Charity says she saw that young lady standing at his side, her hand on his leg. "She was flipping her eyelids at him," Charity told me, "and you know what that means."

Indeed I do. And though I am certain young ladies have been "flipping their eyelids" at Major Haynes for years, I cannot help but wonder if Miss Scott holds some special place in his heart. If Roger still thinks of me with affection and will marry me when the war is over, shall Nell Scott be my sister-in-law?

I shudder to think of it, yet stranger things have happened. I have only to look at where I am, and with whom, to know that nothing is inconceivable. War makes all of us bold.

Flanna blew out her cheeks in relief as the train picked up speed, sending a rush of warm wind through the railroad car. The summer heat was nearly unbearable, assaulting them like a silent enemy. Dressed in undershirt, shirt, blouse, and a wool dress coat, Flanna's own internal furnace burned until rivulets of sweat streamed down her face and she thought she might faint.

"Might as well make yourselves comfortable, boys," Sergeant Marvin called out. Standing near the open door, he dropped his rifle and began to unbutton his dress coat. "Ain't no one here to impress, so lighten your load as much as you want."

The other men immediately followed suit, doffing overcoats and dress coats, even shirts and shoes. Flanna undressed down to her trousers and shirt, then stuffed her outer garments under a strap of her knapsack. Why did the army give them so many clothes in the heat of summer?

The uncomfortable benches held knapsacks and propped up a line of rifles. The men sat on the floor, leaning against the walls or each other, while a lucky few stretched out in the center and pretended to doze. The ubiquitous poker game ensued, and a host of cigars and other forms of tobacco magically appeared from shirtsleeves and coat pockets. A couple of men pounded holes into the narrow wooden sides of the boxcar, creating windows of a sort, and Flanna let the wind flow over her face, grateful for every breath of moving air.

A whiskey bottle appeared from a haversack and began to move from hand to hand and mouth to mouth. Albert Valentine lifted his soulful eyes and offered Flanna a swig from his flask with the admonition, "Better drink it while you can. We're on our way to meet death, you know."

Flanna held up her hand, refusing. "If that's the case, you'll understand why I prefer to keep all my wits about me."

Valentine shrugged and swigged from his flask, then smacked his lips in appreciation. A rising devil-may-care mood permeated the car, and as the alcohol began to take effect, some of the men began to pound on the others in a spirit of riotous jesting.

Easing away from the merriment, Charity curled into a ball on the floor beneath one of the benches. Flanna sat beside her, resting her elbow on the bench. Across the crowded aisle, she glimpsed Matthew Larry, the company's chronic borrower and shirker. The man had proved himself a nuisance already, since he refused to clean up after himself and routinely slept through guard duty. O'Neil had assured Flanna that Larry was nothing but lazy when he reported sick this morning, abandoning his place in the line as the company marched to the depot.

Haunted by the suspicion that she and the others might have judged Matthew Larry too harshly, Flanna squinted at the man. He lay on his side, his face pale, his upper lip lined with tiny pearls of sweat. She recalled that he had visited the latrine at least half a dozen times before roll call.

Flanna frowned slightly as she watched him. He was more likely than any man in the company to feign illness, but why would he pretend to be sick today when there was no real work to be done? He'd copped out of drill practice twice last week due to "dizziness and weak bowels," but had eaten as heartily as any man at supper.

The man shivered in his sleep, and Flanna felt her adrenaline level begin to rise. This man might be *very* sick. Dr. Gulick was supposed to appear at roll call to take an accounting of those who were ill, but he had not visited the camp this morning. Flanna suspected the surgeon spent the morning in a tavern, bolstering his courage and his spirits with whiskey.

She bent her knees and locked her arms around them, making a mental note to keep an eye on Matthew Larry. Gulick was a poor excuse for a doctor, but there would be other physicians in the Washington camp. Once the train stopped, she'd ask the sergeant to make sure Larry went to a proper hospital.

"Don't you cheat me, you vile snake!" Diltz roared from the midst of the poker game, and Flanna idly turned her eyes to the sound of his tirade, surprised at how little his outbursts affected her now. Diltz was a hotheaded fool, unafraid even to hurl curses at an officer, and he spent most of his free time assigned to guard duty or in the guardhouse. If there was whiskey in the tent, he'd certainly find it, and he was the last person Flanna would trust with a secret. But, she mused, turning her eyes to the gray outskirts of Boston rolling by the window, Diltz was the kind of man she'd want next to her when it came time for battle...*if* it ever came time for battle.

Roger had been confident that the struggle would not last long. In the hope that he was right, Flanna prayed for peace...and hoped that the leaders of the North and South would come to their senses before the Twenty-fifth Massachusetts stepped onto a battlefield.

She would never be able to fire at an army in which her loved ones might march. Beneath every gray Rebel cap she'd see Wesley's face, or Arthur's, or Brennan's, or Carroll's. And since her present comrades would depend on her to hold her place in line, she prayed that God would soon send victory, compromise, or even defeat. Anything that would end this great civil war.

Fourteen

Saturday, September 7

We have arrived in the Union camp outside Washington. General McClellan has placed us here to guard the capital, though I see no signs of Rebel aggression or activity. I have in fact, seen nothing but men, mud, and muck. It rained several days before our arrival, and, after disembarking at the train station outside the city, we were marched under a hot sun to our camp, several miles away in Maryland.

While Andrew Green gazed wistfully at the foliage around us, Philip Hart voiced my feelings more appropriately. "If there is anything particularly attractive in marching from ten to twenty miles a day under a scorching sun with a good mule load and sinking up to one's knees in the 'sacred soil' at each step," said Hart, "my mind is not of a sufficiently poetical nature to appreciate it."

As uncomfortable and tired as we are, sweet Charity and I are in good spirits. For though we are yet in Maryland, we have heard talk of a great movement south, as soon as McClellan prepares the Federal force. They say Lincoln is anxious for the

*army to move, and so are many of the gentlemen
in Congress. But no one is more ready to go than I.
Shall we be home in time for Christmas?
Nothing would bring me more pleasure.*

Alden read the newspaper article, folded the paper, and placed it on the colonel's desk. Colonel Farnham's eyes locked tight upon him, and neither man spoke for a long time.

Outside the tent, Alden could hear the busy sounds of men and horses, but those sounds seemed miles away.

"You knew him?" Farnham finally asked, using his knuckle to wipe small sparkles of sweat off his upper lip.

Alden nodded, still reeling from the news. "Yes sir. General Lyon was a friend from West Point." His hands tightened on the arm of the chair. "He was a good teacher, a good man."

Farnham lightly touched his forehead in a subdued salute. "God rest him. I didn't think the Rebs would get him. Not this soon."

Alden brought his hand to his chin, thinking. The loss of Brigadier General Nathaniel Lyon was a tragedy for the Union, but even more unsettling was the news of Confederate victory in the West. Half of Missouri, a slave state that had remained loyal to the Union, now lay in Confederate hands.

Alden had read the details in the newspaper story. The Missouri catastrophe had begun when a crowd of secessionists pelted a group of Lyon's men with stones. The general's men shot back, killing twenty-eight people, including a baby in its mother's arms. The secessionists quickly raised an army, but Lyon chased them to the quiet area known as Wilson's Creek. There he died, a victim of his own zeal.

"They were defending their own people, their own women and children," Farnham remarked, stretching his long legs before him. "We, too, will be the invaders. As long as we're moving south, it will go hard for us."

Alden thought of the innocent baby, then for some shapeless reason Flanna O'Connor's image filtered into his brain. He was on his way to invade her country. Though she was safe in New York, she had spoken often of her brother and cousins. How could he know that her loved ones did not lie ahead in some Confederate camp?

He couldn't think about that possibility. If he dwelled on it, if he looked for her green eyes and red hair on every Reb that appeared in the woods, he'd be unable to do his duty. And he was an officer in the army, trained since youth to follow orders and succeed on the battlefield. To kill the enemy.

"Well, we'll just have to keep the men's spirits up," the colonel said. The wariness in his eyes had frozen into a blue as cold as ice, though his lips stayed curved in a pleasant smile. "Can I count on you to do that, Major?"

"Of course, sir." Hearing dismissal in the colonel's tone, Alden stood and snapped a salute. "I will not let you down."

The colonel returned his salute. "I knew you wouldn't."

With Charity at her side, Flanna stepped out of the tent, eager for a breath of fresh air. Dr. Gulick had posted an order that all tent flaps should be kept lowered, for the cooler winds of autumn might bring typhoid fever, but the air inside fairly vibrated in a symphony of stinks. Unwashed bodies, the ammoniac smell of urine, and other pungent and immodest odors drove her outside to breathe the crisp, cool air of autumn.

She glanced down at the fire pit and saw Matthew Larry's canteen serving as a skillet. Diltz had hit upon the notion of inserting a match and a bit of gunpowder into a canteen. The resulting explosion ripped the canteen's seams, producing two lightweight frying pans.

Larry himself was dead, the first of their mess to die in Gulick's hospital tent. As they left the train, Flanna had urged Sergeant Marvin to speak to Dr. Gulick about sending Larry to a Washington hospital, but the doctor would not listen. "That one's always playing possum," he had said, shrugging away the sergeant's concerns. "He's not leaving us. If he's truly sick, I'll take care of him once we reach camp."

After three days on the train and the tiring march into Maryland, Matthew Larry's strength ebbed away, and there was little Gulick could do. Larry entered the Union camp on a stretcher, jabbering and muttering insanities in his fever, his clothing shredded by his fretful hands and stinking of sickness.

Flanna had guessed the verdict before Dr. Gulick pronounced it—the high fever, headache, coughing, and rose-colored spots could only have been caused by typhoid. And though Larry was the only one of Flanna's messmates to succumb to the disease, several others within Company M were affected.

While the men of the Twenty-fifth Massachusetts drilled in this Maryland camp and waited for General McClellan to take action, disease stalked the tents and pulled men from the ranks, often as many as two-thirds of a regiment. Typhoid wasn't the only disease, of course; a variety of illnesses seemed to plague the camp. In the six weeks since they had arrived in Maryland, a startling number had already died. A dozen of the dead were from Flanna's own regiment, and Dr. Gulick would give no name for their illness save "looseness of the bowels." Gulick blamed the disease on the night air, but Flanna knew there had to be a more definite cause.

She became convinced that the growing rate of disease resulted from ignorance, laziness, and ineffectiveness. Her training led her to believe that part of the reason for illness lay in the camp latrines, or sinks. These shallow trenches, far too near the tents for Flanna's comfort, were left uncovered for long periods of time. The stifling odors that rose from these ditches were enough to sicken even the healthiest man. Another problem sprang from the reluctance of many soldiers, especially those from rural areas, to even use the latrines. Like Flanna, these overly modest men crept into the woods when nature called, but unlike Flanna, they did not carry a shovel and practice biblical hygiene.

Not only did most of the men ignore the terrible sinks, but even the men who used them ignored certain safeguards. Army regulations called for fresh earth to be turned into the sinks on a daily basis, but the increasingly repugnant odor repelled those who were supposed to tend the latrines.

Nor did the men attend to personal cleanliness. Though Sergeant Marvin frequently reminded his men that army regulations called for each man to wash his hands and face daily, few men bothered. Flanna changed her undergarments at least every other day and gave them to Charity for washing in the creek.

Flanna knew that a number of her messmates had not changed their clothing since induction. Some of them, she realized, had no other clothing to change into, for they deemed extra garments an added weight and hindrance. In the heat of summer they had shed their overcoats, dress coats, extra shirts, and clean trousers, and few bothered to include those garments in their bedrolls when the army moved to Washington. Now that October's chill had arrived, they were regretting their decisions. Charity's help was again a blessing. While Flanna carried as much weight as her fellow soldiers, Charity wore Flanna's heavy overcoat and carried extra garments in her bedroll.

And, unlike her soldier companions, Flanna scrubbed her hands and knuckles clean each morning, often visiting the creek to fill her canteen two or three times in a day. O'Neil teased her about her constant scrubbing and high-toned manners, but when Flanna pointed out that she had not yet suffered a case of the "Maryland quickstep," he stopped teasing and began to follow her example.

Though she had never thought of herself as a doctor for men, she could not help being affected by the suffering around her, particularly when she saw how Dr. Gulick treated his patients. Each morning after breakfast, one of the company's duty sergeants lined up all the ambulatory sick patients and marched them down to the surgeon's tent. One morning Flanna followed out of idle curiosity, and the cursory examination Dr. Gulick gave each patient horrified her.

No matter what the patient's complaint—loose bowels, bellyache, headache, or fever—the doctor wagged his bearded chin and called out a number that referred to a treatment. His assistant jotted the number on a slip, then gave it to the soldier, who took it to the surgeon's assistant for dosing. As she listened, Flanna discovered that the good doctor never varied in his order of prescriptions, calling out "six," then "nine," then "eleven," before repeating the series again. Number eleven, she discovered, was "vinum," or a stiff shot of whiskey. The more clever men had already figured out how to feign sickness after breakfast and fall into line just where the doctor's "eleven" prescription would fall.

Prescription six was eight grains each of calomel and rhubarb, followed by a saline cathartic, which moved the bowels—just the thing, Flanna realized, that a patient with diarrhea *didn't* need. Prescription nine was a mixture of carbonate of ammonia, turpentine, quinine, and brandy. Those who recovered from their illnesses obviously did so in *spite* of the doctor's remedies.

As much as Flanna despised Gulick's practice of medicine, her disguise required that she remain silent. She had been able to account for her manners and book knowledge by explaining that her father was a doctor, but she thought it best not to advertise that she had earned a degree in medicine herself. If the men knew that Franklin O'Connor was a doctor, they'd want to know why he hadn't enlisted as a surgeon. Flanna couldn't explain that regimental surgeons occupied positions of authority and power—attention Flanna would rather avoid if she hoped to maintain her charade.

She might have been able to completely disguise her medical knowledge if another of her messmates had not become sick. Warmhearted Andrew Green was one of her quieter comrades. With four older brothers in the service, Green knew how to get along with others and was well liked in spite of his reluctance to participate in rough games and teasing. At night, after taps, when the others moaned in their sleep or wept silently and longed for home, Green often enthralled them by quietly weaving stories of ancient heroes and mythic creatures or naming the bird that sang in the night. "The bravest birds sing in the dark," he said, his voice rising and falling in an easy rhythm. "Because they know God will bring light on the morrow."

Sometimes by the campfire Green would point to the sky and name the constellations, and once as they foraged for firewood, he paused to marvel at the beauty of a flaming maple tree. He reveled in the unfamiliar flora of the area and used his free time to write poetry about nature and his loved ones at home.

Even Herbert Diltz had a soft spot for Andrew Green, and this morning Diltz had been the one to notice that the young man did not rise from his bed. Sergeant Marvin had moved to Green's side and nudged him with his boot, then knelt and pressed his palm to the boy's forehead.

"The boy's burning up," Marvin called, his voice rough with anxiety. "Anybody got water in their canteen?"

Flanna immediately pulled out her clean shirt and wet it with water, then offered it to the sergeant. "Let me see him, sir," she whispered, kneeling by Green's side.

The sergeant stood and stepped back, more than willing to let her help. Flanna pressed her fingers lightly to Green's hot wrist and found that his pulse was elevated. Perhaps typhoid. Perhaps measles, though the spots had not yet begun to show. In either case, he needed a doctor—a real one.

"He needs to go see the doctor," she said, standing. "Right away."

Sergeant Marvin scanned the tent for men who were already dressed. "Diltz, you and Valentine take him to see the doc. And Valentine—not a word about death and dying, do you hear? This boy's going to be okay."

Diltz and Valentine moved to lift Green, and Flanna stepped back to her bedroll and picked up her jacket. Dr. Gulick would not do anything for Green; a six, nine, or eleven treatment might even worsen Green's condition. And Andrew Green's mother, wherever she was, did not deserve to risk five sons in war and lose one in camp.

Flanna caught Charity's eye, then pulled her maid outside for a badly needed breath of fresh air. "Later this afternoon, after inspection," she whispered, buttoning her cuffs as they stood by the campfire, "you and I are going to look through those medical wagons outside

Gulick's tent. I don't know what he's stashed away out there, but he's going to give Andrew Green something that will help."

A pensive shimmer lit the shadows of Charity's eyes, then her mouth curved in a slow smile. "I was wondering, Doctor," she said, her voice deep and dusty, "when you was going to get busy doing something useful."

"Now you know." Flanna smoothed her hair, then pulled on her cap, positioning it so low that the brim nearly rode her brow. "And soon we'll see if we can make a difference."

<hr>

"O'Neil, would you be having a minute to spare for a friend?" Standing slightly apart from the others, Flanna grinned at Paddy. "Or is that poker hand too bonny to pass up?"

O'Neil let out a snort. "I haven't had a good hand all day. I think the good Lord's trying to punish me for playing poker on Sunday." He dropped his cards in the center of the circle of card players, then stood and stretched. "Excuse me, lads, while I stretch my legs with the wee laddie."

Flanna rolled her eyes at his comment, but was relieved when he sauntered her way. The company had spent a quiet morning in worship services with the chaplain, and most men relaxed throughout Sunday afternoons. O'Neil was apt to be ready for his regular Sunday routine of polishing his boots and his rifle, but there was still time for him to help her before inspection—if he proved willing.

"What's eating at you, young Franklin? Surely you aren't wanting me to teach you how to win at poker. Truth to tell, I haven't got the knack of that game."

"It's not poker I'm interested in." Flanna led him away from the tent. She walked a dozen paces, then pinched her nose and pointed to the sinks. "It's that."

"The sinks?" O'Neil grimaced in distaste. "Have you lost your mind, lad? What in the world would make you bring me out here?"

"They're too close to the camp." Flanna released her nose and turned away, unable to abide the smell. "I don't know why, exactly, but I'm certain the latrines have something to do with all this sickness."

O'Neil's brows flickered as he stared at the sinks, then he thrust his hands into his pockets. "I'll admit the smell enough is likely to churn a man's stomach, but why—"

"There's more to it than that, but I can't explain right now. But if you believe in God's Holy Word, then surely you remember what the Lord said in Deuteronomy 23."

O'Neil lifted a brow. "Remind me, lad."

"After telling his people that they should take care of their business outside the camp—" Her face grew hot with humiliation, but she went on, "God said, 'For the Lord thy God walketh in the midst of thy camp, to deliver thee, and to give up thine enemies before thee; therefore shall thy camp be holy: that he see no unclean thing in thee.' Both Leviticus and Deuteronomy are filled with references to cleanliness and sanitation."

Flanna thrust her hands in her pockets, mimicking O'Neil's broad stance, and something either in the gesture or her words seemed to touch him.

"Och, lad, that's lovely, but why are you tellin' me this? I'm just one man, and I can't very well be filling in the entire trench."

Flanna steeled her voice with resolve. "I want you to go to Major Haynes and tell him that the trenches are too close to the camp. He'll listen to you, I know he will, and perhaps he'll command a detail to cover these ditches and dig others further out."

O'Neil regarded her with an intense but secret expression. "Been thinking about this for a while, have you? Well, feeling as strongly about the situation as you do, why don't you go to the major yourself?"

Flanna looked away and groped for words. She couldn't say she'd had a disagreement with the major; O'Neil would know she was lying. So why not tell the truth? "The major makes me nervous," she finally said. "All the officers do."

"Why? 'Tis not like you're a troublemaker," O'Neil said smoothly, with no expression on his face. "I've heard scarcely a peep out of you since you came. So why you should want to raise this matter with the major is beyond my ken—"

"It's because of Albert Green." Flanna lifted her hands in frustration. "One of our own is sick, Paddy, and I'm trying to do something about it. Now are you going to help me or not?"

O'Neil hesitated for a moment, then he grinned. "Aye, I'll speak to the major," he said, "though I don't know what good it will do."

"Thank you, Paddy." Flanna sighed in relief. "It may do no good at all, but at least we will have tried, right?"

A flash of humor crossed her friend's face. "You're an odd lad, O'Connor." He reached out and thumped Flanna's back, nearly knocking her off her feet. "But I'll do as you ask, if only because those cursed trenches are more than I can bear when the wind blows from the south."

"Thanks."

O'Neil thrust his hands in his pockets and moved away, his laughter floating back to Flanna on a blessed northerly breeze.

∽∾∾∾

"You want me to do what, Private?"

Annoyed by this unexpected intrusion on a peaceful Sunday afternoon, Alden glanced up from his paperwork and stared at the ruddy Irishman. Paddy O'Neil of Company M stood at attention before him, his chest thrust out, his eyes fixed and straight ahead.

"I'd like to request that the sinks be moved, sir." His voice emerged as a nervous croak. "They are too close to our tents, and one of our men has taken sick. I think—well, sir, I believe there is a connection."

Alden leaned back in his chair, his mind whirling. Someone else had grumbled about the sinks' proximity to the tents, someone he respected, but who?

Flanna. As the image focused in his memory, he could see her again, lifting her wide skirts as she moved through the Boston camp, pointing at the latrine trenches and proclaiming them too close to the men. He'd found her objections amusing, attributing them to her genteel sensibilities, but then she'd made some remark about the Bible…

178

He leaned forward and studied the Irishman's broad face. "Why, Private O'Neil, do you believe the sinks are too close?"

"Several reasons, sir." Despite the man's apparent boldness, Alden saw the Adam's apple bob in O'Neil's throat as he nervously swallowed. "First, the smell is unbearable when the wind blows from the south, sir. Second, several of our messmates have taken sick, and we are closest to the sinks, sir. Third—" He paused and gave Alden a narrow, glinting glance. "Do you read the Bible, sir?"

"Yes." Alden leaned back in his chair and crossed his arms. "Yes, Private, I do. You were saying?"

"The Good Book says we should keep a clean camp," O'Neil finished, his face brightening to a tomato shade. "In Deuteropoly."

Alden pressed his hand to his lips, trapping the laughter that threatened to erupt from his throat. The man had obviously been coached, but by whom? And why?

"And were you reading in, um, Deuteropoly this morning? Or perhaps the chaplain brought this passage to your attention?"

"No sir." A smile nudged itself into a corner of O'Neil's mouth, then pushed across his lips. "Truth to tell, sir, I didn't think it right to bring a Bible to war. But I know what the Good Book says, and it says we're to keep a clean camp. We won't be sick as often if we do."

Alden stared at his visitor and let the silence stretch. Of all the complaints and requests that regularly crossed his desk, this one rang with novelty. And yet O'Neil was expressing sentiments he had heard before.

"Did Dr. Gulick send you to me?"

"No sir!" The soldier tossed his head in a gesture of defiance. "That old sot? He doesn't care whether we're sick or not."

"Did you, by chance—" Alden hesitated, knowing the possibility was unlikely. "Have you, Private, been talking to another doctor? For if there is another doctor in our regiment, we could certainly use his abilities."

"No sir." O'Neil spoke in a quiet, firm voice. "I know no other doctor. Now, sir, what can you tell me about the sinks? Can we move them? I'm fairly certain I can rouse enough men from my company to cover the old ones, if you'll give permission to dig new ditches further out."

"Permission granted." Alden picked up his pen to make a note of the matter, then glanced up. O'Neil had not moved. "Is there anything else, Private?"

"No sir. Thank you, sir. He'll be right pleased to hear it."

Alden stopped writing. "*Who* will be pleased?"

"Every man in my tent, Major." O'Neil snapped a salute, which Alden casually returned, then the Irishman spun on his heel and strode out of the tent.

∝⟡∝

The afternoon air stirred with chilly hints of coming winter days as Alden moved through the camp, his eyes alert for any sign of mischief. By now the new recruits had realized that soldiering involved a lot of sitting and standing around, and the chief problem Alden had faced since arriving at the camp was simple boredom. Men with nothing to do had time to make trouble. Already there were reports that men were deserting the camp at night to visit the taverns and bawdy houses that lay on the road to Washington. Alden sighed in frustration. He didn't need that kind of trouble.

His men weren't the only ones who yearned for action. The commanders' tents were rife with rumors that Lincoln himself had grown impatient with McClellan's confounded and endless preparations. At first Alden had been pleased to hear that McClellan believed in making no move until preparations were complete. That pragmatic philosophy was born out of West Point and agreed with Alden's own practical nature. But the Republicans in Congress were hungry for victory, especially since they now smarted under the sting of Bull Run and the tragedy at Wilson's Creek. Colonel Farnham reported that Lincoln seemed painfully aware that cotton-hungry Europe was watching carefully, weighing the wealth of Southern cotton against Northern resolve. And if England aided the Confederacy—well, the war would be lost. No doubt about it.

McClellan seemed intent on running the war his way, ignoring both the president and Congress. Alden had been shocked at the news that Lincoln had visited the general's home, waited patiently in the parlor for the McClellans to return from a wedding party, then silently departed when McClellan's butler announced that the general could not see him, for he had come home and straightaway retired for the night. Such arrogance was incomprehensible.

Days earlier Alden had felt a fierce but disloyal surge of satisfaction when McClellan took a bit of humiliation on the chin. For months he had claimed that over 150,000 Confederates waited within striking distance of Washington, with artillery cannon trained on the great city. But when Rebel pickets withdrew from an exposed position southwest of the capital, those "great cannon" were left behind. Closer inspection by Federal cavalry revealed them to be giant logs, painted black. A scornful newspaper reporter wrote that McClellan had been held hostage by "Quaker guns."

Though Alden felt a bit embarrassed for McClellan, he, too, felt the need for action. He and his men were ready and willing *now;* delay would only result in a dangerous lowering of morale. Already the advent of sickness had damaged the spirit of what had been an eager and robust regiment.

Fortunately, an order had come down involving the Twenty-fifth Massachusetts, and Alden was relieved that his men would finally have a task to perform. The entire regiment had been ordered to advance for a reconnaissance mission. By the end of the week they would move to the Sugar Loaf Mountain Station in Maryland, to reinforce Brigadier General Charles Stone's division. They would probably—and Alden's nerves tensed at the thought—cross the Potomac River into Virginia.

The brigade commander was Colonel Edward Baker, an Oregon senator who was probably less qualified for his position than Alden's mother. But he had supported Lincoln in the war effort after Fort Sumter's fall, and he, like Lincoln, chafed for action. The troops were tired of being restrained by harmless Quaker guns and threats of phantom Rebel troops. The time had come to move out, to do something to end the struggle. Alden, for one, did not want to spend the winter sitting on the frozen ground of Maryland.

But how could they move in their present condition? Alden turned onto the narrow street of Company M and frowned at what he saw there. The first tent had been given over entirely to sick men, and though the tent flaps had been lowered, the odors of illness still wafted through the open entry. More than a quarter of the regiment's men were on the sick list; 250 men would not go forth to duty, but would remain in camp, victims of disease.

Still walking, Alden thrust his hands behind his back, absently wishing that he could summon Flanna O'Connor again. Dr. Gulick had come highly recommended, but the man had done nothing to stop the spread of sickness among the men. Despite her quirks and her reluctance to treat men, Flanna had been a gifted healer. Private Henry Fraser lived because of Flanna's courage and devotion to detail, so why in heaven's name couldn't John Gulick achieve the same measure of success?

Something odd caught his eye, and Alden stopped in the road and turned toward the sick tent, idly wondering what detail seemed out of place. A pair of men stood by the medical supply wagon, a slender youth and his black body servant. Alden frowned as an inner alarm rang. The thin soldier moved with undue caution, his hand reaching toward the tarp over the wagon as if to spy out its contents. What would he be searching for, if not whiskey?

"You there!" Alden's voice rang across the street. The men at a nearby campfire fell silent; the only sounds now were the windy flap of the tent canvas in the wind and a constant groaning from the sick tent.

Slowly, the youth at the wagon turned. The sun shone brightly on his cap, shadowing his face, but there was no denying the tension in his posture.

"What are you doing, soldier?" Alden walked forward, ripping out the words. "Unless Dr. Gulick sent you on some errand, you'd better have a reason for snooping in the medical wagon."

The boy's head lowered as Alden advanced, and the visor of the cap shielded the youth's eyes. Alden could see a quivering chin, freckled skin, and clenched hands.

"I meant no harm, sir." The boy spoke in a husky voice that held a trace of Irish brogue. "I was just curious. Our boys are perishing with hunger and sickness in there, and I thought I might find a wee bit of something to help them."

"You're no doctor. And since you're not, you'd best stay away from this wagon and everything in it." As Alden paused to let the words sink in, he glanced at the youth's body servant. The black man was as shy as his master. His head hung so low Alden could see nothing but his hair.

Alden shook his head as his anger faded. The boy seemed sincere enough, and he hardly seemed the type to make trouble. No sense in taking out all his frustrations on this one boy.

"Listen, lad," he said, stepping closer, "there's been trouble enough, and we've no time for it now. We'll be leaving this place in a few days, and I'd hate to have to discipline you when we're moving out. You'd have to carry a log or march with a rail tied around your neck, and frankly"—he cast a meaningful glance at the lad's slender frame—"I don't know that you'd be able to handle it."

The boy did not answer. Alden didn't know whether the youth's silence sprang from defiance, stubbornness, or guilt.

"Do you hear me, soldier?" Alden straightened, ready to forcibly lift the boy's chin if he didn't respond. "Look me in the eye when I speak to you."

The boy's chin lifted only for an instant, and Alden caught a glimpse of startling eyes as green as grass. "Faith, I cannot help but hear you." The boy lowered his gaze. "Am I dismissed, sir?"

"Yes." Alden stood still as the boy and his servant moved away. He was conscious of a small stirring of curiosity about the lad, but fought it down. There were too many other pressing matters at hand.

Sighing in frustration, Alden moved away to find Dr. Gulick.

Four days passed. On Thursday night, October 17, Flanna waited until after taps, until even Albert Valentine (who rarely slept but usually lay awake and worried in the darkness) breathed in deep, regular breaths. At roll call they had learned that they would move on the morrow, taking the inept Dr. Gulick with them. Sergeant Marvin told his men that the sick, including Andrew Green, would be transferred to the Alexandria Hospital. Though Flanna hoped they would receive better treatment there than in the camp, she had no assurance that they would, and for Andrew Green, at least, she felt a deep and abiding compassion. In some ways he reminded her of her young cousin Gannon, for both loved the things of nature.

"Charity." Flanna nudged the girl's shoulder in the dark. "Come, it's time."

Charity clung to sleep as hard as she could, burying her face in the folds of the overcoat.

"Charles!" Flanna whispered with greater intensity. "Get up! We've got to go!"

Charity sat up, blinked, and then turned to Flanna with wide eyes. "You ain't still going through with it! The major said he'd punish you."

"The major is in bed. He won't see me."

Charity shook her head. "The guards aren't in bed. And I'm not going to carry your knapsack all the way to Virginia if you're busy carrying some log."

"I'll carry whatever I have to," Flanna said, slipping on her shoes, "but I'm not leaving until I know Andrew Green has been properly treated. If it's measles, the spots should have appeared by now."

"I'm not going with you." Charity folded her arms around her bent knees. "You have gone out of your mind. I didn't say nothing when you wanted to join the army, and I didn't say nothing when you told me we'd have to sleep on the ground with all these strange men. The army and these men are helping us get home, but this fool thing means nothing to us. I ain't going to risk getting whipped for sneaking out after dark."

Flanna paused, not knowing how to explain herself. The ties that pulled her toward Andrew Green were as strong as those that pulled her homeward, but Charity wouldn't understand a physician's obligation and the yearning to heal. And she had never taken the Hippocratic oath.

"Then stay here and wait for me." Flanna slipped into her jacket. "Say a prayer, at least."

Flanna shivered as she stepped outside the tent and the shock of cool air hit her face. She hesitated in the shadow of the tent and looked around to be sure no guards stirred in the moonlight.

The camp lay silent under the moon, silver and black with shadows. Pulling her jacket more tightly around her, she moved down the street toward the sick tent, praying that nothing moved in the darkness.

Nothing did. Even the usual troublemakers like Diltz had willingly gone to sleep, knowing that a long march awaited them on the morrow.

Flanna slipped into the sick tent, then crinkled her nose as a storm of odors assaulted her senses. The enclosed chamber reeked of vomit, blood, and urine. Another smell struck her nostrils, a lower and more sinister scent—the stink of fear.

The room lay in complete darkness, for no nurse or guard watched over the sick, and Dr. Gulick was doubtless in his bed, resting for the journey to come.

Flanna moved toward a small table she had seen earlier, then fumbled for the oil lantern and box of matches. Her questing fingers found the items she sought, and she lit the lantern, then shook the flame off the match. Pausing, she lowered the wick into the oil until only the barest light glowed—some of these men were awake and restless with pain, and she didn't want any of them to identify her in the morning. Once the lantern put forth a narrow halo of light, she lifted it high and walked among the pallets, searching for Andrew Green.

She found him on the far side of the tent. Hanging the lantern from the tent's center pole, she knelt at Andrew's side and pinched the skin at his neck. It felt stiff and dry under her fingertips, but at least his fever had broken. Leaning over him, she pushed the hair off his forehead and studied his complexion. His face gleamed with oil and sweat, but no red bumps. No measles. She sighed in relief. Andrew Green would live, but he needed water.

The water bucket in the center of the tent stood empty, and she trudged outside to the water barrel, wincing at every noisy drop that rattled into the pail. But soon the water overflowed and splashed onto her feet, and she trudged back inside. She found a dipper and lifted Andrew's head to give him a drink. He seemed not to notice or care who she was, but drank deeply. As she gently lowered his head back to the ground, he mumbled, "Thank you."

"Water, please." The man next to Andrew must have heard the liquid sounds. "Please—I've had no water." Unable to refuse him, Flanna moved the bucket to his pallet, pouring water from the dipper directly into his mouth. The situation didn't measure up to her standards of cleanliness, so she poured the water from above her patients, not allowing any sick man to touch the dipper with his lips.

The second man, she saw immediately, suffered from an abscessed tooth. "What has Dr. Gulick done for you?" she whispered, searching his eyes for signs of lucidity.

The sick man waved his hand. "Quinine and turpentine," he moaned, his eyes tearing with pain as his jaw moved. "My gut is killing me."

"No wonder." Flanna moved toward the table where she'd found the lantern. An assortment of tools lay scattered there—a hammer, chisel, twine, and an awl. She ran her fingers over the implements until she found what she sought, then paused by the whiskey keg and filled a gourd with the pungent drink.

She turned and moved back to the man, who gratefully accepted the gourd and drained the liquid. Flanna squatted by his side, watching as he smacked his lips. "In a moment," she said, tilting her head to gauge the effects of her improvised anesthetic, "you're going to feel warm and relaxed. I want you to lie back and open your mouth. No matter what happens, do not cry out."

The man nodded with a sleepy smile, and a moment later he lay sprawled at her feet, his arms outstretched, his mouth open to the sky. Flanna fitted the pliers to the broken tooth and yanked; the diseased gum surrendered the tooth as if glad to be rid of it. Flanna frowned as the odors of pus and decay rose from the man's mouth. She poured another tumbler full of whiskey, then pulled the man upright to prevent him from choking. With his head supported by her left hand, she dribbled the liquid into his mouth, then packed the wound with soft cotton. When she had finished, she rolled the soldier onto his side so that any liquid oozing from his mouth would drain out on the blanket.

Though her energy was nearly spent, she looked around at the others, all of whom needed water. To the partially conscious she gave a drink; she pressed cool wet cloths on the others' foreheads. Several weakly complained of stomach pains, so she found a small vial of jalap, a cathartic, among the medical supplies and sprinkled a teaspoon of powder on several tongues. After making certain that each man had a blanket over him, she went to the far side of the tent and lifted a flap for ventilation.

When she was certain she had done the best she could for each patient, she rose and washed her hands, then began the walk back to her own tent. Soon the horizon would begin to brighten in the east. She'd have less than an hour to sleep. But as Flanna's head dropped to the rough fabric of her haversack, she knew the night of hard work was worth the effort.

Fifteen

Prodding stragglers with a direct glance and an abrupt command, Alden moved through the camp and checked the regiment's progress. He was conducting a routine check of how many men would be marching and how many would remain behind in the sick tents, and thus far he'd been dismayed to discover that Companies B, D, K, and L listed more sick today than yesterday. Some cynical part of his nature wanted to attribute the abrupt increase to sheer cowardice, but reason reminded him that sickness had run rampant ever since they arrived at this camp. Most of the men, even those with a touch of fever or a raging case of the Maryland quickstep, were eager to head out to a new area.

He reached Company M's row of tents and paused before its infirmary. Despite Private O'Neil's assertion that moving the sinks would tremendously benefit his company's health, Company M had a full dozen men sick yesterday. Based on his experience with the other companies, Alden mentally added another three to that number—he'd probably discover at least fifteen sick men inside this tent now, and perhaps two or three dead.

He lifted the tent flap and peered inside. Instead of the darkness and stench he expected, bright sunlight and fresh air greeted him, because someone had opened the tent on the other side. There were still a dozen sick men, to be sure, but these were not writhing in the agony he expected. Three were sitting up, awake and alert, and one man was actually laughing and sharing jokes with a comrade.

"What's going on in here?" Alden stepped into the tent and looked around, finally directing his gaze to a young man who sat in a bright patch of sunlight. "You're Private Green, aren't you?"

"Yes sir. Andrew Green." The youth nodded soberly.

"I saw you yesterday." Alden frowned, recalling that the boy had done nothing but lie still, his body weak and his skin like pale parchment. "Are you feeling better?"

"I believe I am, sir." Green smiled with warm spontaneity. "I felt like the very devil yesterday, but today I think I am fit enough to rejoin my messmates."

Alden half-smiled at the soldier's enthusiasm. The fellow might be well enough to leave the sick tent, but his strength wouldn't last through a twenty-mile march. "Take it easy, Green. We'll ease you in when we return." Alden's gaze roved to the next fellow. "And you, soldier—what's your story?"

The man grinned up at Alden, then blinked in the sunlight. "I've an awful pain in my mouth and a raging headache," he said, gently pressing his fingers to his forehead, "but the throbbing in my jaw is gone! The angel came last night and pulled my tooth. See here!" With a flourish, the man fumbled at the blanket where he lay, then held up a bloodied brown tooth.

Alden grimaced at the sight of it. "Your tooth fell out?"

"No, the angel pulled it out." The idiot grinned, and even from this distance Alden could smell whiskey on his breath. "She gave me drink, and then she sat back and said it would hurt but a minute. And then it was all over!"

"There weren't no angel." This observation came from the other side of the room, where another man leaned on his elbow and glowered at the giddy drunk. "There was a soldier, sure, and he went around and gave everybody water. But he weren't no angel."

"A soldier?" Alden thrust his hands behind his back. "Surely you mean Dr. Gulick or his assistant."

"It weren't neither of them fools," the man said, his voice breaking in a horrible, rattling gurgle. "I saw him. It was a soldier, just an ordinary soldier. He woke me up and poured water into my mouth."

"What did this soldier look like?"

"I couldn't see much." The man lowered his head back to his blanket. "It was dark. He was just a shadow."

"Soft." The man with the swollen mouth gently rested his cheek upon his hand. "The angel was soft, with delicate hands and a whispering voice. Even when she pulled my tooth, I kept thinking how soft her touch was."

"Soft as velvet," Private Green murmured, his eyes focused on some indistinct point. "I remember now! I drank water, too, but thought I was dreaming of a waterfall. There was a soft murmuring sound, like a river, and water flowing from somewhere above me."

"Are you men trying to tell me that a velvet shadow passed among you last night?" Alden sighed with exasperation. He'd heard of battle fatigue, of cowardice, and fear and false bravado, but no one had ever warned him that sick men might share a hallucination.

"Whatever it was, it done me a sight more good than that army doctor." The drunk grinned up at Alden with a remarkable space between his teeth. "If Gulick was as liberal with the whiskey as the Velvet Shadow, there'd be far fewer sick men in here."

"And far more drunks in the camp," Alden muttered, turning away. He paused in the open doorway, considering this mysterious "velvet shadow." If the man could be discovered, Alden didn't know whether to commend the mysterious fellow or rebuke him. Absolutely no one was allowed to move about after taps except officers and those on guard duty. Yet the fellow had obviously done these men a great service.

But nothing could be done until the man was apprehended, and since they were leaving the sick behind, the mysterious saint might not appear for several weeks. And Alden had other, more urgent matters to consider.

He stepped outside and watched the men of Company M as they went about the work of dismantling their tents and stowing their gear. They moved with the fumbling, awkward movements of men not quite in the mold of soldiering. But that would change soon enough.

❧

"Men of the Twenty-fifth Massachusetts! Today we begin our march toward the enemy in Virginia!"

An anticipatory shiver rippled through Flanna's limbs as the colonel's voice rang out over the assembly. Today they would begin to move south, and each step would bring her closer to her father…and danger.

Colonel Farnham sat stiffly on his horse, a fine white stallion that pranced anxiously before the assembled troops. "Men," Farnham continued, "General Charles Stone has asked for our assistance. He holds Sugar Loaf Mountain, a position in Maryland, and needs some brave Massachusetts boys to help him make sure the Rebs are running from that part of the country. So we're going up there to do a little reconnoitering in the grand old dominion of Virginia."

The men erupted in a cheer, but Flanna felt as though strong bands were constricting her chest. She turned her head until Alden Haynes appeared in her line of vision. He stood in the line of officers just ahead of her, his golden hair peeking out from beneath his hat. His calm attitude of self-command and relaxation helped soothe her strained nerves.

"Men of the Union!" The sound of the colonel's voice filled the meadow. "The hour for which you have waited has arrived. We are about to enter the enemy's territory. Let every man do his duty. Be cool. Keep ranks as we march on the road, as we file through the woods, as we reclaim the traitors' land. And if, by chance, we should encounter the Rebels, hold your fire until they are in easy range. Then aim low and fire deliberately; listen for the voice of your sergeants. If you follow orders, we will emerge the victor in every contest."

The men cheered, and the colonel pulled his sword from its scabbard and waved it overhead. "For your God and your country!" he yelled, his lined face brightening in an ardent flush.

The colonel spurred his horse and raced down the line; the officers turned to face their companies. At once, a blizzard of commands whirled in the air, the band began to play, and the lines moved. To the stirring rhythms of "John Brown's Body" Flanna stepped out with her fellows and began to march toward the south.

Through the rising din, she breathed one word: "Home."

They marched for three days, sleeping in small, four-man wedge tents as they moved northwestward toward Sugar Loaf Mountain. From what Flanna overheard, she gathered that the Rebs had occupied the train depot at Leesburg, Virginia, but General McCall, whose men held nearby Dranesville, Virginia, to the south, had been scaring the Rebs away with a heavy show of force. Her regiment was to cross the river and approach Leesburg from the east, pressuring any remaining Rebs to move out. "I suppose we'll look for Confederates as we go through the woods," she explained to Charity as they breakfasted on Flanna's ration of hardtack and dried beef. "And I earnestly hope we won't find any."

Flanna wiped her hands on her jacket, then opened her journal long enough to record the date—October 21, 1861. Too nervous to write more, she snapped the book shut and dropped it, with her pen and ink bottle, back into her haversack. They had camped last night at Sugar Loaf Mountain. Today they would cross the Potomac into Virginia, and that realization had painted a shadow even on Paddy O'Neil's jovial face. Albert Valentine's mournful eyes had deepened into pools of black melancholy, and Rufus Crydenwise, a pale-faced mama's boy who never should have enlisted, was fairly weeping into his coffee cup.

Jonah Barker stood to wipe his nose on his sleeve, then glanced at the men around the fire. "Does anyone have any cartridges to spare?" he asked, his voice dull and troubled. "I spilled mine as we crossed that ridge yesterday. I was afraid to stop and pick 'em up."

William Sheahan, a Crimean War veteran who had drifted into Flanna's mess, exploded. "Fool! Do you think we carry extra cartridges just for imbeciles like you?" Standing tall and straight like a towering spruce, he glared at Barker. The scar on his cheek darkened to match the vein that swelled in his forehead. "You are a shame to us, a curse, a jinx! You should have stayed on the farm and left the fighting to men who know what they are doing!"

"Leave him be, Sheahan." Sergeant Marvin stood, opened his cartridge box, and counted out ten dead men. "Here." He thrust them into Barker's hand. "Don't lose these." The sergeant turned and looked at the others, one corner of his moustache twitching. "Anyone else got a few to spare?"

Flanna dug out her cartridge box and pried it open. "I do." Truth be told, she'd willingly give every last cartridge to poor Barker because she didn't plan on shooting anyone. She'd keep her gun loaded for self-defense, and if pressed, she'd shoot at the tops of trees and rocky ledges. But she had no intention of shooting into any Confederate line that might hold Wesley or one of her cousins.

She counted out ten cartridges, then rolled them into Barker's open box. To her surprise, Paddy O'Neil did the same, as did Rufus Crydenwise.

"All right then." The sergeant spoke in a slow drawl, then picked up his rifle. "Let's go. O'Connor, you and that boy of yours bury the fire, then hurry and fall in. We're leaving right quick."

Flanna shoveled sand over the glowing embers of their fire while the others picked up their belongings and moved away. "Are we going to run for it now, Miss Flanna?" Charity whispered, her eyes wide. "We'll be in Virginia as soon as we cross this river. And I've got your other clothes, so you can slip out of that Yankee uniform in the woods. We can find someone to take us back to Charleston—"

"Shh, not now." As she scrubbed the sand from her hands, Flanna glanced up and scanned the milling crowd in the clearing ahead. Apart from the others, near a small thicket, she saw Roger and Alden Haynes, their heads close in conversation.

Flanna's heart contracted in sympathy for both brothers. This was Roger's first foray into the enemy territory, and she knew he had to be anxious. And Alden—though he was cut of military cloth—had never ventured into an enemy's territory or faced an enemy's guns. He would not only have to conduct himself with dignity and valor, he would have to place the men of his regiment above his own needs.

"This would not be a good time, Charity," she whispered, knowing with pulse-pounding certainty that she could not leave Alden Haynes today. "We're still too far north, and the woods might be crawling with men from both armies."

If Charity disagreed, she said nothing. She helped Flanna finish covering the fire and spoke only when Flanna stood to adjust the straps of her heavy knapsack. "I'll pray that God is with us today then. 'Cause the sooner we move south, the sooner we'll get home."

"Right you are." Flanna glanced pointedly at a fellow who had slunk backward toward them, then lowered her voice. "But you can't stay with me while I go out. Servants usually stay in the rear with the supply wagons, so you go with them and wait for me. Don't some of the officers have body servants who'll be waiting there?"

Charity nodded, and in response to the flickering fear in the girl's eyes, Flanna patted her arm. "Don't worry, we'll be fine. This is just a scouting expedition, nothing more."

"Yes ma'am—I mean, yes sir."

"Okay. See you soon." Without a further farewell, Flanna held on to her hat with one hand and ran forward to join her fellows.

⟡

Alden paced on the banks of the Potomac and tried to disguise his annoyance. He should have known that a politician had arranged this reconnaissance, for nothing about the approach to Harrison's Island or the Virginia shore had been well planned. He and his men had crossed the Potomac earlier in the morning, but only four boats—three long, light, flat-bottom bateaux and a small skiff—had been engaged to ferry four regiments and a squadron of cavalry from Harrison's Island to the Virginia landing site. The bateaux carried only thirty men and the skiff only four, ensuring that the river crossing would be difficult and slow. Already the sun stood high in the sky, and the artillery unit had not yet begun to cross.

Alden glanced across the river and moved his gaze through the trees. The area they were supposed to investigate sat high on a ridge known as Ball's Bluff, a hundred-foot-high cliff that could only be reached by walking up a narrow, serpentine path. Colonel Charles Devens, commander of the Fifteenth Massachusetts, had crossed at midnight with three hundred men. After reporting in, he had been ordered to conceal his men and wait for reinforcements. "We'd be happy to support you, Colonel," Alden muttered under his breath, "if we ever get across this cursed river!"

Alden had been ordered to oversee a small detachment to guard Harrison's Island while the other regiments made the crossing from the island to the Virginia shore. The last troops had just been ferried over, and Alden and his men were ready to cross and join their comrades atop the bluff.

"Come on, hurry!" he called, herding the last of his men into a bateau. They piled in, a pair of privates picked up the oars, and Alden climbed in after them, his heart pounding in anticipation. Colonel Baker, with his "First California" regiment—so named to honor Senator Baker when the regiment was in fact the Seventy-first Pennsylvania—had taken the lead position, while Roger and the other Twenty-fifth Massachusetts companies marched somewhere in the center of the line. Alden wasn't sure how his regiment had regrouped, since the men were scattered in the disorganized river crossings.

"Are we going to miss the best of it, Major?"

Alden looked at the man next to him. Idly scraping the callused tip of his forefinger across the blade of his fixed bayonet, the man looked almost relaxed, though a feral light gleamed in the depths of his blue eyes. Alden struggled to recall the man's name. He was from Company M—yes, Sheahan, the one who'd fought in the European war. He was a professional fighter, swarthy and seasoned, and probably a better soldier than most men in the regiment. Alden didn't completely trust him, though, for the man spoke with the broad, slow accent of a Georgia planter.

"The best of what?" Alden reached out to balance himself as the boat wobbled in the swift current. "This is a scouting expedition, not a battle. Word has it that the camp atop this ridge has been abandoned."

"I don't think so." Sheahan's scarred face cracked in a smile. "Can't you feel it? It's in the air; I can smell it. Hunger. Battle lust. This day will end with blood."

"Quiet, Sheahan. You're gloomier than Valentine," Sergeant Marvin called from the front of the boat. Alden caught the sergeant's eye and grimly smiled his thanks. The men didn't need to hear prognostications of doom before their first outing.

Sheahan didn't speak again, but a bright mockery invaded his stare as he studied the bluff above them. Alden turned away from the man and looked out over the rippling waters. As much as he hated to admit it, Sheahan probably knew more about what might happen up there than he did. Alden had studied Napoleonic strategy. He had memorized facts regarding historical battles. He had proved himself as a sharpshooter and swordsman. But he had never smelled powder away from the firing range, never felt blood on his hands.

He didn't particularly want to.

⌘

Flanna caught her breath and forced her heavy feet to climb the steep trail. She had never visited Virginia and had no idea it was so rocky. The path they climbed had not looked so steep from the water, but now every step carried her more upward than forward. The weight of her knapsack threatened to pull her backward into a long line of men who might topple like dominoes if she missed a single step.

The air was cold and damp; the morning's gray promise had been fulfilled with a slow drizzle that soaked her clothing as she walked skyward. Her hands and face felt as cold as glass, but perspiration had dampened her undershirt as her legs worked to push her up the path.

She had congratulated herself on being able to keep up with her companions on the long march to Sugar Loaf Mountain, but she'd never realized that climbing upward would exhaust her strength.

A cold wind blew past her with a soft moaning sound. Her comrades walked without speaking, each man uncomfortably aware that he walked in Johnny Reb's territory. They were moving through Virginia hills, over a Virginia mountain, with red Virginia clay beneath their feet. Flanna heard the far-off knocking of a woodpecker and the liquid duet of a pair of birds from somewhere across the river. But the space along the line of men was quiet, the silence filled with dread.

At last they crested the knoll. Relieved smiles lit the faces of the men who'd arrived the night before. A few of them had stretched out on the grass, their canteens open as they splashed their faces with water. "Quite a climb, eh?" they called to those who came up the narrow trail. "And all for naught. Just look at the encampment we came to spy upon!"

One of the revelers pointed toward the woods, and Flanna saw nothing but a row of pale trees shimmering like silver in the afternoon light. "What?" She looked at the soldier in confusion. "Trees?"

"The idiots who flew over in the spy balloon thought they were a line of tents," the soldier said, grinning. "Guess they never saw a white tree before."

"What's been happening here?" she asked.

The soldier jerked his thumb toward the trees. "The Fifteenth Massachusetts started out for Leesburg as soon as they got up here, but I don't know how far they'll get. Johnny Reb is out there, but we don't know where."

Flanna folded her arms and looked around. She stood in a field of about six acres, open to the cliff and the river on one side, and bordered on three sides by thick trees. Colonel Cogswell and his Fortysecond New York artillery were dragging howitzers up the muddy path, men tugging like pack animals as they struggled to maneuver the heavy guns over the circuitous path.

The soldier grinned when he caught her eye again. "Too steep for the horses. So they make men do what horses cannot."

Flanna opened her mouth, about to reply, but halted when a bugle sounded and Colonel Baker strode into the center of the clearing.

"Fall in, men!" The rich timbre of his orator's voice echoed in the clearing. "To your regiments!"

With a quick farewell to the soldier at her feet, Flanna hastened to join her company. The air of merriment vanished as Baker directed the troops—the Forty-second New York to the left, Wistar's First Cavalry to the fore, Lee's Twentieth Massachusetts to the right, and Farnham's Twenty-fifth Massachusetts to the rear.

"Do they think the Rebs are playing hide and seek?" A young man running to join his regiment turned and tossed the wisecrack over his shoulder. "If they were there, we'd have seen 'em before this."

As if in answer, a volley of rattling shots rent the air. An instant later the young man tumbled to the ground at Flanna's feet, his eyes open to the sky, a dark hole in the center of his forehead. She stifled a scream as she automatically dropped to the ground beside him; then her stomach fell, and the empty place filled with a frightening hollowness.

The trees had disappeared, shrouded in a veil of drifting smoke. They were under attack.

Sixteen

A lden heard the sharp pop of rifle fire and looked up toward the high ridge. He could see nothing from this vantage point, but the men in his boat instinctively clutched their rifles and pointed their bayonets toward the sky.

"Shall we keep rowing, Major?" one of the oarsmen called, his mouth tight and grim.

Alden hesitated, considering his options. If he kept rowing, he could bring these men as reinforcements, but if the commander on the bluff called a retreat, they'd need this pitiful boat to ferry others back to the safety of Harrison's Island.

"Go back!" He shouted the order. "At once, reverse, take us back to the island!"

Sheahan shot him a contemptuous glance—undoubtedly he thought Alden a coward.

Alden waited until the boat shivered and changed direction, then he fixed the swarthy soldier in his sights. "Mr. Sheahan, you and I will remain aboard to row the boat back. We may be needed to help the others retreat."

Sheahan did not answer, but gripped his rifle more tightly as the boat moved into the midst of the river. As a new sort of crashing sound broke above his head, Alden looked up—and what he saw froze his blood. A veritable deluge of men spilled from the crest of the ridge; the rocky brow was blue with retreating men. The ground crumbled beneath their feet, sending them over the edge like a panic-stricken herd. Screams tore the air as men tumbled like rag dolls from the precipice, their bodies fairly bouncing over the ragged, jutting crags.

Alden blinked, quite unable to believe his eyes. Men who ought to have known better were leaping from the cliff with their rifles clutched in their hands. Without removing their heavy knapsacks, they threw themselves into the river and sank beneath the silver water without resurfacing. The side of the mountain, which only a moment before had been green with fern and scrub and seedlings, was wiped smooth as men rained down upon it in mindless retreat.

"Major! The current!"

Horror snaked down Alden's backbone and coiled in his belly as the current caught the boat and pushed it into the hail of men. One poor fellow fell straight on an upward bayonet before Alden could command his men to lower their rifles.

The water churned while a savage and continual thunder rumbled from the ridge. Hands reached out to the boat; desperate men pulled at it from all sides. Alden and his men sprang from the flooded vessel in desperation, joining the scores who struggled, screamed, fought, and gasped in the water. Weak men dragged stronger men under, while the very weakest disappeared without a trace.

Without thinking, Alden slipped out of his knapsack and let it sink to the bottom, then kicked his way toward the Virginia shore. Within moments he stood in knee-deep water, offering help to those who needed it. Most of the men who scrambled toward the bank were from his regiment, but the proud faces he knew were now contorted in the desperate lines of hunted beasts. No trace of the innocent arrogance in which they had marched into Washington remained.

Oh, God, Alden prayed, extending his hand to another gasping soldier, *spare your wrath and have mercy!*

⁂

Flanna felt her heart pounding in time to her running footsteps. She had lain on the ground, frozen with fear, for nearly half an hour, then Colonel Baker came from the right and passed in front of the line of

Union skirmishers. He had opened his mouth to give a command, but a bullet from the trees caught him in the head and he fell, instantly killed.

The line before Flanna shuddered. As the sergeants vainly called for order, the frightened recruits panicked, many of them rushing toward the cliff and the water below. Though the cliff was frightening and the drop formidable, the certainty of the water and the fall seemed preferable to advancing toward whatever forces lay in those trees.

The lines dissolved in mayhem, and finally the order to retreat sounded over the clearing.

All too willing to obey, Flanna turned and ran toward the footpath that had brought her to this deadly place. The trampled ground was slick with rain and the tread of nearly two thousand men, but stout tree trunks and foliage would shield her from sharpshooters' bullets. Others had taken to the path as well, a few of the more frightened ones shedding their heavy knapsacks along the way. Flanna kept hers, for the heavy weight on her back felt like a sheltering hand, guarding her back as it insistently pushed her away from the danger.

She heard shouts and yelling from the distant trees to her right. Looking up, she saw gray forms scurrying from tree trunk to tree trunk. Now the woods were snapping around her, bullets nicking the saplings at her left and making soft thuds in the clay at her feet.

"Two shots per minute," she mumbled, forcing her legs to fly lest she be run over by others on the path. "They can't fire fast enough to get you; they can only fire two shots per minute!"

The thought was utterly insane, of course, for while one individual might only be able to fire two shots per minute, Flanna was certain the entire Rebel army hid in those trees, aiming and firing at leisure as the Yankees ran for the river.

There! Rejoicing at the sight of silver water and blue uniforms, Flanna paused behind a tree at the river's edge. There was no way to cross, for all four boats had vanished, but a line of Union men guarded the landing, their rifles trained on the trees. And there, with his golden hair and clothing dark with water, stood Alden, bawling commands as he organized the men in a defensive position.

She wanted to run forward and kiss him, but she raced along in a zigzag crouch instead, explosively releasing her breath when she reached the safe line of defensive fire. For a moment she stood behind that line, gasping for breath and rejoicing in safety, then a sudden thought struck her—she was no longer entitled to take her womanly ease. She was a soldier in this army, and never had her companions needed her more.

Moving to the end of the line, Flanna knelt on one knee. With trembling fingers she pulled a cartridge from her belt, bit off the plug, and poured the powder down the barrel. The action was nearly second nature now, and the mechanical routine helped calm her nerves. She pushed the bullet in with her thumb, drew her ramrod and shoved the bullet down, then pulled the ramrod out and pulled back the hammer. The men around her shouted, and screams rose from the water, but Flanna blocked the sounds from her mind.

Place a percussion cap on the nib beneath the hammer, Sergeant Marvin's voice echoed in her memory, *then draw a bead on your enemy and fire away.*

Flanna lifted her loaded rifle to her shoulder. If anything came out of those trees, by heaven, she was going to shoot.

A swollen and blood-red sun hung low over Ball's Bluff before the random shots from the trees ceased. As darkness deepened, the Federal army began the work of looking after its wounded and picking up the dead.

Flanna felt numb as she climbed into one of the rescue boats. The battered vessel floated silently over the river, where so many dead lay buried. She looked down and recoiled in horror to see a man she recognized on the shadowed bottom, his foot tangled in the strap of his knapsack, his arms floating upward in an attitude of beseeching.

Flanna clapped her hands over her eyes, trying to banish the sight from her mind and memory.

The brigade established a hasty camp several miles north of the river. The army gathered the wounded, then retreated into Maryland. The wounded—and there were far more than Flanna would have believed possible—rode to camp in the rickety wagons or were dragged in by their comrades. Now they lay on the ground in a straight line, their faces turned toward the starry sky, their voices rising in keening sounds of pain and sorrow, regret and loss.

Dr. Gulick, who had not expected a battle, had left most of his medical supplies in the Maryland camp. He worked now under a hastily constructed lean-to, with a wagon bed as his operating table. Flanna stood in the darkness, numbly watching him saw off injured arms and legs without anesthesia or much regard for his tormented patients.

Flanna had thought her body and mind totally exhausted, but something in her quickened as she watched and listened to the screams of agony. Roger or Alden could be among those bodies on the ground, and she wouldn't amputate a rat's leg without first administering something to kill the pain…

Energized by a steadfast determination, she advanced toward the doctor's tent as a pair of men brought in a soldier who had been wounded in the leg. The man's coat was streaked with blood and red Virginia clay, and his trousers below the knee were slick with blood. Flanna's heart congealed into a small lump of terror when the man lifted his head and shone a smile around the circle. Paddy O'Neil!

Flanna inched closer, insinuating herself between two of the doctor's burly assistants. "Paddy!"

The Irishman turned and grinned at her. "Ah, wee O'Connor, 'tis good to see you. Sure, and didn't I tell you this would be an easy day? You made it out without a scratch, did you now?"

"Aye, Paddy." She gazed at him in despair. She wanted to help; she could certainly do more than Dr. Gulick, but she had no supplies, nothing with which to operate.

At a nod from Gulick, one of the assistants cut at O'Neil's trousers, exposing a shattered leg. The bullet had entered just below the knee.

"I'm sorry, son." Gulick turned to pick up his saw. "It's got to come off. I've got no chloroform or ether, but there's whiskey if you want a minute to liquor up before I start cutting."

Flanna expected loud protestation and tears, but O'Neil only eyed the doctor with a moist glance, then pulled a pistol from inside his coat. Flanna choked back a gasp—she knew Sheahan and a few of the others had pistols, but Paddy had never mentioned his.

With a humorless smile, O'Neil pointed the gun at Gulick and said, "You'll not be cutting me tonight, doctor. The man that puts a hand on me dies."

"What the—" Gulick dropped his saw into the dirt, and a murmur ran through the crowd of observers.

"Soldier,"—Gulick's face went white beneath its sheen of sweat—"you don't understand. Gangrene will set in if I don't do something for you now. You'll not only lose the leg—you'll lose your life."

"If I die," Paddy answered, his voice suddenly husky, "I'll be taking both me legs to the Promised Land, mind you. How else am I going to walk up to the pearly gates?" Holding the gun steady, he shifted his gaze until he caught Flanna's eye. "O'Connor! Tell this fool that he won't be cutting on me with that filthy saw!"

Not knowing what else to do, Flanna stepped forward. "Don't touch him, Doctor. Give him to me, and I'll tend him."

O'Neil grinned good-naturedly at this, but Dr. Gulick's face clouded in anger. "Let the blamed fool keep his leg and die then," he snapped, gesturing to his assistants. "I don't have time to stand here and argue with an idiot. Take him away and bring me the next one!"

Four men stepped forward and lifted O'Neil from the wagon bed, then one of the assistants looked at Flanna. "You really want him?" he asked, one brow lifting. "Where shall they put him?"

Flanna's thoughts raced. "By the water." She pointed toward a small creek at the edge of the camp. "And after they put him down, I'll need blankets, bandages, alcohol—anything you can bring me."

"I can't release those things without the doctor's permission."

Flanna threw back her shoulders and looked the soldier directly in the eye. "Dr. Gulick is a butcher," she said, rancor sharpening her voice. "I can help this man and others, too, but I need supplies. So if you care one whit about these fellows, you'll bring everything you can from that medical wagon."

The startled soldier looked away, then nodded slowly as the others carried O'Neil toward the creek.

An hour later, Flanna had O'Neil's pistol in her belt and his leg in her lap. She had found a few men from her company—William Sheahan, Rufus Crydenwise, and Sergeant Marvin—and they held torches high as she worked on O'Neil's wound. Not one of them questioned her abilities or how she knew what to do, and no one disputed her when she demanded that they heat water in their fry pans so she could clean any instruments applied to the wound. A little flutter of alarm passed through the group when she asked for Sergeant Marvin's hunting knife, but then the men pressed forward in curious delight.

Her patient cared for nothing. O'Neil had passed out long ago, after sipping liberally from Sergeant Marvin's liquor flask.

Jonah Barker, whose only battle injury was a long facial scratch he received crashing into a sapling, served as Flanna's assistant. Without a single hesitation, he used a pair of clean forks to separate the torn flesh of O'Neil's leg while Flanna probed for the bullet with the sergeant's blade. Minié balls, she soon discovered, looked harmless enough when inside a cartridge, but the soft lead slugs expanded in the rifle barrel and produced a devastating wound on impact. The bullet had severely lacerated the flesh of O'Neil's calf before burying itself in the tibia. The bone itself was cracked, but not broken. Paddy was lucky.

"I'm going to have to dig this out." Flanna lifted her head and motioned for Rufus to hold the torch closer. "Steady there, Rufus, or I'll have to lay you out next. You're not a fainter, are you?"

"No—I'm not much of anything." He gave her an abashed smile and moved the light closer.

Flanna glanced down again, then suddenly remembered. "Charity—Charles! Has anyone seen Charles? He's very good at this, and if anyone has seen him—"

"I'll go look." Sergeant Marvin handed his torch to a curious onlooker, then moved away.

Flanna hunkered back down and applied herself to the task at hand. Paddy O'Neil wouldn't be marching for a while, but he'd live to dance another Irish jig.

⚬⚬⚬⚬

"Major Haynes?" The private who stood alone in the semi-darkness wore a worried expression. Alden pulled himself out of the circle of officers and wondered what else could possibly go wrong. He had been awake for more than thirty-six hours, and the companies of the Twenty-fifth Massachusetts were still scattered like sheep. At present more than seven hundred men who'd gone up to Ball's Bluff were missing and presumed captured; more than two hundred others were dead or wounded.

"What is it, Private?" He stared at the soldier, his mind thick with fatigue. "Can't you find your sergeant?"

"I'm in the medical unit, sir, and Dr. Gulick's right busy. But it's not him I've come about. It's—well, it's the other one, sir."

"What other one?" Alden squinted toward the horizon. Dawn was coming up in streaks and slashes over the treetops, but reveille would not sound this morning. The regiment would need a day to rest, and medical supplies, and transportation for the wounded...He forced his thoughts to focus on the young soldier. "You were saying?"

"A private from Company M. He took a patient away, and doctored him down by the water's edge. I don't know much about medicine, sir, but it looked for all the world like he did surgery." The man's brow furrowed. "And it's the strangest thing, sir, but I think he did a sight better than Dr. Gulick. They say he saved one man's leg, and another fellow's arm."

As wide awake as if he'd just drunk a pot of pure, strong coffee, Alden stepped forward and gripped the man's shirt. "Think carefully, Private. This other doctor—does he have red hair? And is he a small man?"

It was an odd question, but the soldier's face melted in relief. "Yes sir! You know him then! So it's all right? I wasn't sure if I should obey, but he told me to get supplies from the medical wagon, so I did. He seemed to know what he was doing."

Alden released the man, touched his hand to his forehead, then took a quick breath of utter astonishment. It was utterly unthinkable, but not impossible. Flanna O'Connor had never been one to back down from her ambitions, and her driving ambition the last time they talked had involved going home...as an army doctor.

"Is that all, sir?" The private wavered before him.

"No." Alden wiped his hand over his face, then exhaled. "Take me to the place where you left this other doctor. I'd like to have a word with him."

Seventeen

The private who served as one of Gulick's assistants pointed toward a small crowd that had gathered by the creek. Alden dismissed the soldier, then walked silently forward, the events of the last twenty-four hours whirling in his mind like bits of glass in a kaleidoscope. What Alden feared couldn't be true—but how else could he explain the uneasiness that gnawed at his gut?

Around the makeshift surgery a crowd of eager soldiers had volunteered their lanterns, mess equipment, and blankets to comfort the wounded. Inside the circle of soldiers, Sergeant Marvin tended a small fire where water boiled in a split canteen. Right next to the fire, the self-appointed doctor knelt next to a man sitting on a canvas tarp. Two other men lay on blankets on the far side of the fire, and, as the private had reported, one had a bandaged leg, the other a bandaged arm. Unlike Gulick's workplace, there were no severed limbs here.

Watching in complete and utter surprise, Alden recognized the peculiar elements of this man's medical practice—the fire, the pans of water, the clean implements. Like Flanna, this doctor worked slowly and steadily, using instruments that had been boiled. Alden narrowed his eyes, staring at the young soldier's slender form. Were that cap to come off the doctor's head, Aden was almost certain he'd find a mass of coppery hair marked by a single white streak.

He crossed his arms, facing his undeniable and dreadful suspicions. Somehow, at some point, could Flanna O'Connor have made her way to Washington and Ball's Bluff? The thought jagged through him like a thunderbolt.

"I'm afraid that's the best I can do," he heard the doctor tell the present patient, a man who'd taken a Minié ball in the arm. "I've cleaned the wound and removed the bullet, but the bone is shattered. You'll need to go to a hospital to have it set."

"They won't take my arm off, will they?" the man asked, his eyes frankly pleading. "I mean, if you can help me keep it—"

"It must remain clean." The doctor gently lowered the man's bandaged limb to his side. "You tell the hospital doctors to change your bandage every day, to wash their hands and their instruments. It's what the Bible commands."

Alden shivered with a vivid recollection. Flanna had said the same thing about the latrines…and so had O'Neil less than a week ago. Could it be possible? Had she been right under Alden's nose for *weeks?*

"Enough of this," he called, his voice grating in the gray gloom. He shouldered his way through the men until he stood before the doctor. Scarcely aware of his own voice, he mumbled, "Are you finished here?"

"Yes." The doctor brushed his hands on his jacket and stood, but did not lift his gaze to meet Alden's. "Please, don't misunderstand, Major, I meant no harm." The voice was dusky, fragile, and shaking. Flanna's voice…or had his wistful imagination deceived him? "But Gulick takes the shortest way when he doesn't have to. These men will need their limbs."

Desperate to settle the question, Alden glanced around at the curious observers. "Get along, all of you," he ordered, placing his hands on his hips. "Take these wounded men back to their companies and make them comfortable. This soldier has finished for the night."

He waited for a moment as the observers hastened to aid the wounded, then the group began to disperse. Alden cleared his throat when a pair of men lingered by the fire. "Is there some problem? I ordered you to get back to your company."

"Private O'Connor is one of our messmates." Alden recognized the man who spoke—William Sheahan, the veteran. "He's plumb tuckered, and I thought I'd show him where we're bedding down."

Alden's last doubts blew away at the mention of the private's name. *O'Connor?* Flanna would have the audacity…and the honesty…to enlist under her family name.

Tamping down his emotions, Alden gestured toward the retreating men. "I need a word with this soldier. Now you two get along with the others. I'll take care of Private O'Connor."

Sheahan's brows drew downward in a frown, but he and his companion left, leaving Alden alone with the little private. He closed his eyes for a moment, wondering if perhaps he'd taken leave of his senses. This Private O'Connor *had* to be Flanna, yet he couldn't bear the thought of her being here, bearing up under all they'd endured in the long march and the tragedy by the river. He'd been heartsick even at the thought of *Roger* climbing up that cliff. If he had known Flanna was among the men, he'd have moved heaven and earth to stop her.

"Major Haynes?" Flanna's voice was lower, huskier than it had been when she spoke to the men. "If I've done wrong, I'll gladly endure the consequences, but if not, let me go. There are others I could help."

Alden rubbed a hand over his face, considering his options. The thought of genteel Flanna O'Connor living among Union troops was so absurd he actually began to laugh, though his emotions stood a good distance away from real humor.

"How long," his voice cracked as he looked at her, "did you think you could get away with it? Didn't you realize you were bound to eventually encounter me or Roger? We would know you, Flanna, no matter what you chose to wear."

She lifted her head then, her green eyes peering out from deep wells like caves of bone. He saw a tiny flicker of shock widen her eyes and panic tighten the corners of her mouth, then her features relaxed. "How did you know?" Her voice was her own again, dusky and cultured.

"It's not every day that a private begins to operate on his fellows—and does well enough that the others actually bring their messmates to him." He folded his arms. "Still, I wasn't certain until I saw this." He nodded toward the pan of water in the fire. "You did the same thing when you operated on Private Fraser."

"Private Fraser?" She looked away toward the rippling creek, her eyes clouding as if with memories. "And how is that soldier faring?"

Alden shook his head. "I'm sorry. According to the captain of Company B, Henry Fraser drowned yesterday."

A change came over Flanna's features, a sudden shock of sick realization. She swayed on her feet, and Alden stepped forward to steady her.

"Oh, did I do wrong?" She sagged against his arms. "I should have said something! That poor girl should never have—I should never have—oh, Alden!"

She lifted her face, and through the dark shadow cast by her soldier's cap he saw tears running down her cheeks.

"There, don't fret." He patted her shoulder as he pulled her close. She had to be utterly exhausted; no wonder she babbled things that made no sense. "You are a brave girl, Flanna, and you've done a great deal of good today."

"I couldn't—do—enough." She gulped in air as her tears began to flow in earnest. "Up there on the hill, I couldn't do anything! Men were dropping around me, and I couldn't shoot, I couldn't help them, I couldn't do anything but run!"

"Hush now." He pulled her into the circle of his arms, and felt strangely comforted as she slipped her arms about his waist and leaned against him. "You're with me now, and I'll take care of you."

She didn't answer, but pressed her face to his chest and wept in long, gulping sobs that shook her shoulders and dampened his coat. Not caring about anything else, Alden held her close and forgot about the war, about his brother, about everything but the courageous woman in his arms.

Time enough to think about those things tomorrow.

⌀

Flanna awoke to a smattering of birdcalls and the sound of men's voices. The sun had risen and life bustled outside the canvas wall.

Awareness hit her like a punch in the stomach and she sat up, realizing that she was not where she ought to be. She was in a large round tent, away from her messmates, and the sun had already risen to the level of the treetops. She'd slept through reveille—and no one had attempted to wake her.

"Morning, Miss Flanna."

She turned. Charity sat cross-legged on a blanket behind her, her dark face wreathed in a smile. "Glad to see you're finally waking up."

Flanna pressed her hand to her head, trying to clear her thoughts. "What—what day is it?"

Charity pushed a cup of coffee toward her mistress. "It's Wednesday, far as I can tell. October 23."

Flanna took the cup. "And we went up the mountain—"

"Two days ago." Charity gave her a compassionate look. "Major Haynes found me and told me he knew what you was trying to do. He put you to bed here in this tent and gave orders that no one was to disturb you, no matter what. He even has a guard standing outside the door."

Flanna sipped the coffee and tried to focus her clouded thoughts. "Did he seem angry?"

Charity snorted softly. "I thought he would be, but no. He told me to let you sleep as long as you wanted, then I was to come and get him so he can talk to you."

"Don't go yet." Flanna lifted her knees and rested an elbow upon them, propping her head on her hand. What would Alden do now? He'd have her put out of the army, of course. He was military through and through, and this deception flew in the face of every last regulation. He'd probably scold her, just to fulfill his duty, and he'd make her put on a dress as soon as he could requisition one. He'd probably forbid her any contact with her messmates, even with O'Neil, who had become as close as a brother.

But he hadn't seemed angry when he confronted her. Flanna didn't know how he found her, but in some way she had felt relieved to enter his arms and surrender the burden she'd been carrying. She wasn't meant to be a soldier. She wasn't meant to doctor men either; so many things had been forced upon her. But the reason for her charade was as valid as ever, and she wouldn't let Alden expose her if it meant she'd have to return to Boston. She'd just have to find a way to convince him to let her go home. But how?

"Charity," she whispered, lowering the cold coffee cup to the ground, "what are we to do now? Virginia is so close—"

"Land's sake, Miss Flanna!" Charity's voice rang with reproach. "You ain't thinking of running away now, are you? Those woods are full of soldiers, and they'll shoot you before you even see them. Don't forget about that line of dead men laid out on the ground the other night. I'm not aiming to be one of them, and neither should you."

"I haven't forgotten." Flanna crossed her arms on her knees and lowered her head, wanting to block out the sights and sounds of the war.

Charity was right; she couldn't run. Her original idea of slipping away into the woods seemed totally foolish, for she had seen how fire could flash from those trees and cut men into pieces. In a blue uniform, even in civilian man's clothes, she wouldn't stand a chance.

"Are you ready for me to fetch the major?"

Flanna nodded without lifting her head. Charity scooted forward and hurried out of the tent.

Flanna looked up and propped her head on her hand. Alden Haynes would have a plan, of course, and she would have no choice but to follow it, at least until she could think of something on her own. But until they returned to camp, she would have to remain in uniform as part of the army.

❧

Half an hour later, Alden Haynes cleared his throat outside the tent, waiting for permission to enter.

A bemused smile crept to Flanna's lips. Here they were, in the midst of the wilderness, yet Alden still insisted on drawing-room manners. "Come in, Major," she called, running her fingers through her hair again. Odd, that she had stopped caring about her appearance until this moment.

He came through the doorway with his hat in his hand, then stopped and looked at her intently. Careful to keep any expression from her face, Flanna met his gaze. She didn't know what he was thinking, but she didn't want to anger him while he held authority over her life. While she'd been waiting it had occurred to her that he might feel personally offended by her deception. And while she doubted that he'd recommend that she be sent to prison, she might very well be confined to house arrest in Washington like the infamous Mrs. Rose Greenhow. If she'd wanted censure and confinement, she would have stayed in Boston.

Alden did not speak for a long moment, and Flanna finally broke the silence. "Should you be in here without a chaperone, Major Haynes? After all, you are an officer, and I an unmarried lady."

"Forgive me for forgetting that you are naturally shy and modest." His words were loaded with ridicule, and he arched a golden eyebrow as he settled onto Charity's blanket. "But surely you can understand my lapse in memory. After all, you have been sleeping among some of the most thoroughly ill-bred men in Massachusetts. You, my own brother's fiancée—"

"Not quite." She lifted a finger to correct him. "We agreed that the engagement would not be discussed until after the war."

"I see."

They exchanged polite smiles, the type that men and women give each other at formal dinners and cotillions.

"In any case, I shall send you home." Alden looked down and absently swiped at a leaf on his coat. "I don't know how you managed to fool everyone, but this army is no place for a woman." His voice gentled as he lifted his gaze. "I'm certain you see that now."

"'Tis no place for anyone." She hesitated, knowing that she was treading on dangerous ground. "You're sending me home—to Charleston?"

"To Boston."

"No." She met his gaze without flinching. "I left Boston, and I won't go back there until I see my father. I'm going home."

Alden closed his eyes, then exhaled an audible breath. "I thought you might be stubborn about this. All right—there may be a way. Once we get to Washington, I'll talk to Colonel Farnham. Perhaps we can arrange a safe passage for you, or an exchange. I understand that others have crossed into enemy territory under a flag of truce."

Flanna paused and considered his suggestion. If they returned to Washington within the week, she might be home by Christmastime…but what sort of Christmas would it be? Her cousins and brother were doubtless encamped in woods like these. Her father would keep the house dark and cold, not willing to enjoy any comfort while his loved ones suffered deprivation. But he'd feel better if she were home. And together they'd wait out the war and pray for the boys.

Flanna lifted her chin and assumed all the dignity she could muster. "If you can do that for me, Major, I promise to be a good soldier until we arrive back in Washington."

Another thought abruptly occurred to her—one that had been pushed aside in her contemplation of the future. "Who have you told?" she asked. "Do my messmates know the truth about me?"

"No." Alden leaned back, a frown puckering the skin between his eyes into fine wrinkles. "I'd be foolish to tell anyone that we were traveling with a young woman. Your messmates wouldn't know how to handle the news. Half would curse you, half would want to manhandle you—though, of course, I'd have to shoot anyone who insulted you with so much as a rude glance."

"I'm sorry. I didn't intend to put you in this difficult position."

"I haven't even told Roger." His voice deepened. "I suppose I ought to tell him, but Roger's such a blustering sort, he'd make a fuss and the word would be out." Flanna looked up, and the wounded look in his eyes pierced her soul. "Forgive me for not telling him. I suppose you're worried and you want very much to see him."

"Was he wounded in the battle?"

"No."

"Then let him be, please." She lowered her eyes from Alden's direct gaze. "I wouldn't hurt Roger for the world, and this—well, he wouldn't be happy about it. You know him better than I do, and I trust your judgment. You are wise not to tell him."

She leaned forward and lifted the edge of the canvas at her side, peering out at the camp. Her messmates would be sitting around the fire swapping stories, each man coping with the recent horror as best he could.

"What did you tell them about me?" She dropped the canvas and turned back to Alden. "My messmates, I mean. Where do they think I've gone?"

Alden rubbed a hand over his chin, and she heard the faint rasp of two days' stubble. "They think you're under guard for stealing medical supplies. They're pretty aggravated with me, for you've become the hero of Company M. But I couldn't let you keep living with them."

"Yes, you can." Flanna broke into an open, honest smile. "Major, you're stuck with me until we get back to Washington."

"But I'm going to send you away. You can't stay in the army."

"Very well, but why should you inconvenience yourself by trying to shelter me? Charity and I were faring quite well within Company M."

He quirked his eyebrow. "You can't mean that you want to go back there. I couldn't allow it. First, I cannot be responsible for your safety among those fellows, and second"—he lowered his voice—"you are a known Confederate sympathizer. I'd be committing treason if I allowed you to return to your company. If anything went wrong, anything at all, they'd say you had something to do with it. They'd be blaming you for the ambush on Ball's Bluff if they knew who you were."

"No one will know." She pasted on a nonchalant smile. "I've maintained my disguise thus far, and I can continue for a few more weeks or months, no matter how long it takes."

"You will not continue one moment longer than necessary." She heard bridled anger in his voice and knew she was testing the limits of his tolerance. "I should tell the colonel now."

"Why? You can't protect me alone, you have too many other responsibilities. And you can't tell everyone I'm confined to the guard-house until we get back to Washington."

"You can't keep up this disguise! If I had seen your face clearly even once, I would have known you were a woman!"

"You have a knack for recognizing women?" Flanna's mouth trembled with the need to smile. "I don't think you do. If you had, you'd have known that Henry Fraser was not from Carolina. Henry was really Henrietta Fraser, a poor country girl desperate enough for bounty money to enlist in the army. She didn't call for me in Boston because I'm from the South—she asked for me because I was a woman!"

Alden's face went blank with shock, and Flanna congratulated herself on a point well made.

"So you see," she glanced out the doorway, "out there I can be a man and no one will know."

Beneath the smooth surface of his handsome face there was a suggestion of movement and flowing, as though a hidden spring was trying to break through. "I would have known you," he whispered, a trace of unguarded tenderness lighting his eyes as he looked at her. "I would know you anywhere."

Flanna halted, caught off guard by his tone. His eyes seemed to hold more than brotherly affection and friendship, but she couldn't consider any further complications now. She had other plans. She had to go home.

"You didn't know me," she said simply. "You saw me by the medicine wagon, you spoke to me, you ordered me to look you in the eye, but you didn't know me."

He shrugged off her objection. "I was distracted."

"Please, Alden." She transferred her gaze to her hands. "I want to see my father. I'll do anything you say once we reach Washington, but please allow me to continue as I was. The men trust me, and I can help them, but only as a man. The sick ones wouldn't let a woman near them."

"You are the Velvet Shadow." His eyes squinted with amusement. "I should have realized. You were tending the men in Company M's sick tent."

"I can keep on helping them if you hold your tongue. Dr. Gulick is inept, and usually too drunk to know what he's doing. Please, Alden, for the sake of my comrades, don't say anything. Not yet."

He stared at her with deadly concentration, his smile fading. "You know they'll drum me out of camp if the colonel finds out I knew the truth."

Flanna flushed in shame. She hadn't wanted to place him at risk; she'd never willingly bring him pain. She opened her mouth to tell him so, but he held up his hand and cut her off.

"After we reach Washington, you can go to the hospital and live with the nurses. We'll find you proper clothing and make arrangements for an exchange with the Rebels."

Flanna nodded humbly. "Thank you, Alden."

He stood and moved forward, but paused to glance over his shoulder. "Go back to your company, but know that I will be watching."

Eighteen

Wednesday, October 23, 1861
My tent of solitude

I will soon rejoin my messmates, but am enjoy-
ing a few moments of rare privacy. As I sit here in
the doorway of my "prison tent," the whole land
seems alive with birdsong and the liquid accompaniment of the small creek. This is a lovely spot. If I
could forget the horror of two days past, I could
almost enjoy this place.

Now that I have heard and smelled and seen
war at close range, I am in no hurry to "see the elephant"—or face battle—again. I was honestly terrified up on that bluff—not so much afraid that I
would be killed or hurt, but that I would quake in
the face of the test and run into the hills. At least,
God be praised, I remained until I heard the order
to retreat.

Later I was afraid that the groans of the
wounded and dying would make me shake so that
my hand could not hold a knife, but God gave me
strength to stand and do my duty.

Now I pray he will give me the strength to see
my purpose through to the end. I came here in

*order to go home to those who love me, and no
matter how dear these men have grown, or how
great their needs, I must remember that this is not
my place, nor my calling.*

*Neither is Alden Haynes mine. As he left my tent
this morning, a letter fell from his pocket, a missive
from Miss Nell Scott. It obviously means a great deal
to him if he has carried it in his coat for these
many days since we left camp. I left the letter on the
ground, certain that someone else will pick it up
and give it to him. I cannot bring myself to do it.*

The men welcomed Flanna back with more enthusiasm than she had imagined possible. Paddy O'Neil sat propped up by the fire, his leg lying flat on the ground, his hands lifting in applause as William Sheahan and Herbert Diltz clapped Flanna on the back and welcomed her to their campfire. Apparently it was dinnertime, for most of the men had opened their haversacks and were nibbling on whatever they could find.

"You're still here?" she asked O'Neil as she sank to a cleared space by the fire.

"Well, naturally, the hospital wagons aren't coming till tomorrow." O'Neil's face flushed in the cooling air. "So we're all goin' back together."

"But you're not with the other wounded," Flanna said, taking the tin cup someone handed her. She sniffed at it in appreciation. Coffee—fragrant and strong.

"Why would he want to be with the other wounded?" Diltz spat into the fire. "That fool Gulick didn't want to see hide nor hair of our friend O'Neil, so he sent him back to us. And now that you're here, O'Connor, we won't have any worries about him at all!"

The men laughed, then Sergeant Marvin spoke. "Where'd you learn doctorin'?" He crossed one arm across his thin chest. "Some of the boys thought it kind of strange that you knew what to do. We know you're educated an' all like that"—he looked at her, his eyes sharp and assessing—"but if you know medicine, why aren't you with the medical detail?"

Flanna took a long swallow of her coffee, then set the cup on the ground. "Truth to tell, my father is a doctor." She stared at her cup. "I learned a lot from watching him. I went to medical school, but the war began before I could establish a practice." She looked up and met the sergeant's speculative stare. "I didn't enlist as a surgeon because I had no experience with men, nor time to gain any."

"I'll be wanting to have you for my doctor always," O'Neil crowed. "And so would any of the boys. 'Tis a terrible fate awaiting any man who throws his body on Gulick's table."

"Oh, you can throw yourself up there," Sheahan added. "Just remember to pack a pistol under your belt before you do!"

The men laughed, then someone told an insulting joke about officers, and they cackled again. Flanna sat silently, sipping her coffee and looking around the circle of sweaty, grimy faces. William Sheahan, Sergeant Marvin, and Albert Valentine were well and accounted for, though Valentine's dark eyes seemed a shade more melancholy, if such a thing was possible. Diltz was too mean to die, and Jonah Barker too clumsy to make a good target. Rufus Crydenwise, who sat by the sergeant's side and stared at the fire, laughed at the free-flowing jokes, though his eyes streamed with tears in a simple overflow of feeling.

Flanna closed her eyes, picturing the absent ones. Matthew Larry lay buried somewhere in Maryland, a victim of disease, and Andrew Green waited back at camp. Philip Hart, the company's prize forager, was missing, either dead or captured, and so was Freddie Smith, the dandy who spent more time polishing his enameled long-legged boots than his gun.

Flanna's thoughts filtered back to the ascent on Ball's Bluff. Freddie Smith had marched in front of her, grumbling occasionally about the red clay and complaining that it wouldn't wash out of his trousers, for red clay stained wool terribly.

"You look tired, O'Connor."

O'Neil's lilting voice brought Flanna out of her reverie, and she shot him a smile across the fire. "Well, naturally, what do you expect? The entire time I was under guard I kept figuring how to get out and rejoin you fellows." She wiped her hand across her nose and grinned around the circle. "I know there's not a one of you who can manage without me."

"Ah, listen to the wee lad!"

"What bunkum!"

"I do believe the little gallnipper's got the big head!"

Flanna ducked as a storm of twigs and leaves rained down on her, then the men sat in companionable silence as they ate. Flanna reached behind her for her own haversack. Expecting to reconnoiter the area and return quickly, they had drawn six days' rations before leaving the camp in Maryland. Today was their sixth day out, and Flanna knew they'd be hungry tomorrow.

She fumbled in the bottom of her bag and felt two squares of hardtack, the flour-and-water cracker that inspired more jokes than the officers. She brought out one square and lifted it to her lips.

"O'Connor, you ain't gonna eat that without blessing it first, are you?" the sergeant called, a mischievous light in his eye.

"Um, well, no." Flanna lowered the biscuit, embarrassed. Throughout their time together she'd been quietly offering a prayer before eating. She was amazed that anyone had noticed.

The sergeant straightened and held up his hand for silence. "Quiet, all! I'm gonna pray now for Dr. O'Connor's dinner."

Flanna smiled, but a flicker of apprehension coursed through her. The sergeant had inadvertently used her real name, and if she became known throughout the regiment as "Dr. O'Connor," Roger or Dr. Gulick might be tempted to investigate the coincidence.

The sergeant bowed his head and spoke in a deep, booming voice:

"Oh, Lord of love,
Look from above, upon us hungry sinners.
Of what we ask 'tis not in vain,

For you love us raw beginners.
What has been done can be done again,
So forgive us when we're slackers.
Please turn our water into wine,
And *bless* and *break* these crackers!"

"Good grief." Flanna shook her head as hysterical mayhem broke out across the circle. O'Neil laughed so hard he absently slapped his bandaged leg. "'Tis quite enough, lads," he pleaded, tears of mirth streaking down his face as it twisted in pain. "Och! Don't make me laugh again."

"Hey, Sergeant!" Jonah Barker called. "This morning I was eating a piece of hardtack and I bit into something soft. Can you guess what it was?"

The circle grew silent. Given Jonah's penchant for ill luck, it could have been anything. "A worm?" Valentine suggested.

Jonah grinned. "No, by golly, it was a tenpenny nail."

The sergeant snorted with the half-choked mirth of a man who seldom laughs, then the circle rocked with the hilarity of revelers. Laughter floated up from Flanna's own throat, and she turned to catch Charity's eye, then paused. Charity had just appeared, for she hadn't been in the circle when Flanna returned. Where had the girl been keeping herself?

Taking advantage of the prevalent lighthearted mood, Rufus Crydenwise pulled a harmonica from his pocket and began to play "Yankee Doodle." The men joined in the song, but Flanna merely listened, not wanting to startle her messmates with her classically trained alto.

The sunset spread itself like a peacock's tail, luminous and brilliant, across the horizon as they lifted their voices in defiance of the darkening sky. But as the stars sprang out in the indigo vault of the heavens, nostalgia and sentiment overruled their bright spirits. The songs slowed and softened, and "John Brown's Body" gave way to "When This Cruel War Is Over" and "The Sweet By and By."

Rufus began to play another song, and Flanna could have fallen over when Herbert Diltz stood to sing it alone, his eyes shining in the firelight, his clear tenor rising to the night sky in unearthly clarity. She had never heard the song before, but it seemed especially poignant now.

"Just before the battle, Mother,
I am thinking most of you.
While upon the field we're watching,
With an enemy in view.
Comrades brave around me lying,
Filled with thoughts of home and God,
For well they know that on the morrow,
Some will sleep beneath the sod.
Farewell, Mother, you may never press me to
   your heart again,
But oh, you'll not forget me, Mother, if I'm listed
   with the slain.
Hear the battle cry of freedom, how it swells
   upon the air,
Oh yes, we'll rally round the standard, or we'll
   perish nobly there."

When Flanna was certain that not a man would be left dry-eyed, Sergeant Marvin stood and placed his hands on his hips. "Well, men, I hate to break up this little soiree, but we've miles to march in the morning. So let's beat the bugle and get some sleep. Maybe we'll be fresher than the others and move into camp first."

Grumbling good-naturedly, the men rose from their places and fumbled among their knapsacks for blankets. Flanna unfurled hers and staked out a place between Charity and Paddy O'Neil. That soldier's eyes were closed when she lay down, but she hoped he'd wake before too long. She wanted to ask him a question.

The night was clear and cool, and Flanna folded her arms tight around her chest and shivered. Silver filigree laced the branches of the oaks, and above them a cloud reached out and grappled with the moon for possession of the night. Beside her, O'Neil snorted and grunted with pain.

"O'Neil?"

"Aye?"

"You awake?"

He let out a long, audible breath. "Am now, sure enough."

"Can I ask you something?"

"Don't I know I couldn't stop you?"

"Right." Flanna paused, listening to the silence as she gathered her thoughts. "Have you ever wanted something really bad, and then when you were about to get it, realized that you didn't want it at all?"

She turned her head, listening, but heard nothing but the lost and lonely cry of an owl in the dark.

"O'Neil?"

"Hush, I'm considerin' the question."

She waited a moment more. Silence, thick as wool, wrapped itself around her, then O'Neil spoke: "I try not to want things," he said, his tone light and playful. "There are only two things to worry about, lad. Either you are well or you are sick, and if you are well, there is nothing to worry about. But if you are sick, there are two things to worry about. Either you will get well, or you will die. If you get well, there is nothing to worry about. But if you die, there are only two things to worry about. Either you will go to heaven or hell. If you go to heaven, there is nothing to worry about. But if you go to hell, you'll be so bloomin' busy shaking hands with friends you won't have time to worry!"

He laughed at his own joke, muffling the sound in his coat so he wouldn't wake the others. Flanna wanted to laugh, but couldn't. First, she could find nothing funny in his devil-may-care attitude about heaven and hell. Second, though she had done her best to set his leg, he was not yet out of danger. A thousand things could happen between here and Maryland, and a thousand other calamities could befall him once he entered the army hospital.

"I'm serious, O'Neil," she whispered. "Stop laughing!"

"I'm serious too." His tone was still playful, but she caught a glimpse of his eyes in the moonlight. They were deadly earnest. "You asked whether I ever wanted anything really bad. Truth to tell, the only thing I'll be wanting now is to be home again with my sweet wife, Maggie. I left her behind with our unborn babe, and I pray every night that I make it home to her."

Flanna curled tighter under her blanket and hugged her knees. She hadn't even known that O'Neil was married. Compared with her wish to go home, his prayer seemed much more urgent.

"Go to sleep, O'Neil," she whispered, just before lowering her head to her knees. "I'll pray for you tonight."

Dawn came reluctantly, glowing sullen through a clouded sky. Alden stopped short in dismay when he thrust his head out of his small tent. The clouds above were swollen and heavy with rain, and if there was anything he dreaded more than a march with wounded, it was a march with wounded in the mud and pouring rain.

He fastened the last button on his uniform, then saluted Colonel Farnham as the regimental commander stepped out of his tent. No bugler would sound reveille this morning, for the woods might be thick with Rebels. Instead, the sergeants and corporals moved quietly through the camp, rousing men with a gentle nudge or tap on the shoulder.

Alden felt a small stirring of guilt as the colonel returned his salute. Every rule and principle of the military demanded that Alden report that he had discovered a woman in the regiment—two, in fact, if Flanna had spoken the truth about Henrietta Fraser. But how could he argue against Flanna's logic and indisputable bravery? She had gone up to Ball's Bluff with her comrades even though her heart probably yearned to embrace the Confederate cause. She had nursed and aided the wounded, going without rest so that others would not suffer. How could Alden betray so strong a heart?

The odds stood in her favor—she might not be discovered at all. After all, she had been unquestioningly accepted by the men of

Company M. And Roger, who was the only other man who might easily recognize her, lived with Company K, which marched at the front of the regiment. The odds of those two encountering each other in the next few days were small indeed, particularly on the long march back to Maryland.

After this march, then, Alden could stand before the colonel and reveal everything. He'd be sure to mention Flanna's heroism and to describe how she'd risked Dr. Gulick's censure to operate on men who would have lost limbs but for her quick thinking and diligence. Would that all the wounded could have felt her ministering hands! Alden suspected she would want to remain with her company until he could arrange for her transport. He was half-inclined to let her remain, but such deception flew in the face of everything military, and he was a general's son, not easily persuaded to bend the rules.

Two voices argued in his head, the cool voice of reason and the ardent voice of passion. Reason wanted her to go back to Boston, or even to Charleston, anywhere safe. Passion wanted to keep her close, to watch her fulfill her dream of medicine, to marvel at her quiet competence and thrill to the sight of those emerald eyes. But they walked a dangerous road, and if something happened to Flanna, Roger would never forgive him…nor would Alden ever forgive himself.

A distant rumble echoed among the hills, and Alden looked up. Soft rain spattered his hair and his cheeks, blurring his sight like tears.

He pulled his cap down until the brim shielded his eyes, then thrust his hands behind his back and walked into the center of the camp, urging the stragglers to make ready for the long march.

Richmond

I have fought against the people of the North
Because I believed they were seeking
To wrest from the South its dearest rights.
But I have never cherished toward them
Bitter or vindictive feelings,
And I have never seen the day
When I did not pray for them.

ROBERT E. LEE, CONFEDERATE GENERAL

Nineteen
ᷓᷓᷓᷓ

Friday, December 20, 1861

A most terrible thing happened today in camp.
We were about our usual business—waiting, waiting, always waiting for Little Mac to do something—when our company was ordered to assist an
artillery corps as they moved cannon. The work
would not have been hard, except for the mud,
which made it difficult for the horses to gain trac-
tion on the roads. In one tragic moment, a horse
slipped, the wagon slid down the hill, and a young
private was pinned beneath the wagon wheel bearing the weight of a cannon so heavy it took four
horses to budge it.

O'Neil saw the accident and called for me, and
as I came forward I stopped in midstep and stared
at the poor soldier. My heart started beating loud
enough to be heard a yard away. The poor boy was
literally cut in two, but the pressure of the wagon
kept him alive, somehow deadening even his pain
and preventing his upper half from knowing that
the lower half had been severed.

I fell to my knees beside the youth, and though
I wore a smile, my heart begged God for some

miracle, some wisdom of words, something to say. For I knew that this man would die as soon as the wagon rolled forward.

The artillery sergeant was anxious to move on, but O'Neil and Sergeant Marvin led him away, pointing out what should have been obvious to any thinking man. Meanwhile, the hapless private held my hand and gave me a trembling smile. "Is it bad?" he asked, his hands still warm with life.

Oh, merciful heaven, what could I give him but the truth? "Yes," I answered, settling to the ground beside him. "If there is anything you want me to write for you, tell me now. I will see that your loved ones receive your final words."

I cannot record all we went through together, Private Albert James and I. Emotions flickered over his face like summer lightning—first anger, then fear, then despair. He raged, then quaked, then wept. Finally, nearly an hour after I sat down, a peace settled on his features and he dictated the following words to his mother in New York: "Dear Mother: I may not again see you, but do not fear for your tired soldier boy. Death has no fears for me. My hope is still firm in Jesus. Meet me and Father in heaven with all my dear friends. I have no special message to send you, but bid you a happy farewell. Your affectionate soldier son, Private Albert James."

As soon as he had finished these words, Private James's hand clenched in mine, and I knew it would be no mercy to keep the wagon upon him. The artillery sergeant blew his whistle, and O'Neil lifted me by the shoulders and pulled me away as the wagon moved.

I did not look back. I knew Private James was no longer among us, but in heaven. I could not help but remember something my father once told me: "When the Jews save one life, it is as if they have saved the whole world, for, like Adam, each man carries the seed of future generations within him." Even so, a world died today when Albert James breathed his last. His children, grandchildren, and great-grandchildren will never be, for they all died in him.

I do not think I shall ever think of death—or life—in the same way again.

While we were away at Ball's Bluff, Andrew Green was allowed a short visit home to recover from his sickness. He greeted us with great joy on our return and later told me that a strange feeling of discontent had overtaken him at home. "I even had an eager longing for hardtack and army rations," he said, his eyes upon the distant horizon. "I found that I no longer had much in common with my old friends. They did not know what it felt like to march in the pelting rain or sleep beneath the stars. They talked of the weather and business and parties while I gazed at them, dumbfounded. In my illness, I had waltzed with death, and now my eyes see everything in a different light. But they would not understand."

I understand what Andrew Green meant. God alone is the sustainer of my soul. He guards my every footstep, the path of everyone who follows him. My life, the lives of my children and grandchildren, are in his hands.

And he has chosen me to heal—a most humbling and heavy responsibility.

The brief, frigid days of December were at their shortest when Alden sent a messenger to summon Private Franklin O'Connor to his tent. As the messenger hurried away, Alden leaned back and pressed his hands to his desk, grateful for the one bit of good news before him. He'd spent every free moment of the last two months trying to find a way to ease Flanna out of her role as Franklin O'Connor and into a more suitable position, and at last an idea had occurred to him.

He'd had every intention of reporting Flanna's situation to Colonel Farnham as soon as they returned to the Maryland camp at the end of October, but there had been so many questions to answer about Ball's Bluff, so many other pressing tasks, that before he knew it, November had come and gone.

Flanna seemed content to wait for him to arrange something. She did not come to see him, though he took great pains to check on her well-being. Whether she pulled guard duty or struggled to dig trenches in the mud, she worked without complaining. And since her fame as a sort of folk healer had spread throughout Company M, men now sought out her tent to discuss their ailments, but always quietly, for no one wanted to arouse Dr. Gulick's ire. Alden even found it amusing that her messmates, particularly the muscular Herbert Diltz, had begun to serve as the Velvet Shadow's bodyguard, not allowing any suspicious characters into the tent unless O'Connor wished it.

"Major Haynes?"

He looked up. Flanna seemed as thin as a wire hanger beneath that tattered uniform, yet her beauty still had the power to cause a crisis in his vocabulary.

He had to clear his throat before he could speak. "Private O'Connor. Thank you for coming."

She nodded, her eyes expectant. "Have you some news for me?"

"Yes." He motioned toward a chair opposite his desk. "Won't you sit while we talk?"

"You wouldn't ask any of the other men to sit, Major." Her tone was faintly accusing.

"I might." His eyes focused on her strong, slim fingers. For the past month those hands had been engaged in the service of his regiment, and he'd give anything to show his gratitude—including the offer he was about to make.

"Please, Flanna." He motioned toward the chair. "Do you know that you have been nominated for a promotion? Sergeant Marvin says he won't rest until you have been named a sergeant, or at least a corporal."

Twin stains of scarlet appeared on her cheeks as she sat down. "Sergeant Marvin is a very generous man."

"I don't think he's that generous. He only rewards those who show great devotion to duty."

She smiled and looked down, waiting. Alden clasped his hands, tightening one upon the other as all his loneliness and confusion welded together in one upsurge of yearning. Had he deliberately procrastinated in sending her away because he enjoyed knowing she was near? Impossible! She was his brother's sweetheart. Alden had no right to feel anything toward her but brotherly affection, but Roger didn't appreciate—wouldn't appreciate—all she'd done in the service of his own regiment.

Alden made an effort to bridle his rebellious thoughts. "Have you seen Roger?"

She jerked her head upward. "Why? Have you told him?"

"No." Alden gave her a dry, one-sided smile. "Not yet, in any case. I didn't think it wise to tell him while you were still with Company M. I'll tell him as soon as we work things out."

She gave a short laugh, touched with embarrassment. "You're right, of course. Roger would have a fit if he knew." A smile trembled over her lips. "So why have you called me here, Major? Surely it was not to tell me that I've earned a promotion."

"No." He gripped the edges of his desk again, then took a deep breath. "I believe I have found a way for you to go home. Last month, Captain Samuel Du Pont attacked Port Royal Sound, just south of Charleston. Within hours, the Confederates abandoned Fort Walker,

Fort Beauregard, and the Sea Islands. Those properties are now firmly in our control, and the army is now registering volunteer nurses and teachers to serve the abandoned slaves."

He studied her face for a moment, analyzing her reaction. "If I can arrange an escort, you and Charity could travel safely to Port Royal. If you press your case with the commander once you arrive there, I'm sure he would be willing to arrange a flag of truce for you to be escorted home."

For a brief moment her face seemed to open, and Alden could see his words take hold. He saw relief, a quick flicker of fear, and something else—regret?

"I could go home?" Her voice was soft with disbelief.

"Yes, Flanna…if that's what you want."

He hadn't meant to add that final condition, but the words fell from his lips before he could stop them. Her eyes opened, met his, and across her pale and beautiful face a dim flush raced like a fever. "If that's what I want?" Uncertainty crept into her expression. "Why wouldn't I want to go home? That's what I've always wanted."

"Of course it is, and now you can go. I was only thinking of Roger."

She looked away with a pained expression. "Are you always so considerate of your brother?"

Embarrassed without knowing why, Alden looked down and shuffled the papers on his desk. "I believe in family. When my father died, I was left to care for Roger and Mother. Part of my responsibility to Roger includes taking care of you."

"So responsible." Her voice was light, mocking. "Very well then. Make whatever arrangements you must. If you can think only of Roger, you must send me away, for Roger would rather swear off politics than allow his intended bride to fraternize with the enlisted men."

Alden ignored her jibe. "You'll have to resume your female attire, of course, but I can procure a tent for you and Charity while you are waiting for an escort. We should have no problem arranging for you to travel as a nurse."

"When would this happen?"

"As soon as possible, I suppose. I'll have a dressmaker make something for you, and then we'll pull you out of Company M and set you up somewhere at the edge of camp—with the officers' wives."

"I understand."

"And I'll tell Roger that you're here. I'm sure you'll want to see him, and I know he'll want to see you." He drew in a deep breath and looked down at his papers. "Trust me. I'll take care of everything."

"I trust you." He felt her glance rest on him briefly, but he didn't meet her gaze. "Thank you very much, Alden." She stood and lingered by his desk for a moment, but when he still didn't meet her gaze, she stepped back and snapped a salute, a sharp movement utterly at odds with the softness he'd heard in her voice.

Alden returned the salute, then swallowed the despair in his throat as he watched her go.

Flanna clenched her hands against the cold as she walked toward her tent. He would send her away, would he? She had been careful not to cause any trouble or bring undue attention to herself. Each man who came to her tent for treatment knew that he could not mention her name outside Company M, for she'd told them all that Dr. Gulick resented her and would certainly have her disciplined if he knew she was practicing medicine without his approval.

"Mr. Franklin!" Charity tore herself away from a small knot of servants and sprinted to intersect Flanna's path. "What in the world is wrong with you? You look as mad as a wet tomcat!"

"He's sending us away." Her temper flaring, Flanna stopped in the road and crossed her arms. "Alden Haynes wants me to go to Port Royal as a nurse and beg the commander there to send us to Charleston."

Charity's lips puckered into a rosette, then unpuckered enough to ask, "But—isn't that what you wanted to do?"

Flanna bit down on her lip, irritated at the confused current moving through her. "Of course it is. I want to go home."

"So what's the problem?"

"It's—" Flanna hesitated, her thoughts whirling as her new identity collided with the life she'd known before. "It's not the leaving that pains me. It's that he's acting so smug about it. And he keeps insisting that he's doing it all for Roger's sake!"

Charity shot her a penetrating look. "Miss Flanna," she said, lowering her voice, "your trouble is that your head's in one place and your heart's in another. You're gonna have to decide which one you're gonna follow to get yourself out of this mess."

As Flanna stared at her in astonishment, Charity lifted her head and walked back to the boisterous circle of servants. Flanna's anger deflated as she watched her go, and ruefully she accepted the terrible truth. Charity was right.

⁓⁓

The shadows under the wagons were already cold and blue when Roger burst into the circle around the officer's campfire. "Alden! I received your message! What's happened?"

Alden stood and put out his hand. "Come with me, brother. Let's talk in my tent."

Roger followed Alden into his tent, then folded into the empty chair before Alden's small desk. "What is the dire emergency?" he asked, lines of concentration deepening along his brows and under his eyes. "Has something happened to Mother?"

Alden stood motionless behind the desk. "Mother's fine. The news concerns Flanna."

"Is she all right? Has there been an accident?"

"She's here, Roger. In camp."

Roger's expression of concern vanished, wiped away by astonishment. "Flanna's here?" He grinned and gave Alden a look of jaunty superiority. "What a clever girl! That's marvelous! How'd she ever get permission to visit me?"

Alden moved to the tin coffeepot and poured two cups. "Take this," he said, handing one of the mugs to Roger. "Drink up. You may find the story a little difficult to believe."

"Forget the story. Where is she? I'm dying to see her!" Roger crossed his legs and lifted a brow. "Won't the other fellows be jealous when I bring her 'round?"

Alden sank into his chair, then ran his finger over the rim of his coffee cup as he searched for words. He'd been dreading this moment for weeks. "I don't think you'll want to show her around…yet." He set the cup on his desk and stared at it, avoiding Roger's eyes. "She never went to New York, you see. She's been with our regiment since we left Boston."

Roger's jaw dropped. "The devil you say!"

Alden's mouth twisted in bitter amusement. "I was surprised too. Apparently she enlisted the week before we left. She is a private in Company M, and every man there knows her as Franklin O'Connor— a young Irishman with a talent for the medical arts."

Roger clamped his jaw tight and stared at the ground.

"I wouldn't have known her myself," Alden went on, choosing his words with care, "but after Ball's Bluff I heard about a plucky private who insisted upon treating the hothead who had pointed a pistol at Dr. Gulick. When I went to check out the report, I saw this private operating…and then I knew."

"You found Flanna at Ball's Bluff." Roger stared at Alden with absolutely no expression on his face. "And you did not tell me?"

"I wanted to tell you. I confronted her, and she confessed that she'd done it all in order to go south and to reach Charleston. Charity is with her, so she's not alone."

"You didn't tell me." Roger's mouth twisted as he slammed his hand onto the desk. "By all that's holy, Alden, why didn't you say something?"

"How could I tell you?" Alden fired back, his tone loaded with rebuke. "I knew you'd react like this! I knew you'd be angry, and at the time there was nothing I could do but bring Flanna back with us. If I exposed her, I'd not only be ridding our regiment of the best doctor we've ever had, but I'd be subjecting her to a trial—possibly even prison."

"You should have told me!"

"I couldn't trust you!" Alden frowned in exasperation. "Good heavens, Roger, you are a good leader, but you often speak without thinking! And I couldn't risk exposing Flanna until I found an answer to her predicament. Do you know what they'd have done with her at Ball's Bluff if I had told the colonel that I'd found a Confederate woman in the ranks? We were destroyed, and she would have been the most convenient scapegoat. They might have accused her of being a spy—they might have *executed* her!"

A cold, congested expression settled on Roger's face; his hands began to rub at the knees of his trousers.

"I've just spoken to her," Alden went on, hoping that his words were reaching some still-receptive part of Roger's brain. "And she's willing to give up her disguise and leave the army. We will say nothing of what happened or how she came to be here. Soon I'll speak to the colonel about a talented and devoted nurse, Miss Flanna O'Connor, and recommend that she be transported to Port Royal." A reluctant grin tugged at his mouth. "Knowing Flanna as I do, I imagine she'll convince the fort commander that his best interests lie in arranging a flag of truce so she can go home to Charleston as soon as possible."

His smile faded when he looked up; Roger's implacable expression was unnerving. "Don't you see? This is for the best. After the war, you can go to Charleston and make your peace with her. She'll spend this uncertain time in the bosom of her family—where she wants to be. If you love her, surely you want her to be happy!"

Roger's face was a marble effigy of contempt. "You should have told me," he repeated. "You are my brother, and she is the woman I plan to marry. You should have come to me immediately so I could force her to return to Boston."

Alden sighed and drummed his fingers on the desk. Lately he'd heard reports of Lincoln's frustration with General McClellan's stubborn refusal to move forward, but McClellan could not possibly be as stubborn as Roger Winfield Haynes.

"Perhaps I should have told you," he admitted, "but that is over and done. Why don't you concentrate now on Flanna's happiness?"

"I *am* thinking of her happiness!" Sudden anger lit Roger's eyes. "The foolish girl should have married me in Boston. She'd be safe with Mother, not living here in the mud and dust—" His eyes suddenly blazed into Alden's with an extraordinary expression of alarm. "You say she's been living with *men?* I swan, Alden! Men, sleeping around my sweet Flanna!"

"Your sweet Flanna has managed very well. You need not fear for her virtue or her reputation, for no one knows who she really is." Alden hesitated to voice his next thoughts, but a mocking voice inside insisted upon an answer. "Roger, do you truly love her?"

Roger's blue eyes glared into his, shooting sparks in all directions. "Love her? I adore her!" He stood, stiff dignity marking every line of his face. "How can you ask such a question? I intend to honor her, to respect her, to keep her in comfort and ease, to show her the world and let the world revere her as I do—"

"Yes, of course," Alden interrupted, "but what of her dreams? She is far more than a pretty porcelain doll, you know."

He paused as he heard the soft puff of footsteps outside, and a moment later a civilian's figure appeared in the tent opening. The man wore a dapper dark suit, and a pair of spectacles bridged his round face. "Major Haynes? I am Thomas Beckman. The guard told me I would find you here."

"Yes, Mr. Beckman, come in. I've been expecting you." Alden stood and welcomed the man with a handshake. "Mr. Beckman, this is my brother, Captain Roger Haynes of Company K. Roger, Mr. Beckman is a tailor and dressmaker."

Offering the merchant a distracted nod, Roger shook his hand.

Alden looked at Roger as he sat on the edge of his desk. "Mr. Beckman is here on behalf of our friend, Miss O'Connor. You will recall that the lady needs some traveling clothes."

Roger drew his lips into a tight smile. "Yes, of course. Very good."

"I brought some samples," Mr. Beckman said, opening a book of fabric swatches. "I have several gowns already made, they adjust to fit with ties and laces. But you did not specify what sort of apparel the lady will be needing." He lowered his chin and peered out across the top of his glasses. "Perhaps the lady is nearby? She could choose her own—"

"No," Alden interrupted. Crossing one arm over his chest, he lifted a finger to his lips and smiled. "The lady is indisposed at the moment and unable to receive visitors. She has every confidence in me."

Roger gave Alden a quick, denying glance. "In me, you mean." He bowed slightly to Mr. Beckman. "Miss O'Connor is my fiancée. I believe I know her tastes better than any man alive."

"Very well." Mr. Beckman turned several pages of a catalog, pointing to several workday fabrics. "The ladies do seem to like these plaids for traveling. The material is sturdy and holds up well even in damp weather."

"That looks very nice." Alden pointed to a green plaid. The color would complement Flanna's eyes, and it matched a perky bonnet she'd worn in Boston.

"Plaid!" Roger's voice brimmed with disbelief. "You'd dress my betrothed in common plaid?" He turned to the merchant and grimaced in good humor. "My brother is a soldier, sir. He knows nothing of the feminine nature or fashion. Please, show me your finer fabrics."

"Of course, sir." A wide smile gathered up the wrinkles by the merchant's full mouth as he turned to swatches of satin and velvet. "I can see that you are a man of exacting taste, and these are our finest materials. These dresses are tailored by hand, of course, but the extra expense is a small price to pay for quality."

"This is more like it." Roger stared thoughtfully at the fabrics for a moment, then ran his fingertips over a rich red velvet. "That would be wonderful for my Flanna. She has red hair, you see, lustrous lengths of it. A gown of this material would make her shine like a fair ruby in a setting of pure gold."

Alden rubbed his temple, not daring to mention that Flanna's lustrous lengths were long gone.

"Very good, sir." Mr. Beckman snapped the book shut. "Any particular style? A ball gown, perhaps?"

"She needs traveling dresses," Alden interrupted, his voice flat. "I doubt she'll be attending any balls in the midst of the war."

Mr. Beckman laughed. "Oh, but the Washington social season is in full swing! The ladies are so patriotic, they struggle to outdo each other. We've sold more red, white, and blue gowns and bonnets in the past month than in the last ten years."

"Make her a dress of the red velvet." Roger hooked his thumbs into his belt. "Spare no expense, but you'd better do as my brother suggests and make it fit for traveling. Oh, and outfit the gown with"— he waved his hand—"whatever she needs."

"Ah." Mr. Beckman's brow lifted in understanding. "She will need a full set of…inexpressibles?"

"Exactly." Roger ignored Alden's glare. "Imagine that you are providing for a lady who needs everything. She is a medium-sized woman, about"—he held his hand out to his shoulder—"this tall. And slender."

"Sounds like the size of my Marianna."

"You'd better make her two dresses," Alden said. His wages had been sitting at the bottom of his bag for months, waiting to be spent. "Make the second one out of the green plaid."

The merchant nodded. "Very well, gentleman, I'll have the garments for you in two days."

"Tomorrow, please," Alden said, shaking the man's hand in farewell. "I'll reward you generously for a speedy delivery."

"Of course, sir. Thank you very much." The merchant smiled again, then backed out of the tent, clutching his catalog to his side.

Roger ran his hand absently through his hair, then dropped his hand to his belt and turned to Alden. "One thing perplexes me, brother. I can almost understand why you feared for Flanna's safety and didn't tell me that she was here." His eyes flared, hot with resentment. "But since when have you become so concerned about her welfare that you'd part with your hard-earned wages?"

Alden shrugged and moved to the security of his desk. "She will be my sister, won't she? Since I don't smoke or drink, there's little else for me to spend my wages on."

"I can take care of her." Roger pressed his hands to the desk, then leaned toward Alden until their eyes were only inches apart. "She's my betrothed."

Alden crossed his arms and calmly met his brother's gaze. "I haven't forgotten."

"See that you don't." Roger straightened and tugged down the hem of his coat. "And since you don't think I can hold my tongue or cool my ardor, heaven forbid that I should spoil her little game. I believe I'll refrain from visiting her until she's decently dressed and ready to resume her rightful role."

Alden gave him a brittle smile. "See that you do."

Twenty

Saturday, 8 P.M., December 21

Charity did not show up for dinner this afternoon. I suppose it is just as well, for after my discussion with Major Haynes I was hungry enough to eat
a rider off his horse and snap at the stirrups. I'm
afraid I ate a full day's ration, and can only hope
that Charity's new friends, whoever they are, are
sharing their rations as liberally as I usually do.

A number of the officers have colored servants
to handle the laundry and their cooking. Charity
became acquainted with several of them while we
were fighting at Ball's Bluff, and she seems to prefer
their company to that of my messmates. After our
conversation tonight, I can understand why.

One of the men asked about "Charles," and I
gruffly replied that he was a free colored and could
go where he pleased. Whereupon Diltz remarked
that he thought nothing at all of darkies; he'd as
soon shoot them as free them.

I was surprised and said so. After all, wasn't
that why these men joined the army? After Fort
Sumter, the Boston churches had spoken of nothing
but the evils of slavery. But Diltz only looked at me

and laughed. "The runaway slaves that come over the border think freedom means freedom from work," he said, his voice drawing the others to the fire like fascinated moths. "The blacks I've seen in camp are nothing but nuisances. They have been dependents and treated like children for so long that they are children, nothing else."

"I don't have nothin' against the coloreds," Sergeant Marvin said, and we all fell silent to listen, for rarely does he offer an opinion. "But I don't want to lose my job to one. I hear Old Abe intends to send them off and colonize them in Haiti or Africa. If our bein' here frees the coloreds, fine, but I am not in favor of freeing them and leaving them to mingle among us. You can be sure the government is already making preparations to send them away."

Andrew Green put down his notebook and pen and looked up at the sergeant, his eyes shining with wetness. "I used to feel the same way, Sergeant," said he, "until one afternoon when I met an old black man at the train station. He was born in America, just like me, but he was scarred from head to foot where he had been whipped. He showed me his back—'twas a great solid mass of ridges from his shoulders to his hips. That beat all the sermons I ever heard. I'm here because my country called me. If my dyin' helps preserve the Union, I'll meet death without complaint. But if my dyin' helps stop that kind of evil, I'll go joyfully to meet death, honored to do my part so that others can live free."

Andrew's speech said it all for me. Though Diltz, Valentine, and O'Neil continued to argue about the vices and virtues of the black race, I thought of the slaves on Wesley's plantation. Were they still

*there? Or had they fled toward the seashore in
hopes of meeting the Federals at Port Royal?*

*O'Neil told me that Abe Lincoln would let the
South keep its slaves if peace could be made and the
Union preserved. Already Lincoln has promised the
Union's Border States that they can preserve their
system of slavery.*

*But I believe we held the wolf by the ears for too
long—and now he has escaped our grasp. May God's
will be done.*

Flanna closed her journal and crossed her legs, then pulled a slab
of salt pork from her haversack. Scattered fires dotted the darkness
beyond Company M's street, and she stared absently at them, a confused haze of feelings dulling her senses as she nibbled on the meat.

"O'Connor! Didn't you hear me, lad?" Flanna jerked her head
around. Paddy O'Neil was squatting behind her, his hand extended.
"I asked you to pass me the coffeepot."

"Sorry." She pulled the pot from its bed of coals and carefully
passed it to Paddy, then returned to her scant supper. A high, melodic
tenor floated over from the next campfire, and Flanna relaxed as she
listened to the music.

She was going to miss all this—the music, the men, even the mayhem. As soon as she donned a dress, she would be forced to surrender
her role as their friend, messmate, and doctor. For though none of them
hesitated now to come to her with medical problems or for a dose of
calomel to cure the Maryland quickstep, she knew none of them would
feel at ease in her presence once she revealed that she was a woman.

Roger—who surely knew her secret by now—would insist that she
surrender her disguise immediately. And though Alden had demonstrated
remarkable restraint thus far, he would support Roger. Both brothers
would ask her to give up all she had gained as a soldier of Company M.

But what else could she do? If she wanted to go home, common sense told her that she'd have to agree to Alden's plan. Franklin

O'Connor would have to walk into a tent and vanish so Miss Flanna O'Connor, the nurse, could take her place. Soon she'd be wearing a corset again, and pantalets, and a hoop skirt so wide that no man could come within three feet of her without tilting the birdcage beneath her skirt and risking an immodest glimpse of the lace at her ankles.

She reached for her bayonet, stuck it through the meaty middle of her salt pork, then held it over the fire. Rufus Crydenwise squatted next to her, his arms on his knees.

"O'Connor," he said, a slow flush creeping up from the flesh at his neck, "can I ask you somethin'?"

"Ask away."

Rufus squirmed in his jacket, then leaned toward her, lowering his voice. "I think I got lice. I'm itching something fierce, and at night I can feel things crawling over my skin."

Flanna crinkled her nose and pulled her bayonet from the fire. "When's the last time you bathed?"

The boy—though he was twenty-two, Flanna couldn't help but think of Rufus as a helpless boy—shrugged and ran his fingers through his hair. Flanna lifted her chin, then made a face. Even in the fire-tinted darkness she could see the tiny white specks sprinkled throughout his brown curls.

"Oh, Rufus!" She dropped her bayonet and scrambled backward. "You're lousy! Ugh!"

His face went as scarlet as a ruptured artery. "What can I do about it?"

Kneeling a safe distance away, Flanna exhaled loudly and tried to think. "First, ask Diltz to cut your hair real short—he's handy with a blade. Second, soak a cloth in kerosene, then wrap your head in it. Wear it for twenty-four hours, and you'll kill any remaining nits. Third, go down to the river and take a bath, or better yet, get a pass and go to a bathhouse in town."

"But what about now?" He ran his hand over his jacket, his fingers busily scratching at the wool coat.

"Take off all the clothes you can," Flanna said, one corner of her mouth twisting. "And we'll see if we can find a big enough pot to boil 'em in. Hot water ought to kill the little buggers."

"Is that why you wash your hands so much?" Andrew Green looked up from the guitar he'd been picking. "Are you afraid of lice?"

"No more than anything else." Flanna picked up her bayonet, brushed the dirt from the meat, then popped the last bite into her mouth. She chewed, ignoring the gritty texture of sand on her teeth, and smiled at Green. "Didn't your mama ever tell you to wash your hands before supper?"

She looked around for Charity, hoping to ask her to scout out a large pot, but she was nowhere in sight. She'd been leaving Flanna alone a lot, but Flanna hated to rebuke her. Life in the camp had been slow. Aside from morning drill (McClellan was a drilling fanatic), there was not much work to do. So they sat around playing cards, swapping stories, and complaining about everything from the food to the officers. The sergeant, Diltz, and Sheahan played poker nearly every afternoon, and Flanna joked that they won the same ten dollars from each other over and over again.

She glanced back at Rufus, who was still scratching. "If we can't find a pot, lad, you find yourself a nice busy anthill and leave your clothes there overnight. The ants will eat the lice right up."

"Just don't forget to brush the ants away in the morning," Sheahan called. "Or the ants might eat *you* up!"

"O'Connor!" Flanna looked up at the sound of Paddy O'Neil's voice and saw that he had moved inside the tent. He lay on his blanket, his wounded leg stretched out before him. Having avoided the Union hospital altogether, O'Neil seemed well and hearty, with nothing but a slight limp to show that he'd been hit. Flanna insisted that he limped now only when he wanted to be excused from drill.

"What is it?" she called, ducking beneath the canvas tent flap. In the candlelight, she saw that Paddy held a letter in his hand. From the worried look on his face she feared he'd received bad news.

"My sweet Maggie has me worried." O'Neil held the letter up and began to read in a falsetto voice. "Och, my darling, our babe is growin' so! Just last night he kicked me so hard I couldn't sleep."

O'Neil lowered the letter. "Is that normal, for the babe to be hurtin' her?" A glazed look of despair began to spread over his face. "'Cause I can't abide the thought that the wee one is hurting sweet Maggie. I shudder to think she's in pain on my account."

"You fine eejit, don't you know that all babies kick their mothers?" Sinking to the ground next to Paddy, Flanna wrapped her arms around her bent knees and decided it would be best not to broach the subject of labor pains. "And what are you going to do about it, you bein' here and Maggie at home? You'll trust the good Lord to take care of her, and stop filling your mind with these foolish worries."

O'Neil scowled at her, his ruddy brows knitting together. "I'll not have you make fun of me, you wee stripling! Besides"—he smiled as his flesh colored—"what do I know about having babies? And for that matter, what would you be knowing about it?"

"Naturally, no more than you." Flanna gave him a slow smile, then stretched out on the ground, not caring that her hair brushed the dirt, that the boy outside had lice, that the man next to her smelled of sweat and grime. Things that would have sent her reeling across the room six months ago now mattered not at all, and all the silly rules and conventions she'd held so close to her heart seemed about as pointless as scratching a wooden leg. But if Roger had his way, she'd soon be a lady again, wrapped in corsets and silk and a touch-me-not air of isolation.

She folded her hands across her chest and closed her eyes, sighing loudly.

"Tired, O'Connor?" O'Neil asked. "If it's rest you're wanting, I could sit outside to read."

"Stay where you are, O'Neil," she answered, not opening her eyes. "Right now I could sleep in the middle of a stampede if I wanted to."

She heard him chuckle, then he fell silent, doubtless rereading his letter. Flanna did want quiet and time alone, but she wanted to think, not to sleep. Over the course of the afternoon, one fact had crystallized and become abundantly clear—she did not want to leave her messmates. Alden might get her a dress, a new identity, and a tent of her own, but when Franklin O'Connor disappeared, so would her easy and open relationship with these men. And until it was time to go home, they were the only family she had.

She rolled onto her side, pillowing her head on her arm, and silently swiped at the tear that rolled from her eye. How foolish she'd been at fifteen, thinking herself too ladylike to play with Wesley and her cousins! She had thought the world revolved around beaux and balls until Mammy died. In that hour, nothing mattered but medicine, and though everyone said Flanna could charm the red off an apple, she couldn't stop Mammy's lifeblood from draining away. "Go with God," Mammy had whispered when she realized the end was near. "Do your papa proud, honey. And remember that your Mammy will be waiting for you just inside those pearly gates."

Flanna let the words wash through her, shivering her skin like the touch of a gentle ghost. The medicine was important. Not the dresses and proprieties, but the men and their care.

Roger and Alden would just have to understand.

༺❦༻

Charity pushed Beau's hand away from her waist, then clapped a hand over her mouth to silence her giggles. "You is bad, Beau!" She stepped back into the shadows near the cargo wagons, knowing he would follow. They were completely alone here, for the soldiers had all gone to their tents and the other servants had bedded down. Like whites in society everywhere, the army didn't care what the servants did after hours.

"You come here, woman." Beau's arm went around her waist and drew her back into the moonlight, and Charity caught her breath at the strength in his arms. Seemingly oblivious to the cold, he wore a common shirt with the sleeves rolled up to his elbows. The skin of his hard arms gleamed like polished ebony in the silver light. "Is you gonna speak to your mistress or not?"

"I will." Lost in the dark power of his gaze, Charity whispered the words. "But I can't just yet, Beau. I've got to know—"

"What?" His silky voice held a challenge.

"I've got to know if you really mean it."

His hand tightened upon her waist, and for one dizzying minute Charity thought he could snap her in half if he wanted to. Beau was stronger than any man she'd ever known, snake-muscled from long hours on the plantation from which he'd escaped. He worked now for Colonel Farnham, but he'd assured Charity that he'd leave everything and take her away from the army if she'd just agree to go.

"I don't lie, woman. I said I'd marry you, and I will, as soon as you want. But you gots to come away from this place first. Don't neither of us belong in the middle of a war."

"Oh, Beau." Charity threw her arms around those massive shoulders and clung tightly for a moment, closing her eyes against her fears. She'd been meeting Beau for weeks now, amazed at his persistence and his gentle courtship, but even the most patient men had a limit to their endurance.

"Beau, it's not that I don't love you—I do. It's just that I can't leave Miss Flanna now. She's still far from home, and she's not as strong as she thinks she is."

"Charity." Beau's wide hand cradled her head against his chest. "Girl, when are you gonna break free? I's ready to go—you just say the word."

Charity lifted her head and met his gaze. "I've got to give her a little more time, Beau. Mister Alden knows her secret, so it won't be long now. If I can just get her closer to home, I'll feel better about leavin'."

Beau sighed in frustration, but his arms drew her closer. "You say the word, honey, and we're gonna go. You just let me know when."

Secure in the strength of his embrace, Charity nodded.

~ প ~

The next afternoon, after Sunday services, Flanna thanked the drummer boy who'd been sent to fetch her, then stepped inside Alden's tent.

His eyes snapped at the sight of her, but then he turned and abruptly gestured toward a soldier sitting with his back to Flanna.

"Private O'Connor." Alden's voice sounded stilted and unnatural. "There is someone here to see you."

She closed her eyes, knowing without being told that Roger sat in the chair before her. She heard a creaking sound as he turned, then the sharp intake of his breath: "By all that's holy, Flanna! What have you done?"

"Hello, Roger." She opened her eyes and forced a smile. "It is good to see you."

"Flanna!" She felt a small, fierce surge of satisfaction under her annoyance as his eyes bulged and his face went white. Apparently the diplomatic politician was not *completely* unflappable.

She looked at Alden. "I thought you'd tell him."

Alden gave her a bland smile. "I did."

Roger leaned forward, his hands moving in wide, meaningless circles. "Of course he told me, but I never dreamed—I mean I couldn't imagine—" He peered at her, his eyes narrowing. "Sakes alive! You've cut off all your hair!"

"It was necessary," Flanna said, running her hand over her bare neck. Recoiling from Roger's hot eyes, she looked at Alden and tried on a smile that felt a size too small. "I'm glad you sent for me. I have something to tell you."

"And we have something for you." Gesturing broadly with his right arm, Alden indicated two large boxes on his desk.

"Those are for me?" she asked, perplexed.

"Yes." Roger rose from his chair and scooped the first box into his arms, then bowed and offered it to Flanna. "My dear, I know you must have a very good reason for this charade, but I am happy to tell you that it is finished. Please." He waited until she took the box, then thrust his hands behind his back and grinned in pleasure. "Open it. I picked out the fabric just for you."

"Oh dear." Suspecting what lay uppermost in both brothers' minds, Flanna returned the box to the desk and lifted the lid. Beneath a layer of delicate tissue paper she found a showy velvet gown, complete with silk flowers at the bodice and lace at the hem. She took it from the box, straining to lift the yards and yards of heavy fabric, and discovered a corset, pantalets, chemise, and steel-banded hoop skirt at the bottom of the box.

She looked at Alden and arched her brow. "Has Mrs. Lincoln invited me for tea?"

Alden's mouth twitched with amusement as Roger leapt to the extravagant gown's defense. "Flanna, darling, it will suit you so well! You are a beautiful woman, and you should dress like one. When you walk through the camp in this, every man will smile at you. Even the general will be impressed."

"Impressed by you." Flanna dropped the gown back into the box. "Roger, dear, I have no intention of wearing such a gaudy gown, not here, and not anytime soon."

"Flanna." Roger stepped forward and pressed his hands to her shoulders. "Darling, you've been through a very difficult experience. I wish you had confided in me, but we'll talk about those regrets another day. Right now it is in my power to help you. You will be my wife as soon as we're finished here, and it's time you began to act like the lady you are. Take the dress, and let Alden escort you to the tent he's prepared. As soon as he can arrange for your transfer to Port Royal, he will. But until then let me behold the lovely Flanna I adore!"

Flanna stared past Roger to Alden, but he wasn't watching her. He was staring instead at the second box, the customary expression of good humor missing from the curve of his mouth.

"Alden," Flanna pleaded, "help me!"

He shot her a half-embarrassed look as he tapped on the lid of the other box. "This might be better," he said, his voice sounding tired.

Sighing in exasperation, she opened the second box. It contained another dress, but a far more suitable one of sturdy cotton fabric. The full pleated skirt could be worn without a stiffening hoop, and the material was green plaid. Her favorite color.

"It is better," she said softly, not wanting to hurt either man's feelings. What did men know of women's things? "When the time comes to leave, I'll wear the green dress and take the red gown with me. And I thank you both for your concern."

"What do you mean, when the time comes?" Roger wore a prim and forbidding expression. "Flanna, we had these dresses prepared so you can wear them now. Alden has a tent set up—"

"So you've said." Flanna threw up her hands, not knowing how to explain. "Gentlemen, I appreciate all you've done for me, I really do. But I am quite comfortable with my messmates, and they are at ease with me."

"What are you saying?" Roger asked, each word a splinter of ice.

Flanna squared her shoulders. "I want to stay with my company until I'm allowed to go south. Then I'll go quietly, but I don't want to walk around this camp as a woman. My messmates will be embarrassed to think they've spoken their thoughts so freely."

"*They'll* be embarrassed?" Roger's face went pale, with a deep red patch over his angular cheekbones, as though she had slapped him hard on both cheeks. "Flanna, who cares about those men? I care about *you* and the reputation you are so thoughtlessly trashing!"

Flanna swallowed hard and tried not to reveal her rising anger. "I care about those men," she said, nearly choking on her own words. "And I assure you that Flanna O'Connor's reputation is quite safe. But what does one girl's reputation matter now? When men are dying, Roger, when drunken doctors are cutting off the legs of young boys, and hundreds are dying of typhoid, who cares anything about a reputation?"

"I care." Roger spoke in a low voice, taut with anger. "And when this war is over, things will return to the way they were. I'll still be running for office, and you'll still be my fiancée. And then you will care very much, Flanna. And you'll be sorry that you did not heed my words."

"But the war is not over." Her heart hammered; her breathing came in ragged gulps. "And until I can leave this camp, until the day

I can climb into a buggy and know that I am on my way home, I will remain with my men. They trust me—and I trust them."

Roger did not answer. He stood there, tall and angry, as defiance poured hotly from his dark eyes. "Till the war is over then," he said, his voice inflamed and belligerent. "I'll come for you in Charleston. But do not expect me to see you, talk with you, or provide for you as long as you insist upon this ridiculous denial of everything you ought to be."

Flanna drew a long, quivering breath, mastering the passion that shook her. "I expect nothing from you."

Roger chuckled with a dry and cynical sound, then turned to his brother. "So, Alden,"—he took his hat from the stand where he had tossed it—"I leave her in your hands. Please arrange that transport as quickly as possible."

"I'll try."

With one last reproachful look, Roger fitted his cap to his head, saluted his brother, and stomped out of the tent.

Flanna sagged in relief. She had expected him to be displeased, but she had not imagined he would be so angry. She had never seen anything but a smiling, carefree Roger. He was a charmer and persuader, not really the type to lose his temper…

Aware that Alden watched her, she dropped her lashes to hide the hurt in her eyes.

"He sets a great store by you," Alden said, his own voice thick and unsteady. "He's only concerned for your well-being."

She bit back tears of disappointment. "He doesn't even know me. Not anymore."

Alden cleared his throat, probably about to make some other attempt at casual conversation, but Flanna held up her hand. "I'll be going now," she said, rigidly holding her tears in check. "I'll come for the dresses when you tell me it's time to go. Until then, you know where to find me."

"That I do," Alden said. She didn't wait for a formal leave-taking, but hurried out the door, hoping to find a place where she could shed her tears in private.

Twenty-One

Wednesday, January 1, 1862

    Happy New Year's to you, Father, and you, Wesley, wherever you are! I am sad to think that I will not spend this day with you, but with every day that passes, I console myself with the thought that I am one day closer to seeing you again.

    There have been bright spots in this dreary winter. First was the news, gleaned from an old newspaper, that there were no South Carolina regiments upon the ridge at Ball's Bluff. We shot at men of several Mississippi regiments, along with men of the Virginia cavalry. The Confederate losses were 33 killed, 115 wounded, and one missing. Our losses were 49 killed, 158 wounded, and 714 captured.

    We were delighted to hear that the Rebs captured our messmates Philip Hart and Freddie Smith. We may soon welcome them again if the Confederates agree to an exchange of prisoners! (I wonder if Freddie has grown accustomed to dirt—I hear the prison camps are uncommonly harsh and cruel.)

    I find that I am starving for reports of the outside world. From England comes the news that

Prince Albert is dead. His wife, Queen Victoria, claimed to have been the happiest wife in England. (Will I ever make a happy wife? The likelihood seems dimmer with each passing day.)

The newspaper reports that a fire burned Charleston before Christmas. The city has burned at least twice before, and I can only hope and pray that my family was spared great loss. At the conclusion of the report in the New York Tribune, Horace Greeley wrote, "South Carolina is the meanest and the vainest state in the Union and nobody will feel any compunction at laying it waste." Interesting that he does not acknowledge that my state has already counted itself out of the Union.

The news about Charleston would have put me in the lowest of spirits, except for one surprise—Major Alden Haynes appeared outside our tent last night. In a brief bit of ceremony he presented me with a medical bag completely furnished with scalpels, sutures, bandages, and an assortment of common dosing powders. I was moved beyond words, but my messmates made up for my silence, pounding the major on the back and assuring him that he was a capital fellow. I think poor Alden was embarrassed, but he could not speak freely, of course. When the commotion died down, he told me that he had arranged for me to visit the Alexandria Hospital several afternoons a week. He said nothing more, but from his apologetic manner I intuited his meaning. I believe he feels sorry that it has taken so long to arrange a way for me to go to Port Royal, and so he intends to occupy my time with medical matters until I am able to go.

*I was pleased. And so the new year begins the
way last year ended—with a dark cloud, sprinkling
of hope, and an earnest prayer.*

Weeks passed. Flanna knew Alden was trying his best to arrange her transport to Port Royal, but the wheels of war and Washington turned slowly. In mid-January he told her that General McClellan insisted that the area around the Sea Islands was yet too unsettled for civilians. Over ten thousand slaves had been abandoned when their owners fled during the Port Royal bombardment, and these "contrabands," not legally free and yet not enslaved, were in dire need of management. Alden had heard talk of a ship intended to aid these South Carolina blacks, but the ship would not sail until late March or early April.

Flanna swallowed her disappointment as well as she could. In the interim, she was delighted when Alden arranged for Franklin O'Connor to serve as an escort for soldiers traveling to and from the Alexandria Hospital. Many of the wounded from Bull Run and Ball's Bluff still convalesced there, along with soldiers who fell sick in camp. After riding in the wagon with the sick, Flanna wandered through the hospital wards, watching, listening, and learning. She dared not speak her mind at the hospital for fear of revealing too much about herself, but she enjoyed indulging her medical curiosity far away from Dr. Gulick's gimlet glance.

Located in an old seminary, the Alexandria Hospital was an irregular structure badly adapted to hospital purposes. Its abrupt halls and cramped stairways were damp and drafty, its wards too small for comfort. An unhealthy odor pervaded the building even on brisk, breezy days.

Though she enjoyed her visits, Flanna shuddered every time she crossed the hospital threshold. One afternoon she discovered the cause of the vile odors—a heap of filthy trash had been allowed to accumulate in the cellar. Because there were no indoor water closets or baths, nurses had to carry chamber pots to a dumping place. At some time in the recent past, someone had decided it was far easier to dump chamber pots in the cellar than to properly dispose of the waste.

Fortunately, Flanna had been in the army long enough to know how the system worked. On her next visit, she tacked a stern sign to the cellar door. The next nurse to come by with a chamber pot paused at the top of the stairs to read it. "No dumping by order of Colonel Sacks?" She frowned and looked at Flanna, who loitered in the hallway. "Who is Colonel Sacks?"

"A very terrible, awful man." Flanna pretended to shudder. "All chamber pots must be dumped in the ditch outside, or he'll have even the nurses out digging trenches. The colonel is awfully fond of trenches."

The woman took one look at Flanna's callused palms, then moved to the door that led out into the yard. "I'll not dig, not even for Old Abe himself," she muttered, her voice echoing off the damp stone walls. "No sir, I'll walk to Richmond and dump these blasted pots on Jeff Davis's head before I'll pick up a shovel."

And so Colonel Sacks was born. Flanna left his threats on dirty equipment trays, next to untidy bandages, and tacked to the walls above unwashed floors. She left other notes hinting that the colonel might drop in for a surprise inspection, and gradually conditions at the Alexandria Hospital began to improve.

Unfortunately, Colonel Sacks could not intimidate the hospital visitors. Though there were several dedicated lay-nurses whom Flanna admired, the majority of visitors to the hospital made her writhe in shame. There were two types: the pious and the flashy. The pious folk walked slowly and solemnly up and down the wards, casting horrified glances at the patients. After intense whispered consultations with the surgeons, these men and women offered to pray for the soldiers' souls. After doing so, they swiftly retired without smiling upon a single soldier or bestowing a word of comfort or cheer. The pious women were far worse than the men, for they went gawking through the wards as if they'd never seen a man before, peeping into every curtained couch and venting their pent-up feelings in outbursts of "Oh, Lord have mercy!" and "Look, dear, how terrible war is!" One such pair of women—they always seemed to hunt in pairs—paused near the doorway of one ward and clasped their dainty hankies to their noses, exclaiming, "Heavens, what a smell! Worse than fried onions!"

The flashy visitors—young men who ought to be in the army—were no less annoying. These young dandies, usually accompanied by wasp-waisted, almond-eyed, cherry-lipped damsels, behaved as tourists. They moved throughout the hospital like summer shadows, leaving no trace of their goodwill behind but a lingering scent of perfume and a slightly sickened expression on the patients' faces.

When Rufus Crydenwise was sent to the hospital for an infected toe, Flanna sat by his bedside for two days, watching in horror as doctors in blood-stained coats prodded his foot and debated whether or not he'd find it difficult to march with a toe missing. One surgeon moistened his finger with saliva, then dabbed the toe with spit, declaring that it merely needed a tobacco poultice.

Flanna waited until after the "experts" moved away, then she fetched a bottle of alcohol and a basin of clean water. "I'm not going to let them take your toe off," she assured Rufus as she washed the swollen digit with alcohol and water. "They'll have to get through me to take it, and though I'm not the biggest fellow in the company, I may be the most stubborn."

Rufus grinned at her, wincing as she dabbed at the swollen area.

Flanna offered a weak smile as she shrugged. "Sorry."

"That's all right. You're not nearly as bad as some of those Washington women." He folded his hands behind his head and braced himself against the pain. "Lots of ladies come here to visit. Though they've tried, they haven't rubbed the skin off my face yet."

Flanna grinned, imagining the sentimental pawing the poor boy endured, then she cleared her throat. "Rufus, I think I can help. There's pus under the skin, you see, and the skin needs to be broken. If you'll let me lance the toe and clean it, I think it'll be better by tomorrow."

His smile vanished. "You won't let them take the toe?"

"I said I wouldn't." She grinned at him. "Wasn't I right about the lice? You shaved your head and cleaned your clothes, and didn't the lice go away?"

Rufus nodded, but fear, stark and vivid, glittered in his eyes. "But this is different. 'Cause if they take my toe, it'll gangrene, and then I'll lose my foot. Heck, I might even lose my leg—"

"You're not going to lose anything." After glancing around to be sure no one paid her any mind, Flanna opened her bag and pulled out her scalpel. Without hesitation, she swished the blade in alcohol, then made one swift, sure cut on Rufus's toe.

He yelped, then slapped his hand over his own mouth. The fellow in the next bed, a man whose eyes had been burned when his rifle overheated and exploded, turned his sightless eyes toward Rufus. "You all right over there?" His mouth grinned crookedly beneath his bandaged eyes. "Did she hurt you?"

Flanna kept working, though anxiety spurted through her. The blind man couldn't see her, but he'd heard enough to guess she was a woman.

"I'm not hurt," Rufus answered, gritting his teeth against the pain as Flanna poured alcohol into the oozing wound. "And you'd better apologize to the private here. He's little, but he's one tough son of a nut."

An impenitent grin flashed across that wounded face. "My mistake."

Indeed. Flanna continued her work, wondering if Rufus would remember the man's remark, but the boy was clenching his teeth and straining against the iron bars of the headboard, probably cursing the day she walked into Company M.

She smiled to herself and kept working.

⁓

Dr. Garvey paused outside one of the wards. "And here, of course, we have several patients from your regiment, Major."

Alden paused in the doorway, bored with his tour of the hospital. He'd come only because Colonel Farnham insisted that his officers be acquainted with all procedures regarding the wounded.

McClellan had some grandiose plan to fully educate his soldiers before sending them out to battle. This was just one aspect of what Alden and the other infantry officers had privately begun to refer to as "the grand stall."

His eyes flitted over the men in the beds and the spare figures of two nurses in dark dresses. A young woman stood in the corner, vainly trying to encourage a sick man to take a cup of tea, and a soldier sat in a rectangle of sunlight at his buddy's bedside, dabbing at the man's foot with a cotton cloth.

He took a wincing breath as the sun sparked on the soldier's copper hair. Flanna!

Dr. Garvey must have heard his gasp, for he straightened as his gaze took in Flanna's ministrations. "What in the name of—" he began, striding into the room. "Soldier! What do you think you are doing?"

Flanna looked up, surprise siphoning the blood from her face. She opened her mouth as if to speak, then dropped her hand to her side.

"Answer me! What have you done to this patient?" The doctor grasped the wounded man's toe and twisted it, causing the boy to howl in pain.

"Stop—no!" The poor boy kicked his foot free of the doctor's hand and lowered it, slowly, to the bed. "It's all right." His jaw was clamped hard and he breathed through his mouth with a heavy panting sound, but he met the doctor's hard gaze. "This is O'Connor, from my company. I told him to take care of my foot."

"You told him?" The doctor's voice dripped with contempt. "You are my patient! What right have you to decide anything?"

"Beggin' your pardon, Doctor,"—the young man glared at the surgeon with burning, reproachful eyes—"but as it's my foot and my toe, I figured I ought to have some say in the matter."

"This is my hospital, my hospital bed, and you are my patient. You have no say in anything, for you are nothing but a lowly private."

"Excuse me, Doctor." Alden came forward, his hands behind his back, studiously avoiding Flanna's gaze. "With all due respect, you're wrong about that. This is an army hospital, this is an army bed, and at the moment, this soldier belongs to Uncle Sam."

The doctor flashed Alden a look of disdain. "Mind your step, sir."

"I intend to." Alden turned to the patient, trying to place the young man's name. "You are from the great state of Massachusetts?"

"Yes sir." The boy cast a glance of well-mannered dislike toward the doctor, then looked at Alden. "I'm Rufus Crydenwise, Company M, of the Twenty-fifth Massachusetts."

Alden smiled. "Then you are one of my men."

"Yes, Major." A smile found its way through the boy's mask of uncertainty. "Indeed, sir, I am, and so is Private O'Connor."

Alden turned to Flanna. "Are you, Private?"

Her long lashes shuttered her eyes, and he had to strain to hear her voice. "Yes sir."

"If you're proud, speak up."

Her eyes flashed at him then, gleaming green and dangerous in the sunlight. "Yes sir," she said, her voice cold and exact.

"I fail to see what this has to do—" the doctor began, but Alden interrupted.

"Do you, Private, intend to harm your companion?"

"No sir." She frowned with cold fury.

"Well then." Alden turned to the doctor and smiled. "I believe we've established that there is nothing amiss here. Private O'Connor is merely tending to his companion as men often do out in the field. And since Private Crydenwise has no objection—"

"Major." The doctor stood very still, his eyes narrow. "I have important things to do and have no time for this foolishness. If these men want to doctor each other, have them do it someplace else, not in my hospital. And as for you, if you've seen enough, I'd like to get back to my work."

Alden inclined his head. "Thank you, sir, for your time. I believe I'll have Private O'Connor escort me back to camp."

The doctor gave an irritable tug at his sleeve. "That would be a most excellent idea, Major. Good day."

Dr. Garvey moved away, his footsteps thundering over the wooden floors. Relaxing, Alden looked at the young man in the bed. "You all right, soldier? O'Connor didn't hurt you too badly?"

"Naw." A broad smile lifted the youth's pendulous cheeks. "It just stung a little, that's all."

"Good." He turned to Flanna, noting her flushed cheeks. "Pack your bag, Private, and let's depart. I trust you have no further business here?"

"No," she whispered, thrusting several implements into her medical bag.

"Good." Alden moved toward the doorway and waited while she said her farewells to Crydenwise. She moved confidently over her patient, checking the toe one last time and removing the rag she'd used to clean it.

Alden felt an inexplicable, lazy smile sweep over his face as he watched her. Flanna knew what she was doing, and she had not flinched before Dr. Garvey's commanding gaze. But she hadn't spoken up for herself either. Alden leaned against the doorframe, thinking. When the war was over, Roger would dress her in red velvet ball gowns and set her on a shelf in his house, a lovely figurine for his fellow politicians to view and admire. And Flanna would surrender her calling in order to please him, for she was a lady, thoroughly schooled in obedience and genteel deference to one's husband.

He saw her lean over Crydenwise, her eyes soft with concern, her hand lightly brushing the short stubble that grew on his head. Though she wore a shapeless uniform and a shadow of dirt unmistakably smudged that alabaster cheek, Alden thought she'd never seemed lovelier than at that moment.

Twenty-Two

Sunday, February 9, 1862

Yesterday Union forces captured Roanoke Island, North Carolina, and today the chaplain gave thanks for this victory. General Henry Wise and his Confederate garrison of over two thousand men were taken prisoner. Were any of my cousins among them? Was Wesley?

I spent the afternoon praying, not for one army or the other, but for the men in both armies. For Wesley and Alden, for Roger and my cousins.

Sunday, March 9

We sit and wait in Maryland while others fight. The battle of Pea Ridge, Arkansas, was fought two days ago, with heavy losses on both sides. They say the dead include two Confederate generals, McCulloch and McIntosh. Again the chaplain gave thanks, while I prayed for Wesley and Aunt Marsali's boys.

I have also begun to understand why the seas are not safe for civilians. Alden appeared at our fire last night to tell us of a battle on the sea. A Confederate ironclad, the Virginia, destroyed two

Union frigates at Hampton Roads, Virginia. I must confess to feeling a bit of pride of the Confederate victory. The Virginia had been rebuilt from the raised hull of the Union ship Merrimac, which the Federals had burned to the waterline when they pulled out of the Norfolk navy yard last year.

Monday, March 10

One of the men received a bundle of Boston papers in the mail. I must admit I have mixed feelings after reading them. There is much talk about peace and about slavery. There are many in the North who are against the idea of freeing the slaves, as are many of the men in my company. One editorial stated that peace had to come, so we might as well have it now and avoid killing so many of our beloved men. I cannot help but agree. The army around me is bored and dissatisfied. So many want to go home, to return to their farms and businesses and families. I fear that unless something happens soon, many will desert in the spring.

Flanna listened to the news with a rising feeling of dismay. Orders from General George McClellan arrived before her permission to depart for Port Royal. In response to Lincoln's repeated urgings for action, on March 17 McClellan sent his troops the following order, which was read in every camp: "I will bring you now face to face with the Rebels. I am to watch over you as a parent over his children, and you may know that your general loves you from the depths of his heart. It shall be my care…to gain success with the least possible loss."

General Montgomery Meigs organized a great flotilla, and over the next three weeks the amassed Army of the Potomac was ferried to Fortress Monroe, located at the tip of the York-James Peninsula in

Virginia. Over the seven months of his command, McClellan had done little but assemble an army, but what an army! Flanna listened in amazement as Sergeant Marvin told Company M that 121,500 men, 14,000 horses, 1,150 wagons, 44 batteries of artillery, 74 ambulances, pontoon bridges, tons of provisions, tents, and telegraph wire would be transported southward.

Flanna and Charity listened to the announcement with mixed emotions. Flanna was disappointed that the trip to Port Royal had not yet materialized, but at least they were moving southward! Soon they'd be in Virginia, and if they got close to Richmond, she and Charity might be able to slip away with very little trouble.

The thought of impending battle did not concern her much, for McClellan had proved that he was unwilling to fight. A master of preparation, organization, and drill, he seemed to lack the heart for sending men into dangerous situations. She worried far more about running away and becoming lost in the woods than she did about another battle.

She had expected Alden to approach her in Maryland with some excuse to prevent her from moving out with the regiment, but he did not. She was not surprised, then, when he sought her out aboard the ship that carried them down the Potomac and into Chesapeake Bay.

She and Charity were standing at the rail between Rufus and Paddy O'Neil, when Alden approached from behind. "Excuse me, boys." His voice cut through their soft nighttime conversation. "I wonder if I might have a word with Private O'Connor."

O'Neil and Crydenwise tugged on the brims of their caps and moved away, probably thinking that the major had come to deliver some sort of rebuke. Flanna dismissed Charity with a downward glance, half-afraid her messmates were right, but Alden merely stepped into the empty space beside her and stared over the railing, watching the moonlight spread silvery ripples across the dark surface of the river.

A creeping uneasiness rose in Flanna's heart. Why had he come, if not to share bad news? Had something happened to Roger? She hadn't seen him in days, and hadn't spoken to him since that terrible day in Alden's tent.

"Is something wrong? If there is trouble, just tell me, please."

"Trouble?" His mouth twisted in something not quite a smile. He leaned out over the railing of the ship, staring at the coastline, the wind catching his words so that Flanna had to bend forward to hear him. "What could possibly be wrong? I promised to see you safely to Charleston, but I am leading you into the wilderness instead. I promised Roger I'd protect you, and I'll be lucky if I can even find you once we land in Virginia." He turned and looked at her, his blue eyes piercing the distance between them. "I'm sorry, Flanna, that I failed you. I tried everything I could think of short of going AWOL and delivering you to Charleston myself. I even prayed you'd take sick and have to remain behind in the hospital."

"Not a very nice prayer, Major."

"I was desperate." His gaze met hers, and she felt her heart turn over in response. "One night I nearly came to your tent to accuse you of falling asleep on guard duty, or some such thing, so you'd face a court martial, anything to keep you from this venture."

"You could have simply told Colonel Farnham the truth."

"No, I couldn't have. I asked you to trust me…and I couldn't betray that trust."

She cleared her throat, pretending not to be affected by this un-expected proof of his affection—no, she corrected herself, his *loyalty*. His affection resided with Miss Nell Scott, who had remained in Boston like a good girl.

She would have patted his arm in gratitude, but remembered the men milling around them and chose to move a half-step closer instead. "Major Haynes," she said, gazing into the thickening night, "do not feel discouraged. I know you tried, and I know you want me safe. But I have come to believe that we are all in God's hands." She lifted her eyes to the sky, where the stars blazed like gems in a night as cold as the grave. "Look there." She pointed upward. "Such beauty, such bright-ness, and on such a night! We are on our way to do battle, but God still works among us. I want to go home, yes, but I am happy that God is using me here. I believe I am where I am supposed to be."

"Still, I worry," he said, with a creditable attempt at coolness, marred only by the thickness of his voice. "John Magruder is the Confederate general dug in at Yorktown. He is a brave man, but more than that, he is clever."

"You know him?"

Alden nodded. "He fought with my father in the Mexican War. He's a Virginian with expensive tastes, and an amateur actor besides." A trace of laughter lined his voice. "Once, during the Mexican War, he staged a performance of *Othello*. Ulysses S. Grant, dressed in crinolines, tried out for the part of Desdemona."

Flanna stifled the sudden urge to giggle by rubbing a finger hard over her lips. She'd never heard of Grant, but the thought of a man in crinolines was enough to make her titter with laughter.

Alden's smile faded. "McClellan believes there are a hundred thousand Rebels dug in at Yorktown, but I'd be surprised if there are even ten thousand. Remember the Quaker guns the Rebs posted outside Washington? I'd be surprised if there aren't a hundred more at Yorktown, all painted to make us think there's a huge army down there."

A spasm of panic shot across Flanna's body like the trilling of an alarm bell. Her brother might well be at Yorktown, along with her cousins!

"So what if this Magruder is just being clever?" She looked up at him with an effort. "If McClellan thinks there are ten thousand men, so be it. He won't fight, and we'll be safe."

"Think about it." Alden's mellow baritone simmered with barely checked passion. "If McClellan hesitates, we will sit out in the spring rain for weeks. The men will grow tired and bored; morale will suffer. Many will take sick in the damp weather, and we'll lose more men to fever and typhoid than we would lose in battle. Our provisions will dwindle. If the Rebs manage to cut us off, we'll be eating squirrel and rabbit, if we're lucky enough to find them."

Flanna stood silent, her thoughts racing as Alden gestured broadly over the water. "The men aboard this ship want the war to be finished so they can go home to their wives and children and farms! The more McClellan hesitates, the more heartsick his army becomes. He talks about loving his men like children, but you can ruin a child with kindness!"

He fell silent, seemingly exhausted with the fervency of his feelings. Flanna bit her lip, realizing that her own concerns and desires seemed insignificant compared to those facing the men who led this army.

"I'm sorry," she whispered, her words sounding mild and flimsy in the cool air. "Of course you're right, Alden. I didn't think. I must seem awfully foolish sometimes."

"Don't do that!" A swift shadow of anger swept across his face. "Don't demean yourself! You are not foolish. You are a sight more intelligent than half the men on this boat, but you allow others to push you around just because"—he halted suddenly, remembering where he was, and lowered his voice to whisper in her ear—"just because they're men!"

Totally bewildered by his behavior, Flanna stepped back. "No one pushes me around!"

"Oh no?" He laughed softly, his vivid blue eyes glittering. "What about that scene I witnessed at Alexandria Hospital? You were taking care of that young soldier, yet when the doctor came, you retreated like a scolded schoolgirl!"

"He was a doctor." Flanna pressed her fingertips to her temple; it was difficult to think straight when standing so close to Alden.

"You're a doctor."

"But he didn't know that."

"You could have told him."

"No, I couldn't." She wavered, trying to understand his point. "Alden, you know I can't tell anyone."

"Being a doctor has nothing to do with your secret." He faced her now, and she could see no lingering gleam of amusement in his black-lashed eyes. "Private O'Connor, you must learn to speak up for yourself. God gave you a brain—use it. He gave you a tongue, and I've heard you use it to good effect when you're confronted by a strong-willed woman like my mother. So why do you sheathe all your common sense when confronted with a difficult man?"

She stepped back, momentarily stunned. What did he know of the confrontations she'd faced? She once sat before an entire examining board and spoke her mind; she grew up with a big brother and seven rambunctious cousins, daring them to best her in all sorts of verbal and physical games. And yet—

Her mind came to an abrupt halt, as if hitting a wall. Hadn't Mammy and Aunt Marsali taught her how to respond to men? On her fifteenth birthday, they had called her into the house and confronted her in her bedroom. There she learned lessons about what proper ladies could and could not do. "Miss Flanna, you can't be arguin' with young men no more," Mammy had said. "You gots to hide your book learning and that sharp tongue."

"Men are like the earth, and we are like the moon," Aunt Marsali added. "They think there is only one side of us because that is all they see—and sometimes you must allow them to believe that, Flanna. For when a woman's will is as strong as the man's who wants to govern her, half her strength must be dedicated to concealment."

Flanna absorbed those lessons without question. She was taught—and she believed—that men ought to assume authority over women, for a woman's world centered on her family. A woman did not need to vote or express her opinion in mixed company, for she ruled her husband through his heart, and he spoke for her. According to everything Flanna had been taught, when a woman was confronted with a difficult man, she had no choice but to demur, for her husband would surely take up her case.

But Flanna had no husband yet. No father or brother at hand to help. No one but Roger, who so disapproved of her actions that he had been avoiding her, and Alden, whose very glance unsettled her so much that every coherent thought flew out of her head.

She drew in a breath, searching for words that would not come. "You don't understand." She clutched at the ship's rail as if it were the only solid reality in a tilting world. "You're a man; you've always been a man. I was trained to be…something else."

"Why?" His voice was tender now, his look gentle and understanding. "Why would anyone tell you to be anything other than what you are? Dr. O'Connor, you are a wonder."

He took a quick breath as if he would say more, then set his jaw and returned his gaze toward the shoreline. Flanna said nothing, but stood beside him, her heart lifting with the first words of honest encouragement she'd heard in months.

The wind whispered across the river, the various conversations of other men wrapped around them like water around the ship. Alden wanted her to stand alone. Most amazing of all, he believed she could. Why, then, did she have to cling to the railing and fight an overwhelming need to stand closer to him?

After the space of several moments, he turned from the rail and nodded to a pair of passing officers. "It'll be time to bed down soon," he said, his voice remarkably casual. "Find the men of your company and remain with them. I've smelled whiskey several times this evening, and if it's flowing at all, there's bound to be trouble of one sort or another."

"Yes sir." She tugged on the rim of her cap, gave him a timid smile, and then went below.

Twenty-Three

Tuesday, April 15

We have entered Virginia and set up our camp.
I am delighted to be in the South again, but my
first impression was that the Negroes are everywhere, going about their work with an air of
importance I've never observed before. They are the
contrabands of which I have heard so much—not
yet free, but no longer enslaved. My messmates gape
at them, for though they have grown used to
"Charles," they have never seen so many coloreds in
one place.

When we alighted, however, our first greeters
were the army mules. A veritable herd of them were
hitched to and eating out of pontoon boats. O'Neil
says that mules are hungrier even than soldiers and
are particularly fond of pontoon boats and rubber
blankets. I would never have believed that a mule
could eat a boat...but, then again, I would never
have believed that I could eat hardtack either.

I have never seen such a colorful mix of men as
I saw at the landing. The Zouaves, who wear red
caps, white leggings, and baggy trousers, strutted
like peacocks around those of us who wore plain

infantry blue. The cavalry fellows wear short jackets with a yellow stripe at the sleeve—an easy target in the woods, O'Neil assured me. He had a point—why don't they wear green or brown? Even nature camouflages its creatures.

We all came ashore and hurried to our posts, though some of us (me included) had no clear idea what those posts were to be. I stayed with my messmates and kept my head low, not wanting to hinder Roger or Alden with my presence. They have rather enough to think about.

The people who lived here before we invaded have moved aside and watch us curiously. My messmates, who have never traveled in the South, hold varying opinions about the land I love. Freddie Smith, who was returned to us before we left Washington, says that Southern women "are void of the roseate hue of health and beauty that adorns our Northern belles." Philip Hart, also returned in a prisoner exchange, says that the Virginia women who walk outside our camp each night are "nasty, slab-sided, long-haired specimens of humanity. I would as soon kiss a dried codfish as one of them." I can understand why he feels ill will toward them, for I saw several of these women piously hold their handkerchiefs to their noses as they approached our Yankee camp. They will inspire no love for the South with that attitude.

Sweet Andrew Green, bless his heart, is quite enamored of a young lady who sells milk to the men for a quarter. Andrew confided in me, "I have found the sweetest girl that ever man looked upon. She is about your size and form, O'Connor, with large deep brown eyes that sparkle like stars. I declare, I was

never so bewitched before." He sighed and looked
away toward the ditch that separates us from the
secesh damsel he adores. "Oh, this war," he sighs.

This afternoon, hoping to buy something to eat
besides hardtack, salt beef, or coffee, O'Neil and I
visited a woman in one of the dwellings outside our
camp. She looked at me with tears in her eyes, and
proclaimed that she had a son in the Confederate
army. How I wanted to comfort her! Together we
could have prayed over our boys, for the sight of her
tears made me want to weep for Wesley and my
brave cousins.

While we visited the woman, O'Neil expressed
the opinion that we were on our way to Richmond
and would end the war as soon as we had reached
that city. "No," said our hostess, "you will all drink
hot blood before you all get that far!"

I pray she is mistaken.

Alden's gloomy predictions came true. The Army of the Potomac
camped in a continual spring drizzle, waiting for McClellan to move.
But the Union General was in no hurry. Convinced that the entire
Confederate army waited in Yorktown, McClellan ordered his men
to dig ditches and build defensive earthworks.

Flanna bent and shoveled until she thought her back would break.
Each night her messmates gathered around their campfire and munched
on tasteless hardtack and salty sowbelly, too tired to complain about
anything but the mindless work. "All talk and no fight," Sergeant
Marvin groused. "I don't see the sense in piling up earth to keep us
from the Rebs. If we don't get at each other sometime, when will the
war end? I'd like to quit ditching and get to fighting."

Though she could not admire McClellan's reluctance, Flanna was
nonetheless grateful for it. At night they could hear sounds from the
Confederates—music from army bands, the pop of an occasional

sharpshooter, the whooping yelps of men at play—and she trembled to think that her loved ones might lie on the other side of those muddy breastworks. She could not help but believe that Alden was right—the Confederate general was only bluffing. If the Confederates had been able, they would have driven the Yankees from Virginia before the first landing. The fact that they sat and waited, too, convinced Flanna that they were waiting for reinforcements.

Hundreds of men fell sick during the waiting time. Dr. Gulick was so harassed by the sheer numbers of men needing attention that Alden allowed Flanna to set up her own dispensary tent, where she treated men who suffered from digestive upsets and other assorted ailments. One man who wandered into her tent had slept the night before in a bed of dry leaves. He awoke the next morning in a panic, discovering that during the night an army of wood ticks had sought the warmth of his body.

Using tweezers, Flanna carefully pulled all the ticks from the man's scalp and back, then handed him the tweezers when he announced that he preferred to pluck the "villainous secesh ticks" from his chest and limbs. She had turned her back to her patient and was rummaging through a crate of medical supplies when Dr. Gulick stalked into the tent.

He stood before Flanna like a dark and vigilant presence. Sweat had made clear runnels in the dust on his face and neck, and his cheeks were flushed, as though he'd been running. After one quick glance around the tent, he took a deep breath, barreled his chest, and pointed at the crate Flanna was unpacking.

"What on earth do you think you are doing?" His soft voice was filled with a quiet, controlled menace that aroused her old fears and uncertainties.

Flanna flinched and retreated a step before his thunderous expression. Charity, she noticed from the corner of her eye, ran out of the tent like a rat fleeing a sinking ship.

"I'm tending one of my fellow soldiers." Her voice was shakier than she intended.

Dr. Gulick ignored the patient and advanced toward Flanna. "Who gave you leave to set up this tent?" His gray eyes darkened like thunderclouds. "And who gave you permission to take my medical supplies? That box belongs in my tent."

Flanna lowered her gaze, feeling as though he'd hit her in the stomach. She'd known this was a risky endeavor. Alden had told her to work quietly and not call attention to herself. Neither of them had dreamed the doctor would have the time or the inclination to seek her out. Apparently they had underestimated Gulick.

"You will return that box to my tent immediately," the doctor ordered, the muscles in his face tightening into a mask of rage. "Snap to it! And you"—he whirled on Flanna's bewildered patient—"put your shirt on and get back to digging. You're not sick! I can tell by looking that you're as healthy as a May morning."

"These varmints—" the man began, pointing at his reddened skin.

"A little bloodletting is good for a body! Now get a move on!"

Flanna closed her eyes, feeling a strange lurch of recognition. This was the same narrow-minded incompetence she had come to disdain at the Medical College. Gulick was a fool and would never change. Unfortunately, the men would suffer for his stupidity.

She felt herself trembling as her mood veered swiftly to anger. "You"— she whirled around to face Gulick—"will get out of my tent. Major Haynes established this dispensary with Colonel Farnham's permission. I requisitioned these supplies, and you'll take them from me over my dead body."

She stood straight and tall, every muscle in her body speaking defiance.

The doctor's breath came raggedly in impotent anger. "You dare challenge me?"

"Yes sir." She shot him a cold look. "I do."

"You're not a doctor. You know nothing, you little imbecile!"

"I am a doctor."

"You think you can dose a man with calomel and call yourself a physician? I don't know which hill you crawled out from under, but you're a quack, if you're anything at all, you superstitious little runt."

Flanna forced dignity into her voice. "I know how to treat my patients. And if you are any doctor at all, you will get back to your tent and wait upon the men there. I understand there are more sick today than yesterday."

He lurched toward her, one square hand uplifted as if he would slap her for her impertinence, then his eyes darted toward the back of the tent.

He halted in midstep, his hand falling to his side. "I'm going." He gave Flanna a glare hot enough to sear her eyebrows. "But if I hear that you have harmed one patient, young man, I'll have you drummed out of camp—no, imprisoned! And I will be watching you!"

He left the tent as suddenly as he'd come. The space he had occupied seemed to vibrate softly, and Flanna felt her knees grow weak. She put out a hand to steady herself against the table.

"I'm very impressed, Dr. O'Connor."

She turned to see Alden standing behind her, with Charity at his side. Her patient had disappeared.

"Oh." Flanna moved to a chair and fell into it. "It was nothing, really. Dr. Gulick has always been...difficult."

Alden came forward and peered out the front opening of the tent as if to make certain Gulick had disappeared. "I don't think he'll bother you again." He turned back to face her and gave Charity a warm smile. "Thank you for fetching me, Charity. But it appears our Dr. O'Connor has everything under control."

"Lawdy, I was scared." Charity fanned herself with her hand as she came forward. "I've never seen a man so angry as that doctor. Why, he was about to slug you! Is he jealous or just meaner than a snake?"

"He's probably more concerned about losing his medical supplies than his patients," Alden answered. The faint beginnings of a smile marked his mouth.

"Why should he care about bandages and chloroform?" Flanna shook her head. "He has plenty; there's no shortage at the moment."

"You're forgetting about the whiskey." Alden squatted on the earthen floor beside Flanna's chair. "Every regiment gets a ration of rotgut for medicinal purposes, and the good doctor has doubtless noticed that he is a jug or two short. I had part of his allotment sent to you."

Stunned by the thought, Flanna laughed until tears rolled from the corners of her eyes. She paused to wipe them away, then noticed that Alden was still kneeling beside her. He was smiling, and in his smile she saw a warmth she didn't expect.

"Was there something else, Major?" She wiped the last of the wetness from her eyes. "Perhaps you slept with a tick or two last night?"

"Afraid not." Still smiling at her, he stood up. "But I must congratulate you. You are learning, Private O'Connor. You are changing."

She sniffed as he left and her heart settled back to its even keel. Didn't war change everyone?

⁂

At roll call on Saturday morning, May 3, the Union army learned that McClellan planned to begin bombarding the Confederate position on Monday, May 5. Flanna and Charity watched the artillery corps haul the last Federal guns into place, some so heavy that it took several horses to pull them to the top of the earthworks.

But the Confederates cared nothing about McClellan's carefully laid plans. As the monstrous guns pointed toward Yorktown, Confederate cannon began to bombard the Yankee position, shells and shot pouring into the camp from one line to the other. The flashes of gunfire and arches of trailing smoke created a pyrotechnic display unlike anything Flanna had ever seen.

Not a man slept Sunday night. Most huddled behind the earthworks, their hands over their ears, their eyes wide to the sky above, always looking for that one shell that might be intended for them.

Flanna ducked into the dirt as one particularly loud shell screamed over her head. When she lifted her eyes again, she was surprised to see Major Alden Haynes crouching in the dirt in front of her.

"Major Haynes?" Her heart flooded with relief at the sight of him, fit and well. Since the shells had begun to fly, she and her messmates had not dared venture out of their trench.

"Private O'Connor, I need to speak with you." His voice sounded uneasy, and the look in his eye sent a shiver down her spine.

"Speak, Major." They both instinctively ducked as another shell rocketed overhead, but this one flew with the wailing sound of a winter's wind, not the loud whistling that meant it was coming their way.

Alden turned and sat in the dirt, his back to the piled earth. He bent low so that his words reached her ears alone. "Flanna, you can't stay here. This is real fighting, and there may be a real battle on the morrow. I owe it to Roger to see you safely away."

Always Roger. She pressed her lips together and waited for the dull thump that meant the wailing shell had landed. They both cocked their heads, listening for the sound, and slumped in relief when it came.

"Major Haynes." Her gaze flew up to study his face. "I want you to know that I am honestly grateful for your concern. You have taken good care of me, and I appreciate it, even if Roger doesn't. But I've learned something in the last few months—something they did not teach me in medical school. I've learned that the Bible is right when it says that to everything there is a season—a time to be born, and a time to die. And I believe God will preserve me until it is my time."

"Surely you don't believe that God protects those who take foolish risks." In spite of his reserve, a tinge of exasperation lined his voice. "I want to protect you from those risks, Flanna."

"I'm not being any more foolish than you are." She watched the play of emotions on his face. "Do you remember some weeks ago when a young boy was crushed under one of the artillery wagons? I sat with him for an hour and helped him make his peace with God. And when it was done, I realized that for some reason I cannot understand, it pleased my sovereign God to take that boy home."

"War is a dangerous business, even in camp." Alden looked away into the darkness. "Soldiers have to be prepared for death. You, on the other hand, should not be expected to face those risks. Let me send you away. You've been an escort, and it would be natural for me to choose you to escort some of the wounded back to Washington."

"No." Knowing that the darkness cloaked her movements, Flanna reached out and slipped her hand over his. "We must all be ready for death, Alden. Once, in Charleston, a young lady was climbing into a carriage when her crinoline caught on the carriage step. The groom made a great noisy to-do as he attempted to free her, and the girl screamed in frustration. At that noise the horse bolted, dragging the poor girl for blocks before the carriage could be stopped. They called my father, but nothing could be done. That girl died on her way to a barbecue on a peaceful summer morning."

Flanna's heart squeezed in pain at the memory. "So you see, Alden, death can come anywhere, at any time, in God's sovereign will. God holds my life, and he has seen fit to make me a part of this company, at home with these men. I will not leave them unless I have a clear indication that God wants me to depart. I will not go simply because I fear death. I don't."

He looked at her, his eyes compelling and magnetic in the gloom, then his free hand swept behind her neck. Her heart pounded as he held her at arm's length for a moment, then the silence shattered with an angry howl. "Look out! Here comes another cook stove!" The shell screamed overhead and Alden drew Flanna's head to his chest, shielding her until the canister landed somewhere near the center of the camp.

Within Alden's arms, Flanna felt an unwelcome surge of excitement that had nothing whatever to do with the shell rocketing overhead. Her heart jolted, her pulse pounded, and she heard an answering uneven rhythm within Alden's own chest.

Could he possibly feel what she felt?

He released her after the explosion, and she looked at him, her eyes searching his, but she saw nothing there but an aloof and protective pride. "Good night then," he said, standing. He brushed the dirt off his uniform, gave her a distracted smile, then turned and walked away.

A blurred, red sun finally rose above the clouded eastern horizon. Tension hung in the air like dense smoke, waiting to descend and smother any man foolish enough to acknowledge his fear. As the rain began to fall again, Flanna and her company quietly loaded their cartridge boxes, formed lines, and advanced through the mud. Flanna gripped her rifle and moved out to the drummers' steady beat, marveling at the eerie silence of the landscape ahead.

When the foremost company breasted the earthworks, the sergeant lifted his hand. "The Rebs are gone!" he yelled, his voice echoing over the flat land between camps. "Every last one of 'em!"

Flanna and the others quickened their pace. Within moments they stood in a deserted Confederate camp, staring at refuse that pointed to a hasty departure. The ground around the campfires was strewn with heaps of oyster shells, empty bottles, cans of preserved fruit and vegetables. Flanna found a loaf of unbaked bread nestled in a kneading trough, and a slab of pork dripping over a still-warm fire.

"They're all gone," Sergeant Marvin said, coming to stand beside Flanna. The corner of his drooping moustache lifted in a wry smile. "Imagine that."

Flanna closed her eyes. Thank God, they'd gotten away. General Magruder, whoever he was, God bless his cleverness.

The Army of the Potomac halted while General McClellan conferred with his officers. Flanna knew he'd pronounce the effort a great success, though the Rebel army had escaped and the war would continue.

Exhausted by the thought, she sank to the ground by some Rebel's discarded campfire. A pan of beaten biscuits lay upon the coals, and she picked one up and stared at it. Had Wesley or one of her cousins taken that half-moon bite?

"Miss Flanna," Charity whispered, crouching as she came near, "I wants to talk to you."

"Talk." Flanna leaned upon her rifle, watching the others forage for useful items. After the tension of the morning, she felt strangely relieved...even elated. No Rebels would die today, and none of her messmates would be torn apart.

"Miss Flanna, I was thinking about going home."

"I know, Charity." Flanna sighed. "I'd have slipped away long before this, but we couldn't—not with the Rebels camped right here in our path. But now we may find a way. We'll be moving further into Virginia, maybe even into Richmond."

"I know." Something in the girl's voice struck Flanna as odd, and she turned to look at her maid. Despite Charity's cropped hair and dirty clothes, a sort of passionate beauty shone from her face, an elegance Flanna had never seen about Charity before.

"Charity," Flanna began, puzzled and more than a little nervous, "what's happened to you?"

The maid lifted her head. "I met a man," she said simply, feather-like laugh lines crinkling around her dark eyes. "He's a body servant to one of the Yankee officers, and he wants to marry me."

Ripples of shock erupted from the midst of Flanna's chest. "He knows you're a woman?" She grabbed Charity's arm in a furious grip. "You told him?"

Radiating offended dignity, Charity shook her head. "Miss Flanna, I didn't tell anyone about your secret. Beau says he knew I was a woman the first time he looked at me. And he never asked me about your reasons—I don't think he cares much. But he wants to marry me, and I'm going to let him. We've been waiting a long while, and now's the time."

Flanna released Charity's arm and stared at the fire in stunned silence. She tried not to cry, but her chin wobbled and her eyes filled in spite of herself.

Charity bent low to look in Flanna's eyes. "Are you cryin' 'cause you're happy for me?"

"No!" Flanna gasped in disbelief. "I'm crying because you're leaving me! I'll be alone! Charity, how could you? I thought—I thought we were friends."

Charity's left brow shot up in surprise. "Friends? Miss Flanna, I was your maid, nothing more. I ain't even been that since we left Boston 'cause you ain't had any money to pay me. Truth is, you've always treated me more like a slave than a friend. And it's time I moved on."

"Like a *slave?*" Flanna's shock yielded quickly to hurt. "How can you say that? I am personally opposed to slavery; I've said so a thousand times. You were always paid good wages."

"Miss Flanna, what's the difference in paying wages over the long haul and paying them up front when you buys a slave? Truth is, the difference between a slave and a free colored is that freedom means I can go when I wants to. And I wants to go now." Visibly trembling with intensity, Charity swallowed hard and squared her shoulders. "If I is free like you say, you won't stop me from going. And if I is your friend, you'll want me to be happy more than you want a maid."

Flanna felt the bitter gall of guilt burn the back of her throat, then she gave herself a stern mental shake and fumbled for another argument. "What about your mother and father in Charleston?" she asked, dismayed to hear a faint thread of hysteria in her voice. "Have you forgotten about them?"

"No ma'am, I ain't forgotten." Charity looked away, her eyes soft with pain. "I love my parents, but I can't know if they'll still be there when this war is over. I can't know that I'll even make it home. You're shooting for an awful faraway star, Miss Flanna, and I don't know if you're gonna make it. So I figures I needs to be happy now, and Beau makes me happy." She blinked, then focused her gaze on Flanna again. "I wish you the best, but I can't go with you no more. Not one more step. Beau and I, we're thinking of going back to Washington with the next load of sick soldiers. We'll live someplace up there, at least until the war's over."

Still reeling with disbelief, Flanna lowered her head to her hands. She had thought she could endure the worst the war had to offer, but she'd never imagined she'd have to endure it alone.

"Miss Flanna." Charity straightened and lifted her chin. "Miss Flanna, don't you be going on about this. You have always treated me good, but you have always treated me like a child. Well, folks like you tend to forget—children grow up. Truth is, I don't need you, Miss Flanna. And it's about time you learn that you don't need me neither."

The truth crashed into Flanna's consciousness like surf hurling against a rocky shore. Blank and amazed, she sat very still, her hands clasped around her head, her eyes wide. Charity didn't need her—what an unexpected, inconceivable thought! Flanna had grown up feeling responsible for Charity's clothing, education, and wages, and yet she had ceased to provide those things months ago. And though it might be possible that she didn't need Charity, that truth would be harder to accept.

But Charity was right—what was freedom if not the right to chart the course of one's own life? Right now Charity had more freedom than Flanna did, for not only was Flanna caught in an enemy army, she was trapped in a false identity.

"I'm sorry, Charity." Flanna's voice cracked with sardonic weariness. "I'm sorry for...everything. Go, be married. I'm happy for you."

Charity just sat there in the hush, her arms folded loosely across her knees, then she reached out and patted Flanna's arm. "Miss Flanna, don't feel sad!" she said, her face alight with eagerness. "You ought to get married too. Forget about going home till after the war, and get yourself out of this mess before you get killed."

Flanna's eyes screwed tight to trap the sudden rush of tears. "Roger won't marry me," she said in a choked voice. "Not now, not like this. Not until after the war."

"I wasn't talking about Roger." Charity squeezed Flanna's arm. "There's another man that loves you, only you is too stubborn to see it."

Flanna's mouth dropped open. "You can't mean Paddy O'Neil!"

"No." Charity looked at Flanna in amused wonder. "I'm talking about Major Haynes. The man is crazy in love with you, and if you can't see it, well, you're blinder than most of the men around this place."

"Alden?" Flanna muttered, half-laughing, half-crying. "Why, he feels nothing for me but responsibility. I'm nothing but a burden to him, a trial he'd rather send to Charleston than be mindful of."

"Land's sakes, Miss Flanna." Charity shook her head in wonder. "You're smart, but you can be awful thick sometimes. I know how you feel about Mister Alden. I've been with you eight years, and I know you. I saw you looking at him that morning before you went up that mountain at Ball's Bluff. And I know you decided you'd rather take your chances against the Rebels than slip through the woods and leave Major Haynes."

"You can't believe that!" Flanna burst out, wholly taken aback. "Why—that's not true at all! I had very good reasons for not leaving then, and I have good reasons for not leaving now—including the fact that I'd be wandering in the woods alone, since you're abandoning me!"

"I am sorry about that." Charity patted Flanna's arm. "But you have a good head on your shoulders. If you just keep your eyes open and your head down, you're gonna be all right."

"Sure." Flanna squeezed her maid's hand with a warmth she didn't quite feel. "I'd stand up and hug you, but the fellows would think that very strange."

"Don't mind me." Charity released Flanna's hand and stood up, then stepped away…toward the new life she'd begun to establish weeks ago.

Flanna had been blind to that too. "God go with you," she called, a heaviness centering in her chest as Charity moved away. *At least he is still with me.*

Flanna sat silently for a long time, only half-aware of the men moving around her. From somewhere off to her right, a soldier snorted and wheezed into the depths of his handkerchief, and Flanna unconsciously noted that he could use a draught of syrup to clear his sinuses.

She pressed her hand over her mouth, smothering a wave of hysterical laughter. Oh, how Aunt Marsali would laugh if she could see Flanna now! The belle of Charleston, the girl who'd refused seven different marriage proposals by the age of eighteen because she wanted to be a doctor! Her cousins, who had teased her unmercifully about being too prim and highfalutin, would sell their prize jumpers for a chance to see Flanna O'Connor sitting in the mud beside a tray of cold biscuits, her hair hacked off and her maid sashaying away.

She was alone. Completely and totally alone. If she wandered off into the woods right now, no one would come looking for her. Oh, a few of the fellows from her company might notice her absence, and perhaps the sergeant and O'Neil would scout around in the bushes. When they told Major Haynes that Franklin O'Connor was AWOL, Alden would feel so responsible to Roger that he'd send out a detail to look for her. But if she disappeared in the late afternoon, he'd have to wait until morning, and Flanna could be miles away by sunrise.

But she couldn't leave alone! Shaking her head, Flanna tucked away her thoughts of escape. Charity's departure would leave an extraordinary void in her life, for properly bred young women did not go out in public without a maid or an escort of some sort, and they certainly didn't traipse around in the woods like some kind of backwoods hermit.

"But you're no longer a properly bred young woman," Flanna whispered, reminding herself of the inescapable truth. She was a Yankee soldier, and she could go anywhere she darned well pleased. She'd found the courage to stand up to Dr. Gulick, and she could stand up to anyone who stood in her path—as long as he wasn't too much bigger and didn't carry a gun.

Who was she kidding? A skeptical inner voice cut through her thoughts. She was *afraid* to step out on her own, absolutely terrified of what might happen out there in the woods. She had told Alden Haynes that she wasn't afraid to die, and that was true, but the thought of being alone paralyzed her with fear. At least here, in the army, she still had Roger nearby and Alden and the men of Company M to keep her company. And she had the memory of men like Andrew Green, who had assured her that the bravest birds sang in the dark because they knew God would bring sunrise soon enough.

She was not completely alone, then…but she would never find her way back to her loved ones unless she learned how to let go.

"'Trust in the Lord with all thine heart,'" she said softly, pressing her hands to her cheeks as tears slid hot and wet between her fingers, "'and he shall direct thy paths.'" She wept silently, not daring to draw attention to herself, and hastily wiped her eyes when a long shadow fell over hers.

"O'Connor?" The voice was Paddy O'Neil's. "You all right, lad?"

"Fine, O'Neil, just a wee bit weary." She wiped her hands on her coat, then looked up and gave him a wavering smile. "What are they saying now? Did we run the Rebs all the way to Richmond?"

"Ah, no, we didn't, though I wish we had." He crouched in the dirt next to her, then picked up a stone and casually tossed it into the charred remains of the Confederate fire pit. "Truth to tell, they're sayin' that we're goin' to advance as soon as we can. Little Mac is intent upon takin' Richmond. If he can do it, Major Haynes says the war will be over and done."

Flanna smiled, finding great satisfaction in the possibility. She squinted up at O'Neil. "I'd like that, wouldn't you?"

His ruddy face split into a wide grin. "Sure, and haven't I said so? I'd like nothing better than to board a train back to Boston, there to hug my sweet wife and baby. I've yet to learn if it was a boy or a girl."

"Well, it's one or the other, I promise you that." Flanna sighed as her gaze fell upon O'Neil's rifle. Except for target practice, she had not fired her weapon once. Suddenly she desperately wanted to quit the war without ever having to squeeze that trigger in battle.

She lifted her eyes toward the western horizon. Somewhere in those outstretched miles ahead the Confederate army marched in retreat, and just beyond them lay Richmond, capital of the Confederacy and a central transportation hub for the South. Despite her fears, the knowledge tempted her. If she could gather her courage and slip away at an opportune moment, she could make her way to Richmond, wire her father, and take the train home to Charleston. She had an advantage now, for Alden carried a dress she could wear during her escape, and not even a nearsighted Rebel would confuse a woman in wide skirts with a Union soldier.

For her, at least, the war would be over the moment she crossed the threshold of her father's house.

Twenty-Four

Tuesday, May 6, 1862

The rains have ended; it is a beautiful day. Birds sing in the thickets that shadow our dead.

The first real fighting I have seen commenced from Williamsburg, where the Confederates tried to impede our forward movement. My company was spared from fighting, as the Twenty-fifth Massachusetts marched at the back of the lines. We were not spared, however, the work of caring for the wounded.

Afterward, the field of battle presented a ghastly appearance. In one small hollow I counted sixty dead, Confederates and Federals mingled together.

We found one of the dead Rebels sitting upright, his rifle aimed over the top of a fallen tree, his finger still curled upon the trigger. A Union soldier lay beside him, shot through the belly. Beside the Federal lay a Testament, and on his breast lay two ambrotype pictures—one of a group of children, another of a young woman. At least he had the images of his loved ones to prevent him from dying alone.

Does Wesley carry my picture? Does he have a sweetheart? My heart breaks when I think of him and of how we were separated. When this war is over, if we both survive it, I do not want to be separated from my loved ones again.

I pray we may soon end this horrible war.

The wounded Union soldiers are taken to Dr. Gulick's tent; by some unspoken understanding my messmates quietly bring the injured Rebels to me. I asked O'Neil why they assumed I would look with compassion upon Rebels, and he grinned at me. "Well, naturally, they know you're the Velvet Shadow. Anyone who would risk sneaking out after taps to tend another has the sort o' compassion these fellows need."

Strangely enough, the Confederates grin at us with great glee, as if we were long-lost cousins. One fellow promised to trade tobacco for coffee, and another offered a packet of Richmond newspapers for anything we had at hand. Diltz asked one Rebel who had taken a shot in the arm why the Confederates left so many good clothes and blankets behind in their retreat. "We're God-fearin' men," the wounded man answered. "We obey the injunction to clothe the naked and feed the hungry—ain't that you'uns?"

I examine each Rebel soldier with great fear, afraid I will discover Wesley or one of my beloved cousins. I did recognize William Hartley, a boy I knew from church. He was always the liveliest in Sunday school, quick with a ready answer. He died on my table.

I wonder what I will say when I see his mother in Charleston.

rendered

Thursday, May 15

We are marching. Along the way a profusion of castaway overcoats and blankets bloom over the road, dropped by men too weary to add an ounce to their knapsacks. I tossed my overcoat without regret, for I still think of it as Charity's and would rather not be reminded of my loss. No one minds losing these belongings; we can pick up others on the road ahead.

Today we came upon White House Landing, where George Washington once courted Martha Curtis. General Robert E. Lee's wife had tacked a note to the door, asking that the army not desecrate Washington's home. General McClellan has pitched his tent on the lawn of the house and posted guards to prevent looters from taking souvenirs. Mrs. Lee herself passed through our lines under a white flag of truce. O'Neil and I watched her go, her mouth thin and set in a straight line, her belongings packed into a single trunk. My heart broke for her, for this war has also torn me from the home I love.

Saturday, May 17

Despite General McClellan's order, Mrs. Lee's house was set afire as we pulled out to move northward. Unnamed stragglers (not of our company) apparently hate General Lee more than they revere General Washington.

Tuesday, May 20

Richmond is just nine miles to the west. Our advance has been slow. The men have taken to calling General McClellan the "Virginia Creeper."

Saturday, May 24

Today Sergeant Marvin led us up a hill from which we could see the spires of the Richmond churches. My heart pounded as I stared at those spires, only five miles away! Five miles! I could walk into Richmond in just over an hour—if not for the Confederate army that lies in my way.

I am still nursing the wounded from the fighting at Williamsburg. The Confederates have all been taken away to prison, but ambulatory soldiers who would not come see the Velvet Shadow in daylight come to our campfire at night, seeking some trivial bit of care Dr. Gulick would not give. Last night I treated a soldier who lost his thumbnail to shrapnel. Another came to me with a scalp wound—a bullet took off a three-inch strip of hair from the top of his head. Another had a ball pass into the toe of his brogan, between his two toes, and out the sole of his shoe. Though he was uninjured, he seemed to need my assurance that he would be okay. Many of the men are superstitious; they feel they are invincible to all but the single bullet intended for them. The lad whose shoe had been pierced by a Minié ball wasn't sure whether that bullet was intended for him or not. I prayed for wisdom, then told him God had meant it only for his shoe. He went away content.

Monday, May 26

I sat awhile today with a wounded soldier who delighted in telling of the fight at Williamsburg. "We were none of us too proud, not even those who had the dignity of an officer's shoulder straps to support, to dodge behind a tree or stump when the

*bullets began to sing over our heads," he told me. "I
called out to a comrade, 'Why don't you get behind
a tree?' and he answered, 'Confound it, there ain't
trees enough for the officers.'"*

*At this the young man leaned toward me and
whispered confidentially, "I don't mean to be
accusing officers of cowardice, but I found out that
they show the same general inclination not to get
shot that privates do."*

*No one is shooting at the moment. The Rebels
run in front of us, but Little Mac sits here in the
mud, waiting for reinforcements. And despite my
brave proclamations that I do not fear death, I
have been much shaken of late. Charity, my right
arm, is gone, and I stare death in the face every
day when I work with the wounded. It is not the
prospect of my death that makes me consider leaving the army—it is the death of my friends. How
can I remain, knowing that I may one day close
Sergeant Marvin's eyes or listen in vain for the
beating of Diltz's heart? When I think that I may be
called upon to pull a bullet from Alden's chest, my
hands tremble.*

God, show me what to do!

On Friday, May 30, while McClellan waited for reinforcements,
Flanna sat by the fire with her messmates and contemplated leaving
the Army of the Potomac. Charity and her Beau had already gone,
and Flanna knew she could disappear just as easily.

Why shouldn't she? She had been too afraid to run before, but
now she feared remaining more than she feared going. As a soldier,
she was of little use to her company, and as a doctor she felt completely inadequate. Treating men for fever and dysentery was one
thing; calming a frantic man while sawing off his leg was quite another.

At Ball's Bluff she had acted on an impulse and helped a few men, but the carnage at Williamsburg had shown her that she lacked the experience to deal with war injuries.

In medical school she had learned how to deliver babies, not amputate limbs. And if any of the men she had come to respect and admire should die under her hands, she did not think she would be able to continue as a surgeon.

For several days she had withdrawn from her messmates in order to pray and beg God for a sign, and tonight it had come. Albert Valentine, whose only talent seemed to be the uncanny ability to find the cloud behind every silver lining, had picked up Philip Hart's guitar and begun to sing.

> "Do they miss me at home, do they miss me?
> 'Twould be an assurance most dear
> To know at this moment some loved one
> Is saying, 'I wish he were here.'
> Too few of the group at the fireside,
> Are thinking of me as I roam,
> Ah, yes, 'twould be joy beyond measure
> To know that they miss me at home,
> To know that they miss me at home."

The words of the song burned in Flanna's brain. Lately she'd spent so much energy thinking about the men around her that she had spent little time thinking of her father, whose heart probably broke a little each day that she and Wesley stayed away. The time had come to leave. She sat only five miles from the heart of the Confederacy—nothing could hold her back now.

So why did she feel so reluctant to go?

Her gaze moved around the fireside circle, lingering for a moment on each man's countenance. Though a steady rain had been falling for hours, Sergeant Marvin sat with Freddie Smith, Rufus Crydenwise, and William Sheahan under a tarp, their attention dedicated to their nightly poker game. Valentine sat a little removed from the others, his fingers still caressing the guitar. O'Neil sat in the opening of his small tent, his eyes narrowed in concentration as he scratched out a letter to his dear Maggie.

Flanna's heart squeezed in anguish. She might never see these men again. They were her companions, her comrades, and they had become her friends.

She pulled her damp blanket closer around her shoulders and stared past the fire into her own thoughts. These men were dear to her, but Charity was right, two others meant far more. To one she owed a parting word, to the other she owed…everything. If not for Alden Haynes's care, she could not have come this far.

She glanced up at the water-dappled canvas over her head. It was a perfect night for her departure. No one would follow her in the rain, and her footprints would be washed away by morning. It was also the perfect time. Tattoo would not sound for another hour, and if she hurried, she could catch Roger by one of the Company K campfires.

She stood, stuffed her blanket under the tarp, and stepped away from the fire. She might as well leave everything; it would look suspicious if she took even a blanket. Perhaps, with luck, they'd think that a bear got wee Franklin O'Connor and ate up every trace.

O'Neil's voice called after her as she moved out into the darkness. "Got some errand to run in this weather, O'Connor? If you see O'Leary from Company B, ask if he has any coffee. The man owes me half a pound."

"I'll ask," Flanna answered, lifting her hand in the only farewell she could give him.

≈≈≈

Company K had spread their tents in a curving line over the next ridge. Flanna walked toward them with long, purposeful strides, not certain what she should say to Roger. He'd kept his distance as they moved inland, and some part of her wondered if he really cared for her at all. He had promised to leave her alone, and in that he had more than kept his word.

She slowed her pace when she reached the row of two-man tents. Like those of her company, the men gathered around small fires for warmth and companionship, shielding themselves from the rain with blankets and tarps. She had the impression that she stared at clusters of dark-shelled turtles who occasionally thrust their heads out to peer past the campfire.

Flanna heard Roger before she saw him. His voice rose from a campfire dug under a massive oak. She hesitated in the darkness, listening as he spun a tale of great courage and even greater unlikelihood.

"The balls made rather strange music as they screamed within an inch of my head," he was saying, his molten voice pouring over the men in the fire circle. "I had a bullet strike me on the top of my hat just as I was going to fire, then a piece of shell struck my rifle. I had heard the colonel say that the Rebs had as strong a position as could possibly exist, but I was so excited Old Scratch himself couldn't have stopped me. I rushed toward them, loading and firing as fast as I could see a Rebel to shoot, and at last the varmints began to run for the woods. The firing sounded like the roll of thunder, and I got rather more excited than I wish to be again. I didn't think of getting hit, of course, but it was almost a miracle that I wasn't."

Flanna shifted until she saw him, hunched like an old woman beneath his tarp. He paused from his storytelling and scratched the beard that had grown, thick and full, on his cheeks. "The Rebel prisoners we took said they'd never seen anything like it, of course. And on the ground there I saw some of the most horrid sights I've ever seen. Poor Thomas Withington—did you see him? Both eyes shot out. And he'd been standing right behind me in the line."

"Captain," one of the men drawled, "I don't recall seeing you in that charge at all."

"I was too far in front of you, my good man." Roger leaned forward and slapped his knee. "Now, if I could have that coffeepot, I think I could die happy on this spot."

From outside the circle, Flanna cleared her throat. "Captain Haynes?"

Startled, Roger looked up and peered out into the darkness. He frowned for a moment, not recognizing her in the shadows.

"Captain Haynes, it's Private O'Connor. May I have a word with you?"

Roger took a deep breath and adjusted his smile. "Certainly, Private."

Flanna turned away, shivering in the rain as he left the circle of his men and came toward her. "Let's walk under the tree to get out of the wet," he suggested, his voice cool and clear in the night air. She followed him, and as soon as they reached the other side of the sprawling oak he grabbed her arm and whirled her around to face him. "Flanna, are you crazy? Why have you come here?"

Her lips parted in surprise. "I came—to see how you were."

"I'm fine." He released her and stepped back into the dappled firelight, his brows a brooding knot over his eyes. "Now tell me the truth— why have you really come? I told you I didn't want to see you while you were"—he waved his hand in a gesture of disgust—"like this."

She struggled to maintain an even, conciliatory tone. "I came here because I wanted to tell you something important."

"Yes?" A half-smile crossed his face. "Wait, don't tell me—you have finally had enough of this foolishness and you want me to send you home. Very good. I thought this might happen." He thrust his hands behind his back and eyed her with pained tolerance. "I'll have Alden send Mother a wire that she's to expect you. We'll take one of those dresses from Alden's trunk and outfit you properly, then one of the officers can escort you back to Washington. It will take a few days, but—"

"Let me speak, Roger." Flanna tilted her head and looked at him, oddly grateful for his outburst. He had just solved her problem. She hadn't been able to figure out how she could tell him good-bye without revealing her intention to desert, but Roger had just given her the perfect plan.

"Well?" Roger frowned, his eyes level under drawn brows. "Am I right?"

"Yes." She sighed heavily. "You're right, Roger, as always. But I want the dress tonight, for I'm tired of this wet uniform. Can you get it for me—without letting Alden know? He'll only make a big fuss, and he needs to concentrate on his work."

"Of course I can get it." He gave her a bright look of eagerness. "But what about your quarters? You can't stay with your company. I'll have to set up a tent for you at the rear of the line, and that may take some time. But Alden won't need to know anything. There will be dispatches flying between here and Washington, so we ought to be able to get you back to Boston with little trouble."

He lifted his chin and looked at her, the glitter in his eyes both possessive and accusing. "It is very considerate of you to think of my brother." Light bitterness spiced his voice. "Lately I have become very aware of how often Alden thinks of you. You have made quite an impression on him, you know."

Flanna lowered her eyes, glad of the darkness that hid the hot flush in her cheeks. "He feels very responsible for me, and I am sorry to burden him. Yet, I would like to think that I have not merely used the army. I hope I have given something back to it."

"A very noble sentiment, my dear. Perhaps we can find a discreet way to mention your nursing activities when I run for office."

Flanna sighed again. "Whatever you decide, Roger."

"This is best, you know," he said, possessive desperation in his voice. "Mother will take good care of you until the war is over."

"I know."

She stood silently in the hush, wanting to say so much more, yet unable to open her heart. She had come to tell him she could not ever marry him, but her disappearance would burn that bridge for her. In the morning, when he looked for her and discovered her gone, he would know that she had kept her resolution to go home…and his oft-tested patience would vanish like a bursting bubble.

And yet…her heart softened as she studied his dear face. He was a charming man, pleasant and bright, all she had ever wanted…once. She would always think of him fondly.

"Thank you, Roger," she whispered, hoping he would remember that she had left him with a grateful smile. "You have been very kind to me."

"Wait here." Roger stepped closer, his eyes artless and serene. With a warm wave of breath in her ear, he whispered, "I'll return in a moment."

Flanna leaned against the tree and slid slowly to the ground while some soldier in the distance played "The Old Folks at Home."

Dear Alden—

Flanna paused and tapped her pencil on her knee, thinking. She had ripped a page from her journal for the purpose of writing a farewell note, but now that the moment had come she could not think of what she wanted to say. The hunger to leave gnawed at her, and yet she could not go without telling Alden of the feelings that had arisen in her heart. She felt gratitude, affection, and admiration for him, but how could she express herself without seeming to ask that he reciprocate her feelings? She had already been far too much of a burden. And if Charity was right and Alden did feel some inappropriate emotion for Flanna, time and distance would eradicate it. He should go home and marry Miss Nell Scott, a proper Boston lady.

Something rustled in the oak branches above Flanna's head, sending a sudden shower over her. She stiffened and looked up, then relaxed when the leaves grew silent. Probably a squirrel. She was as jumpy as a bird in cat country, all because she was about to confess love to the man who was not free to love her—who would never love her as long as Roger claimed her affections.

> *I have struggled to know what I should write*
> *to you, and it is only because I am certain I*
> *shall never see you again that I dare to be bold.*
> *Alden, you have my gratitude and my admira-*
> *tion forever. You alone saw all that I could be,*

and if you had not encouraged me to be true to my calling I would never have found the courage to exercise the gifts God has given me. You have helped me see that I am complete in God. As a woman, I am not less than a man, though it has always given me great pleasure to submit to your loving leadership.

You have given me the courage to step out on my own, though my heart breaks at the thought of not seeing you again. But know that wherever I go, I will carry in my heart the lessons you have taught. Though I am a woman, I am not weak. Though I am soft, I am not soft-headed. And though I may be lonely, I am never alone.

I will pray for you every night, begging God to carry you safely home.

With all my affection,
Flanna O'Connor

She folded the letter and sealed it in an envelope, then scrawled Alden's name across the front. She had just slipped it back into her jacket when the sound of approaching footsteps announced Roger's return. She saw him clearly; he walked quickly and hunched over, the dressmaker's box on his hip.

A moment later he entered the shelter of the oak and handed the box to her. "There's a tent for women at the back of the camp," he said, frowning as he placed the box into her hands. "I'm sorry, but the women there are camp followers. I've no doubt you won't want to be associated with them, but you need only remain there until the next envoy leaves for Washington."

"I shan't mind." Flanna shifted the box to her own hip, then gave Roger a careful smile. "Thank you, Roger. May God go with you until we meet again."

She couldn't see his face in the shadows, but she felt his hand on her shoulder. "Be safe, Flanna." He softened his words by squeezing her arm. "I will join you as soon as I can."

He released her then and moved away, as silently as a shadow. Flanna waited under the oak until she saw him reenter the circle of his men, then she walked carefully through the sodden leaves toward her own messmates. She had one more task—a letter to place where O'Neil would be certain to find it—and then she would be done with the Army of the Potomac.

She looked up. The sky was thick and black with clouds, weeping steadily enough to cover any trail she might leave behind. God could not have arranged a finer night.

Twenty-Five

Flanna stumbled into the woods, watching the darkness thicken and congeal around her. Above the trees, stark white streaks of lightning cracked through the black sky, lighting her way in random flashes.

Flanna trembled and her teeth chattered, as much from fear as from the freezing rain. When she had walked for ten minutes, she paused in a sheltered copse and opened the sodden dress box. She fumbled among the contents and sighed in relief that Roger had picked up the green plaid dress, not the ridiculous red velvet gown. Under the protective cover of the trees, Flanna shed her wet coat, shirt, trousers, and undergarments, then slipped into the chemise, pantalets, and dress. Thank goodness the hoop skirt was in the other box; she'd never manage one in these woods. The dress itself was heavy and cumbersome around her ankles, and not nearly as warm as the wool coat of her uniform. Reluctantly, Flanna slipped the coat over her dress. She'd get rid of it in the morning, though any Rebel who found it was liable to panic at the thought of Federals in the woods.

After dressing, Flanna tore the dress box into tiny pieces, then scattered them through the woods, knowing the pieces would be lost in the mud. She stuffed her undershirt and drawers into a knot-hole, then threw her trousers under a bush. She had only brought two things away with her—her journal, which she had always kept buttoned inside her coat, and her medical bag, which she had quietly pulled out of her knapsack when she left Alden's letter in O'Neil's tent.

She couldn't part with the medical bag. Common sense told her that she might need it, and sentiment reminded her that it had been a gift—from Alden.

She hesitated, looking back through the dark shadows through which she'd come. Tattoo would sound at any moment, summoning the men to their quarters, and afterward the pickets would shoot at anything they saw moving in the brush. She had to get away, and quickly.

A sob rose in her throat as she pushed forward, and sudden tears blinded her eyes and mingled with the rain that streamed down her face. Jagged and painful regrets kept her company as she walked. She should have told Paddy good-bye. She should have told Valentine that she'd pray for him. She should have thanked the sergeant for tolerating her weaknesses, and she wanted just once to punch Diltz in the arm and run like mad. She wanted to copy down one of Andrew Green's poems and assure Freddie Smith that there was more to life than fripperies and foolishness.

Most of all, she wanted to feel Alden's arms around her once again, feel his head resting against hers like the night when the shells were flying and he'd held her. She had felt so close to him that night, but she would never feel close to him again. When the sun rose on the morrow, she'd be a Rebel, a South Carolina Confederate.

Alden and the others would be her sworn enemies.

She walked for over an hour, then stopped, judging that she'd covered at least two miles. At this point she should be in neutral territory, beyond both the Union and Confederate pickets.

Groping with her hands, she found a hollowed-out spot near the bottom of a slanting pine tree. She curled up at its base, hugging her knees to her chest and using her soldier's coat as a blanket. She leaned her head back on the scabbed tree trunk and stared at the sky. She would rest here and wait until morning before moving further. The Confederates had undoubtedly posted guards around the roads into Richmond, and she could not travel safely in the dark.

She had thought she'd be too cold and nervous to rest, but a profound, peaceful weariness settled on her like a cloak. After a while her eyelids drifted shut and her body relaxed into the trusting limpness of sleep.

⌘

A handful of fat raindrops spattered on Flanna's face. Instantly awake, she opened her eyes in sudden panic, unable to tell the hour. A dull gray light filled the woods in a light fog rising from the luxuriant foliage, cloaking the forest in a steamy carpet.

Daylight. Morning.

Flanna stood, stuffed her soldier's coat into the hollow of the tree and gripped her medical bag. She stepped out of her hiding place and turned, confused. Though the rain had stopped, she couldn't see the sun through the morning haze, and the towering trees obliterated any glimpse of the horizon.

She felt an icy finger touch the base of her spine. Had she come this far just to get lost in the woods—alone?

No. She could find her way.

Trust in the Lord with all thine heart, and lean not unto thine own understanding. God had not created her helpless. She had a brain, and a good one, and she knew how to use it.

In all thy ways acknowledge him, and he shall direct thy paths. He would guide her path...if she could only start walking.

She turned again, shielding her eyes from the dripping raindrops, then noticed how the light streamed through the canopy of trees. The diagonal gray bands had to slant toward their source—in the east.

Sighing in gratitude, Flanna turned west. She lifted her heavy skirts and began to move through the thick undergrowth, kicking her way through tangled vines and praying that she wouldn't encounter any snakes. At least she wore her heavy men's brogans. Fortunately, Roger hadn't thought to order her a pair of dainty slippers.

Thunder boomed somewhere to the north, and she lengthened her stride, fearing that the heavens might open in earnest before she reached Richmond. "You had the right idea, Charity," she murmured, yanking her dress from the branches and briars that tugged at her skirt. "You followed your heart and went with the man you loved. I wish I could do the same…but Alden wouldn't have me."

The heaviness in Flanna's chest felt like a millstone, weighing her down far more than the wet skirts that dragged around her ankles. With every step, her heart pulled her back toward the man who had changed her life, but reason spurred her forward. Alden would always see her as Roger's sweetheart; his fanatical sense of duty would prod him to provide for his brother as long as he lived. What Roger wanted Roger got, so Alden could stand tall and assure his mother, his dead father, and God above that he had fulfilled his obligation, no matter what the cost.

A tree limb snatched at her, and Flanna tore herself away with a choking cry. How in the world had she come to this place? She ought to be safe in Charleston at her father's hearth, content in the warmth of his love. She should have been knitting socks for Confederate boys instead of sewing those confounded havelocks. She should have given her heart to some devoted young man from South Carolina, and not to a headstrong, stubborn Yankee officer who would never allow himself to love her.

She balled her free hand into a hard fist, fighting back the emotions she couldn't allow to distract her. She wouldn't look back. These thick woods were a curtain, and all she had to do was pass through them and find a northwest road, for it would lead her to Richmond and the Confederacy. These gray and blue shadows would soon yield to sunlight; this ragged carpet would vanish when she reached plowed earth. And she would find her way home to Charleston.

She was finally ready to fulfill the promise she'd made to her father and Mammy. Images of the future crowded her mind, pushing in like unwelcome guests. Once she got home, she'd establish her women's medical practice and deal with assorted female troubles and predictable complaints. The joy of an occasional obstetric delivery would be offset by the daily grind of dealing with simpering women who fainted to be fashionable or because their corsets were too tight. In a year, maybe two, she would marry a nice Southern gentleman—if she could find a war survivor who wasn't too intimidated by a woman with a calling. She would respect him, obey him, and be grateful to him for saving her from permanent spinsterhood, but she would never love him. Flanna doubted that she could ever care for anyone the way she cared for Alden Haynes.

The thunder sounded again, echoing through the gray haze, and Flanna halted in midstride, her thoughts sharpening to an ice pick's point. That wasn't thunder! That rhythmic, pounding rumble was the sound of artillery fire.

She froze as sheer black fright swept through her. What had happened? Either the Rebels struck unexpectedly, or reveille sounded early in the Union camp and the men learned of the attack at roll call. Another thought whipped into her brain. No wonder Roger had no trouble retrieving her dress last night! Alden had not been in his tent; he had probably been in an officers' meeting. The Virginia Creeper must have decided to advance.

Trembling at the sounds of battle, Flanna stared through the woods in hypnotized horror. She stood in the no-man's land between two armies; she had to move. She lowered her head and hurried forward as her heart pounded, each separate thump like a heavy blow to her chest. The blurred images of matted vines and thick foliage faded as her eyes colored with the memory of Alden's face as he had looked on the night they were shelled outside Yorktown. She recalled the concern in his eyes, the determination in his jaw, the strength in his face. The Twenty-fifth Massachusetts had marched at the rear of the fighting at Williamsburg, so they would likely be at the front of the fighting now. And Alden would be on the front line with his men, his sword drawn and pointed toward the enemy as he urged them forward. And while the enlisted men knelt or sprawled on their bellies and aimed their rifles over fallen logs and muddy earthen mounds, Alden would stand upright to shout encouragement, his noble head exposed to shell and shot.

She halted as a scream clawed in her throat. How could she leave now? The life she had imagined in Charleston paled in comparison to the life she was leaving behind. Her men needed her. There'd be a gap in the line next to Paddy O'Neil, for wee Franklin O'Connor wouldn't be there to fill it. And if something happened to Paddy, Alden would never receive her letter; he'd never know how much he'd done for her. And if something happened to Alden—

She trembled as she imagined Alden on Dr. Gulick's table.

Abandoning her plans, Flanna turned sharply toward the sound of fighting. Nothing mattered anymore, nothing but Alden. And she would find him or die trying.

Distracted by movement in a stand of scrub oaks, Alden tilted his head and stared as a flock of sparrows rose from the greenery, fluttering and circling above the field in a state of utter bewilderment. Beyond the line of embankments, the artillery had been blasting canisters loaded with grapeshot into the Confederates for nearly an hour. Those Rebel lines ought to be weaker now.

"Major," a man called from the line, a look of pained concentration on his face, "can I be excused? Nature's calling real insistently."

"Stay in your place, soldier." Alden shook his head and pressed his heel to his horse's ribs, urging the skittish mare forward. Amazing how many men marched to the front line and suddenly remembered that they'd forgotten to visit the latrine or repair their rifles.

Alden rode parallel to the line, using the flat side of his saber to prod the stragglers forward. "The artillery's been softening them up for some time now, boys," he called, reining in his horse. "We're moving out soon, for God and the Union. Let's show them what Massachusetts men are made of!"

The men cheered and the drummers began to play. The line filled in and undulated softly as men scrambled over the trenches and the mounded earthworks, then stepped onto the open field. There had been no artillery fire from the Rebs, so they were safe to wait outside the embankments.

Alden kicked the mare and trotted down the line, mentally checking off the companies in his command. Company L marched in this part of the line, supported by Company K. He caught a glimpse of Roger's profile and saw that his brother wore a cold, hard-pinched expression on his face. Alden nodded grimly and moved down the line, then slowed as he recognized the men of Company M.

His eyes studied every form in the line, searching for Flanna. He didn't see her.

"Major!" A ruddy-faced soldier looked back over his shoulder and jerked his chin toward Alden. "I got a message for you—a letter."

"Let it wait, Private." Alden's gaze moved on down the line, relieved that Flanna had listened to him and stayed behind. He didn't care whether she was playing sick or working in the medical tent, at least she had sense enough to realize that she couldn't very well tramp into battle with these men.

Alden turned his mount and retraced his path, automatically soothing the mare as she snorted and danced beneath the saddle. A smudge of sun dappled through the heavy cloud cover, and though the prospect of sunlight should have cheered him, Alden felt a distant anxiety.

They had been expecting the Rebs to attack. Colonel Farnham had told his officers to move at morning's first light, and yet the rains had upset McClellan's master plan. Last night's rain had brought the Chickahominy, a trickling river in the midst of this peninsula, to flood stage, effectively cutting the general's grand army in two. Rather than face the entire Union force, the Rebs had wisely directed all their efforts against the Federal troops on the southern side of the swollen river.

Alden reached into his pocket and pulled out a map he'd hastily drawn the night before. One penciled line indicated the Nine-mile Road; two dots marked its intersections with the Williamsburg Old Stage Road and the Richmond and York River Railroad. The locals called the Old Stage intersection Seven Pines, and the depot at the railroad intersection was named Fair Oaks. Alden and his regiment stood less than a mile from Fair Oaks.

After memorizing the locations, Alden folded the map and thrust it back into his coat. Like a wolf seeking out its enemy's weakness, the Confederates had surmised that this half of the Union army was the less prepared, and so the attack had come.

Alden's orders were specific. His troops were to support the picket line and prepare to move forward at the colonel's command. Two regiments of the brigade had already been detached, and skirmishers had been sent to detect the extent of the Confederate lines. The enemy no doubt believed that an energetic morning attack would defeat the Federal regiments on the southern side of the river before the other portion of the army could cross. The Rebs would be fighting on boggy, swampy fields and woods, but they were defending their capital and their cause.

This would not be an easy battle.

God, help the right. And help me do my duty.

A sharp burst of signal fire sounded behind the trees, and Alden barked the order to move out. The mare back-stepped, eyeing the trench and embankment with suspicion, but Alden touched his boot to her ribs. The horse cleared trench and mound in one graceful leap, then moved contentedly behind the men, the grass making wet slicking sounds against her legs. As he rode, Alden stared at the ground in grim curiosity. A mass shedding was taking place, the men dropping anything and everything that might be a hindrance in battle. Overcoats, blankets, and canteens littered the earth, and Alden felt the corner of his mouth lift in a wry smile when he saw a blizzard of playing cards whirling in the wind. Someone, no doubt, had just forsworn gambling in a last-minute attempt to enjoin God's protection.

"'Tis a messy day, Major!" the regimental standard-bearer called over his shoulder as the blue and white flag flapped over his head.

The men were wading through a virtual swamp; some of them splashed through puddles and found themselves in knee-deep water. This would be a difficult fight, for powder cartridges would not fire if wet, and most of the men were accustomed to kneeling or lying on the ground to load and fire.

"Keep it up," Alden called, strengthening his voice. "We'll take this land inch by inch if we have to!" He heard the sound of gunshots, dry and thin as snapping twigs, then a shrill, exultant, savage cry from the woods.

"Listen to the Rebs screaming," one man yelled. "They can't wait for us to come."

"Yell back at them," Alden called. "Center up, close up those gaps, keep the line tight. If the man next to you falls, keep going!"

Alden tensed as the noise of battle intensified. The sound of the bullets varied from a sharp crack to a hum, then a whistle. One blew by his ear with a strange meowing sound, as if a Rebel had thrown a kitten at him. The line buckled as his men stopped to aim and fire, though clouds of smoke from the Confederates' rifle pits made it difficult to aim at anything.

"Keep it up, boys, keep going," Alden yelled, resisting his own urge to duck as bullets whizzed past him. "Fire at will! Show them that Massachusetts men aren't afraid to fight for freedom!"

The standard-bearer fell, hitting the damp ground with a wet smack as the regimental colors fluttered down over him. Alden immediately kicked his horse into a canter and moved into the man's empty position. He reached out for the flagpole, which another soldier placed in his hand.

"Onward!" He braced the flagpole in his stirrup and held the banner high for the others to see. "Our colors are still flying!"

As the line of attack closed in on the Confederates, the hail of lead thickened. The mare snorted and shook her head, unnerved by the hum of bullets and the crackle of musketry. Clods of earth flew up in front of the line, turning what had been an emerald field into a muddy mess. Unavoidably, one by one, the men in Alden's line fell. He ordered his men into new positions, frantically trying to keep the line closed, but the time of organized warfare had ended. From this point each man would fight on his own.

A shot whizzed by, stinging Alden's ear. He lifted his hand and pulled it away, surprised to find a streak of blood on his fingertips.

"Enough of this," he muttered, sliding off his horse. He turned the mare away from the battle line, pulled his rifle from its scabbard, then swatted the animal's bony rear. The grateful animal bolted and was gone.

Wanting to leave the regimental flag with someone else, Alden looked around. The sight of movement from behind a tree startled him, and Alden dropped the colors and crouched behind a bush, not certain what he would encounter. Through the veil of greenery he saw a soldier squatting behind a stout oak, a cartridge in his hand. As Alden watched, perplexed, the man bit the cartridge and ripped it open, then poured a handful of gunpowder into his palm. After casting a surreptitious glance over his shoulder, he spat into the powder and rubbed the moistened mixture on his face, then he obliterated the traces of gunpowder on his hands with mud. When he had finished, he turned and sank to the ground, his back against the tree, his eyes closed, his rifle in his hand, still unfired.

Alden stared in stunned disbelief. The little coward! By all appearances anyone would think he had been out fighting on the front lines, but the shiftless sneak would undoubtedly remain here until retreat.

Alden charged forward. "You, there!" He pulled his pistol from the holster at his waist. "Get up right now or, by heaven, I'll shoot you myself."

The coward's hands lifted in a don't-shoot posture as Alden approached, his eyes showing white all around like a panicked horse.

"I saw your little act and the application of your war paint." Alden shook with impotent rage. "You will get up now, and you will march toward your fellows, proudly carrying our regimental colors. To make sure you do, I will march right behind you."

The fellow's powder-blackened lips parted in a wide smile as he stood. "Why, Alden, why would I want to do that? The man who carries the colors might as well wear a sign that says Shoot Me."

Alden stared wordlessly at Roger, his heart pounding.

"Say something, brother." Roger slowly lowered his hands, warming Alden with that ever-so-charming smile. "You aren't really angry, are you? I would have gone to the front with my company," his hands moved to his stomach, "but I've an awful bellyache and I really didn't think I should be fighting. You wouldn't want me to have an attack of the quickstep out there on the field, would you?"

Alden hesitated, weighing his anger against his responsibility to protect his brother. Mother would never forgive him for deliberately placing Roger in harm's way.

Seething with anger, humiliation, and frustration, he lowered his pistol.

"You are a disgrace to your company, your men, and Massachusetts." His voice vibrated with restrained fury. "Stay here, guard the regiment's standard, play your little game. But as long as you persist in wearing that uniform, you are not to speak to me again."

He turned and walked toward the battle, leaving Roger in the cowardly shadows. And a few moments later, when a shot knocked Alden to the ground, he closed his eyes in resignation to God's will.

At least his mother would be spared one son.

⚜

Flanna took cover while the battle surged in front of her. She had wanted to run and find Alden, but she knew she would have been simply a target for both sides if she entered the battlefield.

After two days she finally got her chance. Under flags of truce soldiers of both armies moved out to collect the dead and wounded. Flanna moved among them, too, not caring whether the men at her feet wore butternut brown, the prevailing uniform among the home-dressed Confederates, or Union blue. She closed the eyes of the dead and brought water to the wounded, trying to make them as comfortable as possible until a litter could arrive. Both Union and Confederate soldiers watched as she went about her grim task, and each side assumed she belonged to them. Which, in a way, she supposed she did.

As she worked, she interrogated the Union litter bearers. While the Confederate wounded had access to a hospital in Richmond, the Union wounded had only the regimental surgeons' tents at the rear of the army.

"So what is happening to these men?" she demanded, placing her hands on her hips as she interrogated one young drummer boy.

The boy blinked up at her, doubtless confused by her manner, her unconventional coiffure, and her mud- and blood-stained dress. "We're taking 'em to the railway depot at the rear." He swatted away a fly that buzzed around his bloody hands. "Though I haven't seen or heard a train in days. They're just lyin' out there, shivering."

"Is someone giving them food and water?" Softening her tone, Flanna stooped slightly and looked the young man in the eye. "Did the general or the surgeon appoint someone to care for these men, or are they lying in the rain?"

The boy nodded slightly. "That's it, ma'am, you have it right. They're all just lyin' there, with no one to help. If it was me"—he paused and chewed his lip thoughtfully—"yep, if it was me, I'd rather be dead. They're calling and crying, but no one listens. And after the trains pick them up, if the trains ever come, they'll have to lie at the wharf and wait for a boat."

Flanna turned away, hiding the storm of frustration and anger that surely showed on her face. General McClellan might enjoy preparing for war, but he had obviously made no preparation for its brutal aftermath.

"Thank you, young man." She turned and gave the boy a patient smile, then knelt down and smoothed the forehead of the wounded infantryman at her feet. He was unconscious. Considering all that lay ahead of him, that was probably a mercy.

The boy and his companion lifted the litter and trudged back through the mud toward the Union lines. Flanna stood and pressed her hands to her back, easing the stiffness out of her joints. She had slept only a few hours of the last forty-eight, and had eaten nothing but two pieces of hardtack and a slab of dried beef from a dead Federal's haversack. The rains had vanished, but the sun still hid its face, dropping only occasional shafts of light through breaks in the overhanging clouds.

The foragers were out in force, too, hiding their dirty work under the pretext of caring for the wounded. Every dead man she had come across had already lost his rifle and pistol, and more than a few were missing their shoes and the brass buttons from their coats—buttons that would serve as ghoulish souvenirs. She had come across one Federal soldier taking a toothbrush from a dead Confederate's knapsack; upon seeing her, the man merely grinned and thrust it in his pocket.

Flanna stiffened as a bitter wail rose from beyond a sloping hill beyond. She moved toward the grassy knoll, then paused at the sight of a fallen soldier and a comrade who knelt at his side. The survivor's moaning cry went on and on, lancing the silence, and Flanna frowned as she drew nearer. The fallen man wore gray, the survivor, blue. And the scarred face that now turned toward her belonged to William Sheahan, the veteran of Company M.

She came to an abrupt halt, her heart jumping in her chest, but Sheahan only glanced at her, then turned back to the dead soldier in the field. "It's James." He spoke in a broken whisper, then made a harsh keening sound in his throat. "Jimmy, why'd you leave home? You should have stayed with the folks and not come to war. I never wanted to see you like this, boy."

Flanna closed her eyes, her heart aching with pain. She had known Sheahan was from Georgia, but he had never spoken of family or friends back home. She had never dreamed that a heart lay beneath that granite strength, and the sight of his mourning unsettled her.

"I'm very sorry," she whispered, coming close enough to place her hand on his shoulder. Sheahan didn't look up, but cradled the boy's head in his lap and made soft, shushing sounds.

Flanna drew in a deep breath, released it slowly, and left Sheahan to his mourning, knowing there was little she could do. Another soldier lay before her, only the tips of his boots visible through the tall grass. She hurried toward him, her jaw tightening, then stiffened in shock. Paddy O'Neil lay on his back on a patch of matted red grass, his face grimed with black powder, his hair sparking like copper in the sun. Except for the traces of gunpowder on his face, he could have been napping in the quiet warmth of afternoon.

She knelt by his side and pressed her hand to his face. "O'Neil? Can you hear me?"

He groaned, and his eyelids fluttered like the throats of baby birds. Then the blue eyes opened and a drowsy smile spread across his face. "O'Connor." His voice was a weak and tremulous whisper. His eyelids drooped and closed again as he spoke, but the sleepy smile remained. "Now I know I'm dreaming. You look like a woman, O'Connor."

"Where are you hit, O'Neil?" Flanna frantically patted his body. There were no torn places in his shirt, no obvious wounds anywhere...

"Don't tell the others," he said in an aching, husky voice she scarcely recognized. "I was hit in the back, but...don't want the others to think I was running. I had just turned around...to check on Green."

A new anguish seared her heart when Flanna looked up and spied another familiar form in a bed of tangled vines. Andrew Green lay completely still, his eyes wide and blank as windowpanes. The sensitive soul they had mirrored had long since flown.

"You don't have to worry about Green." Flanna reached out and clasped O'Neil's hand between both her own. "You just lie still. Help is coming."

"I can't...see you." His eyelids no longer fluttered. "And I can't feel much of anything."

"It's okay, O'Neil." Flanna leaned forward to speak directly in his ear. "I'm with you."

"Tell Maggie...I'll be wanting to meet her in heaven." His smile faded a little, as if that admission had used up the last of his strength. "Tell her...I'll wait."

"O'Neil!" Flanna pressed her hands to his chest, then leaned forward to listen for the sounds of breathing. There were none. In a surge of panic she ripped open his coat, tore at his shirt, and pressed her ear to his chest, but...nothing.

Paddy O'Neil was dead. And in the grass, where she'd flung it when she tore open his coat, Flanna saw the letter she had written to Alden. Paddy had not had a chance to deliver it.

Flanna sank back to her knees and brought her hand to her mouth, overwhelmed by a sense of loss far beyond tears. This, then, was the field where the Twenty-fifth Massachusetts fought. Paddy lay here, and Andrew…

Her teeth chattered, her body trembled at the thought that others of her company might lie in the trampled earth beyond.

Twenty-Six

She didn't know how long she sat beside Paddy, but the field had begun to fill with mist and gray-blue light by the time she composed herself enough to continue her search for the wounded. She could not work much longer, for the western sky was already blazing with violent copper and coral shades. Soon the sun would set, and the wounded would spend another night on the battlefield...if any remained alive.

Flanna clenched her jaw to kill the sob in her throat. If there were others, she would find them.

With a heavy heart she walked over the scarred field, her eyes searching behind every tangle of leaves for a glimpse of blue or gray or butternut. The pain and grief of this place clung to her like the gray smoke that hung over the battlefield, socked in by low-hanging clouds. A harrowing headache pounded her forehead while her heart mourned the bitter knowledge that Alden had not received her letter. He had opened her eyes, inspired her to act, and changed her life. She owed him everything, but he would never know it.

Flanna's eyes caught another form in the brush, and she moved doggedly toward it. She felt drained, as hollow and lifeless as the bodies she'd examined and left for the gravediggers. Her back ached between her shoulder blades; the images of brush and mud and trees seemed to quiver before her weary eyes.

"Hello?" she called, stumbling toward the soldier in blue. He lay on his side, his back and shoulder toward her, and even from this distance she could see that his shoulder had taken a brutal hit. She squinted in concern at the sight of his shoulder strap—an officer. "Can you hear me, sir?"

His head stirred and lifted, and something in his profile caught at Flanna's heart.

She stopped, her hand flying to her throat, then she rushed forward. Flanna felt her nerves begin to tense. "Alden?" She fell beside him in the muddy hollow where he had fallen, her practiced eye taking in the hoofprint on his pant leg, the bloody hole in his uniform, the cut above his right eye. "Alden, can you speak?"

He gave her a faint but glorious smile that Flanna would have accepted as her last view of earth. "I can speak tolerably well." His voice was low and controlled, but Flanna could hear an undertone of desolation in it. "Is the battle ours? Have we advanced?"

"The battle belonged to no one." Flanna gripped his shoulder and carefully lowered him onto his back. She gently pressed her fingers to the wound at his shoulder and nodded when he grimaced in pain. Pain was good. He could feel, and he hadn't yet bled to death, so his heart had been spared. But there was no corresponding wound at his back, which meant that the bullet remained within him. It could shift or cause putrefaction and infection if not removed.

She looked up and scanned the horizon, judging that less than half an hour of daylight remained. If she left him here, he wouldn't be picked up until morning. And then he'd lie in a long line of wounded patients outside the surgeons' tents. If he was lucky enough to survive Gulick's table, he'd lie on the ground and wait for the train, then he'd lie amid the stinking flies and dirt while he waited for the boat to Washington, where he'd be treated in that filthy Alexandria Hospital.

He'd never make it. The wound didn't look serious, and that would work to his disadvantage, for he'd be shuffled about from place to place while his body fought to repel the foreign object inside it.

Flanna blew out her cheeks, then made her decision. Alden wouldn't like it, but in his present condition he couldn't protest.

Pasting on a stiff smile, she prayed that she would not betray her agitation and fear. "Alden, you must trust me now." She lifted his shoulder again, struggling to free the bloody coat from his arm. "And you must ask no questions. I am only acting for your own good."

"What are you talking about?" He inhaled in a soft hiss as she lifted the opposite shoulder, momentarily forcing his weight upon the wound.

She yanked his coat free and tossed it aside, noticing that a pair of letters protruded from the inner pocket. Alden's thoughts. She wouldn't leave them for foragers.

She picked up the letters and tossed them inside her medical bag, then turned back to Alden. He was trying to moisten his lips and speak.

"Be quiet, rest, and let me look at you." Alden shivered slightly in the chilly air, and Flanna noted his cooling body temperature even as she ripped his undershirt away from his neck and studied the entrance wound. The Minié ball had struck the flesh above his heart, probably shattering the collarbone. He might be able to walk, but if his heart began to pound, the increased rate of circulation could result in a disastrous loss of blood. She could not apply a tourniquet to that wound, nor could she stop a bone fragment from slipping out of place and puncturing his lung if he were jostled.

"Alden." She pressed her hands to his shoulders and looked steadily into his eyes. "I must remove that bullet. And I can't do it here."

He had to be in shock from the pain. His eyes were soft and dreamy, as gentle as a child's. He drew a ragged breath. "I trust you."

"Good." She pressed her hand to his cheek. "I'll be right back."

⊷∾⊷

Back in the Union camp, Roger sat with his comrades and watched as the wounded were brought in. His brother had not been seen in two days, and Roger's stomach churned when he thought of their last meeting. Alden had looked at him with loathing and disgust in his eyes, but why couldn't he understand that they were fundamentally different? Alden was the soldier, the West Point instructor; Roger had never been anything but a charmer and persuader. He was destined to battle in the courtroom and the chambers of Congress, not here. He fought with the weapons of words and ideas, not rifles and cannon.

Roger gazed at the men in his command, a thinner number than had been present three nights ago when Flanna called to him from the rain. At least she had escaped the slaughter. Roger hadn't looked for her, but he imagined her to be somewhere at the rear of the camp, probably up to her arms in wounded men.

He shook his head, imagining her in that horrid plaid dress, her hair blowing in the wind like a homeless child's. Her compassion would do him credit when they were married, but he'd have to convince her not to become so directly involved in her causes. Respectable women always maintained a discreet distance from the raw issues of life; she could speak intelligently and forcefully about medicine without ever having to touch another patient. Ideally, of course, once they were married she would forget about medicine altogether.

"Got a smoke, Captain?" one of the men called, his brow lifting with the question. Roger pulled a package of freshly rolled cigars from his pocket, then tossed it to the man without comment. He stood and stretched his legs, wondering how he'd find the courage to write his mother should the worst prove true. Mother adored Alden; the news of his death would destroy her.

"Captain Haynes!" A high, girlish voice called from the darkness beyond his fire, and Roger's heart skipped a beat, fearing that Flanna had come from the medical tents with bad news.

"What?"

"A message for you."

Roger squinted into the darkness. The summons had not come from Flanna, but from one of the young drummer boys. He relaxed and stepped away from the fire, resting his hand on his belt. "What message?"

"This, sir." The young man held up a letter and slanted it toward the campfire. Roger could see that someone had written "Major Haynes" on the envelope. The handwriting was feminine and remarkably similar to Flanna's.

"Major Haynes is my brother." Roger took the envelope from the boy's hand. "How did you come by this?"

"We found it on a dead man, sir. Private O'Neil, from Company M."

Roger tapped the envelope against his fingertips, thinking. O'Neil's name meant nothing to him, but Company M certainly did.

"Thank you." Roger nodded, dismissing the boy, then walked back to the campfire. The men around him sat silent for the most part, each man consumed by his own thoughts, regrets, and private relief.

Ignoring the warning voice that whispered in his head, Roger broke the seal and pulled out the letter, still damp from the rain and the sweat of battle. A deep, surprising pain smote his breast as he read; the feeling intensified as he read the note a second time.

When he had finished, he crumpled the letter in his hand and stared at the fire. An unexpected weed of jealousy sprang up in his heart, stinging like nettles. He tossed the wadded paper into the fire, then shoved his hands in his pockets and hunched his shoulders forward, trying to hide from the pain.

How could he have been so blind? His sweetheart loved his brother; that much was clear enough. From the first word, Flanna had expressed more honest admiration and caring for Alden than she ever had for Roger.

And what did she mean by saying that she would never see Alden again? She certainly would, for as Roger's wife she would see Alden at every family gathering…unless the letter was a calculated lie. A test. An attempt to force Alden's hand, to goad him into doing something he would never have done without an open threat.

You have given me the courage to step out on my own…

Roger looked out into the darkness, unable to stop himself from pondering the impossible. Had Alden and Flanna run away together? It seemed inconceivable that Alden would desert his post and his men, but before this night Roger would never have believed Flanna capable of deception.

He laughed aloud, realizing the illogic of his thoughts. Why, Flanna was a natural deceiver! She'd deceived him from the first, hiding in this camp as a man, without telling him, her fiancé, anything at all. But Alden had known. Alden had spent a great deal of time with her, helping her establish that silly dispensary, encouraging her in foolish and inappropriate ideas. And Alden had brought her to Virginia, against all common sense, against Roger's wishes, and why? Because he loved her!

The admission flowered from a place beyond all logic and experience, but Roger could not deny it. And the letter, Flanna's loving farewell, was intended to provoke Alden to action.

The thoughts that had been chasing each other through Roger's brain suddenly fell into a neat and obedient order. That was exactly why she had done it! She had written this letter before the battle, but Alden hadn't received it because this man O'Neil had died. And so Flanna had waited and confronted Alden after the first day of battle, knowing he could easily desert his post in the confusion. They both knew he'd be listed as one of the missing while they ran away together.

"So this is why you brought her to Virginia," he muttered.

The man next to Roger turned with a quizzical glance. "You okay, Captain?"

"Fine," Roger answered, crossing his arms. "Just fine."

They were out there together. Somewhere in the woods or in Richmond itself, they had their arms wrapped around each other. Perhaps even now they were laughing at the brother they'd left behind.

The surge of rage caught him unaware, like white-hot lightning through his chest and belly. Roger gasped, half-choked with it, then clamped the anger down tight, hoarding it like coals in a hearth.

He would find them. Tomorrow he'd search through the camp for Flanna and Alden, just to give them the benefit of the doubt, and when he didn't find them, he'd set out on his own. During this lull, while men still walked around in an after-battle daze, Roger would slip away too. Some things were bigger than war, more pervasive, more fundamental.

At that moment, Roger felt far less animosity toward the secessionists than he did toward Flanna and Alden. A cheating woman and a disloyal brother were far greater sinners than mere secessionists.

Twenty-Seven

~∞~

Six days after the battle at Fair Oaks, Flanna paused beside the bedside of a wounded Confederate soldier. The man had been hit in the thigh, and the leg amputated. Even with her skill, Flanna could see no other way to save the man's life. He seemed to bear her no ill will, though, and now he lay on a cot in the house and stared at the ceiling with his hands folded across his chest.

"You okay, Private?" Flanna asked.

His eyes did not move from the ceiling, but he nodded slightly. "Yes sir, I'm just glad it's over. Glad I'm out. Glad I'm alive."

His eyes flickered toward her for an instant. "You been in battle, Doc?"

Flanna pulled over a nearby stool and lowered herself to it. "I was at Ball's Bluff."

He lifted a shoulder in a slight shrug. "I weren't there. But I heard about it." A slow, shy smile blossomed out of his beard. "I heard we set the Yanks running right off the edge of a cliff."

Flanna lowered her eyes, alarmed that she had nearly forgotten where she was. She was in Richmond, in the guise of a *Confederate* doctor, tending *Rebel* soldiers. If she wasn't careful, she'd be talking about how she'd been quaking in her boots as she ran down the mountain…with the Yankees.

"It was something," she offered noncommittally. She reached out and pressed her hand to the man's forehead. No signs of fever. Good.

"Were you nervous, Doc?" His bright blue eyes squinted up at her, then one hand came up to wipe a string of wetness from his eyes.

"Yes," Flanna answered, looking away. "I was nervous."

The Rebel nodded and folded his hands again. "I was scared as a jackrabbit, and ready to run," he said, his eyes lighting with some indefinable emotion. "The bullets scared me most—that constant hissing sound. The captain said to move out, and I tried, but I felt sick at my stomach and started sweating all over. I didn't think my legs could hold me up, much less carry me to meet those bullets. But I ran, and I kept running, even when my comrades fell over in the grass."

He paused a moment, and Flanna let the silence stretch, knowing that he needed to talk. Most of these men had been in this house for nearly a week, and they'd had no chance for conversation, no opportunity to share their feelings and their pain.

"The thing that scared me even more," his voice quavered, "was that after a minute, I couldn't feel anything."

When he did not speak again, Flanna squeezed his shoulder. "You're alive now, Private, and you're feeling lots of things. Trust in God with all your heart, and he will guide your path."

He didn't answer for a moment, but tears fell from his eyes and made dark patches in his brown hair. "Were you ever that afraid, Doc? So afraid you couldn't feel nothin'?"

Flanna looked away, remembering the hour when she brought Alden to the Confederate doctors. She, too, had felt a cold perspiration and a weakness in the knees—indeed, she'd later thought that only the stiffness of her blood-stained skirt had held her upright. And she hadn't cared about living or dying. Alden's safety was all that mattered.

"Yes, soldier, I have been that afraid."

◦◦◦◦

Though he could not find the strength to open his eyes, Alden heard a myriad of sounds: voices, murmurs, whispers. The voices faded to a brief inaudible exchange, then a door closed with a definite and final click. And yet the sounds continued; the place seemed alive with them.

Someone screamed, someone cried, and every once in a great while the sheets over him rustled as they lifted and fell.

He drifted in and out of a thin, cruel sleep. He dreamed of men falling around him, shells exploding in a shrieking frenzy, soldiers splintering apart before his eyes. He choked on air thick with black smoke and struggled to move forward, joining men who shoved and stumbled over each other as they pushed through the mire. And then something hit him, and he fell. The others kept going, unaware that he had fallen. His hands clawed at the mud; his body sang with pain as a panicked horse galloped over his legs.

The darkness gradually deepened, and he slept for what felt like a very long time. Then he felt someone lift a weight from his chest, and something cold splashed on a burning area in his shoulder.

Groaning, he locked a scream behind his teeth and writhed in pain.

His eyes flew open. Flanna stood beside him, a pitcher in her hand. "Thank goodness." She smiled at him as if she'd just kissed him awake instead of shattering every nerve in his body. "I was beginning to wonder if I'd killed you."

"Good grief!" Alden gave her a black look. "What are you trying to do?"

"Hush." She leaned over, examined his shoulder, then nodded with satisfaction and taped a clean bandage into place. "I have done nothing but try to save your life. But you must hold your tongue, or you may get us both killed."

Her voice brimmed with depth and authority, and Alden knew she wasn't joking. He lifted his heavy head and glanced around him. He lay on a cot in what appeared to be a private home. Two other soldiers lay near him, their faces drawn and pinched in suffering even while they slept. A small table stood near the door, with a washbasin and pitcher arranged on a pretty, embroidered doily.

"Where am I?" He lowered his head to meet Flanna's gaze.

"You are a guest in the home of Mrs. Ellen Corey," Flanna answered, her voice now as smooth as silk. "In Richmond."

Richmond?

"Did we beat the Rebs back? Is the war over?"

"Stop talking foolishness, soldier," she snapped, glancing abruptly toward the hallway. "Do you think we'd let the Yankees into Richmond? Not by a long shot."

Alden let his head fall to the pillow as the significance of her words took hold. The Confederate army wouldn't treat Union prisoners in Richmond; there were far too many wounded Confederates for that sort of largess. Which could only mean that—

Flanna placed her hand upon his chest, stilling the question on his lips. For the first time he noticed that beneath her starched apron she wore an oversized shirt and dark men's trousers. Her hair was slicked back away from her forehead, barely touching her collar.

"I can see that you don't remember much." Her eyes warned him, *Be still and listen.* "Right after you led your men to face the Federals' charge, you were hit in the shoulder. I found you and brought you back here." A little smile quivered in the corner of her mouth. "I removed the bullet, cleaned your wound, and put your arm in a sling. You'll be fine as long as you don't try to rejoin your regiment, sir. The Fifth South Carolina and Colonel Giles will just have to get along without you for a while."

Alden opened his mouth to protest, but she was quicker.

"Of course," she went on, her voice pitched low so that only he could hear, "they weren't about to let a woman operate on you. What Yankees lack in manners they make up for in common sense, Alden, I'll give you that. It might be twenty years before a Southern man allows a woman to come near him with a scalpel."

"Excuse me," he interrupted in a tense, clipped voice that forbade any foolishness. "But who are you today?"

If she hadn't been wearing pants, an observer might have thought she cast him a flirtatious smile. "I'm Dr. Franklin O'Connor, of the Fifth South Carolina—everyone knows that. I've been here several days, tending all you nice Confederate boys."

Alden closed his eyes, then exhaled loudly. He knew he ought to be grateful that his life had been spared, yet this wasn't right.

Flanna was claiming him as a Confederate, but this particular disguise was an affront to his honor and the vows of loyalty he'd taken as an officer.

"Alden." Her tone deepened as she leaned closer. "I know you think this is wrong. And as soon as you're better, I'll do whatever you want me to do with you. But I had to save your life. The Union has no hospitals, and scores of men are dying right now by the railroad tracks. There is no one to help them."

He met her determined gaze. "I ought to be with them."

"You wouldn't have survived the journey!"

He flinched at something he heard in her voice, something jagged and sharp, like words torn by a bayonet. She bit her lip and remained silent for a moment, and when she spoke again, her voice rang with cool authority. "You don't know what it's like out there. The Confederacy has never seen a tide of casualties like this. The folks of Richmond and even Petersburg have been taking omnibuses and private carriages to the battlefields to collect the wounded. The injured are being piled into stores, tobacco warehouses, factories, private homes, and tents, and *still* there isn't room for everyone. Men with perfectly trivial injuries are dying because they can't walk and there is no one to bring them food and water. Even the ones who made it into town are having a rough time of it. The Richmond papers have been begging people to bring ice and food to the hospitals, and ladies are tearing up their old cotton dresses for bandages."

Unspoken pain glowed in her eyes, and he swallowed hard, realizing that she had risked a great deal to save his life. He reached up and squeezed her hand. "Thank you," he said simply, knowing he could not undo what had been done. For some reason God had used her to save him when he ought to be dead in the field with his comrades. Who was he to question the Almighty? Better to trust this woman's compassion and rest in God's plan. If it meant he spent the rest of the war in a Confederate prison camp, well, there were less honorable ways to end a military career.

Aware of passing footsteps in the hallway, he released her hand. "I didn't think anyone would come." His voice fell as the memory brushed him. For some reason he felt compelled to talk about what had happened. "I felt the bullet hit, and I tumbled to the ground like a drunken man, but I did not feel any pain. Instead I thought that someone had hit me terribly hard." He gave her a crooked smile. "I could not even tell where I had been hit, and thought perhaps I shouldn't look. Perhaps it was best not to know."

He lifted his eyes to the ceiling, letting his gaze rove over the water stains from the floor above. "I had little hope of seeing the next sunrise. I thought of more things in that next hour than I could write in a year. I thought of my dead father's brave example and prayed for my worried mother, wondering if she would ever learn what had happened to me. And I thought of you."

A cynical inner voice railed at him—*what a thing to admit to your brother's sweetheart!*—but Alden clenched his fist. He had suffered much for his brother and his country, and he deserved a moment of honesty! In the hours that he had lain on his back and stared at the weeping gray sky, he had thought about the people he would miss if he died. Flanna's oval face was the one that filled his imagination and fired his will to live.

But he no longer stood at death's door. And Flanna was still his brother's fiancée.

Reining in his defiant emotions, he avoided her eyes and kept his gaze fastened to the ceiling. "I longed for someone to come. I was shaken by the thought that I might die alone. I thought none of my regiment would ever find me, and that I might be buried in a common grave like the one we dug at Ball's Bluff. I prayed for daylight and the sunrise…and that someone would come, someone who would sit with me while I died. I knew God was with me, but I wanted to…touch someone."

"I would have come, Alden, if I had known how to find you. I sat with Paddy O'Neil." Flanna's voice went soft with the memory. "He died talking to me."

Alden blinked back a sudden rush of tears. "I shook so badly I thought I would jar all my bones out of place. I wanted water. I wanted to die…but not alone."

"You're not alone now." Her small hand floated up from the bedside and touched his cheek with tenderness. "You're not going to die, Alden, and I'm not going to leave you. When you're well, I'll help you do whatever you want to do." Her voice dropped to a hushed bedside whisper. "I'll even go downstairs and put on a dress, if that would please you. I'm done with surgery—I'm your nurse now."

"Why should you stay here?" He swiveled his head to better look at her. "You wanted to go home. Surely you can now."

Her lovely face twisted in a small grimace of pain, as if someone had suddenly struck her. "I have placed my trust in Mrs. Ellen Corey, mistress of this house. I had to, you see, for I needed men's clothing in order to operate on you and the others. The Confederate doctors would never have listened to me otherwise."

She looked toward the window, and Alden shifted as far as his wounded body would allow in order to study her. "You helped others?" he asked, gently urging her to continue.

"Yes. Mrs. Corey was very understanding." Flanna pulled a handkerchief from her pocket and dabbed at her eyes. "These clothes were her son's. He died at Manassas." She lifted one shoulder in a slight shrug. "In any case, when I found you, I took off your blue coat. Without it, you looked like any other wounded man on the battlefield. I brought you in on a wagon with Confederate wounded, but I couldn't leave you in the hospital." Her face twisted in horror. "I saw how they were operating, and I couldn't leave you there! So I sought out Mrs. Corey, for in her face I saw kindness and compassion. I pulled her aside, explained as much of my story as I dared, and she brought me here and gave me her son's clothes. I had you brought here with the others, and I operated on you downstairs in her kitchen."

She smiled, but her smile held only a ghost of its former warmth. "Amazing, what a pair of trousers will accomplish. I barked orders like

Gulick on his best day, and they brought everything I needed—bandages, chloroform, sutures."

"It wasn't the trousers." He eased into a smile. "It was you." He shook his head slightly, marveling at her determination. Her story thus far was one of success, so why did a shadow linger in her eyes?

"What else, Flanna?"

She hesitated only a moment, but the muscles in her slender throat tightened and betrayed her emotion. "You should know, Alden, that I had left the camp before I found you. I knew Richmond was only a few miles away, and I thought I could make it into town. I had Roger bring me one of the dresses from your tent, and I had nearly made it out of the woods when I heard the guns and turned back." Her voice faded to a hushed stillness. "I wrote you a letter, but—well, you didn't receive it. But I have your letters, the two I found in your coat."

"Letters?" Alden frowned.

"One to your mother, and one to Miss Nell Scott." She paused to tuck a stray strand of hair behind her ear, and Alden saw that her eyes burned with infinite distress. "I'll post them for you, when I think it's safe. Right now it wouldn't be wise to post letters to Boston from Mrs. Corey's house."

Alden nodded, still concerned about the sorrow in her eyes. "Do what you think best. But go on—why did you turn back? I thought you wanted to go home."

"I did." Her voice filled with anguish. "But I knew home would wait, while men might need me on the battlefield. So I did what I could for you and the others, and as soon as I came here, Mrs. Corey helped me send a wire to Charleston—two wires, actually. The first was to my father, and it said I'd be coming home as soon as he could wire the money for travel. When there was no reply, we wired my Aunt Marsali…and learned that my father died in December. I had read about the Charleston fire in an old newspaper, but I had no idea my father was involved."

Alden reached for her hand and felt her shudder as she drew in a sharp breath. "I heard the entire story from one of the Carolina boys. It seems that when the Union overran the Sea Islands, the planters and their slaves took refuge in Charleston. On December 11, a group of slave refugees started a campfire near the sash and blind factory on Hasell Street. Somehow the fire spread out of control, and the winds took it. And then"—her voice faltered, but she swallowed, squared her shoulders, and continued—"the fire moved down Queen Street, where the authorities blew up fourteen homes in order to save the hospitals, the Medical College, and the Orphan House."

Flanna clasped her free hand over Alden's and stared vacantly downward. "My home was one of those destroyed. And though everyone had been warned, apparently my father went back into the house at the last minute to fetch something. He was killed when the house fell in on him."

Floundering in a maelstrom of emotion, Alden stared at her. It wasn't fair! She had dared so much and risked everything to reach her father. God could not mean to repay her sacrifice with this sort of tragedy.

He curled his hand around her fingers, wanting to comfort her. He yearned to sit up and draw her into his arms, but if he held her…Better to lie still and be grateful that his wound prevented him from bringing her close.

Pain still flickered in those beautiful green eyes when she lifted her gaze to meet Alden's. "I'm so sorry," he whispered, a stab of guilt pricking his breast. He had felt sorry for himself until he heard Flanna's story. "I'd give anything to make it all right."

"Thank you, Alden." She squeezed his hand. "I'll let you sleep now," she whispered, pulling away, "and we'll talk more tomorrow…about what you must do."

"One thing?" He lifted his head.

"Yes?"

"You don't need the trousers, Flanna. Not anymore."

The glow of her small smile warmed him from across the room.

❧

The only room of Mrs. Corey's home not given over to the wounded was her tiny pantry. At sunset, after all the well-meaning visitors had been shooed out of the house, Flanna and her hostess sat on stools in that tiny space, two weary Southern women sharing a pot of tea. Flanna now wore a plain workday skirt, blouse, and apron that the widow Corey had thoughtfully provided. The green plaid dress was soaking in a basement washtub, still undeniably soiled with blood-stains at the hem, skirt, and sleeves.

Some of the blood on that skirt was Alden's, and Flanna knew she'd never look at that dress without remembering that she had at least been able to save his life. Her letter had never reached him, yet his letter to Nell Scott rested in her medical bag, so God's will was plainly evident. God had used her to save Alden for Nell. When Alden was fully recovered, Flanna would search for some way to send him back to the Union army, then she would look for some place of service in the Confederacy. Perhaps she would remain with Mrs. Corey, for this house was likely to be needed as a hospital as long as Jeff Davis called Richmond his capital.

Flanna sipped her tea, smiled at the widow, and tried not to think about the forty-five sick men in this house under her care. Technically, of course, they were the responsibility of the Confederate army surgeons, but none of those gentlemen had been able to visit in the last two days. Flanna and Mrs. Corey had handled all the nursing and medical care.

Flanna was amazed by Mrs. Corey's strength. She had listened to Flanna's story with wide eyes and an open heart, and from the first moment she had been willing to do anything to help the wounded...no matter which general they served.

"It is amazing," Mrs. Corey said now, gracefully placing her cup in the center of her saucer, "that you would want to go to medical school. I can't imagine a young lady of your charm answering any call but that of wife and mother."

"Truthfully, Mrs. Corey, I had hoped that I might still fulfill that calling." Flanna placed her teacup on a shelf next to a bag of corn meal. "But medicine was my first love. I felt a responsibility to the women of my community. So many were too modest to let my father treat them."

"How many of these men would be too modest to let you operate if they knew you were a woman?" The widow smiled, a quick curve of her thin, dry lips. "Quite a few, my dear. Modesty is a virtue claimed by both sexes."

"It's not modesty that prevents them from accepting a female doctor." Flanna cast her gaze downward. "It's fear. They can't believe that a woman could possibly know what she is doing. Their modesty is perfectly capable of allowing a woman to bathe them, change their bandages, hold their heads over a basin, and empty their slop jars." She lifted her teacup and smiled at her hostess over the rim. "They just don't want a woman coming toward them with a sharp blade."

"Still, I wish there were enough doctors to take care of these men." The widow fretted with the lace collar at her throat. "It just doesn't seem natural that you should have to disguise yourself as you did. Trousers aren't becoming, my dear. You are much more lovely in womanly garb."

Flanna shook her head, dismissing the compliment. "I would be happy to give the care of these men over to a male doctor," she said, then quickly lifted a finger. "No—I spoke too soon. I would not, for I have seen how army surgeons operate. You would recoil, Mrs. Corey, if you knew how things are. I have seen surgeons in blood-stained garments operating without anesthetic, chopping off limbs with a saw." She shuddered. "No, dear lady. One thing I have learned is that I must stand firm. I know what is best for these men, and I will do all I can to provide it for them."

Both women fell silent as the sound of footsteps thundered across the front porch. "Who can that be?" The widow's hand flew nervously to her throat as she stood and stepped out of the pantry. "We can't take any others—there simply is no more room."

"Should I go with you?" Flanna slipped from her stool, not waiting for an answer.

"Stay in the shadows if you please," Mrs. Corey called, moving through the hall toward the front door. "No offense, my dear, but you are a stranger in town."

Flanna remained in the kitchen, automatically moving toward the pile of weapons they had confiscated from the men brought to the house. Several rifles stood propped against the wall, but Flanna lifted a short pistol and checked to be certain it was loaded, then caught herself. What was she doing? These were her people; this was Richmond! The only thing she had to fear was Alden's discovery, and no one else but Mrs. Corey knew the truth of his identity. Leaving the pistol, she moved toward the kitchen doorway and looked toward the foyer.

Mrs. Corey opened the door. In the lantern light Flanna saw a Confederate officer standing on the porch. In a long double-breasted tunic of cadet gray, fronted with two rows of buttons and trimmed at the edges and collar with a blue stripe, he was the most nattily dressed soldier Flanna had seen in months. A group of at least six other men waited behind him in the dark.

"Excuse me, ma'am." The soldier doffed his cap before the venerable widow. "We've heard a most remarkable report from a captured prisoner, and my colonel says I have to check it out before we can send the fellow off to prison."

"A captured prisoner?" Mrs. Corey gasped and coiled back into the flickering shadows of her doorway.

"Oh, there's no need to fear." The officer smiled indulgently, like a father amused by the antics of a child. "We have him most securely in chains. But he keeps babbling about spies, so the colonel thought we'd best do a house-to-house search before we take him away."

"Spies?" The widow squeaked the word. "In Richmond?"

"Of course, ma'am." The officer's gaze left Mrs. Corey's face and moved into the house, resting briefly upon Flanna before glancing up the stairs. "I know you have wounded in the house. Have you anyone else? Anyone who has appeared since the Federals moved into the area?"

"Why, no."

Flanna closed her eyes as the widow's voice trembled. Unless this man was a complete fool, he had to see that Mrs. Corey was nervous. And though Flanna had every confidence in the benevolent widow, she couldn't know if the woman trusted her completely.

"Ma'am." The officer's firm voice verged on the threatening. "You won't mind, then, if we come in and look around?"

"Why—there are sick men in here," the widow answered in a rush of words. "You can't just come tramping through here when men are trying to sleep! They need their rest, sir; they need their strength! If you expect them to be up and soon fighting for the Cause, you'd best find another house to disturb."

"We promise we'll be quiet." The officer pushed past Mrs. Corey, gesturing for his men to follow. A parade of footsteps thumped on the porch steps, and Flanna hesitated in the hallway, not certain whether she should retreat.

"Who might you be?" the officer asked, his eyes pinning Flanna to the wall.

"Flanna O'Connor, visiting from Charleston." Flanna spoke in her best Southern drawl, folding her arms as she leaned against the wall. "I am a nurse, and I must agree with Mrs. Corey, sir—these men must not be disturbed. They have given of themselves on the battlefield; let them regain their strength in peace."

"We were told we might be looking for someone from South Carolina." The officer's eyes shone with the stimulation of alcohol and adventure. "A doctor from South Carolina, or so our prisoner said."

Flanna lifted her chin as her heart leapt uncomfortably into the back of her throat, then she glanced toward the doorway. A line of men had filed into the house, and Roger stood among them, his hands tied together at his waist, a purple bruise marking his cheek.

"Flanna." His voice wasn't much louder than a whisper, but the effect was as great as if he'd shouted in the hallway. The officer stepped toward her, instantly alert, and Flanna flinched as though an electric spark had arced between them.

"This woman?" The officer pointed at Flanna and turned to Roger with an incredulous expression on his face. "This is a doctor?"

"Yes." Roger's eyes closed as if he were suddenly very weary.

The officer stepped backward and stared, then his lips curved in an expression that hardly deserved to be called a smile. "By heaven, I knew the Yankees were perverted and profane." He whispered as if the words were too terrible to utter in a normal voice. "But this beats all I have heard of. Women undertaking work no modest lady would ever seek, cutting off the hair that God himself gave for a covering—"

"Ask her where the Yankee officer is," Roger said, his voice resigned and defeated. "I guarantee that he is hiding in this house."

More shaken than she cared to admit, Flanna stared at Roger. How could he know Alden was with her?

"What makes you think there's a Yankee in this house?" Her eyes drilled into him. "And what is all this talk about spies?"

"I read the letter." Roger's brows rose, graceful wings of scorn. "The letter you wrote my brother. I know you love him."

The Confederate officer stepped so close that Flanna could smell whiskey on his breath. "Where is he?" His eyes glittered like a snake slithering toward a paralyzed bird. "Tell me, or I'll march this prisoner through every room in this house until I drag the Yankee out by his heels. If you care at all for this Yankee spy, you'll speak now."

Flanna dropped her eyes before the officer's steady gaze and glanced at Mrs. Corey. The widow stood with her back to the door, her eyes wide with fear and concern for the others.

Roger said nothing, but glared down his nose at her like some avenging angel. Did he have any idea what he was doing?

She looked down at her hands, and laced her fingers at her waist. For Alden's sake, she would have to tell the truth. His wound was far from healed; he should not be handled roughly. If she cooperated, perhaps they would be gentle with him.

"Upstairs." Her throat clotted with unuttered shouts and protests. "In the first bedroom. He's the man nearest the door, the one with the shoulder wound."

Roger's head lifted sharply. He stared at Flanna as the officer gestured for two of his men to follow and then bounded up the stairs.

Roger's brow creased with worry. "Alden's wounded?"

"He was nearly dead." Flanna pushed herself off the wall and walked toward him, fury almost choking her. "Perhaps he will die now, if these buffoons manhandle him."

"Oh, Flanna." Roger's face wilted in sudden regret. "I didn't know. I thought you two were trying to run away together. You disappeared at the same time, and then I saw the letter—"

Hot tears bordered her eyes as she stared at him in silent fury. Roger lifted his hands and stepped toward her, but she jerked her head away, repulsed by the thought of his touch.

"He's up there," the captain called, descending the stairs. He looked at Mrs. Corey and smiled. "I'm assuming, of course, that you knew nothing about this, ma'am."

"She's innocent." Flanna stepped forward. "She is a good woman, and she's done nothing wrong."

"I wasn't blaming her. She hasn't been consorting with Yankees." The officer's smile disappeared, and a muscle flicked at his jaw as he motioned another man toward Flanna. "Tie her hands and take her too. The colonel won't believe this story."

Flanna set her chin in a stubborn line as the soldier came toward her. "I'm sorry, ma'am." He held up his hands as if afraid to touch an example of debased Southern womanhood. "But I've got my orders."

"Bind away," she countered icily, offering him her hands. The soldier pulled a length of rope from his belt and proceeded to wrap her wrists, grimacing every time his flesh touched hers.

Heavy footsteps creaked the stairs, and Flanna looked up to see the other two men supporting Alden as they descended. He was awake, his eyes wide and confused until he saw Flanna and Roger in the foyer. "Ah," he murmured, his expression clearing as his gaze met Roger's, "we meet again. Why am I not surprised?"

From lowered lids, Flanna shot a commanding, reproachful look at Roger, then followed the Confederates out into the night.

Twenty-Eight

Flanna sat between Roger and Alden in the back of a wagon as the Confederates took them away from Mrs. Corey's house. Even at the late hour of candle-lighting, the streets of Richmond were crowded. Baggage wagons heaped with trunks, boxes, and baskets rumbled over the streets. Uniformed men filled the walkways while brightly dressed female camp followers loitered on street corners, eager to ply their trade. Flanna noticed that most of the houses they passed looked deserted, but golden lamplight shone from several. She suspected that those homes, like Mrs. Corey's, were filled with the wounded and dying.

Flanna lowered her gaze and concentrated on Alden. He sat beside her, forced to sit upright in the wagon. His captors had allowed him to put on a shirt and trousers, but he wore no coat, and the stark white bandage was clearly visible through the thin cotton shirt. His face was pale, and sweat bordered his forehead and upper lip. At every pothole and jostle of the wagon a muscle flicked in his face, and Flanna knew he was in pain.

The horses stopped before a stately building fronted by six imposing columns. At a signal from the Confederate captain, Flanna and Roger climbed out and waited on the marble steps while the guards dragged Alden from the wagon. A curious crowd surged around them—men in uniform, politicians in suits, curious ladies in the refined bonnets of gentlewomen—and then they were ushered into the building and down a long hallway. Finally the three of them were deposited in a stuffy, windowless room and told to wait.

"I expect the colonel will want to know about this immediately," the arresting officer said, his gaze sweeping over Flanna as he lingered in the doorway. "But you can just sit right here until he's available. Might not be until tomorrow morning."

"Wait, please." Flanna wiped her hands on her apron and tried on a flimsy smile. "If you can find my brother, he will assure you that I'm a loyal South Carolinian. His name is Wesley O'Connor, and he's from Charleston. I'm sure he's in the army."

"What regiment?"

Flanna's face fell. "I don't know."

The officer shot her a withering glance. "You call yourself a loyal Confederate and yet you don't even know where this brother of yours is fighting?"

Flanna lifted her chin, not willing to let herself be put down by this brute. "I am a loyal American, sir!"

"I think we caught ourselves a genuine spy," he said, eyeing her with a calculating expression. "An honest-to-goodness piece of Yankee trash that talks like a Southern belle."

Without giving her a chance to respond, the man stepped through the doorway and closed the door. Flanna ran to it, but heard a clear click as the key turned in the lock.

She turned around and leaned against the door, her feelings as bleak as the room in which they'd been confined. The only light came from a high window above the door, and she knew that would fade as soon as night fell and everyone went home. The furniture—a single chair and a bench against the wall—was scuffed and scarred. The floor was dusty tile; the walls weepy plaster that smelled of dust and mildew.

"Well, that's it then." Roger sank into the wooden chair. "The war's over for us. They'll send us to prison, of course, but we'll be released as soon as McClellan comes up and takes Richmond."

Flanna stared at Roger in astonishment. Had he not learned anything during these past months? "McClellan will never take Richmond!

He's retreating right now! The man can't stand bloodshed—he won't fight."

"What would you know about it?" A shadow of annoyance crossed Roger's face. "You don't know politics, and you don't know men."

"I know about Little Mac," Flanna said, crossing the room. The soldiers had dropped Alden on the floor. He now slumped against the wall, and Flanna feared he would fall over at any minute. "Here, Alden, lie flat." She knelt beside him. "Is the floor cold? Let me find something—"

She looked up at Roger, who still wore his blue dress coat. "Give me your coat," she said, her mind racing. "Did you wear it into town? What were you thinking, Roger?"

"I was angry." He leaned forward and shrugged out of his coat, then tossed it to her. "I thought you both had deserted the army. I came through the Confederate lines with my hands up. I knew I'd be arrested immediately, but I didn't care. I wanted to find you."

"Whatever for?" Flanna had been spreading the coat on the floor for Alden to lie on, but she stopped and stared at Roger. "What were you going to do when you found us?"

Roger released a choked, desperate laugh. "I don't know. I hadn't considered that." His gaze returned to her. "I just didn't want to lose you."

She felt her heart shrivel at his hurt expression. "Roger," she softened her voice, "you never had me. I'm sorry, but I didn't join the army to follow you. I just wanted to go home."

Turning away from Roger, Flanna put her hand on Alden's shoulders and eased him to the floor. He mumbled something she couldn't understand, so she shushed him and urged him to rest.

She sat silently for some time, studying him. He had not shaved in over a week; a golden brown beard covered his cheeks, softening that determined chin, that strong jaw. Even in sleep, his face seemed marked by anxiety and grief. The cut above his forehead was healing nicely, but loss shadowed his eyes and his face seemed narrower than it had been on that Christmas Day when they first met.

That thought had barely crossed her mind before another followed: *Alden was not hers.* After the war, he would return to Boston and marry Nell Scott, the faithful young lady who had remained at home and fulfilled a woman's proper role. While Flanna slogged through mud and shivered in the freezing rain, Miss Scott had been kneeling by her cozy fireplace and praying for Alden, her delicate fingers clasped together, her long hair spilling over her shoulders like a waterfall...

Flanna slammed the door on her imaginings. Bad enough that she should save him for another woman; she didn't have to torture herself in the process.

When at last Alden's breathing slowed and deepened, she crossed her legs under her skirt and turned to Roger.

"I suggest you get some sleep too." She looked at his sorrowful face and did her best to smile. Perhaps she had been too harsh with him.

"Flanna, I didn't know." Roger's voice echoed with entreaty. "I didn't know he was wounded. I'm afraid I've made an awful mess of things, but I was so crazy with jealousy. I read the letter, you see, and I know you so well I knew what you were saying."

Feeling utterly miserable, Flanna closed her eyes. "I'm sorry, Roger."

"It's okay. I can understand. Alden's always been the brave one, the responsible one." A thread of desperation edged his voice. "I should have known you'd fall in love with him."

"You don't have to worry about that." Flanna crossed her arms and rested them upon her knees, watching the shadows lengthen in the room. Was Nell Scott sitting by the fire now, thinking of Alden as she penned another letter? "I could never give Alden my heart." *Because he would never accept it.*

Roger cleared his throat. "But now that I've ruined things for all of us—"

"Maybe things aren't so bad." Flanna spoke with a conviction she didn't feel. "But we won't know anything until the morning. So get some sleep, Roger, and we'll talk tomorrow."

He nodded slowly, then pointed to the chair. "Would you like to sit?"

"No. I never could sleep in a chair, not even in medical school." Flanna stretched out on the cold floor and rested her head on one arm. Streams of dust rose to tickle her nose, and sand gritted against her skin, but she was content. Alden was safe, and he slept only a few feet away.

"Flanna?" Roger's disembodied voice floated toward her in the darkness.

"What, Roger?"

"We are friends, aren't we?"

She smiled, amazed at his persistence. He was the perfect politician because he never gave up, never acknowledged defeat.

"Yes, Roger," she called, her voice husky with exhaustion. "We're friends."

"Some marriages"—he paused a moment—"some very *good* marriages are established on friendship, Flanna."

Flanna closed her eyes and sighed in exasperation. Like a child who has been denied a privilege he thought he had earned, he needed to know he would have something to call his own.

But he would never have her. Alden had given her heart wings, and she could never settle down in a loveless marriage. She would die alone and a spinster before she would marry a man she did not love.

"Go to sleep, Roger." Her voice echoed in the room's emptiness. "I expect that we will need our strength for tomorrow."

He did not answer, but the chair creaked as he settled into it. Flanna rested her cheek on her clasped hands and willed herself to sleep.

⁂

Through a haze of exhaustion and pain, Alden heard two voices buzzing around him. Something in his brain urged him to wakefulness, and his eyes opened to complete darkness as Roger assured Flanna that friendship would prove a good foundation for marriage.

Of course it would. Flanna was too accomplished, and Roger far too persuasive for them to be anything but happy together.

Alden let his heavy eyelids fall. The dreams he allowed himself were an exercise in futility, and he would do himself a favor if he put them aside altogether. He had no business even thinking about his brother's sweetheart.

∽৯৯৹

Flanna woke the next morning to the sound of argument. Both brothers were awake and sitting up; both blazed with fury as they faced each other.

"You still haven't explained why you were absent without leave," Alden was saying, his face bright with anger. "If I were your commanding officer—"

"But you're not," Roger snapped. "And I've been trying to tell you, but you won't listen. You were gone, Flanna was gone, and I figured you were gone together. But none of that is important now—we've got to decide how to help Flanna now."

"She should tell the truth," Alden said. "No one would blame her for trying to come home."

"But she aided the enemy, and they'll consider her a spy," Roger countered. "Do you want her executed or thrown into prison?"

"She's not a spy." Though stained with fatigue, Alden's face glowed as though lighted from within. "You must give away information to be a spy. She's given no information to anybody."

"She impersonated a Confederate army surgeon!" Roger's eyes were flat and dark in the dim light, unreadable, but there was no mistaking the passion in his voice. "They will not appreciate that! And they will be incensed to learn that she brought you, a Yankee officer, to a Confederate hospital for treatment."

"Stop, stop!" Flanna held up her hand, then wearily ran her fingers through her sleep-tousled hair. "Both of you must be quiet. There is nothing to debate. This Confederate colonel will decide whatever he wants to decide, and that is all there is to it."

"You could lie." Roger tilted his brow and looked at her uncertainly. "Tell him you were held captive by the Union army. Tell him you were caught behind the lines when the army came ashore on the

345

peninsula, and when you saw Alden wounded you thought he was a Confederate. Tell them you were confused, that you're only a woman, that you had no idea what was going on—"

"I'll say no such thing." She crossed her arms and glared at him. "I won't lie."

"It's not a lie; it's an elaboration. Politicians do it all the time—"

"Heaven spare me from politicians then." She closed her eyes, wondering if he would ever understand. "Roger, I am a woman, but I can think, I can reason, and I know very well what is going on. And what I did will be wrong in their eyes, but it was right in God's. I just used the gifts he has given me."

"So you're bringing God into the discussion?" Alden looked at her with a smile glowing in his eyes.

"Yes." Flanna's voice was firm and final. "For God Almighty is neither Confederate nor Federal. He is truth, and he is right, and he knows that my heart is innocent."

"Well then." Alden leaned peacefully against the wall, a beatific smile creasing his tanned face. "Let us hope the officer who hears our case has consulted the Almighty on our behalf."

Colonel James L. Kemper, of the First Virginia regiment, sat in a chair at the front of the courtroom, flanked by several other officers in brushed gray coats with gleaming brass buttons. General Robert E. Lee had just been appointed commander of the army at Richmond, an aide explained as he ushered Flanna, Roger, and Alden into the oak-paneled chamber, and Major General James Longstreet commanded the right wing. But neither man could be spared for a military trial, so Colonel Kemper had been tapped to hear this case.

The accused did not have to wait long for the proceedings to get under way. Once Flanna and the brothers had been seated in a row of wooden chairs before the tribunal, one of the colonel's aides stood and read the indictment. "Charge—that this woman, Flanna O'Connor, with premeditation, did willfully impersonate a doctor of the Confederate army with the avowed purpose of giving aid and comfort to the enemy."

Flanna risked a glance at the colonel. He sat absolutely still, his eyes as hard as dried peas and his mouth drawn up into a disapproving knot.

"These two men, sir," the aide lowered the list of formal charges as he pointed to Roger and Alden, "are officers in the Union army. We will file no charges against them. The wounded officer was brought here by the machinations of this woman, and the other freely surrendered himself to our pickets."

"A deserter?" the colonel asked.

"Yes," the aide answered, and Flanna saw Roger flush at the word.

"Your honor, I object to these military proceedings." Roger stood and inclined his head in a gesture of respect. "This woman obviously has no place in either army. Since she is a civilian, she is beyond this court's jurisdiction. You have no authority over her."

The colonel pressed his hands together and leaned forward, his dark eyes sinking into nets of wrinkles as he smiled. "Thank you for attempting to educate me. I have eyes—I can see that this is a woman. But she has been tampering with the army, sir, and under very serious circumstances. So I find I must deal with her."

Those dark and wary eyes now turned to Flanna and studied her above a strained smile. "Miss O'Connor, did you bring this Yankee officer into one of our hospitals for treatment?"

"Yes sir." She tried to maintain her curt tone. "He was very badly wounded, and I knew there were no Union hospitals behind the lines. He would have died if I had not brought him to Richmond."

"Surely the Union army has regimental surgeons."

"Yes, but the surgeon for Major Haynes's regiment is inept."

The colonel's feathery brows shot up to his hairline. "And how would you know anything about this Yankee surgeon?"

"I know because…" She glanced at Alden, and the warmth in his eyes gave her courage. "I know because I am a degreed physician, sir. And I have been traveling with the Twenty-fifth Massachusetts since last summer."

A light twittering sound broke out among the observers at the back of the room, and Flanna blushed when she realized what they had inferred.

"I am not a camp follower," she proclaimed, imposing an iron control on herself. "I would not have you thinking that my virtue was compromised in any way." She lifted her chin and straightened into a militant posture. "I wore a soldier's clothes, sir, and enlisted as Franklin O'Connor."

Astonishment blossomed on the colonel's face, then he snorted in derision. "You expect me to believe that?"

"Believe what you like." Pride kept her from arguing. "But while I traveled with the army, I observed several regimental surgeons at work—many of them are butchers, including the surgeon attached to the Twenty-fifth Massachusetts. Major Haynes would have died in the Union camp if he had been fortunate enough to receive any care at all."

The colonel lifted an eyebrow in amused contempt. "Then why, Dr. O'Connor," he said, faintly underlining the title with scorn, "did you choose to bring this particular Yankee officer to Richmond when there were scores of other men who needed treatment?"

Caught off guard by the question, Flanna blanched. Why bring Alden? She wanted to shout, "Because he means everything to me," but she couldn't give that answer. The judge wouldn't understand, Alden would be mortified by her confession of a love he couldn't return, and poor Roger would be further humiliated.

"Why did I bring Major Haynes?" Her stomach knotted under the colonel's withering glare.

"That was my question, young woman."

Flanna gripped her hands and decided to revert to Southern tactics. She was a lady, schooled in all the strategies of feminine charm. Perhaps this gentleman colonel could be convinced to grant her a moment's grace.

She deepened her voice and her accent. "I must confess that I hesitate to tell you, sir, since it involves a personal matter." She looked up, hoping to disarm him with a pair of fluttering lashes and her prettiest smile—

He wasn't buying it. Her flirtation rippled over him like water over a rock; his granite expression remained unchanged. "Speak up, young lady!"

So much for Southern charm. Flanna wiped the smile from her face, quietly relieved that Aunt Marsali's lessons meant nothing here.

"Well—" She glanced at Roger. "I know you may not approve, but I acted to save Alden Haynes because for some time I have thought of him as my future brother-in-law. Roger and I had an understanding before the war began."

The colonel's eyes widened into glittering ovals of repudiation. "You, Miss O'Connor, have already gone to the devil. You may as well go to the Yankees too!" He flushed in fury and slammed his hand on the armrest of his chair. "We shall waste no more time with this." He motioned toward his aide. "The proper judgment is clear. Flanna O'Connor, you are remanded into the care of Mrs. Ellen Corey and placed under house arrest. If you're a doctor, you ought to make a good nurse. You will work in Mrs. Corey's house as a nurse until the business of war is finished."

The colonel's mouth pulled into a sour grin as he looked at Roger and Alden. "The two Yankee officers are sentenced to Libby Prison until the war is over."

Flanna pressed her hand over her face as her throat ached with regret. She did not mind her sentence, for she liked the widow Corey and Charleston no longer tugged at her heart. But neither Roger nor Alden deserved a prison term.

"Come, my dear."

Flanna looked up. The widow stood by her side and her arm slipped around Flanna's waist. "Let me take you home."

"Wait, please." Flanna stepped out of the widow's embrace and turned to Alden and Roger, who stood between uniformed guards. "Roger, I'm so sorry," she whispered, reaching out to take his hand. He tried to smile at her, but his features only flinched uncomfortably.

"And Alden—" She took his hand, too, and held it tightly. "I never meant for this to happen. If I had known I would bring you such pain, I would never have acted as I did."

"If you hadn't, I'd be dead." The warmth of Alden's smile echoed in his voice. "Take care, Flanna. God go with you."

Flanna released their hands, and the soldiers led both men out of the courtroom. She stared at the space they had occupied a moment before, and it seemed to her that it now contained a dark and palpable emptiness. She stood in the void and heard her heart break— a small, clean sound, like the snapping of a twig underfoot.

...and he shall direct thy paths. Where was God taking her?

A light touch patted her shoulder. "Let's go home." The widow Corey spoke with staid calmness. "You'll feel better after a cup of tea."

Flanna took an abrupt step toward the door, then allowed Mrs. Corey to take her hand and lead her out of the courtroom.

A pair of volunteer nurses had managed to move the wounded out of Mrs. Corey's kitchen by the time Flanna and the widow returned. Mrs. Corey told Flanna to sit at the table while she prepared a bit of lunch.

"I'm so sorry," Flanna murmured again, drowning in waves of guilt. "There's a guard outside your door now, and all because of me. You are too kind to suffer this way."

"Pshaw! Why should I mind having a handsome soldier on my front porch?" The widow's blue eyes snapped with mischief. "Don't you worry your pretty head about me. There's a lot of life left in these bones, and I'm not as addled as I might seem."

"You don't seem at all addled." Flanna stared at her hands. Right now she was the one who couldn't seem to pull her thoughts together.

"I've heard that we should expect a visitor later this afternoon," the widow said, her heavy teakettle wavering as she lifted it from the stove. "A man from a South Carolina unit. He was one of our patients the other day—do you remember him? You pulled a piece of shell from his leg."

Flanna shook her head, her memories obscured by the events of the morning. "I'm sorry."

The widow sat a teacup before Flanna and added a pinch of tea leaves, all she could spare since the blockade had dried up supplies. "You talked to him for quite a while. And you mentioned your brother, Wesley."

Flanna nodded absently. "I remember now. He had shrapnel near the tibia; it just missed the artery."

"I received a note from that young man this morning." The widow patted her bosom, which crackled under her touch. "He's returning this afternoon to thank you."

"No thanks are necessary," Flanna murmured, lifting her teacup. "He should save his strength for marching."

The widow sat down and gently stirred her cup, her eyes abstracted. "I don't know that the army is going anywhere. Some say they will camp out here until the war is over. Richmond can't be allowed to fall, you know."

She rattled on about Jeff Davis and the Confederate treasury, but Flanna's thoughts wandered toward Alden and Roger and the place called Libby Prison.

"Mrs. Corey," she asked, putting her hand on the woman's frail wrist, "tell me about Libby Prison. Will Roger and Alden be treated well there?"

The widow's silver brows drew together in an agonized expression. "Dearie, you don't want to know about that place."

"Yes, I do." Flanna's eyes never left the widow's face. "Mrs. Corey, I have great respect for Roger Haynes, and I love his brother more than life itself. So you must tell me—what have I done by bringing them here?"

The lady's dark eyes flashed a gentle but firm warning. "Libby Prison is not for the faint of heart. I visited there one Saturday with some ladies from my church, but I could never go again. You don't want to know—"

"Tell me, please!"

Mrs. Corey exhaled loudly, then looked away. "The prison is a converted ship's chandlery." Her hand toyed with the tatted lace doily in the center of the table. "It's a dark and cold place, with only six big rooms for over a thousand prisoners. And I've heard—though I don't know if it's true—that the men are kept barely alive on quarter rations. The Confederacy must feed her own men, you see, before she can feed her prisoners."

A cold lump grew in Flanna's stomach and spread chilly tendrils of apprehension through her body. She couldn't bear the thought of Alden growing thin and weak. His body needed food and rest to heal itself, and he would be allowed neither in a prison.

"Dear God," Flanna dropped her head onto her hand, "show me what to do! There has to be a way!" Forgetting Mrs. Corey, Flanna yielded to the compulsive sobs that shook her and lowered her head to the table, watering the wood with her tears.

⁓

"Flanna?"

Mrs. Corey's cackling voice slashed Flanna's sleep like a knife. She lifted her head from the table, noticing that her arms tingled from poor circulation. She wasn't sure how long she had slept, but her head felt as though it had filled with cotton.

"Flanna, dear." Mrs. Corey's slippers whispered across the wooden floor as she scooted into the room. "You have a visitor. Sit up, let's wipe your eyes and smooth that hair of yours." The lady's little hands patted Flanna's cheeks and hair, pulling her into some sort of presentable appearance.

Flanna blinked, trying to force her confused emotions into order. "What time is it?" she murmured, her voice heavy with exhaustion.

"About four o'clock, I should think." The widow took a step back and studied Flanna with a critical eye. "I expect you'll do," she said, clasping her hands at her waist. She glanced up and nodded toward someone who stood in the hallway. "You may come in now."

Another patient? Flanna turned at the thump of heavy boots upon the floor. A Confederate soldier came toward her, but his trousers were whole, his gray coat stained only with mud and grass, not blood. At the last moment she looked at his face, expecting to see a bruised eye or bloodied cut that needed her attention, but it was only Wesley.

Wesley! She stared wordlessly at him, her heart pounding; then she jumped up and ran to him, throwing her arms around his neck.

He lifted her from the floor in his embrace and lightly scolded her for the sobs that broke from her lips. "There now, is that any way to be greeting your long-lost brother?"

"Wesley, I'm so happy to see you!" He lowered her to the floor and Flanna stepped back, thinking that she might actually burst from the swell of joy in her heart. Wesley was whole, thank God, and well, though his face was ruddier than she had ever seen it. He wore a beard now, which added to the manly aura around him, and the sun had parched the skin around his eyes and forehead. A gold captain's braid hung from the shoulder of his uniform. So, he was an officer!

"Welcome to Richmond, little sister." Wesley tossed his hat on the kitchen table, then winked at the widow. "Mrs. Corey tells me that you've gotten yourself into a bit of a scrape." His mouth opened in mock horror as his hand smoothed her hair. "And what's this? In faith, I never expected to find you bald!"

"I'm not bald." Flanna smacked his hand. "And yes, I've really made a mess of things. Not for me, so much, but for two very dear men."

Without waiting for permission, Wesley pulled out a chair and sat down, and Flanna took the seat opposite him. From the other side of the kitchen, Mrs. Corey hummed and put another kettle of water on to boil.

"Would one of them be the Roger Haynes you wrote me of?" Wesley asked, one corner of his mouth turning up in a wry smile. "The charming, successful man you thought you might marry?"

"Yes—and no." Flanna sighed and opened her hands. "Yes, it's Roger, and no, I will not marry him, though we are great friends. It's his brother, Alden, that I love." Her smile faded. "He loves someone else, a girl back home. But I'm the one who dragged him behind enemy lines. Now he's wounded and in prison, and he'll die there unless I can do something."

"You?" His left brow shot up in surprise. "Genteel little Flanna, who would rather sit at home than go riding and soil her brocade slippers?"

His cynicism grated on her. "I'm not wearing brocade slippers anymore."

"So I understand." Wesley cut a quick look at Mrs. Corey, and Flanna frowned. What had the widow told him while Flanna slept?

Wesley reached across the table and took her hand in his. "Flanna, you were constantly surprising me when you were a little lass. Once you got a thought into your wee head, nothing could stop you from doing what you set out to do." He laughed, a deep and rich sound that warmed Flanna's heart. "You gave me and the cousins quite a bit of competition until you decided you'd rather sip tea and chatter than tangle with us."

She shook her head, impatient with his reminiscences. "Wesley—"

He lifted his hand, cutting her off. "'Tis a bit strange, don't you think, that you should come full circle? For here you are, full grown into a bonny lass and chasing after the boys again. But this time you're in over your head, darlin'."

She sat silently, a hot tear rolling down her cheek.

Wesley leaned forward, his eyes suddenly somber. "I trust you heard about the fire? About Papa?"

She nodded, and some of the stiffness seemed to melt out of Wesley's shoulders. "I'm glad you know, and relieved I am for not having to tell you. Papa died the way he lived, trying to help someone. I know he wouldn't want us to grieve."

"But—" Flanna's promise weighed upon her, choking her. "I promised to go home and help him, Wes. That's all I've wanted to do for these many months—"

"Hush, darlin'." He reached out and grabbed her hand. "Papa wouldn't want you to stake your future upon his past. The world's a different place, and the Charleston you knew is already changed. If

Papa were here, he'd tell you to get on with your life, and since he's not here, I'll do the telling for him. You're a bright girl, Flanna, and God led you away from us. To my way of thinking, he'll keep on leading you. All you have to do is trust him."

Trust God? If Wesley only knew how hard that was! She *wanted* to trust God's plan for her life, but he had led her over a path filled with so many obstacles.

Flanna knew that tears were flowing down her face, but she was not truly crying. The tears came from a simple overflow of regret, hurt, loss, and love.

Wesley's eyes darkened with emotion. "Aw, don't cry, lass! Your brother's here. And since your life seems now entwined with two other men, I'm going to help you free those fine lads, Yankees though they may be."

A hot and awful joy swept through her, then despair reared its ugly head. "I can't do anything, Wesley! I'm under arrest and there's a guard outside. Mrs. Corey is under strict orders not to allow me out of the house."

"Ah, lass." His white teeth flashed amid his red beard. "Mrs. Corey is your friend; how can you be forgetting that?"

"What do you mean?"

Wesley did not answer, but pointed behind Flanna. As her thoughts swirled in confusion, Flanna turned and saw the widow standing behind her. Mrs. Corey's arms were filled with folded clothing. "This was to be Willie's new uniform," the lady said, gently fingering the soft gray coat on the top of the stack. "I meant to give it to him at Christmas. But Christmas never came last year."

The widow offered the clothing to Flanna with a small smile. "Willie would be pleased to help you, Miss Flanna. I've watched how you treated these boys, and I know your heart is in the right place." She placed the garments on the table, then stepped back. "But you'd better hurry. They transport the prisoners every afternoon near sunset. If you're going to reach those men before they reach the prison, you'd best go now."

Flanna choked back a sob of gratitude as Wesley's smile widened in approval. "Think you can manage putting on a man's uniform, sister?"

Flanna met his grin with a larger smile of her own. "Brother, you'd be surprised how well I can manage."

Twenty-Nine

⁂

Ten minutes later, Flanna finished slicking her hair back with Macassar oil, then stepped out of the pantry wearing the light blue trousers and gray coat of a Confederate infantryman. Wesley whistled in appreciation as she twirled for his inspection.

"Add this," Mrs. Corey said, taking a cap from a pile of discarded clothing she'd collected from the wounded. She tossed it to Flanna, then moved to the stack of weapons and closed her hand around a rifle barrel. "You should take this too."

Flanna slipped the cap over her hair and stared at the rifle musket in Mrs. Corey's grasp. "Are you certain you want to give me that?" Her eyes met the widow's. "When they find out I've escaped, they won't appreciate the fact that you gave me a rifle."

"It's not loaded." The widow pushed the gun toward Flanna, then took a hasty half-step back as if glad to be rid of it. "I don't have any bullets or powder, so the gun will be useless to you if you get into trouble. But how are they to know?"

"How indeed?" Wesley asked, picking up his own knapsack and rifle.

Overwhelmed by gratitude, Flanna propped the rifle against the table, then clasped the older woman in a brief embrace. "I wish I had known Willie," she whispered in Mrs. Corey's ear. "With a mother like you, he must have been a very special young man."

Tears trembled on the widow's sparse lashes as she patted Flanna's shoulder. "I packed your green dress in your knapsack. Promise me you'll change as soon as you can. You'll be safer traveling as a woman."

"Yes ma'am, I promise."

The widow patted the tiny curls at her ears in a distracted gesture. "I also put some cornbread in the knapsack, as well as your medical bag and your book."

Her journal. In the horrors of the last few days, Flanna had nearly forgotten about it. "Thank you."

She gave the widow a kiss on the cheek, then picked up the rifle and knapsack. As the widow sighed loudly and sank into a chair, Flanna and Wesley walked toward the front of the house. A thrill of frightened anticipation touched Flanna's spine as she paused by the door.

"Just act like you know what you're doing," Wesley said, reading her face. "Salute the officers, ignore the others. The guard saw me come in, and he'll assume you were with me."

"And if he questions me?" Flanna quailed at the thought of being arrested again. The colonel would not be as merciful a second time, particularly if she was apprehended while trying to free two Union officers. And what might happen to Wesley if she failed?

Wesley cocked his head at a jaunty angle. "If he questions you, just turn around and march back inside the house. But nothing ventured, nothing gained."

Flanna swallowed hard, then slung her rifle over her shoulder, and reminded herself that she'd been marching and drilling for months. If any woman on earth knew how to walk like a soldier, she did.

"Let's go."

Wesley swung the door wide. Flanna blinked in the bright flood of sunlight, then followed her brother down the stairs.

⋘∘⋙

An hour later Flanna and Wesley stood outside the same majestic white building where she had been taken the day before. There were no crowds this time, just a handful of soldiers loitering in the shade of the columns. A cool breeze was sweeping away the heat of the day, and the western sky had begun to glow with crimson and gold.

Flanna felt her hands go slick with sweat as an entire regiment of Confederate soldiers came around a street corner, marching in straight lines as the drums and fifes played a sprightly version of "Dixie." Flanna turned slightly and thrust her hands in her pockets as they passed.

"Nice job, Private," Wesley joked, puffing on the end of a cigar he'd fished from his pocket. "Remember—wait patiently, stay calm. You know what you are doing."

The hands on the city clock moved slowly, marking the time. Six o'clock, and yet no sign of prisoners.

"Are you sure this is the right door?" Flanna glanced up at Wesley. "What if they've taken them out another way?"

"Hold your horses, lass." Wesley's eyes scanned the street as he lifted the cigar to his lips. He drew heavily on it, making the tip glow bright, then held it out and stared at it. "Nasty habit," he said, a thin plume of smoke drifting from his pursed lips. "But it's all I have to keep me warm most nights."

Flanna leaned back against a pillar, wishing she had something to do with her hands. The swollen sun hung low in the west, so if the guards waited much longer they'd be transporting prisoners in the dark. What had delayed them? Had Alden taken a turn for the worse? Or were they merely delayed by some other trial?

"Look sharp, Private." Wesley's voice brought her out of her reverie. Flanna glanced up to see the double doors opening. Two Confederate guards appeared, followed by Alden and Roger. Both were bound at the wrists, and both walked with their heads bowed. Someone had draped a dark blanket over Alden's shoulders, but the sight of his pale profile made Flanna's heart twist in misery.

"You there, Sergeant," Wesley called out, lifting his cigar in the guard's direction. "We have orders to relieve you."

"Orders?" The sergeant came forward, frowning. "I know nothing of any orders."

Wesley jerked his chin toward the prisoners. "These are the men bound for Libby Prison?"

"Yes."

"Well then." Wesley pulled a folded sheet of paper from his pocket and made a great fuss of unfolding it with one hand while he held his cigar with the other. "I've got these orders commanding me and the wee one to escort these men to Libby Prison by six o'clock." The line of his mouth curved, a mere twitch in his bearded face. "Seein' as how these men are already late, it'll be my tail that ends up bein' catawampusly chawed up by the colonel. Unless you insist on taking them in."

"I didn't know anything about six o'clock." The muscles of the sergeant's throat moved in a convulsive swallow. "And it weren't my fault that they're just now bein' released. The colonel said to hold 'em until he was good and ready to let 'em go."

Wesley suddenly whirled toward Flanna. "You there! Hold that rifle on those prisoners, you fool!"

Flanna jumped in honest surprise, then swung her rifle off her back and pointed it toward Alden and Roger. Roger's brows lifted when their eyes met, but for once he said nothing.

"Well." The sergeant hesitated, not bothering to look at the paper fluttering in Wesley's hand. "If you've got orders…"

"My good man." Wesley laughed and slipped his arm around the sergeant's shoulders. "If I were you, I'd thank my lucky stars that someone else will take the browbeating. Take advantage, boy! I hear Miss Rose has opened her tavern for business. Instead of arguing with me, you could be down there debating the weather with a right fair-looking wench."

The captain's nose quivered like a leaf in the wind. "Miss Rose is back? I thought she'd left the city."

"She did leave." Wesley turned and pointed down the street. "But when our boys held the Federals, she came back, bringing all her girls with her."

"Well then." The sergeant thrust his hands in his pockets and broke into a leisurely smile. "I suppose I could use an hour or two of feminine companionship."

"And jealous I am, mind you." Wesley jabbed the sergeant's arm, then pointed his own rifle toward the prisoners. "And if you'll excuse me, I'll be taking these Yanks off your hands."

As the sergeant called to his companion and moved away down the street, Wesley jerked the muzzle of his rifle toward Roger and Alden. "Get along now," he said, his voice as dry as a desert. "Let's get you two settled in a more proper place."

Alden turned, and Flanna gasped as she caught sight of a nasty bruise around his eye. The cut in his forehead had opened, and a dark red stream of blood marked the side of his face. Had they beaten him?

Alden looked up then and caught Flanna's eye. His expression clouded in confusion for a moment, then he seemed to relax. Without a word, he and Roger walked between Wesley and Flanna out onto the street.

꧁꧂

They turned down a nearly deserted road and walked for nearly a mile without speaking. Wesley set the pace and led the way with Roger, while Flanna followed with Alden. Her heart squeezed in compassion when she noticed that Alden had begun to drag his feet; his strength ebbed with every step.

Warehouses lined the road, so pedestrian traffic was light. Flanna waited until there was no one around to hear, then hissed at her brother. "Wesley! We're losing Alden. We've got to stop."

"It's not safe yet," Wesley insisted, moving relentlessly through the darkening gloom. "Soon, though. I know a place."

"I'm all right," Alden added, in a voice that seemed to come from far away.

Flanna yearned to slip under Alden's arm and support him, but in the guise of a Confederate soldier she could not. Eventually, though, the warehouses fell away, and they found themselves on a wide dirt road. Flanna slung her rifle over her shoulder and slipped her arm around Alden's waist, helping him in the gathering darkness. The glow of candles and lamps seeped through the shutters and lace curtains of several homes on the road, reminding Flanna that they had been walking for some time. She sighed in relief when Wesley finally turned toward a small slave cabin that lay at least fifty feet behind a great white house whose windows were blank with darkness.

The little whitewashed cabin gleamed in the light from a full moon. "The owners of the house fled when McClellan landed," Wesley explained, holding the door open as Flanna led Alden inside. "I don't dare take you into the big house, but this place should be safe for the night."

"What about the slaves?" Flanna asked. She eased Alden to the floor, then knelt to untie the ropes that bound his wrists.

"Gone with their owners, probably." Wesley closed the door behind him, then fumbled in his pocket for a flint. In a moment he had lit a small lamp that sat on the table, the only piece of furniture in the room.

As the lamp flickered and brightened the small space, Wesley untied Roger, then extended his hand. "I'm Wesley O'Connor, Flanna's brother. I'm pleased to meet you."

Roger's mouth split into a smile that lit his eyes like the sun. "I've never been so happy to meet a Confederate soldier in all my life," Roger said, briskly shaking Wesley's hand. "Thank you, sir, for coming to our rescue."

"'Tis all Flanna's doing." Wesley extended his hand to Alden, too, who shook it with the same warmth. "I couldn't very well leave my sister under house arrest in a heathen town like Richmond."

"Heathen?" Intense astonishment marked Roger's face.

"Full of politicians," Wesley explained. He glanced around the room for a moment, then turned to Flanna. "There's a fireplace, but I wouldn't light it. The smoke might draw attention to you."

"I know."

"And you'll have to move quickly tomorrow. My guess is that these two will be missed tonight, and searchers will be out at first light."

"Don't worry." Distracted by thoughts of her patient, Flanna studied Alden's battered face, trying to determine the extent of the damage.

Wesley tugged on her arm. "Listen, Flanna, pay attention. You'll need to particularly watch out for the conscription agents. Since April they've been out in force, snatching up every able-bodied man not in uniform. Those who resist are shot—or worse."

She accepted this new threat, then swallowed hard and managed a feeble answer. "We'll be careful."

Wesley caught her wrist, and she wondered if he could feel the banging of her pulse. "I'd love to stay with you, lass, but I'll be in a peck o' trouble if I'm absent after tattoo. And I'd only make your situation worse if I am caught with you."

"I know. You've already done so much." Moving into her brother's embrace, Flanna pressed her cheek to his chest as her heart swelled with gratitude and love. She held him tight and breathed in his scent, the mingled flavors of tobacco, leather, and horses. "Thank you, Wesley. May God keep you safe until we meet again."

"You too." His voice faded, losing its steely edge. "Where will you go? I'm not quite sure I want to leave you with two Yankees."

Flanna lifted her head. "We'll probably try to rejoin our regiment." She ran her fingertips over his brow and tried to smooth away the deep line of concern on his forehead. "There's nothing left for me in Charleston, Wes. Not since Papa died."

"I know." His eyes were misty and wistful as he looked at her, then he abruptly cut a glance toward Roger. "She has a dress in her knapsack. Make certain that she puts it on in the morning." His dry smile flattened. "I'm certain you are honorable gentlemen, or Flanna wouldn't set such a store by you, but I can't have her catching a stray bullet because some trigger-happy idiot thinks she's a soldier. So promise me that you won't set foot outside this cabin tomorrow unless she's wearing that dress."

"You have our word upon it, sir," Roger answered, his eyes grave.

Wesley reached out and held Flanna in a close embrace, patting her back and murmuring soft endearments as he said farewell. A thousand emotions whirled inside her—love, sorrow, joy, despair, hope, fear. After a few moments she pulled away, wiped a tear from her cheek, and gave him the warmest smile she could manage. "You'd best be going, lad." She clung to his hand for a moment, swinging it in a gentle rhythm. "I always found your hiding places when we were children, and I will find you again when this is all over. Rest assured, Wesley O'Connor—I'll see you again."

An answering smile lit his face like the striking of a match, then he released her hand and stepped through the open door into the black night.

Flanna watched the door swing on its leather hinges and heard the soft groan of wood.

"He's a noble man, your brother."

She turned at Alden's voice and gave him a weary smile. "Yes, he is. I never realized it until now."

"Come." Alden held out his hand and she accepted it, sinking to the earthen floor between him and Roger.

"I hope you'll understand that I'm too tired to talk." Roger's voice scraped terribly, as though he were laboring to produce it. "And since we've a long day tomorrow, I suppose we should all try to sleep."

"Good idea," Flanna answered, helping Alden push himself away from the wall so he could lie down. She looked toward Roger after Alden was settled, but he had already lain down with his back toward her. Flanna stretched out, too, grateful that at least their flight had taken place in June, for without a fire this cabin would have been unbearably cold in winter.

Silence filled the small shelter as the lantern glowed, and somehow, despite her fear and the circumstances, Flanna withdrew into a dreamless sleep.

❧

Alden woke to a sharp tug on his sleeve. He opened his swollen eyelids, then shuddered as the memory of the previous day came flooding back. After that mock trial, the guards had taken him and Roger to a holding cell, where a burly man in a plain white shirt and breeches decided that since Alden was the higher-ranking officer, he deserved the more thorough beating. The interrogation began—queries about Union troop strength and strategy, to which Alden had no answers—then the man's fist smashed into Alden's face and ribs until he passed out.

Finally they left him and Roger alone, only to rouse them near sunset. The burly man had swiped a towel over Alden's bloody face and tossed a blanket across his bruised shoulders, then pointed toward two guards who waited in the hallway. Alden had thought they'd awaken today in the bowels of the notorious Libby Prison, but here they were, safe and free…and all because of the woman who lay curled on the ground beside him, her cheek stained with mud from the dirt floor.

Blue-veiled dawn had begun to creep into the room. Though the lamp had gone out, Alden could see Roger's gray form crouching at his feet.

"I figured we ought to talk before we go any further," Roger said. Something like a smile twitched into existence and out again amid the shadows of his dark beard.

"Good idea." With a great effort, Alden sat up and brushed the dirt from his shoulders. At some point in the night, Flanna had covered him with the blanket; now he draped it over her.

Roger cleared his throat. "Do you know where the army is?"

Alden pressed his hand to his forehead and tried to remember the layout of the land. He had been unconscious when Flanna brought him to Richmond, so he had no idea of the distance or the topography of the surrounding area.

"You know the area better than I do." He squinted across the room. "You walked in, right?"

Roger snorted softly. "Strolled right into the middle of a Rebel camp."

Alden rolled his eyes in bewildered disbelief. "Why on earth, Roger, would you do such a thing?"

"Oh, I don't know. Why did Othello kill Desdemona?" Roger looked toward the door, then glanced at Flanna's sleeping form. "Madness, I suppose. Jealousy. Frustration. I knew, you see, that Flanna wanted to leave, because I read the farewell letter she wrote you. And when I couldn't find you—well, I was just crazy enough to act without thinking."

"She only wanted to go home." Alden bent his knees, stifling a groan as his body rebelled at the movement. "I don't know what was in that letter, but I can guarantee that you misinterpreted it. You are the one who adores her; you want to marry her." He lowered his gaze into Roger's eyes. "I would never take her from you."

"She doesn't want me!" Roger threw up his hand, then raked it through his hair. "Can't you get that through your thick skull? She loves you, Alden."

"She doesn't."

"She does!"

"Perhaps she doesn't know what she wants."

A single shriek interrupted their argument, and Alden turned to see Flanna awake and propped on her elbows. Her eyes blazed like emeralds in a face as pale as paper.

"Who are you to say what I want or don't want?" A faint tremor lined her voice. "You, Alden Haynes, are the one who told me to speak up for myself!"

Alden opened his mouth to answer, but the defiant look in her eye stopped him.

"I will speak for myself," she went on, pushing herself up from the floor. "And neither you, nor Roger, nor the Confederate army will dare to speak for me."

"Flanna, perhaps this can wait." Always the diplomat, Roger spoke in a smooth and charming voice. "The sun will rise soon, and we need to decide upon a plan."

"Our plan can wait." She glared first at Alden, then at Roger. "I don't know why I bother with you two. If I didn't love you both, I'd send both of you on your merry way."

Roger blinked in surprise. "You love us both?"

"Yes." She crossed her legs and rested her arms upon them, then lowered her head into her hands. "I love you both, in very different ways." She looked at Roger. "You, I love as a friend, almost in the same way I love Wesley. You are a dear man, you are talented, and I will always be grateful to you for squiring me around Boston and helping me feel at home. But I fear you want the woman I once was, not the woman I have become. So you and I, Roger, must remain friends. I cannot be the sort of wife you want."

"Flanna, you can! You are!"

"No. I am a doctor, and I will not stop practicing medicine." She smiled, but with a distracted, inward look, as though she was mentally cataloguing her thoughts. "Roger, I've had a lot of time to think in the past few days, and going back to the South has been good for me. I saw slavery again, but in the past week I've looked at it from a different perspective." Her eyes shimmered in the dim light. "Losing Charity has been good for me too. I learned that children grow up, and when they do, it's time to let them be independent."

"Flanna,"—impatience lined Roger's voice—"we can talk about slavery later."

"No, we can't." She tilted her head at him. "Because there's little difference in the way I treated Charity and the way you want to treat me. She wasn't a slave, but I guided her actions and her thoughts— at least, I wanted to. And if I were to become your wife, you would want to guide my actions and my thoughts—motivated by love, perhaps, but still you'd see me as little more than a child. And I'm not a child, Roger. I'm a doctor."

Her eyes brimmed with tenderness and passion as she caught Alden's gaze. "I will never be able to excuse slavery again. Mature human beings—be they black or white, male or female—have the right to make their own decisions and control their own destinies." She reached out to Roger, but her hand fell short of touching him. "Charity had the right to live her own life, and so do I."

She swiveled her gaze and looked at Alden with something very fragile in her eyes. "You, sir," she said, her voice shaking, "taught me to believe in the gifts God gave me. You told me to speak up for my ideals, for the truths I knew were right. You have created in me a will of iron, and I will not break. I cannot help but love you for that, though I know you cannot reciprocate my feelings. So I will wish you well, and pray that God will richly bless your future."

A glaze seemed to come down over her swimming eyes, and Alden struggled against his own impulse to reach out and hold her. She loved him with the same sort of affection a young girl might give an inspiring uncle or a mentor. If her feelings ran deeper, she would have given him some sign, but Alden could see no invitation in her eyes, only resignation and loss.

Very well then. He had almost begun to believe that God could demonstrate his mercy, but this was another call to exercise duty and honor.

Alden glanced away, unable to look at Flanna without revealing his own emotions. He loved her desperately, he wanted to continue to explore and understand her, but his brother stood between them. Roger still loved her; even now his countenance glowed with the intensity of his feelings.

Tell her, he urged Roger silently, meeting his brother's eye. *Tell her that you've changed, that you want her to continue her work. Tell her you used to think women were created to bear children and look attractive upon a man's arm, but you've since learned that they are God's crowning creation.*

But Flanna wasn't looking at Roger. Her gaze remained fixed to Alden's face, as if she expected a reply.

Alden took a deep breath, looked her straight in the eye, and gave her the truth he thought she needed to hear. "I didn't create your will of iron. Or your strength, or your beauty, or your intelligence. Such things are gifts of God, Flanna. I only encouraged you not to hide them under a bushel."

The gold in her green eyes flickered with pain. "I think you have ruined me for marriage," she whispered. "I know few men who can tolerate a woman like me."

Alden flinched, knowing that she spoke the truth. He had unconsciously encouraged her to break free of her shell because *he* loved the emerging woman within, but few men, including Roger, would appreciate the fiery angel she had become.

Yet Roger held first claim on her affections.

The cackling voice of a solitary rooster broke the silence. "Morning comes," Roger said, standing. "We have to go." His eyes met Flanna's, and his tone softened slightly. "You need to change, dear. You promised your brother."

"We'll wait outside." Alden gathered his strength and pushed himself off the floor, then stepped out into the first rays of morning. Roger followed, and the two of them stood silently outside the cabin, neither man willing to voice his thoughts as sunrise painted the colors of a new day.

Thirty

Why didn't I just stay in Boston?

Roger considered the question as he waited. His law practice had been thriving, and the war had surely brought a flood of cases relating to wills, inheritances, and business liability. He should have remained at home to hold Mother's hand and comfort her, rather than going off to play at soldiering.

For that was all he had done. When it came time for Roger to face the elephant, he had proved worthless. At Ball's Bluff he had turned and run like a scalded dog; at Fair Oaks he had hidden himself behind a tree. Worst of all, Alden knew he was a coward...and excused him.

Better that Flanna should have Alden, for the two of them were made of the same stern stuff. Like some sort of determined Joan of Arc, Flanna had wandered right onto the field of battle, risking death and capture to find the man she loved. And Alden gloried in battle, risking his life for the cause of God and country, somehow able to find meaning in the sacrifice and suffering.

Yes, they belonged together, no matter how stubbornly each of them denied the truth. Roger had whited too many sepulchers to be easily deceived, and he knew these two better than they knew themselves. They loved each other.

But Alden would never admit his feelings for Flanna while Roger stood in the way. And Roger, having once proclaimed his feelings for her, could not very well deny them. And, heaven help him, he did adore her.

The white house was just beginning to shine in the first tangerine tints of the rising sun when Flanna stepped out of the cabin, dressed in the green plaid dress Alden had commissioned in Washington. Roger felt a moment of annoyance, then swallowed his irritation when he noticed that rusty bloodstains marked the hem.

"What have we in the way of weapons?" he asked, peering back inside the cabin. Flanna's rifle stood there and he picked it up, then lifted the pieces of her discarded Confederate uniform to see if she'd thought to bring a dagger or pistol.

"I have only the rifle," she called from outside, "and it's not loaded."

"No cartridges?" Roger heard Alden ask. "No powder?"

Roger slipped Flanna's knapsack onto his back, then stepped back out into the yard. "There's nothing." His lips thinned with irritation as he handed the rifle to Flanna. "You carry this. If we're in trouble, you can always use it as a club."

Flanna took the gun, then jerked her head toward the row of trees beyond the house. "That is east." Wonder and dread mingled in her voice. "And we'd better move quickly if we want to stay ahead of the patrols." Her silky brows rose in concern as the sun revealed the violently purple bruises on Alden's face. "It will be harder walking through the woods," she said, in a distracted voice, "but the roads will be too dangerous."

She stepped closer to Alden as if she would support his weight, but Roger pulled her away, insinuating his own bulk beneath his brother's arm. "I'm stronger," he said in answer to her questioning look. "And faster. So let's be on our way."

"Wait."

Roger bit back his impatience as Alden hesitated.

"Flanna," Alden asked, "are you certain you don't want to go home? Roger and I can return to the regiment alone. You could find a safe place outside the city. Within a week, maybe two, I'm certain you could find a way back to Charleston."

"My home in Charleston is gone." She lifted her shining face and seemed to find her mirror in Alden's eyes. "For now, at least, my home is with you."

Roger closed his eyes against the nauseated sinking of despair, then forced a light note into his voice. "If you two don't hush, the Rebs will have us for breakfast." He stepped forward, tugging on Alden's weight. "Let's go. The regiment waits in the east, not here."

Flanna set off at a fair pace, and, like a horse drawn to the carrot, Alden fell into step beside Roger and followed her.

Flanna moved ahead with the rifle in her arms, wishing over and over again that she hadn't promised Wesley and Mrs. Corey that she'd wear a dress. The heavy fabric was hot, the narrow waist impeded her breathing, and every branch and vine clung to the full skirt, slowing her progress.

They moved steadily southeast, knowing that the Union army waited somewhere in the trees beyond. Flanna had not heard any sounds of battle during her few days in Richmond, but the fighting could resume at any moment.

"They've replaced Joe Johnston with this Robert E. Lee," she remarked offhandedly as they walked. "Johnston took a bullet at Fair Oaks. The men I nursed seemed enthusiastic at the idea of serving under Lee; they say he is nothing if not audacious."

"Let's hope his audacity holds him in Richmond until we reach our picket line," Roger joked, his eyes anxiously sweeping the horizon.

Flanna followed his gaze. The Rebels were camped out here, too, and Jeb Stuart's infamous cavalry was said to be traversing the countryside and taunting the Yankees.

They fell silent again, walking quickly across an open field. Flanna sighed in relief when they entered a forest; she felt much less exposed here than in the meadow. The forest whispered to itself around them; the faint patter of dewdrops on the leaves blended with the subdued rustle and rub of leaves and branches. They'd been walking for nearly two hours, covering a distance of at least seven miles, and Flanna sensed that they ought to encounter something soon.

A faintly familiar scent caught Flanna's attention. She sniffed in appreciation, then threw up her hand and stopped the others.

"What?" Roger's eyes widened in alarm.

"A cigar." Flanna stood perfectly still, suddenly grateful for her green dress. The plaid pattern might serve as a bit of camouflage.

She could see no movement in the woods, but straight ahead the ground rose in an abrupt swell. Anything could lie behind that bit of earth.

"Wait here." She put her finger over her lips and dropped the rifle to the ground.

"Flanna, no," Alden warned, but she ignored him and hurried forward. She was faster on her feet than Alden, and Roger was encumbered by his brother's weight. If trouble lay over that hill, at least they'd know to move around it. But Union scouts could be sitting there, and perhaps they'd have a horse to carry Alden back to camp.

She breathed deeply, inhaling the scent again. Yes, it was tobacco, rich and pungent. She thought she could smell coffee, too, but perhaps her empty stomach was merely playing tricks on her.

She reached the rise and debated walking around it. But any men who stood on the other side might see her before she saw them, while no one would expect her to appear over the edge of this nearly vertical mound. She walked to the rise, buried her hands in the vines and leafy ground cover that blanketed it, and began to climb, pausing to kick toeholds into the soft earth.

A chorus of birdsong echoed down from the high canopy of the trees, and Flanna took comfort in the utterly normal sound until a murmur of voices caught her ear, the slow and lazy drawl of relaxed men. They were probably pickets, placed out here as the army's eyes and ears. If Flanna was lucky, they'd be concentrating more on their hardtack and coffee than on the rustlings of leaves.

Inch by inch, foot by foot, she hoisted herself up the rise, then pulled herself onto the narrow ridge at the top. Lying flat on the ground, she stared into the concave depression below. She saw three men huddled around a campfire, their eyes fastened to a slab of bacon sizzling over the fire. Flanna's stomach clenched at the sight and smell of food, but she fought her hunger down and studied the strangers. The nearest one wore a white shirt and dark pants; the man next to him wore a dark brown jacket. She frowned. Though men of both armies had taken to wearing clothing removed from the dead, these men did not look at all military. They could be the conscription patrols Wesley had warned her about.

Another man abruptly stepped out from behind a tree at her left, so close Flanna could have spat on him. He tugged at his blue trousers and walked toward the fire, then picked up a coat on the ground.

A gray coat, with a double row of brass buttons. A stripe on the sleeve, just like Wesley's.

A Confederate captain.

Her high hopes vanished in an instant. Flanna pushed herself backward, scurrying away like a rat. Her feet slipped over the edge of the embankment, and prickles of cold dread crawled over her spine as she scrambled down.

Keep calm, she told herself, taking care that her trembling hands did not lose their grip on the vines. The men hadn't seen her. And though there might be a Confederate camp in the woods ahead, they could circle around it. They'd just have to walk further than she had hoped. If Alden's strength waned, she could find a stream and check his bandage. With water and the cornbread from Flanna's knapsack, he ought to be strong enough to make it back to a Union regiment as soon as they found one.

She whirled and ran the instant her feet hit the ground. Like the quick, hot touch of the devil, fear shot through her, urging her to flee. She didn't know exactly who those men at the campfire were, but they weren't friends.

She caught sight of Alden's startled face. "Rebels!" she gasped, her feet flying over clumps of brush and dead leaves. "Go!"

The words had scarcely left her lips when she tripped over her skirts and fell, slamming into the ground with such force that her breath left her body. She lifted her head, dazed and bewildered, and felt strong hands on her upper arms.

"Hurry." Roger pulled her up as though she weighed no more than a sack of feathers. He slipped his arm about her waist while Alden came to her other side. Half-carrying her, they began to move away, but then a sharp, ringing voice shattered the silence.

"Halt, there!" A nasal twang cut through the air like a knife.

Flanna closed her eyes as her heart went into sudden shock. This, too, was her fault. Not only was she responsible for bringing both brothers behind enemy lines, but now these Rebels had heard her clumsy crashing through the brush.

"You'll halt right there if you know what's good for you!"

Roger and Alden stopped, and Flanna felt her legs begin to tremble.

"We're going to be fine, Flanna," Alden said, looking at her. His voice was calm, his gaze steady.

"Turn around, so we can see what we've done caught."

They turned to face the ridge, and Flanna shuddered when she saw all four Rebels standing atop the embankment. Two of the men pointed rifled muskets directly at them.

"Come closer, and let us take a look at you." The Rebel captain stood propped against a tree, panting with exertion from his climb. "Come on up here, so we can see what the cat dragged in."

Roger looked at Alden. "I don't like the looks of this. I only see one uniform—the other three probably have more in common with that brute who beat you than with the regular army." His voice was smooth, but insistent. "You take Flanna and run for the brush over there." He jerked his head toward a stand of thick foliage. "You'll have time to hide yourself in the thickets while I deal with these men."

Flanna flinched at the resolute tone of his voice. "Roger, these men are not politicians." She saw the determined expression on his face and felt a cold blade of foreboding slice into her heart. "You can't charm Southerners, you know, any more than you can trick a trickster. We'll all go forward together, and no one will get hurt."

"Let me do this, Flanna." A faint light twinkled in the depths of his dark eyes as he looked at her.

He turned to Alden next. "Take her, Alden, and go."

Flanna's blood pounded thickly in her ears. "Roger, no!"

Alden's hands fell upon Flanna's arms, holding her back. An unspoken understanding passed between the two brothers, then Alden gave Roger a look of thanks, which Roger acknowledged with just the smallest softening of his eyes.

"Come up here now, or I'll shoot you dead!" the Confederate captain called again.

The next few seconds stretched into an eternity. Roger opened his mouth and screamed, "Go!" and Alden pulled Flanna toward the thicket with a strength born of desperation. As she fell back, Flanna lifted her eyes to the men on the embankment. Caught by surprise, they were slow in lifting their rifles, but Roger moved like a man possessed. In one swift gesture, he swung Flanna's useless rifle off his back and brought it to his shoulder, then squinted down the barrel like a sharpshooter.

Flanna choked back a scream as Alden dragged her into the brush, then his hand clapped across her mouth. She fell back against him, her vision filling with green leaves and blue sky as the sharp crack of rifle fire snapped through the rustle of insects. For one appalling instant, even the continuous birdcalls from the forest canopy ceased, and the woods overflowed with silence.

Unable to control the spasmodic trembling within her, Flanna closed her eyes and turned into Alden's embrace. He shuddered deeply as he held her, then he urged her to her feet. "Hurry," he said, pulling her out of the thicket. "Come, Flanna!"

Gasping for breath, she obeyed, running until she thought her heart would burst.

❦

In the next few hours, Flanna plumbed the full breadth and depth of fear. The four Rebels pursued her and Alden with fiendish glee, shooting randomly into bushes and beyond trees, once sending a bullet through Flanna's sleeve as she and Alden crouched behind a huckleberry bush. The forest rang with their taunts and a yipping, nasal version of the Rebel yell, and if Flanna had once imagined that these men were military, she knew now they were not. The captain was either an impostor or a renegade; the other three probably bounty hunters on the lookout for deserters.

"Come out, come out, wherever you are, missy!" one of them shouted as he took a moment to reload his rifle. "You looked awful sweet! Come on out here and let me show you what a real man looks like!"

Huddled beside Alden behind the huckleberry bush, Flanna felt a bead of perspiration trace a cold path from her armpit down her ribs. What were they to do? She and Alden could not outrun them in the open, for the Rebels were healthy and well fed. She, on the other hand, was half-petrified by fear and the shock of Roger's sacrifice, and Alden was breathing so heavily that the heaving movements of his chest might open his wound at any moment.

"Come on out here, sweet thing!" The man in the Confederate uniform walked slowly ahead of the others, his rifle cradled in his arms. "I won't hurt you. Why are you hiding with that whipped-looking son of a pup? Why, he isn't even worth dragging to the recruiting office, but we'll do you a favor and put him out of his misery. So you come on out now, and let's say a proper how-do-ye-do."

He paused less than thirty feet away, and glanced down at a spindly oak seedling. Flanna watched, transfixed by terror, as he smiled and broke off a small branch, then lazily twirled it between his fingers. "Your man's bleeding, sweet missy," he called, his eyes roving through the woods. "He won't last much longer. But if you come out, we just might help you patch him up."

Flanna tore her eyes from the tormentor and looked at Alden's chest. The wound had opened and bled through the bandage, for a red spot bloomed on Alden's white shirt, bigger and brighter than a full-blown rose.

"Alden!" Panic stole her breath, which came in short, painful gasps. "What are we going to do?"

Alden's eyes were abstracted in thought, but they cleared as she gripped his hand. "Three choices," he said in a clipped, low voice. "Stay, run, or hide."

Flanna blinked. Stay here? Out of the question! In another fifteen steps that phony Confederate would be upon them. Run? Impossible! Alden couldn't run another hundred yards, and she could never outrun her pursuers in this long, heavy skirt. Hide? Where?

"Come on out, little sweetheart!" The leader came closer, so close that Flanna could see the red smear of Alden's blood on the oak leaf.

She looked at Alden then, too afraid to speak. Silently he lifted his hand and pointed toward a rotting log ten feet to his right. The log was partially obscured by a leafy screen in front, and some animal—Flanna didn't want to imagine what kind—had hollowed out a space in the mud beneath the log.

It was a small trough, barely five feet long and three feet wide. But the log lay over it, and it was their only chance.

"Sweetheart!"

She could hear the renegade's heavy breathing now, so Flanna nodded. Alden took her hand and crept forward in a crouch, then knelt and rolled into the hole. Flanna crawled in after him, filling the space between him and the log. With her last remaining strength, she pulled at the log, managing to roll it a few inches to the right, obscuring the opening even more.

A twig snapped beneath the renegade's foot. From inside her hiding place, Flanna could see his heavy boots. He stood at the huckleberry bush and glanced down, then wiped another drop of blood from a huckleberry leaf.

"What's that you got there, Will?"

The sudden voice seemed to come from Flanna's left ear, and she felt Alden shudder against her as a heavy weight fell against the tree. One of the other Rebels stood right above them, his boot resting against the fallen log.

"The man's bleeding pretty bad." The one called Will rubbed Alden's blood on his coat as he scanned the woods. "Don't think they'll make it far, but we'll keep looking."

"What about the other one?"

Will shrugged, then leaned his rifle against the huckleberry bush and paused to bite off a chaw of tobacco. "No use to us dead, is he? But the woman might be a pleasant diversion, and the man worth a dollar or two—more if he's a runaway."

The second man stepped over the log and sat down, his weight pressing the heavy log onto Flanna's anklebone. She gritted her teeth, willing herself not to cry out.

"Should we go on?" The second man rocked slowly on the log, each movement grinding against Flanna's ankle.

"Yep." Will spat out a brown stream of tobacco juice. "I suppose we could check a little further, then double back. She couldn't have got far."

The second man stood then, relieving the pressure on Flanna's leg, and she wanted to weep with relief. The two men called out to the other two, who were searching the woods farther to the east, and soon the sound of their voices faded.

"Alden?" Flanna whispered.

He did not answer.

Turning in the confines of the shallow pit, Flanna wriggled her hand up to Alden's shoulder and drew in her breath when she encountered a warm stickiness. Alden was still bleeding, and there was nothing she could do about it. The Rebels were going to double back, they'd said, and they would undoubtedly return to their campfire to gather their things before moving on. She and Alden could do nothing but wait.

Sighing in surrender, she let her head fall upon his shoulder, taking comfort in the steady warmth of his breath on her face. If they were to die, at least they'd die together. And perhaps death in this shallow grave would be more merciful than death in prison or at the hands of the renegade Rebels.

She lay still for so long that she lost all sense of time. Something—an insect or spider, she couldn't tell which—crawled across her cheek, and she steeled herself to ignore it. Her arms felt too tired and heavy to even bat it away.

A chorus of crickets had begun to sing by the time Alden began to stir. "I'm sorry, Flanna," he apologized, his hand falling upon her neck. "But I think I fell asleep."

"You passed out." Flanna's hand moved to his shoulder and felt the stiffness of dried blood. Good. The blood had coagulated while they rested. If Alden didn't push himself, perhaps the wound would remain sealed until they found shelter.

Flanna squirmed out of the pit, then turned and helped Alden up. He moved slowly, like an old man, and once he straightened she examined him in the fading rays of the sun. The colors of health had completely faded from his face, leaving him wounded and ghostly in the shadows.

She didn't feel very steady herself. She took a step away from the log, then felt the ground shift beneath her feet. Alden caught her, and together they sank to the gnarled surface of the log.

"Why did you let Roger do it?" The question had been uppermost in her mind all afternoon, and only now, when she could see Alden's face, could she ask it.

Alden stared at the ground, his eyes like blue ice. "I don't know if you'll understand."

"Give me a chance."

He winced at the sharp tone in her voice. "I didn't want him to do it. I could have stopped and made a scene, reminding him that I was responsible for him, that I had promised Mother that I'd look after him…"

His voice trailed off, and Flanna gave him a moment to compose his thoughts. "So why didn't you stop him?"

"I did it for Roger." Alden's mouth pulled into a surprised smile, as if he had just realized the truth himself. "Don't you understand? Roger wanted to be a hero. You knew him, but I knew him far better.

It wasn't patriotism or even boosting his chances of election that drove him to enlist. He came to the war because he wanted to be brave—he needed to stand for something and test his mettle. He couldn't do it at Ball's Bluff, and he didn't do it at Fair Oaks, but he rose to the challenge today. He couldn't seem to summon the courage for going into battle for the intangible things like patriotism and honor, but he didn't hesitate to give his life for you and me."

Alden's expression softened into one of fond reminiscence. "You didn't know him as a child, but Roger always had to be the brave one when we played war games. But when we boys got into real trouble, he found it far easier to step back and let me handle things—which I always did." He frowned, as if responsibility were some great sin.

"Alden,"—Flanna took his hand and quietly checked his pulse—"you did what every big brother does. My own Wesley used to tease me unmercifully, but when the cousins ganged up on me, Wesley was quick to intervene. You saw it yourself—he still feels responsible for me."

"But last night he left you to stand on your own." Alden's free hand fell over hers, alarming her with its chilly touch. "I had never allowed Roger that same freedom. But today, he asked for it. And as hard as it was for me, I had to give it."

He looked at her, his eyes large and fierce with pain, and Flanna pulled him into her arms. Burying his face in her shoulder, he went quietly and very thoroughly to pieces.

⟿⟾

They waited until the sun set and the moon rose high enough to light their way through the woods. Logic urged her to keep walking eastward, but Flanna knew without being told that Alden would want to return to the place where his brother died. Roger deserved a decent burial, and Flanna desperately wanted to reclaim her knapsack. Inside were her journal, her medical bag, and at least three loaves of cornbread—and Alden desperately needed food. The conscription agents, or whoever they were, would certainly have moved on by now.

A shining net of stars spanned the ebony dome of heaven, and in the west a silvery glow outlined the curving hills around Richmond. Flanna and Alden walked slowly, her arm about his waist for support, until they found the edge of the woods where Roger had fallen. His body lay there still, unmolested and untouched, and for a heartbreaking moment Flanna wondered if she could have done something to save him. But as Alden dropped to his knees and turned the body, she saw the dark circle in the center of his forehead. If ever a man had died instantly, Roger had.

Alden sat on his knees and leaned forward, using his hands to shovel away the layer of dead leaves. "No, Alden." Flanna touched his shoulder, stopping him. "You haven't the strength for digging."

Tears sparkled in his lashes, and a silver trail marked his pale cheek. "I must."

"Then let me help."

She knelt across from him, cupping her hands as she pushed the earth aside. They worked in tandem until they had hollowed out a shallow trench, then Flanna helped Alden lift Roger and place him inside.

Alden prayed and Flanna listened, her own heart overflowing with unspoken thoughts and feelings. She was burying a man who had loved her, a man who had influenced her life for more than two years. Roger had been the truest of all friends, loving her even though he knew she loved his brother.

She looked up at Alden's shining face. He prayed in a quiet and composed voice, his countenance lifted toward heaven, and his eyes glowed with love and understanding as he asked the Lord to say his farewells to Roger.

What had Nell Scott ever done to deserve such a man?

When Alden had finished praying, Flanna picked up her knapsack and led Alden to a stream where she forced him to eat and drink.

She couldn't tell whether it was because of the food or simple relief that Roger's burial was over, but Alden's spirits seemed to rise as he sat in a patch of moonlight and ate. He insisted that Flanna eat, too, but she merely nibbled at her loaf of cornbread, knowing that Alden needed the lion's share.

"You're looking better," she finally said, leaning over the creek bank as she swished her hands in the water. "Nell will probably write me a thank-you note once you're married."

Alden stopped chewing, and one of his brows shot upward. "Nell who?"

"Nell Scott." Flanna folded her hands in her lap and gave him a controlled smile. They had been through so much together, they might as well bring this secret out into the open. "I know she loves you. Will you be married in Boston or Roxbury?"

He shook his head back and forth, like an ox stunned by the slaughterer's blow. "I'm to marry Nell Scott? This is the first I have heard of it."

Flanna laughed. "What is this, selective amnesia? Of course you're going to marry Nell. You've been writing her since the war began. I have one of your letters to her in my medical bag."

"I remember her writing me." Alden's face suddenly went grim. "But I don't remember anything about a wedding. How could I marry her when I—" His voice broke off, and he narrowed his eyes at Flanna. "You think I'm engaged to Nell Scott? You've always thought so?"

Rattled by the pressure of his gaze, Flanna felt herself flush. "Of course I thought so. One does not write a young lady for months without holding certain intentions—"

"Who wrote the young lady?"

"You did!"

He stiffened as though she had struck him. "Produce the letter."

Without hesitation, she pulled her medical bag from her knapsack, then opened it and fished the letter from its depths. "Here!" With a triumphant flourish, she dangled it before Alden's eyes. "A letter to Miss Nell Scott of Boston."

Flanna wasn't sure, but she thought she saw the beginnings of a smile amid the tangles of his beard. "Read it."

"I don't read other people's mail."

He leaned forward and grabbed her hand, making her skin tingle where he touched her. "Read it, please. If I hold any intentions toward this young woman, I'd like to be reminded of them."

Flanna pulled away, then produced a scalpel from her medicine bag. "I'll make a neat cut, so you can post the letter anyway." She slit the envelope along its upper edge, then pulled out a single sheet. Alden leaned back upon a wide rock and folded his hands, seeming to enjoy her torment.

The shocking events of the day must have dulled his senses, else he would not have forced her to read of his love for another woman.

Flanna opened the letter, held it up to the moonlight, and began to read: "Dear Miss Scott, greetings. I am sorry I have not been able to respond to your thoughtful letters—"

Flanna paused and looked up. Alden merely lifted a brow, then nodded. "Do go on. I've heard nothing about a wedding yet."

Flanna took a deep breath and tried to curb her riotous emotions. "—but we have been marching for many days. The weather here is very wet, and the men are not used to it…" Flanna's voice trailed off as she skimmed the rest of the letter. He wrote about his men, the food, and the countryside, then he ended with a single short sentence: "I asked you to pray for my men before we left, and I would especially ask you to pray for one Franklin O'Connor. He is a most stubborn sort of person, a raw recruit, and I worry about him. Very sincerely yours, Alden Haynes."

She glared at him. "You asked her to pray for me?"

Alden shrugged. "Why not? She was desperate to pray for someone."

"But you said you were worried about me? And that I was *stubborn*?"

"Perhaps worry was too strong a word." He learned forward, and in the moonlight he seemed to study her with a curious intensity. "I wanted to write that I thought about you constantly, but Miss Nell Scott wouldn't understand my concern for a fellow soldier. In truth, Flanna, I've never worried about you. I've never met a woman more capable, or one who intrigued me more."

He reached out and lightly fingered a strand of hair on her cheek. "I think I fell a little in love with you on the day Roger asked me to walk you home—do you remember? I deliberately said something appalling when I left you at your boardinghouse because I thought I might have an easier time of it if you hated me."

"I never hated you." The words bubbled to Flanna's lips from some deep place where she'd hidden them away.

He smiled with beautiful candor. "Every time you and Roger had a spat, I dared to hope you might look in my direction. Then the war began, and I knew you'd despise me for fighting against your loved ones."

"I never despised you."

"And then," he went on, not giving her a chance to unburden her thoughts, "when the three of us waited together in that holding room, I heard Roger say that your friendship would be the basis of a good marriage. And this morning, you made your feelings quite clear—for me you felt gratitude. And in that moment, a word which should have brought genuine happiness served only to tear at my heart."

"Alden." Her heart took a perilous leap toward him. "Alden, I have loved you for months, but I thought you were engaged to Nell Scott. I never dreamed that you could feel anything but affection toward me…and there was Roger."

"Yes," he said, his arm slipping behind her neck and drawing her closer, "and today Roger brought us together."

"He knew." Flanna closed her eyes as Alden's warm breath fanned her cheek. "He read the letter I wrote you. He knew I loved you."

Alden pulled her to his side, and for a long moment they sat together, her head resting on his strong shoulder, his arm holding her close. Flanna pressed her hand to his chest, feeling the beat of his heart through his shirt as she thought about the circumstances that had brought them together.

How could two brothers be so different and yet so alike? Each was devoted to the other; each admired different qualities of the same woman. Flanna knew that Roger had valued her wit, her charm, and her beauty, while Alden esteemed the qualities he had chided her for hiding. And which man had loved her most?

Roger had given his life for her…and Alden had given her life. He had given her the courage to step out of the confining mold of genteel womanhood. While still cherishing her femininity, he had shown her that God had given her unique gifts and then encouraged her to use them.

She lifted her eyes, imprinting his beloved profile upon her heart. The applause of fluttering oak leaves and the quiet ripple of the creek served as a natural accompaniment as Alden kissed her, anguish and promise and faith all mingled in the moment.

And when they stretched out on the rock and waited for sleep, Alden thrust his hand toward the silvery net of stars and closed his fist as if he could pluck one from the sky. "Have you ever thought about the stars, Flanna?" A tinge of wonder lined his voice. "They differ from one another in glory, yet each of them is priceless, beautiful, and bright with the glory of the Creator. In every star, every sunrise, and every wind that blows, I see God's hand. Whenever I was tempted to look at the horrors of war or the frustrations of dealing with General McClellan, I'd step outside my tent and look at the heavens. And then I could see that God remained far above the fray, that he controlled my life and everything that touches it."

He lowered his hand and dropped it to his chest. When he spoke again, his voice was low and oddly gentle. "I don't know what made me love you. But when I look at you, I see God's beauty in your compassion, his strength in your courage, and his mercy in your love. I had never noticed any of those qualities in God before. He was like a supreme commander—giving orders, making sure you obeyed, meting out justice. That has all changed now, and I understand why so many people willingly surrender their lives to him. Wherever we go, whatever tomorrow holds, I know that I have been blessed by you."

Flanna felt the wings of tragedy lightly brush past her, lifting the hairs on her forearm. Was that resignation she heard in his voice? "Tomorrow holds rescue, Alden," she assured him. "We'll set out at first light, and we'll find a Union regiment. I'll personally see that you are taken to a decent hospital, and I'll oversee your care. You're going to be fine, Alden, just fine."

She lifted her head to look at him, but his eyes had closed. She lifted her hand; the surface of her palm was shiny and black in the moonlight.

He was bleeding again, and she had no more bandages to stanch the flow.

❧

An hour later, Flanna knelt by the creek to wash the blood from her hands and tried to steady her pounding heart. She had tried everything she knew to stop Alden's bleeding—a splash of cold water, a grass poultice, even a bandage she fashioned from fabric ripped from her skirt—but nothing seemed to work. Alden's pulse grew weaker with each passing moment, and the heart she had listened to only a short while ago would soon stop beating unless she could get help. But how could she leave Alden when he had told her that he feared dying alone? She herself had tasted the bitter fear of abandonment. This hour, coming so soon after they had finally declared their love to one another, was not the time to forsake the man she loved.

You have to go.

Flanna acknowledged the voice, but not its message. "Leave him?" Her accusing voice stabbed the air. "If I go, will you keep him alive? Or is this your way of setting him free? I let Charity go. Alden let Roger go. And neither of them is ever coming back!"

Trust in the Lord with all thine heart.

She splashed her hands in the frigid water and scrubbed her knuckles until the skin stung. She had depended on God through her examinations and her entrance into the army. She had stepped out in faith when she left the Yankee camp and wandered over the battlefield. But now she had Alden, the love they had struggled so long to express, and the promise of their future! How could she risk something so precious when the odds were against her?

Lean not unto thine own understanding.

"I'm not leaning on understanding." She pulled her dripping hands from the water and wiped them on her torn skirt. "I'm using my head. I've always used my head. It's pulled me through many a situation—"

Suddenly her mind blew open, and with naked clarity she saw the truth in her words and the lie in her heart.

She wasn't trusting God. She was trusting herself.

Throughout her life, she had investigated, made plans, and prepared herself for whatever was to come. As she studied for her examinations, prepared to enter the army, even as she decided to strike out toward Richmond, she had leaned solidly on her own understanding, trusting common sense and hard work to make a way and see her through. She had given lip service to the notions of trust and faith, but God was only her contingency plan, someone to fall back on if her own plans went awry.

Now there was no one to trust but God, no way but his way.

She glanced back at Alden. He lay on the rock, his shirt wrapped around him, his face as pale as candle wax beneath the bruises. The front of his shirt, black with blood, shone darkly in the moonlight.

"How can I leave him?" Her heart breaking, she glanced up at the star-studded sky. "I know now that he is what I have been searching for all this time. I joined the army, knowing he'd be there. I followed him to Virginia, even into battle, because my heart yearned for him. Besides Papa, Alden is the only man who ever loved me enough to let me be the woman you called me to be."

She listened, straining to hear the small voice that had echoed in the deepest part of her heart, but she heard nothing but the warbling song of a bird on a branch overhanging the creek. God was going to be silent, then. He offered no promises, just a simple request. He wanted her faith and surrender, a deliberate commitment to him when she could see no other way. And time—like Alden's strength—was slipping through her fingers.

Flanna's stomach churned and tightened into a knot as fear brushed the edge of her mind. If she left, Alden might wake and die alone, and she would never forgive herself for deserting him. If she remained to comfort him, he would die in her arms, but he would *die*.

She rose to her knees on the muddy creek bank and lifted her eyes, searching for a falling star or some other celestial omen, but nothing moved in the starry black vault overhead. If only she could have some assurance that Alden's strength would last until she returned! She tilted her head, listening for the whisper of the wind, but except for the insistent warbling of that bird, the woods were as silent as the grave.

She sank back, drained of will and thought, then realization came on a slow tide of feeling. *The bird*. What birds sang in the dark? The bravest birds—those who trusted the Creator. The simple creatures who knew nothing of science or the earth's rotation but still trusted that the bright light of morning was not far away.

She rose up and absently brushed clinging leaves and mud from her skirt. She had entrusted her dreams to Alden, and he had protected and encouraged them. Why, then, could she not trust the love of her heart to the almighty God? As a youngster, she had trusted the Almighty's plan of salvation. She could cling to childlike faith again.

After placing a soft kiss on Alden's cold cheek, Flanna climbed the moonlit hill. A chilly breeze swept over the dark ridge, but sunrise could not be far away. If she found a Union camp—*when* she found a camp—there would be men aplenty to help her bring Alden back.

The darkness in the deep woods felt like liquid, and Flanna moved from one moonlit patch to another, hoping to sight a clearing and a road that would lead to help. She walked quickly, her regret at leaving Alden alone overruled by the certainty that God could be trusted with her dreams. Songbirds sang in the dark…because they knew the morning would come.

❦

The stars had just begun to fade behind a sky of dark blue when Flanna saw a solitary ghostly figure in the road. The soldier, undoubtedly a Union picket, leveled his rifle musket and called out in a gruff voice, "Who's there?"

Flanna opened her mouth, but her throat felt thick and heavy; the words wouldn't come. Her knees were liquid, her body light as air.

The gray figure straightened as the musket rose to shoulder height. By all rights he ought to shoot. She was a stranger approaching from hostile territory, but perhaps he might show her mercy.

Her leaden feet moved forward, her skirts dragged over the road. She struggled forward in a hunched posture, her arms wrapped around her center. He might shoot her. If he did, Alden would die, and the struggle would be over. At least they'd be together in eternity.

"Speak now!" the guard called again, moving into a patch of silvery moonlight. "You are approaching a Federal camp!"

"Please!" From somewhere at the center of her being she drew the strength to summon a whisper, husky and dark. "Please help me. I have come on behalf of a Union officer, Major Alden Haynes."

"Major Haynes?" The guard lowered his rifle; he must have recognized the name. As Flanna halted, he inserted two fingers in his mouth and whistled. Within an instant, a pair of guards came running.

Limp with weariness, Flanna dropped to her knees in the dirt. When one of the guards lifted a lantern, she flinched, then squinted into the light. The ghostly figure with the rifle proved to be a boy, probably not more than seventeen.

"My name is O'Connor." She lifted her hand to shield her eyes and spoke in a weary monotone. "I am known to Sergeant Marvin, Company M of the Twenty-fifth Massachusetts. I have left Major Alden Haynes in the woods, and I need your help."

"You better watch her," one of the other guards said, his eyes narrowing as he came closer. "I hear some of those screaming Rebel furies have been trying to sneak into our camps. They're spying for General Lee."

The boy with the rifle frowned, and Flanna breathed an exasperated sigh, understanding his confusion. How could a ragtag woman know Major Haynes and Sergeant Marvin? How could any woman in Virginia know Union officers?

The boy jerked his rifle to his shoulder and pointed it downward. "Tell me the truth, lady—are you a Rebel?"

Flanna swayed slightly on her knees and closed her eyes. She had seen enough rebellion and bloodshed to last a lifetime.

She lifted her head and met the guard's gaze. "No. I am a Bostonian."

Reassured, the boy lowered his gun, then jerked his chin at one of the guards. "Russell, run over to that camp of Massachusetts fellows and see if you can find this Sergeant Marvin. Thomas, you bring the lady a hot cup of coffee; she looks like she could use one."

Flanna gave the young man a grateful smile. He helped her to her feet, and even in the dim glow of lantern light she saw a rich blush stain his cheeks.

Thirty-One

For the second time in a week, Alden awoke to find Flanna standing by his side.

"Shh." She pressed her finger to his mouth as he moistened his lips and struggled to speak. "We're safe within our own regiment."

He lifted his head to see her better. Flanna wore a becoming dress of butternut homespun, while a wide ribbon held her hair back in a most feminine fashion. He smiled for a moment, grateful for her loveliness, then looked past her. He lay on a cot in a large tent, but there were no other patients. "Where—?" he began.

"You're in an officer's tent," she answered his unvoiced question. "McClellan is preparing another attack, but I doubt much will come of it. We've already pulled back from the position we held at Fair Oaks." She bent low and whispered into his ear. "Strange way to wage war, isn't it? Win and fall back. At this rate we'll be safely back in Washington before Christmas."

"Flanna—"

"You need to be quiet."

"No." Alden rallied his strength and struggled to sit up. "I need to speak, woman!"

She gave him a slightly reproachful look, then sank demurely to a stool by the cot. When he pulled himself up and stared at her, she lifted a brow. "So speak."

"What will you do now?" He felt his heart turn over as he looked at her, so lovely, so strong, so loving. "Will you go to my mother's house in Boston?"

"Not on your life." Her husky voice was edged with steel. "I love you, Alden, and I've seen the uncertainties of war. So as long as you stay, I stay. If you want to go home, I'll go with you, but if you're going to risk your life for a cause, the least I can do is support the same cause."

He reached up and scratched his chin, a little startled by the heavy growth that had appeared there. "There's no dissuading you?"

"Absolutely not. Just like your mother and the suffragists, I'll speak my mind. I refuse to be pushed aside."

He frowned, momentarily imagining Flanna in bloomers and parading down the streets of Boston, then he saw the smile hidden in the corner of her mouth. "Come here, Flanna."

She did not dispute him or argue, but moved into the circle of his arms as if she had always belonged there. He held her close as she sat on his lap, and he lifted his hand to stroke her hair, marveling at the soft, coppery strands that glistened in his fingers like burnished threads of sunlight.

Perhaps God's plan for his life held more than a call to duty. This certainly felt like love...and mercy.

"Why am I still alive?" The question slipped from his lips. He felt guilty for asking it, but he needed to know. "I was dying, and ready to do so, for you were with me and Roger was gone—"

A blush ran over her cheeks, but her eyes glowed with an inner fire. "Don't you dare feel guilty about living, Alden. I couldn't let you die. Roger gave his life so you—so *we*—could live. And God guided my steps to bring you back."

She reached out, lacing his fingers with her own.

"You're going to be fine, as strong as ever in a few days. Though Gulick bellowed at me throughout the entire procedure, Colonel Farnham allowed me to perform a transfusion on you." Her smile lingered on him, more warming than the summer sun. "We're truly connected now, Major Haynes. My blood—quite a bit of it—now flows in your veins."

"How—"

"A syringe." Releasing his hand, she lifted her sleeve and showed him a blue bruise in the bend of her arm. "The English physician James Blundel invented the technique in 1818, but not many American doctors seem willing to try it. But for you"—her voice lowered—"I had no choice."

Amazed, Alden brought her closer and wondered if he should feel some guilt for the feeling of relief that swept through him. She had not only given him her love, but she had saved his life in the most profound sense. He struggled for words, but found none adequate to convey the feelings in his heart.

He lifted his hand and tenderly traced the outline of her cheek and jaw, hoping touch could communicate what words could not. She seemed to sense his feelings, for her hand came up to cover his, and she leaned into his palm, closing her eyes.

"We can ask the chaplain to marry us," he said, his heart rising to his throat at the thought.

"A very good idea," she said, opening her eyes to smile at him. "I always wanted to be a June bride." Burying her face in his neck, she breathed a kiss there, and the mere touch of her lips sent a warming shiver through him.

Alden Haynes rested his chin atop the little doctor's head and exhaled a long sigh of contentment.

Thirty-Two

◦━∽◦◦∽━◦

Tuesday, September 23, 1862
Antietam Creek, Maryland

Three separate battles raged in this place only six days ago. By the time the fighting ended, the glorious Union counted 2,108 dead, 10,293 wounded or missing. The papers report that General Lee lost fewer men—some 10,318 killed, wounded, or missing—but that number represents a greater proportion of his army.

Oh, how I wish this war would end!

I have been a bride for three months, but now my beloved Alden is among the missing. And though my heart yearns to look up and see his face, my hands have been so busy in the care of the wounded that I have had no time to wonder or grieve. And yet I pray that he is in the quiet care of some Maryland housewife who will soon send him on his way.

How can I write all that is in my heart? My brain grows numb with the sights and sounds of war.

At Antietam I saw a cornfield in which every stalk was cut off at the ground. In the cornstalks' place the dead lay in neat rows, exactly as they fell in their valiant lines. I saw a road—they now call it Bloody Lane—filled with Confederate dead piled two and three deep. One wounded soldier told me he could have walked to the horizon with dead men as his steppingstones.

The wounded fill every building and have over-flowed into the country, occupying farmhouses, barns, corncribs, and cabins. Wherever there were four walls and a roof, there are wounded who need medical care. I am giving it to the best of my ability.

After being turned away from one hospital tent by a doctor who did not know me by sight or reputation, I went to the battlefield itself—hoping, I must confess, for some sign of Alden. My clothing grew heavy, and I had to stop and wring the blood from the bottom of my skirt before I could continue. As I bent over one man, a bullet passed through my sleeve and struck my patient, killing him instantly.

Though my heart mourns for those who are dead and missing in both armies, I have come to believe that God might hold an opinion about this struggle after all. Yesterday President Lincoln issued what the papers call the Emancipation Proclamation, a decree freeing all slaves held in rebellious states. Though the slaves in Maryland, Missouri, Delaware, and Kentucky are still in bondage, I cannot believe that this condition will continue for long.

A country founded upon the belief that all men are created equal, with fundamental and inalien-able rights guaranteed by the Constitution, cannot justify the bondage or dehumanization of others,

whether black or white, male or female, born or
unborn.

Perhaps it was for this that we went to war. I do
not know if these men realized it when they enlisted
in the army...just as I did not know how I would be
liberated as a result of my bold disguise. I doubt
that even Lincoln envisioned the full effect of this
conflict when he first summoned those brightly
patriotic young men to serve this wounded country.
How strange it is—a war fought to deny freedom to
rebel states might in fact free us all. In our rebellion, we are lost. In submission to a God-appointed
head, we are free.

If this war dignifies the downtrodden, frees the
slaves, and protects this Union for the unborn children yet to come, then the struggle will have been
worth it all.

For the sake of a single unborn child, I must
surrender my work on the battlefield. I have
decided to accept Mrs. Haynes's invitation and
return to Boston. Together she and I will pray for
the end of the war, and we will wait for Alden's
return. And if he does not come home to us, I will
miss him forever, but I will go on.

And when my son is born—for I am certain it
will be a boy—I will name him Alden Roger Haynes.
He will continue in the tradition of two remarkable
men...and my love will keep them alive.

Epilogue

The doorbell buzzed again.

I winced at the nerve-racking sound and hurried to answer it. "I'm coming!" I called, a bit crossly. One quick peek through the peephole confirmed my suspicions, and when I opened the door, Taylor Morgan stood there. Before I could even greet him, he thrust the heavy *Velvet Shadow* manuscript into my arms.

"Flanna's story can't end there." He moved past me without so much as a hello. "You can't leave me hanging, Kathleen. You did the research, so you should know." He whirled in the hall to face me. "What happened to Alden Haynes?"

I shifted the bulky manuscript to my other arm, then back-kicked the door closed. "Haven't you ever read *Gone with the Wind*?" I moved past Taylor into the living room. "Margaret Mitchell left us all hanging. We never knew if Scarlett and Rhett got back together."

"That was fiction." Taylor followed me into the living room, then dropped into my wing chair. "Come on, Kathleen, you've got to tell. Why'd you end the story there?"

I shrugged and sat on the couch. "The story wasn't about whether Alden Haynes lived or died." I moved the bundled pages to the coffee table. "It was about how two people found each other."

Taylor made a small sound of exasperation, and I grinned. "Besides, it took me over four hundred pages to end the story in 1862. Did you want me to take another six hundred pages to carry Flanna through 1865?"

"What happened in 1865?" He leaned forward, instantly alert. "The war ended in April, and—"

"Johnny came marching home." My voice softened as my eyes fell on Flanna's journal on the coffee table. I picked it up, ran my palm over the rough leather binding, and once again felt the force of Flanna's personality through the pages. "Alden Haynes came home from the war, too, in the company of Wesley O'Connor."

"Wesley?" Taylor gaped in surprise.

I nodded. "Yes. Flanna, her two-year-old son, and Mrs. Ernestina Haynes welcomed both men to the Haynes house—quite a gesture for Mrs. Haynes, considering that Wesley had been a slaveholder. But she must have believed that he atoned for his sin in the war. Wesley, you see, had been wounded in the fighting outside Richmond, and a Confederate surgeon had to amputate his arm. No longer able to fight in the field, he was transferred to the prison camp at Belle Isle in the James River. When Alden was captured at Antietam and taken to Belle Isle, the two recognized each other. Alden told Wesley that he had married Flanna, and in a gesture of goodwill, Wesley saved Alden's life."

"How?" Taylor shifted in the wing chair and frowned. "What happened in the prison?"

I sighed, once again feeling the sense of tragedy and loss that had hovered over me while I researched the story. "General Grant put an end to all prisoner exchanges, you know, virtually assuring that all prisoners of war remained incarcerated until the war ended. And by 1865, the Confederate army couldn't feed itself, much less its prisoners. Ninety percent of all survivors from Belle Isle weighed less than one hundred pounds when they were released. The sight was so shocking that Walt Whitman reportedly looked at several skeletal prisoners and cried, 'Can these be men?'

"In an effort to help his brother-in-law, Wesley embroidered Flanna's story a bit. He told his fellow officers that Flanna had saved several

Confederate soldiers—which was true—but just to make sure they treated Alden with a bit of compassion, Wesley said that Flanna had been dressed as a boy and fighting by his side during the war. Apparently Wesley told a ripping yarn. The commander of the camp was impressed enough by Flanna's story and the Yankee that could win her heart that he allowed Wesley to share his rations with Alden Haynes."

Taylor seemed to melt in relief. "So Alden was healthy when he was released."

"Hardly. By the end of the war, both he and Wesley were living on rats, dead fish, and rainwater. The daily rations—which had consisted of a teaspoon of salt, three tablespoons of beans, and half a pint of unsifted cornmeal—ran out long before 1865. But they were alive, and they made it back to Boston. Flanna's journal ends shortly after their homecoming, but from other research I learned that Wesley remained in Boston, doted on his nephew, and died from tuberculosis in 1870 without ever returning to Charleston."

"Was he happy in Massachusetts?" Taylor pushed his bottom lip forward in thought. "I can't imagine that a Rebel soldier would be welcomed in Boston."

I shrugged. "The South was virtually an occupied territory after the war—the Yankees instituted martial law, and South Carolina didn't regain congressional representation until June 1868, three years after the war's end. I'm sure Wesley thought he'd be as happy in Boston as in Charleston. He wouldn't have an easy life in either place, but at least in Boston he had family and friends."

Taylor sat silently, mulling over the information I'd just given him. From outside my window, I heard the hush of cars moving up and down the street, then the whine of a siren. The sounds seemed somehow strange and anachronistic; part of me expected to hear the whicker of horses and the rattle of passing carriages.

"Were there really no women doctors?" Taylor's voice brought me back to reality. "I knew women were pretty much bound to hearth and home in the nineteenth century, but I had no idea they were not allowed to practice medicine."

"The Union army did appoint Dr. Mary Walker as a contract surgeon in 1864," I explained. "Like Flanna, Dr. Walker gave up on proper channels and just dove into the work as a volunteer. After months of unsuccessfully hounding the surgeon general for a commission, she left for the Chattanooga front, where her spying soon resulted in her capture by the Confederates. A Rebel captain, surprised to see a female doctor among the prisoners, wrote his wife that his men were 'all amused and disgusted at the sight of a thing that nothing but the debased and depraved Yankee nation could produce. She was dressed in the full uniform of a Federal Surgeon—not good looking and of course had tongue enough for a regiment of men.'"

Taylor laughed softly, then rested his chin on his hand. His eyes twinkled at me. "So what do you do now? Anika, Aidan, and Flanna—you know all about them. But you're the next heir of Cahira O'Connor, Kathleen. And we're only months away from a new century."

"You know, it's really ironic that you should be so curious about all this." I opened the journal and pulled out a sheaf of paper I'd placed inside. "Since you and the professor urged me to pursue this, I was curious to see whether or not I was directly related to Flanna O'Connor. So I traced her descendants and mapped out her family tree." I glanced down at the paper, then shot Taylor a quick smile. "Very interesting stuff, genealogy."

"Really?" Taylor pulled back his shoulders and lifted his chin. "How so?"

"I'm not descended from Flanna at all, so I must come from another line of the O'Connors. But there was one really interesting line. Alden and Flanna Haynes gave birth to Alden Roger Haynes, born in 1863. Alden Roger married, and his wife gave birth to Felma Frankie Haynes in 1887, who married and gave birth to Lela Johnston in 1915, who married and gave birth to Arthur Johnston Morgan in 1943, who married and fathered Taylor Johnston Morgan in 1973."

The shock of recognition blanched Taylor's features. "You don't mean—"

"You." I nodded, more than a little pleased that I'd be able to hound *him* for a while. "If I'm an heir of Cahira O'Connor, then so are you. Flanna O'Connor is your great-great-grandmother."

Taylor had been interested before that moment, but now the facts overwhelmed him. He sank back into the wing chair and turned away from me, his hand rubbing over his face as if he could somehow wipe the truth away.

"What does this mean?" Abruptly, he turned to me. "What in the world are we supposed to do about it?"

I wanted to laugh. I'd been asking the same question for months, but neither Taylor nor the professor had been able to give me a clear answer.

"Maybe," I leaned forward with my elbows on my knees, "we take what we've learned and we look for some avenue where we can do some good. The professor seemed to think that I'd need something from each one of the other heirs to make a difference when my turn came. He said I should take Anika's spiritual strength, Aidan's creative joy, and some quality of Flanna's—"

"Which one?" Taylor interrupted. "You're not a doctor."

"No, but Flanna was more than a doctor. She had to step outside the role society expected of her. Maybe that's what I'm supposed to do."

Taylor leaned forward, and his eyes twinkled as they met mine. "I don't know, Kathleen. There aren't many things women can't do today. Unless you want to play professional football—"

"No way." I crossed my legs on the sofa and ran my hand through my hair. "Honestly, Taylor, this may be the end of it. Those three women did remarkable things with their lives, and I'm proud to think I'm somehow linked to them. I have learned a lot from this project. Who knows? Maybe we're both supposed to take what we've learned and make the world a better place."

Taylor stood up and gave me a twisted smile. "So—you want to get a bite to eat? Since you've done such a good job with my great-great grandmother, maybe you can shed some light on my unhappy childhood."

"I'd like the food, but I'll pass on the psychoanalysis." I stood up and reached for my shoes, which had disappeared beneath the couch.

Taylor moved out into the hall in a fog of deep thought, and I tried to concentrate on tying my shoelaces. I had enjoyed finishing Flanna O'Connor's story, especially when I discovered the link between the Boston doctor and Taylor Morgan. The next time he insinuated that I was destined to save the world in the twenty-first century, I'd just ask him if he was prepared to play Moneypenny to my James Bond.

He was leaning against the wall, his hands in his pockets, when I came into the hall. "You know why people write historical novels and screenplays?" he said, voicing his thoughts aloud.

I pulled my jacket from the hook in the hall and swung it over my shoulders. "Tell me."

"People write historical stories because they deal with contemporary issues too painful to study at close range."

His eyes moved into mine, glowing with brilliant intelligence while I fumbled in ignorance. "And your point is?"

He opened the front door, but stopped me before I could walk through the doorway. "What are the issues you've been studying? Spiritual corruption in Anika's day, greed and lust in Aidan's, and slavery and prejudice in Flanna's. What if"—his voice dropped in volume, as if he were confiding a deep secret—"what if you will be confronted with all these issues in the coming months? Think about it, Kathleen. God may have been preparing you through all this—"

"I'm hungry, and you promised to feed me." I moved past him into the hallway, then turned and winked at him. "Coming, Moneypenny?"

This time he was left fumbling in the dark. "Money what?" he asked, pulling the door closed. "I don't get it."

"Remind me to introduce you to James Bond sometime," I said, slipping my arm through his as we moved out to the street. "You know, Taylor, you really should get out more often."

He tilted his head and gave me an uncertain smile. "I'd like that, Kathleen. You know, I've had a chance to think about it, and I don't want to end up like the professor. He was a wonderful man, but he was…quite alone."

"You don't have to be alone." I tightened my hold on his arm and pointed to the Chinese restaurant on the corner. "And if you take me for Chinese and promise not to ask how I'm planning to save the world, I'll let you tell me all about your unhappy childhood."

"Deal." He paused at the steps of my apartment and surprised me with a light kiss on the cheek. "Thanks, Kathleen." He smiled down at me. "I have the feeling my life is about to change."

The feeling was mutual, but I wasn't quite ready to tell him so. "Life is always changing," I finally said, hoping that this time he wouldn't lose interest after only a few weeks. "You can count on it."

A frigid wind blew down on us as we left the shelter of my front steps, but I pressed closer to Taylor's warmth and barely even felt the cold.

Author's Note and References

The tragedy of the American Civil War has not been forgotten, nor should it be, for more than 130 years later we are still influenced by the powerful feelings that instigated this conflict. As I researched this period of history, I discovered that my own great-great-great-grandfather, John M. Johnston, joined the Confederate army in 1862 and was among the starving soldiers who surrendered with Lee in 1865. It is impossible to write about these men without feeling a surge of loyalty and affection toward them.

Could a woman really disguise herself and enlist in a Civil War army? Of course, and over four hundred actually did. Motivated by patriotism, bounty money, a love of adventure, or the desire to remain beside their husbands and brothers, they left the traditional roles of womanhood behind and went off to battle. One soldier from a Massachusetts regiment wrote his family: "There was an orderly in one of our regiments and he and the Corporal always slept together. Well, the other night the Corporal had a baby, for the Corporal turned out to be a woman! She has been in three or four fights" (*An Uncommon Soldier*, p. xii).

There is an abundance of material available on the Civil War, and I, unfortunately, could not pursue an exhaustive study. I have, however, taken pains not to contradict the actual facts regarding the battles at Ball's Bluff, Fair Oaks, and Antietam. And while I am certain there was a Twenty-fifth Massachusetts regiment, Alden's Twenty-fifth Massachusetts and its officers are fictional. All other references to specific regiments and commanders are taken from the historical record.

I am extremely grateful for the wealth of information compiled by various authors and experts on the Civil War. Many of the quotes that spill from my characters' lips were actually voiced by men and women who lived during the American Civil War, and I must give credit to the fine authors whose books enabled me to explore these tragic years of our nation's history.

Bergren, Philip. *Old Boston in Early Photographs, 1850-1918.* New York: Dover Publications, Inc., 1990.

Brooke, Elisabeth. *Medicine Women: A Pictorial History of Women Healers.* Wheaton, Ill.: Quest Books, 1997.

Burgess, Lauren Cook, ed. *An Uncommon Soldier.* New York: Oxford University Press, 1994.

Colbert, David, ed. *Eyewitness to America: 500 Years of America in the Words of Those Who Saw It Happen.* New York: Pantheon Books, 1997.

Davis, Kenneth C. *Don't Know Much About the Civil War.* New York: Avon Books, 1996.

Davis, William C., ed. *Touched by Fire: A National Historical Society Photographic Portrait of the Civil War.* New York: Black Dog & Leventhal Publishers, 1997.

Fishel, Edwin C. *The Secret War for the Union.* New York: Houghton Mifflin, 1996.

Fraser, Walter J. *Charleston! Charleston! The History of a Southern City.* Columbia, S.C.: University of South Carolina Press, 1991.

Hall, Richard. *Patriots in Disguise: Women Warriors of the Civil War.* New York: Marlowe & Company, 1994.

Johnson, Robert Underwood, and Clarence Clough Buel, eds. *Battles and Leaders of the Civil War.* 2 vols. Edison, N. J.: Castle, 1887.

Marcus, Robert D., and David Burner. *From Settlement to Reconstruction.* Vol. 1 of *America Firsthand.* New York: St. Martin's Press, 1989.

Massey, Mary Elizabeth. *Women in the Civil War.* Lincoln, Nebr.: University of Nebraska Press, 1994.

McCutcheon, Marc. *Everyday Life in the 1800s.* Cincinnati: Writer's Digest Books, 1993.

Schwartz, Gerald, ed. *A Woman Doctor's Civil War: Esther Hill Hawks' Diary.* Columbia, S.C.: University of South Carolina Press, 1986.

Ward, Geoffrey C. *The Civil War.* New York: Knopf, 1990.

Wiley, Bell I. *The Life of Johnny Reb* and *The Life of Billy Yank.* New York: Book of the Month Club, 1994.

Woodward, C. Vann, ed. *Mary Chesnut's Civil War.* New York: Book of the Month Club, 1994.